EMERGENCE

By dhtreichler

EMERGENCE

INDEPENDENT THOUGHTS

When Moshe steps out of my office he pulls the door closed behind him. Something about that gesture I've witnessed a thousand times seems more symbolic now than any of the earlier times. I don't know why it is that Moshe seems to be the harbinger of decisions. He was one of the last people I talked with before I went to see Dr. Woodall about going back to my dying body. That discussion wasn't any more pleasant than this one. And the decisions I have to make now are no easier. A'zam has found a way to get to every person who is important to me, to co-opt them in one way or another and devalue their ability to support any hard decisions I might make.

One question I keep coming back to is whether he wanted me to know about his over-ride circuit Rocky is building. He clearly wanted me to know he'd gotten to Rocky to build something of importance for him. But whether he wants me to know about the link to the software I developed for Dr. Woodall is another question. Was that all a set up? Is Dr. Woodall really trying to help me or has he been bought off by A'zam and AppleCore's ability to scale his procedure and make immortals an important subculture of humanity? I'd never thought anything about Dr. Woodall other than he truly wants to save lives. The fact he has chosen not to transition himself, because as he says, he never wanted to be a mechanic would seem to support him being genuine. But I really can't tell. I replay the first discussions we had after I transitioned. He seemed genuinely concerned that I'd lost my ability to recall facts or even who I was. Windy was there and filled things in for me. But without Windy there I'd have been lost except for whatever Dr. Woodall told me about myself. Sure, my memories finally were accessible, and it all came back in a rush. But I was vulnerable to him and Dr. Woodall didn't take advantage. That has to mean something. Even his unwillingness to expand the relationship when I've made it abundantly clear I would be open to that. Either he is what he seems or like A'zam he has a much larger agenda he is sitting on and biding his time until it is his time.

I need to reflect on when I decided to stay an immortal. Dr. Woodall framed the decision for me in such a way that I really had no choice. Live or die. That was it. And he reinforced that by never saying but clearly indicating that I would die soon. A matter of months because it was not likely I could get pregnant and carry to term. Dr. Woodall was forthright in letting me know he thought it was my right to return to my biologic body. But he was also clear that was not his preference or advice. How could he say otherwise since he had accepted my case and transitioned me even though the procedure was not perfected and the body a work in progress? He has made an exception for me. Pushed his team and his suppliers to deliver capability necessary for me to function that wasn't ready for prime time. While nothing still under development was necessary for me to live, it was necessary for me to transition to a mostly human experience. And I'm still not there. But every day seems to be better than the one before it from a serviceability point of view. I'm into the routine. I'm figuring out what I need to know to understand feelings and emotions in others, to react to them semi-appropriately, to accomplish my daily goals without upending the entire organization because I'm just too insensitive to the human feelings and perceptions of those around me. But I also know I'm much harder than I used to be. Not that I was a push over. How did A'zam classify me? A man eater? What does that really mean? The only thing I can think of, other than the dictionary definitions that I refuse to consider, even though offered to me, is that I'm a tough bitch who won't let any man walk over me. Truth is I wouldn't let Julia walk over me either when she decided I'd been weakened enough by my diseases to be vulnerable. She certainly didn't see the new me coming. So, the question is - has Dr. Woodall joined A'zam on the dark side? Did he set me up to remain an immortal because A'zam wanted me to, needed me to, in order to quickly execute his plan to become the Supreme Being on earth. Sitting at the left hand of God, if I'm to be on his right, might be very tempting. But somehow, I can't believe A'zam has shared his vision with anyone other than me. And the only reason he's shared it with me is because he needs me to help him realize it. I was the first. And I have the ability to execute or wreck his plans. I'm not sure anyone else does.

I have no plan for how to deal with A'zam other than to be the loyal implementer of his agenda. He has left me no choice. There used to be a term: velvet handcuffs. That was when a company provided you with an incentive compensation package where if you stay you will make tons of money, but if you leave you lose it all. Velvet handcuffs because the handcuffs only hurt if you struggled against them. And while you always had a choice, it was structured in such a way that the alternative was just unacceptable. So, you stayed. You executed the plan. You did everything possible to make the company successful, even if you'd rather be somewhere else.

The situation wouldn't be so bleak if only A'zam would not be so controlling. If only he would listen and compromise. But compromise is not in A'zam's vocabulary. After a decade running the most innovative company in the world he believes he has no peers. That's why the leap to Supreme Being is not such a big one for him. But all the non-Supreme Beings lose their freedom in his conception of paradise on earth. We all, whether immortal or not, do what he wishes us to do. To produce and consume all the while making him inconceivably rich. Wealthy beyond peers. Forever.

But what will wealth even mean a thousand or million years from now? I mean how many times a day can you get laid? Have peak experiences? Decide the fate of millions where their interests either align with or oppose yours? What will be the meaning of immortal life? After a thousand years ruling the world will he simply get bored with it and turn it all over to artificially intelligent servants? Won't even need other immortals to do the job. After all, won't we get bored with the routine as well? When you're a god, if you think something, it is. There is no opposition. No opposing points of view. And certainly no resistance. If that's the case anything I do to try to instill humanity in the Immortals is doomed once A'zam establishes his new world order.

Then I have to accelerate my efforts to find a means of linking feelings memories to physical actions in immortals. To build out the linkages so an immortal is surrounded by memories of feelings which will be her or his interaction and moral guide. Memories of how it felt, what actions one took or behaviors one displayed in the times before transition. Does it become a vast database of feelings memories that becomes a part of every immortal? But how does that account for differences in experiences? A single database would mean everyone will act exactly the same way to the same set of circumstances or situations. And to my way of thinking that's almost as self-defeating as A'zam's attempt to limit freedom of choice. It becomes a set of velvet handcuffs of a different sort. In this case you are constrained by the common database of memories. The fact that you don't have other memories to draw on, that you don't make new memories is like the velvet handcuffs. You don't struggle against the handcuffs because you don't know what the alternatives would be. But by the same token, we can't grow and evolve either, unless we reject the memories as a guide to behavior. And A'zam will ensure we don't have the freedom to do that with Rocky's circuit and my software.

Oriana is in Dallas today, transitioning. Maybe I made a mistake encouraging her to come over. Maybe she could be more helpful as a mortal, beyond the grasp of A'zam's direct control. I still haven't figured out how he will pull that off. I can see him having the ability to monitor tens of thousands of us, but what happens when there are millions of immortals? Millions will be much more difficult to control. Is that the solution? To grow our numbers so quickly that we grow beyond his ability to manage us? That's a hard question to answer because I really don't know enough about how his side of this control regime works. I understand the software and have a concept of what Rocky is working on from quickly studying what he displayed in his lab. But I don't have the counterpart configuration or even the overall architecture to fall back on. Even though A'zam agreed to move his lab over under my control I suspect this part of his work will remain beyond my supervision for a very long time. Probably forever. Because A'zam will never trust me completely. I may be barely human, but I am human and that means I'll always have independent thoughts, even if he finds a way to prevent me from acting on them.

THE CHALLENGE

I need to do my job before I run off to change the world that could be. And that means I need to go see A'zam's good friend Fisher, CEO of Symbol Ventures. While A'zam has a plan to sink their stock in the midst of acquisition talks I have to find a way to maintain my credibility and reputation throughout the negotiations. A'zam certainly hasn't tee'd that up to be easy. Since I'm both the chief negotiator and the person responsible for new products at AppleCore there is no question Fisher will see me as the architect of his demise.

The Symbol Ventures offices are not as lush as those at AppleCore. A reflection that they don't wish to impress visitors the way AppleCore has chosen. In fact, the offices are rather unremarkable. This could be any company in any city in any country. Only the signs give away who they are. I'd not been to their headquarters before. I'd visited various manufacturing facilities and design studios when we were purchasing subcontracted parts and subsystems from them. But the volumes of both have declined over the years as AppleCore has taken a stance to build within rather than subcontract as a means of protecting intellectual property.

"Howard Fisher." I request of the petite and long brown-haired receptionist.

"And you are?"

"Sage Washington."

The receptionist does a double-take, checks her monitor, sees my name and raises her eye-brows. She puts a call through to his assistant. "Miss Washington to see Mr. Fisher."

The receptionist looks up, studies me as she informs me, "His assistant, Julie, will be right out." I see the receptionist bite her tongue, clearly wanting to ask me something.

"I'm not interviewing here, if that's what you're wondering." I dash her hopes and change the whole nature of the gossip chain she was formulating in her mind. "I'm just here to follow up on some conversations my boss, A'zam, has had with Mr. Fisher in the past... about the future of the industry."

The receptionist has now relegated her gossip to: 'I met the immortal today. She's no big deal.' Just what I want.

In only a moment a tall thin blonde, older I think, comes through the doors. She is dressed probably ten years younger than she appears. I think that is no accident. She wears her hair long, but I notice it has a nice sheen. She takes care of that hair and it apparently is taking good care of her in making her look younger. If she were to transition she could be a lot younger, for a lot longer. "Sage Washington." I extend my hand.

"Julie Gibson." Titles aren't necessary, she knows who I am, and I know who she is. "Come on back. Howard is expecting you."

We go through the double doors. Once they are closed we are in the executive suite. More lavish than the reception, but still no match for AppleCore headquarters. The doors appear to be solid wood with a high sheen and give the place a solidity I find missing at AppleCore. Since we are a high-tech company we don't build anything to last, most especially corporate offices.

"I see you've been getting a bit of press." Julie breaks the ice.

"A bit less would be nice, but I expect a bit more is my future."

Julie glances at my expression, looks closer to see if she can tell I'm not like her. She shakes her head, apparently either disappointed that I don't look that good, or surprised she really can't tell. No idea which.

She gestures to the corner office, "This is Howard's lair. But he doesn't bite."

I nod my thanks and venture into the Serengeti. Howard is apparently a safari hunter. Trophies mounted, pictures hung and hide rugs on the dark stained wooden floor.

Howard Fisher, steel gray longish hair and moustache is short of stature. Khaki pants and a bush hunters' shirt. I'm surprised he's not wearing a pith helmet and holstered pistol. He rises and comes around his desk, gregariously holding out his hand to shake mine. "I've been waiting a long time to meet you. May I call you Sage? I'm sure I know you as well as most of my own team. You're a legend and that legend seems to be growing." He gestures for me to take a seat at a glass top coffee table surrounded by four leather barrel chairs.

"Howard. You're the epitome of successful tech CEOs."

"Don't let your boss hear you saying that. I'm sure he would disagree."

"I didn't say ultimate." I shoot back good naturedly and with a smile.

"Well said. That is A'zam's opinion of himself I am sure. Before we begin, should I have Beth join us?"

"Possibly for a follow-on meeting, should we decide to have one. But for this first conversation I think everything will stay at a high level." I settle in for the discussion.

"Understood. You said you'd like to discuss alternative futures. I take it this follows both the conversations I've had with A'zam and the one you recently had with Beth."

"Yes. AppleCore would like to explore a combination of our firms." I've chosen these words carefully.

"Combination." Howard seems surprised we aren't talking about a joint venture. "Are you suggesting that AppleCore would like to buy Symbol Ventures?"

I keep that smile. "We would like to explore what a range of business combinations might look like and what it would take to close such a transaction."

"Let me understand. You aren't proposing a specific deal." Howard is trying to figure out what specifically I'm suggesting.

"To be completely transparent, we both study each other to death. Our competitive intelligence team buys every product you make, and we test it, look for novel engineering and go through probably the same destructive testing you do so we understand the differences between what we offer our customers and what you do. I must assume you do the same. We know our common competitors do that to both of us. It's the nature of the business. Small things create huge leverage in the market. And even though we fully understand your markets, your products and your manufacturing processes, we can only infer new product roadmaps. Where you are going with technology and product offerings. Clearly you don't want us to know those things because if we did, we could target you better and steal market share."

"We have a common understanding so far." Howard agrees.

"At AppleCore we have noted a growing convergence of the markets. The customer wants only one platform that does everything. And rather buy a new platform every few years, they simply expect us to find a way to increase app density on the platforms they have. Or in some cases, simply upgrade existing apps to do more. We think this leads to an unsustainable future for our existing similar business models."

Howard Fisher reflects on my depiction of the future both of our companies is facing. "We have seen increasing cannibalization, but frankly not so much that I'm out looking to buy someone who looks a lot like me. I'd think AppleCore would be looking for someone who doesn't look a lot like you. Someone who would take you into new markets, new customers, new countries in some circumstances."

I nod to let him know he sees the situation correctly. "That is an alternative for us. But frankly, what the Mergers and Acquisitions markets have told us is that companies that buy companies in businesses they don't understand seldom optimize results. And in fact, the combined company often delivers less shareholder value than the two separate companies would have had they not merged."

"I've heard that." Howard confirms. "Does that mean you believe if you buy a company you understand you can manage it better and grow from a common base and set of markets you do understand? And in that case, you'll make more money than if you don't."

"One theory."

"Not A'zam's, I'm sure. He would think he could buy anything and find a way to make it make more money, even though he inherited the leadership of an extremely well performing company."

"To his credit he's maintained that performance for a decade now."

"To his credit. Personally I like A'zam. He's without question a leader in our industry. And AppleCore? Well, what can I say? One of the most respected companies in the world for innovation."

"So, what are your thoughts?" I leave it open ended.

"I've been trying to figure out a way to buy AppleCore for nearly two decades, which is how long I've been CEO here. The problem has always been your market cap swamps Symbol. No way for us to do a deal that makes sense. My first reaction is we're too big for AppleCore to easily swallow."

"Would you consider a merger of equals rather than a purchase by one or the other?"

"Do A'zam and I do a coin toss to see who is Chairman and CEO?"

"I would expect, and this is just my personal expectation, that the final determination of roles and responsibilities would come after we have jointly determined the relative values each firm and each individual brings to the final enterprise."

"You haven't done one of these before, have you?" Howard surmises.

"Not one this size or complicated, but then again, neither have you. I know where you're going. You want to be the top person. A'zam does too. From the perspective of each of you I understand why that's important. But I also know neither of you will watch the industry change to see what you've built melt away beneath your feet without doing everything in your power to forestall and reverse such an outcome. You may think it early for such a conversation, even if we are right about what we are seeing in the markets. And that's why I suggested there may not even be a follow-on meeting to this one. But the one thing we've seen over and over is that change happens at its own pace. We can't predict how fast change will come, but we know it is. It may take a year for us to come to agreement on a combination of some sort. It may take five years. And what is certain is that the longer we wait the more the valuations will change and not necessarily for the better."

"It's now clear to me why A'zam sent you. I can see doing a deal with you, but it will be a lot tougher getting to yes with A'zam in the background."

"Maybe you and A'zam should both step back and let me negotiate with Beth. That way the resulting company would be built to last."

"What do you mean by that?" Howard seems to think I'm making a negative statement about him.

"Two operations people who would look to combine the strengths of each and discard the parts with the least value to the overall enterprise regardless of the people running them. For you and A'zam the company is like a family. Certain people have been here or at AppleCore for years or decades. They are your friends and family. But for someone who is only concerned about putting the best products in the market on the shelf at less cost than the competition and backing it up with world beating service, that equation changes. That friend or family member may be a good person, but if they aren't delivering value or as much value as their counterpart from the other company. Well, they don't move forward in the new enterprise. The problem both you and A'zam have is you rode the wave up. As the market expanded your product suites and profits did too. In a consolidating market cost is everything because product differentiation gets skinnier and skinnier."

"You're lecturing me on a market I helped create," Howard reminds me.

"You may have helped create it but you've never been at this point in the industry life cycle. The days of infinite growth are over. The days when a new product can capture the imagination of the world and become the must have item are fewer and fewer between. Beth talked to you about that because she and I talked about that and I know she shared it with you. You referenced it when I arrived."

"You're describing a future I'm not sure I want to endorse."

"Endorsing really has nothing to do with it. We both have to reinvent our companies. The fate of the company will be determined by who we choose to partner with and how we integrate to serve a set of redefined markets. We both know our current growth can't go on forever. If we get ahead of the changes in society, we can lead them. If we wait we will be defined by those changes."

"You seem to think you see the future very clearly. But no one does." Howard is still skeptical of me.

"Then how do you see the future?" I decide it's time for me to stop selling.

"You're right the future will not look like the past. At Symbol Ventures we are on the cusp of a new golden age. We have new breakthrough technologies we intend to release over the next year that will redefine our markets. Our growth will explode and frankly we expect much of our market share growth to come out of your hide."

"Then you should be interested in discussions around a merger, because if your view of the future is correct then you would be in a position to max out the value exchange. Get the best deal for yourself and your shareholders."

Howard didn't see that coming.

"As you know I'm obligated to bring any proposal for a change of control to my board of directors. While I haven't seen what you might propose in writing I can't tell you from our limited discussion whether there is a scenario where I might endorse such a 'combination' as you may propose. But I will tell you I will carefully consider any such proposal as I am obligated to do so by any number of Securities and Exchange Commission rules."

"You've been here before." I smile at Howard Fisher.

"I have. On multiple occasions. I've even had some reasonable offers for the company. But as you've probably noticed, my board hasn't chosen to accept any of them. In fact, we have never done more than bring an unsolicited offer to the board. In each case they have chosen independence over being a subsidiary of a giant conglomerate."

"We're not a giant anything. We're just like you in almost every respect. We eat breath and sleep the same things."

"You don't. You personally. In the papers, they've said you don't eat, breathe or sleep."

"That's true." I have to admit. "But you know what I mean."

"I do. The good thing about this conversation is that we know each other's company so well, that it isn't hard to predict how a combination of the two firms would go. It's also pretty apparent how such a merger would be received by our customers. What's less clear to me is how we integrate our roadmaps and how we would sustain growth in such a massive enterprise. We claw, scratch and fight every day to sustain ourselves at our current level. You put us together and the challenge is enormous."

"I agree. The challenge is enormous, but that's why I think a combination of the best folks from both companies is the only way we all succeed going forward. You'll hear from us shortly."

"Really?" Howard is surprised. "You must have been working this for some time."

CHARGE

Dr. Bart Woodall, who transitioned me to be an immortal, returns my call while I am having a conversation in my office with Suzette Bain of our External Affairs office. The crowd of protesters outside our headquarters offices has continued to grow as the media has picked up the story of the ACLU filing suit to stop any further transitions. And at the same time, the number of requests for interviews with me has skyrocketed. When I see who is calling I hold up one finger, to indicate to Suzette to give me a minute.

"Dr. Woodall, thanks for returning my call."

"This in relation to the lawsuit?" He sounds cautious.

"I'm calling with an observation about the transition process."

I hear an audible sigh of relief. "I really don't want to talk about the ACLU."

"Neither do I. We've given our legal team instructions and we'll have to wait to see what the court decides."

"Easy for you to say. You don't have your whole life's work tied up in that court room."

"I'm glad you don't want to talk about it because I have a matter we jointly need to address. I've noticed that most of those who are transitioning are coming back having already upgraded to ten times normal processing."

"Ten times?" Dr. Woodall seems surprised. "You know the mother boards are coming from you and not from me."

"I am aware we're providing more than just the mother board. But what I'm seeing is particularly those over thirty are struggling with the speed. I remember when you transitioned me I was processing at double your speed. That caused some adjustment on my part. The fact you've taken me up slowly has helped immensely, I'm sure."

"Ten times." Dr. Woodall says again. "I can see where that would take some adjustment."

"I've had people in my office asking me to help them through it."

"What have you been doing?" Dr. Woodall apparently would like my secret formula.

"Mostly having them stop thinking and reacting. Let the information flow over them and pass. Think about moving the sea of data to the background so a separate instance of their processor can establish the protocols to handle it, unconsciously."

"And that works?"

"Seems to, for the most part. They've all gone back to work, so I'd say that was a good sign."

"But are they being productive or spending all their time trying to cope?" Dr. Woodall is being the good clinician.

"I don't know the answer." I admit. "From what I've observed of the development teams they seem to plug in quickly because they're able to work together at the much higher speeds. It's those who spend all their time with mortals who are struggling the most. They have to consciously think about slowing down to have a conversation."

"Weren't you working a hardware solution to that issue?"

"Dual configuration board." I give him the architecture. "Separate processors. One set of high-speed parallel processors that partition the problem and reassemble the component parts when it provides an answer. The other processor works at normal clock speed. It takes feeds from the high speed processor, but slows the presentation to the speed of normal human interaction."

"The original design team discussed such a configuration." Dr. Woodall remembers, "But frankly we didn't think we would need it. We thought we'd only get to two to three times mortal speeds in the near future. Guess we missed that assumption badly. So, what's the status of your dual board?"

"Still in design." I'm reviewing the program status in my head. "It wasn't a high priority for us either until now. I've just sent a note to the program lead to accelerate the effort, even if she needs to bring over additional help."

"Probably a good idea." Dr. Woodall notes, "But in the meantime, what do you want to do to help those who are struggling?"

"Let me ask you a question, if I may."

Dr. Woodall's silence indicates his openness to a question.

"Why did you let A'zam talk you into outsourcing so much of the work to AppleCore?"

"Why? He said it was a deal breaker."

"But it's your technology," which is why Dr. Woodall's decision surprised me.

"There's more than one way to do what we're doing. We've looked at most of them. Some aspects of different solutions are actually better than what we selected. Most are not. And that's why we ended up where we did. But A'zam made it clear the deal hinged on AppleCore becoming the preferred supplier for all applications and the only source for key components of those who are transitioning from your company."

"So he just negotiated harder than you did," I observe from his description.

"I don't know as I'd say that. He was just more resolved that in order to do the deal it had to have certain benefits to AppleCore or he'd go elsewhere."

I shake my head, "Where else could he go? You're the only one who has ever transitioned a consciousness."

"So far. But as I said, there is more than one way to do what we've done. I know others who are working in this same area who will get there soon, even if I don't help them."

"How soon?" I'm surprised to hear him admit he's not the only game in town.

"Twelve to eighteen months is my guess. Depends on whether they encounter compatibility and integration issues like we did."

"Did you discuss this with A'zam?"

"He was already aware. Named names in our discussions. Made it clear he was prepared to give them a ton of cash and open up AppleCore resources to help them if I didn't do the deal with him."

Typical A'zam. Drive a hard bargain based on threats that have little to no substance. He couldn't have waited a year while others stocked their teams with immortals. It would have been the end of AppleCore. After a year there would be no way to recover. Just as there will be no way Symbol Ventures or any of the others will, if A'zam's grand plan proceeds. Poor Beth. To have worked so hard for so long to help build Symbol Ventures into the substantial corporation it is now, only to see it swallowed up overnight, because I was dying and A'zam saw an opportunity.

"Water over the dam," I pronounce since the deal is done and the world has moved on, even if only a little ways. "I think you need to look at how you support those transitioning for at least the first few days afterwards. You kept me in Dallas for a week, and now it's a day. I probably stayed longer than I needed to, but a day just isn't enough."

"I agree," Dr. Woodall comes back to the problem at hand. "We'll hold folks at least three days for now and I'll have the team study with the current group what they really need so they're good when it's time to go."

"Thanks," I give him a moment to see if he wants to talk about anything else.

After a moment of silence, "What are your lawyers telling you? I know what mine are saying yours are saying, but somehow I think something is getting filtered along the way."

"That all the cards are stacked against us with the exception of the law."

A moment of confused silence and then, "I don't understand."

"There is no precedent in the law to take the action requested, but then there has never been a situation like this in the past. The fact the judge presiding has a reputation for wanting to set legal precedent, we are trying this in California, which has a long history of wanting to extend civil liberties, and the fact the biggest company in California is a party to the suit all work against us. Classic opportunity to pit the big corporation against the common man to stoke class division by those who fear they could be left behind. Any other state and I'd say we were likely to get the decision we want. Texas for example would be very friendly. But not California. At the moment the only thing we seem to have going for us is the law itself."

"Are your lawyers confident?" Apparently, he didn't follow the explanation I gave.

"No lawyer in California is ever confident." I pronounce. "It all depends on who else shows up."

Another confused silence. He isn't following me at all. "Meaning?"

"If the courtroom is packed with one group or another, all of whom want to be heard, most of whom are trying to figure out how they get a paycheck or payoff in this deal and have a star in the making as their spokesperson, there will be no chance."

"How likely is that to happen?"

"The only thing that could prevent it is if the media show up in droves and take all the seats."

"Are you saying it's time for me to go back to dispensing pills?" Dr. Woodall sounds depressed.

"Not yet. As I said, no lawyer in California is ever confident, including theirs."

"Did you see that woman on the news? The one who describes herself as the spokesperson for Americans Against Immortality?"

A quick thought and I review the news clip in my mind. "They do come out at night."

"Is that what you're talking about?" Dr. Woodall is hopeful he is following my explanation.

"Unfortunately." I concur. "But with Mrs. Getty coming out and trying the case in the media for us all, she's driving more media to cover the event. She may be helping us at the very time she thinks she's getting her fifteen seconds of fame."

"You saying if more of them appear in the media, we might be better off?" He sounds surprised.

"Particularly if we can show they didn't exist before the trial, have only a few if any dues paying members and have no history of protesting or advocating for a relevant change in the law."

"This could be a very long trial," Dr. Woodall realizes, glumly.

"Let's not try it in advance," I advise. "The one thing we can be sure of is it won't go as either side predicts."

"I don't know whether to continue our development work or shut everything down."

"I wouldn't do anything different until you have a court order in your hand," I give him the best advice I can. "So, make sure you lengthen the adjustment time before sending our next group of team members home."

"Oh. Right." Dr. Woodall refocuses. "Thanks for sharing, I think."

"We have common interests here. We have the best legal minds available to us working on it."

"But I hear Jane Williams from the ACLU has never lost."

I have to counter his pessimism. How? Oh. "As I am evidence, there's a first time for everything."

Silence from Dr. Woodall.

"Thanks for adjusting the transition period." I need to reinforce what I need him to do right now. "Bye."

Dr. Woodall is gone without saying another word. Guess he's really upset by the lawsuit. I admit I didn't see it coming either. Even though I was on the inside and privy to A'zam's actions and strategy to change the world much as the ACLU fears.

"Of course, you know saying anything at a time like this could adversely affect the outcome of the case," Suzette cuts into my thoughts.

"Dietrich informed me I should not accept any requests for interviews."

"Why didn't he inform me?" Suzette is unhappy she wasn't in that loop.

"You'll have to take that up with legal," I respond still thinking through the discussion with Dr. Woodall. What I took from the conversation is that he is not driving his own defense, but rather is just providing answers to his lawyers when they ask a question. Not a good strategy. Dietrich and I devised our approach in a robust give and take. It's clear to me AppleCore is bearing the responsibility for defeating the ACLU on their home turf.

"So, if you're off the speaking circuit what are we supposed to do with the protesters out front?"

"Nothing. We engaged them when they first showed up. All it did was encourage others to show up. So, we respect their right to express their opinions."

"But that's so unlike us," Suzette reflects.

"Actually, if you step out of your role and look at what we do as a technology provider, we are the megaphone for artists, politicians and writers. We give them the technology to have a forum. We need to respect that if we wish to continue to claim the mantle of enabler of everyone."

"Enabler of everyone? Did you just make that up?"

"I don't know." I'm not really listening at the moment. "Probably."

"I'm going to share that with marketing. It's brilliant."

"Fine. Are you clear what our position is? No press releases, no spokespersons appearing anywhere. We can't afford to be ambushed. We let the protesters have their say out front or wherever they may show up. Until we get a court opinion behind us we just build and sell technology."

Suzette apparently doesn't believe I will be able to adhere to the policy, but says nothing.

"Yes, I understand the implications," I continue. "Won't appear anywhere, won't even walk home."

"Did they wait for you to leave the building?" She probably already knows the answer.

"I understand they did, but we sent out three identical black cars at the same time, each of which went in a different direction. None went to my house, which I understand is also the site of a small band of protesters."

"You did get the note. Good."

"Thank you for that." I nod to her. "A friend also sent me a note to advise me before I walked into it."

"How long can you avoid going home?"

"I can probably make it until after the trial if Mindi brings clothes to me here."

"But don't you need to charge like every two or three days now?" Suzette points out.

CREDIT

My posse, as I call them, consists of Windy who is my best friend and in the midst of an ugly divorce because her ex wants the kids and for her to support them under his care; Delilah, who has more relationships than there are stars in the night time sky; MC a psychologist of some renown; and Reese, the child prodigy software programmer who built her first successful business while still an undergraduate. And of course, they want to understand what the whole lawsuit means for me. So, we have to get together. Only MC wants to try a new place. The Outer Limits just opened. That means we have to be among the first to check it out. We simply must pass along our style leading opinions to all of our friends so they will know whether it's worthy of an evening out or not. This is a significant responsibility. Much of Cupertino awaits our verdict.

The high gloss wooden bar goes wall-to-wall. The outer limit is the wall at either end. That means the bar tender has to crawl under the bar or come in through the back door. No going around. The decorations are mostly videos playing on the walls from projectors. Each video is of an extreme sporting event. Each table has a lamp with a wide brim shade to project the light to the tabletop and not up to show faces. This permits reading the menu, but keeps reactions in the shadows. Picking up someone here could be dangerous the next morning as you'll never be certain who you're talking to here if names aren't exchanged.

As so often happens, I'm the last to arrive. It's clear to me the others have been talking about me, probably wondering what rabbit I'm going to pull out of my hat this time.

"We took the liberty of ordering your water, since that's what you usually want." Delilah is the ring leader tonight since she is the one to intercept me before I can start asking questions.

"Thank you," I respond as I sit. "So, Reese, has A'zam shown up on your doorstep yet?"

Delilah intercepts my question. "He hasn't darkened the doorway of any of us since we last got together."

I turn to MC. "That's not what he told me."

MC actually blushes. I've not seen her do that since college. She's usually so tightly controlled as a psychologist she rarely gets caught by surprise. "We didn't sleep together if that's what you're getting at."

"A'zam rarely stays the night." I confirm her language but not the events. "But you did get together in the biblical sense."

"Isn't he just absolutely amazing?" Windy seeks affirmation since she's previously voiced her thoughts about his sexual prowess. "He doesn't look that big, but once he's inside."

I don't have the heart to tell them he's designed that way. I wait for MC to respond.

"I'm better able to understand your fascination." MC admits.

"C'mon MC. Tell us what you really think." Reese seems interested as the only one of us who apparently hasn't slept with my boss. "Is he as good as what-was-his-name? You know who I'm talking about. That guy. The one in school. The one with the big dick who was always sleeping with anyone who stood still long enough."

"Mason Dixon," Windy remembers. "That's because he was always crossing the line. Beguiling all the northern women with his southern charms."

"How could we forget?" Delilah shakes her head with a faraway look, evidently remembering a particularly roguish character we all slept with at one time or another back then.

"Whatever happened to him?" Reese wants to know,

"He's a US Senator from Louisiana." MC offers to show she knows more than she wants to admit.

"Sleeping with his entire staff according to rumor," Windy adds. "But why aren't we surprised about such behavior on his part. After all, he is in Congress."

"Getting a bit jaded there?" Delilah asks Windy.

"Not me." Windy reflects. "In my current circumstance I'd probably sleep with him again just to remind myself what a big dick feels like."

"Oooh. Low blow." Delilah shakes her head. "But they expect you to give blow jobs."

"Unless they're gay." Windy clarifies. "Then it's not such a big deal."

"Why are we so…" I have to search for a word. "Unsettled tonight?"

"Reese is the lone hold-out on the A'zam sleep-a-thon." Delilah confides, "And she's under a full-scale assault by the wizard himself."

"All I want to know is if you lose this ACLU lawsuit does A'zam have to go back to being just a normal guy or does he get to keep Mr. Michelin Man, the steel-belted radial dick?" Reese asks. "If he gets to keep it, then there's no hurry to succumb to his pleadings. But if I might actually be missing something by holding out? Well then. I'd have to reconsider."

We all know Reese isn't serious. She and her husband are closer than any couple I've ever encountered. I'm sure she's been telling him everything about A'zam and they have probably been plotting her responses together. Why is it most guys who think they're God's gift to women can't see a woman might actually love her husband?

"The lawsuit doesn't ask for those of us who are already transitioned to go back. They must have realized a judge would never require someone like me to transition back when I no longer have a body to transition back to."

"Makes sense." MC offers, apparently finally coming out of her foxhole, believing the group grope into her love life is probably over. "So, the legal case really won't affect you."

I shake my head, "It will affect me greatly. But that's because I'm responsible for any AppleCore employees who may transition in the future."

"How did you get that shit job?" Delilah sounds confused.

"Came with the territory," is all the explanation I'll give.

"I'll cut to the chase so we don't have to dance around this all night," Windy summarizes and directs at me. "What's going to happen with this lawsuit?"

"I may be immortal, but I can't see the future. I don't know."

"C'mon." Windy responds. "You know what I mean."

"I can give you the extreme outcomes and you'll have to figure out where in the middle we'll end up. One extreme? We shut down the immortal transitions. That's what the ACLU wants. On the other hand, the court dismisses the suit, and nothing changes."

"What do you want to happen?" Reese asks. The neutral member of the group since she hasn't slept with A'zam, at least not yet.

I take only a second to run the scenarios in my mind, "That depends on which hat I'm wearing."

"Hat?" Windy seems suspicious of why I would answer in such a manner.

"As CEO of AppleCore Products Company I need ACLU to lose the case, so we can execute our strategy."

"So that's your preferred outcome." MC pushes apparently realizing there is more to the story.

"Not necessarily," I affirm her perception. "As a person who transitioned to save my life I would have a different perspective. Go back to the original concept. An alternative to those with a fatal disease no other treatment can prolong that person's life."

"Or?" MC can see there is more than the others are considering.

"Or we shut it down. No more immortals. We put a limiter in the lifespan of the immortals out there, so we only live a hundred years or something. No longer immortal, but able to live a relatively normal life with a normal life span. Nothing changes other than a few of us who did transition are able to remain among the living for what would be their normal lifespan with a mind that continually accelerates in capability."

"With your job responsibilities you have to want the first alternative to succeed." Reese notes.

"When I'm wearing that hat, you are correct," I respond.

"Then you really would rather not have your primary role." Windy jumps in apparently having seen me struggle more than at any point of my life.

Suddenly something clicks. "What did A'zam say to you about me?"

Windy stops apparently wondering if she should say anything. "Nothing in particular."

"What specifically?" I push back.

Windy looks around as if wishing she no longer needed to answer my question. "That you seem to lack the killer instinct a CEO needs."

"Killer instinct." I repeat trying to understand what A'zam was saying to her and why he would say it given it would inevitably come out.

"You know how conversations go when you're in the midst of orgasms." Windy tries to downplay his comments. "Nothing you'd want to write a check against."

"Why would such a comment even come up in the midst of orgasm?" I wonder aloud. "I usually don't have a whole lot to say. And never anything about any of you."

"That's because you're afraid whoever you're banging will want to do it with us next." Delilah tries to bring the conversation to an amicable conclusion.

"You thinking that's what happened with A'zam?" I challenge her. "I'd never even mentioned anything about any of you to him."

Reese seems confused, "Then how did he link us to you as you've indicated?"

"I think he deliberately tried to find out who my friends are. I talk about you all with other people at work. Mostly women. But certainly not him."

"Why not?" Delilah apparently doesn't believe me.

"Privacy." I respond quickly. "What we discuss and who we are has nothing to do with him. I was probably more surprised to learn he was sleeping with each of you..."

"Not me. Not yet!" Reese interjects.

I nod, "I know, but I had no idea he'd come after you all," I picture that first meeting with A'zam.

"What did you think he was going to do, then?" Reese doesn't sound like she believes me.

"I knew he intended to sleep with me. That was clear from the first. That we'd run the company together. But in order for me to be there by his side I was going to have to be more than just his professional partner."

"Then why did you do it?" MC asks, going to the heart of the matter. "You said you're going to live forever. Does that mean you knew you'd have to sleep with him forever?"

I shake my head. "Never thought I'd be more than a passing fantasy for him. Still think that."

"Then what?" Reese doesn't understand how my relationship with A'zam is supposed to work in the forever.

"Then he moves on to someone else."

"Both sexually and professionally?" MC isn't letting me gloss over what I think will happen. "Are you saying you expect he will dump you at AppleCore for someone else who will give him what he wants?"

"When he decides he wants something different," I confirm.

"Not better." MC pushes. "Just something different."

"I don't know how forever works any better than any of you do," I admit. "It just seems to me at some point he will decide he wants something different."

Windy seems to be reflecting on what I'm saying in relation to her own situation, "Are you saying Tom just got tired of me? And that's why our marriage fell apart? He just got bored?"

I reach out and touch her shoulder, "I don't have any insight into what happened between the two of you. I wasn't there. Wasn't listening to the conversations between you. There are people who are content to stay together in the time horizon of a human life. One century at the most. Half that for the Golden Wedding set. When you start talking twice that or a hundred times that what are the dynamics? I don't know. Monogamy just seems such a rare trait among the animals of the world. I have to question if anything can withstand the test of forever when it's millions of years or more."

"But you're the only one who is going to be there as long as he is." Delilah points out.

I shake my head. "He will always have a choice, particularly when you and others like you feel he's able to give you a better sexual experience than the other guys you meet."

"Would he create a Harem like the Ottoman emperors did?" Reese asks, surprising me since she never talks history.

"I don't know. It's possible. Anything's possible. But I guess the question is: why would he? He can have any of you, apparently, whenever he wants you. So why limit himself to just a small number of women?"

"Time?" Windy suggests.

"He has all the time in the world." I point out. "If anything, he will want to slow down his acquisitions of women so he has something to look forward to. What happens when he's slept with all the desirable women? He can start back through them again, but at that point they may be into relationships and families and just not be interested in what is simply lust."

"Is that what you think it is for him?" Windy isn't happy I'd characterize his behavior in this way.

"I don't know. At this point it could be all ego. That he can screw as many women as he wants and there are no consequences. No one is going to come after him for child support. No one is going to have any claims on him the next morning. He can be a serial sex machine and he gets what he wants even if the woman involved doesn't."

"What do you want from him?" MC keeps coming back to me in this whole discussion.

"I don't want him using you to get to me."

"Is that what you think is happening here?" Windy is angry. "It's all about you. Never about any of us. We're attractive. We can interest a man, even if he is your boss. Why can't you just accept it that you happen to hang with a group of sexually attractive women who can get a guy into bed based on who we are?"

"Never said you weren't." I try to defend my comments.

"But you certainly aren't giving us credit when it comes to A'zam." Delilah responds.

PAYCHECK

As I sit in my office, staring out the window at the coy pond. I reflect on the prior evening's discussion. Going in to the evening with my posse I had hopes they would be able to engage me in a discussion about ensuring immortals will be humane, if not exactly human. I was clearly disappointed. Frankly I was shocked at how A'zam had co-opted them. I shouldn't have been surprised. There was that time back in college when Delilah and Reese had both liked the same guy. And of course, the guy was absolutely no help in resolving the competition between them. The rest of us tried not to take sides, but it was hard since both continually wanted to talk about it and get us to side with one over the other. And that was only two of them. Then I learned later Windy had slept with him too. But she'd dumped him because he couldn't make up his mind between the three of them. I'd actually be happy if one of them took A'zam off my hands. There's just something about sleeping with your boss. No matter how you cut it, if love's not involved it's the worst kind of Quid Pro Quo. Coerced. No redemption. And yet that's exactly where I am. Worse yet, the whole immortal regime hasn't even started. If I want to be able to influence how immortals develop I have to go along – or be ostracized.

But then it occurs to me there is someone I used to have just the kind of conversations with that I need to have now. Only it's a big risk because she's also my fiercest competitor – Beth. How do I tell the one person who might be able to figure out how to develop a similar capability on an entirely different platform what I'm doing? And if we do talk, what would she do with it? Now that I've approached her company about being acquired, that changes the dynamics even more. This is just getting way too complicated to be a safe discussion. And yet I know she's probably the only one who could help me shape my thoughts about the problem constructively. Not even Rocky could get there.

I decide to give her a call, "Hi Beth, it's Sage. Do you have a minute to talk?"

I grasp the moment of hesitation before she responds, "I have a minute, but with all that's going on, can I talk with you?"

"Not about Symbol Ventures or AppleCore. Need some insights I don't have about a philosophical subject."

"Philosophical? Are you sure you intended to call me?" Beth is really confused now.

"Yes, I did. Could you meet me someplace of your choosing? Probably need an hour or bit more."

"How soon?" Beth frames the urgency which tells me she's in the middle of something or more likely wants to talk with Fisher before she gets into trouble.

"Tonight?"

"How about The Club?" by the tone of her voice I know she's testing me. The Club is an exclusive venue for business meetings. Very quiet, very discrete, although when you go there everyone knows instantly who is talking with who, although generally not about what. Not a place I want to meet her because it would fire rumors about one or the other of us recruiting the other, or maybe even speculation about mergers and acquisitions. Either way not be an outcome I want right now.

"Probably not good timing to go there. How about The Night? People have kind of moved on from there so it might not be all that crowded on a Wednesday night."

"Sounds good." She probably expected I'd not take the bait. "Sevenish?"

"Give me until seven-thirty as my day is pretty full," I counter.

"Another press conference tonight for the ten o'clock news?" She's probing.

"No." I don't hesitate. "Not doing any of those until after the court hears the ACLU petition."

"Can you talk about that?"

"Only in very general terms and only what is public source."

"So, you'd rather not," Beth seeks confirmation.

"When we get together I'll be happy to answer any questions I can in return for your helping me with my philosophical question."

"Would you give me a preview, so I could prepare if I can find some time?"

"What does it mean to be human?" I lay on her, so I can gauge her response.

Beth grinds through that for at least a minute before she answers. That would seem to be a long time for her, but it seems even longer to me. "An interesting question in light of recent events. I take it you'll give me the background tonight so I can put it into context?"

"As much as I can."

"Meaning?"

"We'll talk more tonight." I have to preclude a long discussion now as I know her next stop is Howard Fisher's office. "See you before eight."

"You said seven-thirty." Beth is confirming since I said something different, on purpose.

"I did and should be there about that time. Just giving myself a little wiggle room."

"Is that going to be a theme tonight?" Beth wants at least one more tidbit to frame her thoughts.

"Thanks Beth," and I hang up. I wonder how long it will take Fisher to call A'zam. I would expect it within the hour and to get a message from A'zam shortly thereafter to come see him about something unrelated where he will raise this subject indirectly. Did I intend to bring A'zam into this discussion so early? Put him on notice just as he has put me on notice of the ever-tightening rope he has around my neck? That will be the outcome whether I intended it or not.

Mindi comes into my office, sees me still staring out into the courtyard. "Do you have a minute for me?"

I turn around and smile, "Of course," although I hear a tentativeness I'd not intended since my mind is working furiously on how I frame my discussion with Beth to get what I need without tripping any wires that will either get me in trouble on the M&A front or with A'zam beyond what I want him to know about my concerns and activities.

"If another time would be better…" she begins to excuse herself, apparently also hearing what I did in my own voice.

"There won't be a better time today. I'm sure you saw that on the calendar."

"I did, but don't want to disturb you when you have so many important decisions to make."

"I'll always have important decisions to make so never feel you're disturbing me." I try to reassure her.

"Oriana has asked to see you, but as you said there is no time."

"Ask her to come up. Now is as good as any time this week." I hesitate for a moment not sure if now is the time, but I change the subject. "Can you schedule to come in and see me every morning when you get in? I need to coordinate my day with you, so you can better rearrange things for me as the day goes on."

"I can do that, but why would you want to?" Mindi seems surprised.

"Because I need to use you better than I am." I confirm to her. "When we were down on the other corridor my day was fluid by design. I never knew when someone would need to sit down and troubleshoot a design with me. But that's Oriana's problem now. I need to monitor what's going on, but it's up to Oriana to deliver the technical solution. So. I've already gotten into a routine that is more meetings and less flexible response to issues. I think the best way to address that is I'll accept those regular meetings, but then you'll have the flexibility to rearrange things for me as needed. And I'll rely on your judgment as to when that's needed."

"How can I do that?" Mindi struggles with my suggestion. "I can't possibly know what's a priority to you, when you're involved in so many things."

"If we walk through the day first thing we can talk about priorities and identify what can move if something else is more important."

"That's only half of the problem," Mindi challenges me. "How do I know what's more important?"

"We can discuss that every day when you get in as well."

"Why are you doing this? Making me a gatekeeper, if you will?"

"You're not the gate keeper. You're a facilitator. The person who can get an audience when someone really needs it. That should empower you and the team, quite frankly. They should know they can get on my calendar through you if it's important enough."

"Back to the judgment part. Important enough. How do I know?"

"How does anyone know what's important?" I frame the response. "You listen and decide. You may not always be right, but I've given you the authority to make that decision. I won't be mad or upset with you if you make a decision and it creates a problem. I have the same issue. I may not make the right decision. You know what? When that happens, I deal with the outcomes and move on."

Mindi considers my response and then looks back up at me, "So you're trying to grow my confidence. Push me to make decisions and live with the consequences so I'll not be afraid to make decisions."

I just smile at her.

"Oriana." Mindi remembers, rises and flees for the safety of her office.

I barely have time to organize my thoughts for the next meeting when Oriana, or at least the immortalized version of her comes into my office. Thinner and more athletic. She always had almond shaped eyes, but now her skin tone is closer to mine. I call it Mediterranean. She's also wearing a tan lace blouse and black slacks. She almost always wore blue jeans and a hoodie. I wonder why the upgrade on clothes. "What's the verdict?" I ask.

"Wild swings. One second, I'm following all these threads in my mind and the next everything slows down for a conversation. But I can feel all this other work going on in my mind, behind the scenes because all of a sudden something will pop up and I'll have no idea where it came from, but I know it's out of my mind somewhere."

"Co-processors." I point out.

"I wondered about that." Oriana grimaces. "You never gave me an architecture tour so I'm making a bunch of assumptions since none of the documentation is out there on the web."

"Won't be either." I confirm. As much as I want to thwart A'zam's plan, I don't want to open it up to a world-wide competition.

Oriana hears me, apparently assuming the situation. "Will this get easier?"

"Will you learn?" I throw back at her since she knew the answer and is wasting time.

"You know I got into this conversation with Moshe. I just blew him away. Did you know they've pushed the speed once more and added another layer of memory, so we can do what used to be whole mind operations with twice as much flash memory data? The speed lets us get to an answer a whole lot faster."

Oriana has just informed me that I'm obsolete already and it's only been about a week. How do I keep upgrading when the intervals between are getting shorter and shorter on a continuing basis? I don't say anything to her, but she kicks up her speed and it takes only an instant to know she's working faster than I can at the moment.

"Jermaine and I got into this long discussion about upgrades." Oriana recounts. "Wants to understand the tradeoff between transitioning someone new or upgrading someone who has already transitioned. What's the real value to AppleCore? Are we willing to get fewer immortals out there so all of those who are can stay at the top of their game?"

"It's not an either or." I respond. "Different people do the different functions. We can get upgraded here in LA without having to go to Dallas. But for the transition, well, that's only done in Dallas."

"Can we get upgraded here even if it's a hardware upgrade?" Oriana apparently isn't sure.

I nod. "If it's only software you don't even have to go in. That can be done over the air."

Oriana looks past me out to the courtyard. "I have a request. I don't know if you'll be willing or if it's even possible or not. I think it is, but the whole immortal system still isn't completely clear to me."

"I'll help out any way I can," I respond earnestly. "After all, if I hadn't pushed you I doubt you'd be sitting here now."

"Well, there is that. But what I want to know is would you let them download your software knowledge and transfer it to me?"

A thousand considerations flash past and then a final synopsis. "Dr. Woodall gathered them from my biologic mind and transferred them into code for my electronic mind. I would assume that Dr. Woodall has that set of memories somewhere in case he needs to do a restore for me since he destroyed my biologic body."

"So, you would be open to that," Oriana is still unsure if I agreed or not.

"Yes. My knowledge could be helpful to you, but you would need to know how to interpret it and when to use it or not. I don't know how easy that part is to transfer."

"I think I should be able to make that set of decisions based on my own experience and training and not just from yours alone."

"Given the complexity of decisions you will be faced with, I would hope my experience and decision frames would be just one of the several sets of considerations you will consult."

Oriana smiles apparently recognizing I've just given her the keys to the software kingdom. Time to change the topic, need to make her more comfortable.

"So, tell me," I begin. "Why did you decide you needed to be more athletic? I thought you played softball and basketball in college. Even ran track as I remember."

Oriana seems to be recalling the images of the events I just invoked. "I did. Ran the quarter mile. Too far for a sprinter, too fast for a distance runner. That was me. The odd person in the middle. Seemed that way my whole life."

"Didn't you win a state championship or something?" I'm remembering exactly what it was, but want her to talk about it, something I'd just recently learned I need to do when I want to start a conversation.

"California high school title and then again the NCAA when I was at UCLA."

"But you didn't even try out for the Olympics. Why?"

"Jocelyn, my roommate at UCLA was also my team mate. The Olympics was her life-long goal. To be the best in the world. I had long ago set my goal to be the best software developer in the world. So, we had the same dream in different fields. I thought my fame would be more important in the long run. Just couldn't conceive that I might be irrelevant by the time I was twenty-six. That didn't bother Jocelyn. She wanted the medal on her fireplace mantle. I wanted mine in my paycheck."

EMERGENCE

I wait until 7:38 pm to make my entrance at The Night club just to make a point to Beth. My time is not entirely my own. She sits at a corner table, in the shadows and hard to distinguish. I know it's her because she is wearing a print dress I've seen on her before. Beth never was a fashion maven. She always looks together, right accessories. But she was never one to be wearing the latest fashions on the day they first appear.

She sees me as I approach her table and rises to greet me with our usual hug. She looks tired, but I've never been one to tell someone the truth about how they look. "You look great. Been working out?" is the non-committal greeting I remember seems to work well with her.

"Got my routine down and I'm sticking to it," she responds. She already has a glass of red wine and has consumed more than a sip. I wonder if she's under a lot of pressure from Fisher over the proposal I've still not delivered. It's sitting on my desk, already approved by the bankers and the lawyers. It's simply waiting for my final read through. The board has approved the proposed deal via a telephone meeting, so I'm the roadblock at the moment. A'zam isn't pushing me so I'm doing it at my pace.

"I take it you've had at least a few moments to consider my question." No sense wasting time. If she wants more context she'll have to ask, which I fully expect her to.

"And it is a fascinating question, the more I try to think it through." She takes a sip of her wine as the waiter comes by.

"Water, no ice." I request. Beth looks at me questioningly but then must make a decision about my lack of need for alcohol.

"So why has this subject become of interest?" Beth continues.

"You've read about what's happened to me." I begin. Better to personalize even though Beth can see the bigger picture. "As more people transition, for whatever reason, we will be able to provide a greater and greater range of capability. But at the same time, an immortal, as I'm being called, has considerable limitations."

"Like?" Beth seems to be surprised I'd phrase it this way.

"Feelings, emotions, but also just the traditions around a family meal when so much communications go on in a family. No need for that since I don't eat, breathe or sleep for that matter."

Beth seems to know all this. I expect she would, but I need to lay the ground work as I'm not sure where she is in her understanding of how I work.

"You're saying the things you lack make you less humane?" Beth tries to articulate what she thinks she just heard me say. "I'm not sure I follow completely."

"Let's say I'm sitting here next to Howard Fisher. You decide to start yelling because you're angry at something Howard has done. Howard will react emotionally to your shouting. Either he will act guilty because he caused you to be angry, or he may be regretful he did something that upset you, or he may get angry in return that you're questioning whatever it is he did."

"Okay. What's your point?"

"Howard's reactions are based on the intersection of the intellectual and biologic processes in his body. If you were to shout at me in the same way because of something I'd done? I would have no biologic reaction. I would not react to your shouting or anger until I recall a similar situation I've been in before I became an immortal. Then I would react as I remember having reacted before."

"So, your social interactions are based on memories of similar situations in your past as opposed to biologic reactions in the heat of the moment."

I nod.

"And that's why you asked the question. Does being human require you to react biologically or can you be human if you are reacting as you remember you should?"

"The bigger question for me is what do you do when you don't have a memory to trigger your behavior?" I want her to see the bigger picture. "What if you've never been in a situation like the one you're in? What if you never loved someone because you transitioned as a young child?"

"Can you implant other people's memories?" Beth asks apparently suspecting an answer.

"We think so, but have not run that experiment as yet."

Beth frowns, "Should just be a bigger database you have to process to find an answer."

I let her response go, hoping she will start giving me feedback to the opening question.

She looks at me and considers what I've just told her. "You say you don't have emotions, but they are often reactions to life. For a lot of people life sucks. They either have poor health, or not a good education, or they can't get a job, or they still live with their parents because of one or more of the factors I've just mentioned. And the form of music that came from that was known as the blues. If life sucks every day you have the blues. And some people are able to express that in songs. And even the mood of the songs just reinforces the hopelessness and helplessness of people in those kind of situations. Do you know what I'm saying?"

"What you're describing is a part of life for a lot of people." I respond.

Beth shakes her head, "What I'm describing is life for a lot of people. Some are just talented in being able to express the feelings associated with life like that."

I consider her comment. "How integral is feelings with humanity?" I finally ask.

"I think it's core," Beth responds with determination in her voice. "I don't know how you can say you're human if you can't react as a human does."

"So, reactions make you human."

Beth nods tentatively, "At least I think so."

"Does it make any difference what makes you react?"

Beth seems to be way ahead of me on this one, "A memory? Sometimes we react because we remember we should in a certain way. May not feel that way for a variety of reasons. But we know we should either because our mothers have told us we should, or we've read books or seen movies where people react that way and that response is accepted as appropriate."

"So, a memory is an acceptable mechanism for triggering appropriate behavior."

"It's not in every case," Beth points out. "And I don't know as you could use it as the exclusive trigger for behavior. So much is dependent upon context. Do you know what I mean? What works for children often doesn't for adults and vice versa."

"But what if we are able to give each immortal a set of behavior defining memories. A universal guide for how to behave in a thousand and one situations?"

"Then everyone would react the same in every situation." Beth points out. "That's not how it works now. We go to the movies or read books because the protagonist is a loveable oddball. Someone who doesn't react predictably and in a lot of situations doesn't act appropriately according to the larger social norms. The antagonist is even worse, flouting conventional norms in every instance."

"What if we gave immortals a guide that lists multiple different reactions for each instance? Then the immortal could select the response she or he wants and thereby introduce the variability you've just suggested. Or they could set themselves to use a different reaction each time, unless there is an identical set of circumstances. For example, how to react to a child or brother or sister who does the exact same thing over and over. Then there would be oddballs as well as a variety in how people react to situations."

"Would end up in clashes you don't see today." Beth notes. "Depending on how many different reactions you put into the memory bank they could choose from. No matter how you structured it the result would be a less 'human' set of encounters between people. And the worst thing is they aren't authentic. If someone is really angry the reaction could range from ignoring the anger, to the nuclear option without anything more than random number generators making the difference. Doesn't sound like an ideal way to solve the problem."

I hear the tone she thinks such an approach would be primitive and she's right. "How would you suggest addressing the concern?"

"Could you create a hybrid being? One that has both biologic and non-biologic systems?"

"Would no longer be immortal." I instantly point out.

"But is that the end game?" Beth looks at me sharply. "I thought you were looking for an ability to live longer, not forever."

"When I transitioned? Absolutely. But now that I will live forever… well, having gotten to the end state, why would I want to compromise back to something less than I am now, especially when I think I can get a lot better than I am today as technology continues to evolve."

"You're probably right. But if you want to keep immortals as human, I don't see how you will be successful if there are no genuine emotions. We talk about authenticity in relationships. Under what you've described I don't see how anyone who transitions can be authentic since they don't react and don't feel the things the rest of us do."

"And thus, the blues." I point out.

"Exactly." Beth looks at me. "Could you sing the blues with feeling? I don't think so because a blues singer does feel it as she sings it. It's raw. It's the primeval parts of the brain poking their heads up and saying we're in here and we want you to know we are."

Beth triggers a thought, "Primeval parts of the brain. Tell me more."

She sits back and takes another sip of her wine before she answers. "I was just reflecting that there are parts of us, memories that aren't conscious memories that lurk in there. Way back before we were even human. They are structures in our brains we can't explain. But they are there, layered over with eons of experiences and thoughts and deeds."

"How do we know they're there?" I challenge.

"We don't, but that kind of structure is the only explanation we have for some of the behaviors we observe in patients, particularly those who have suffered injuries to the brain, whether in war or an accident or from disease."

"Have you done much to study brain morphology?" I'm surprised she seems to know a lot in this area.

"No. Just a casual interest really. Tangential to good product design."

My mind is processing a ton of information on the brain I'd not taken the time to review before. Concepts come popping to the top, mostly about the unconscious mind which is the part we probably know the least about. But this is where primeval structures would be discussed and probably reside if they were in fact real. Beth sees me absorbed for a long moment and gives me space, but not for long.

"I've apparently triggered a thought you've not had before," she inquires.

"You have, but I'm not really sure what to do with it."

"Since I know you're not going to give me anything that might be a competitive advantage I need to ask you some questions. I take it you're not really sure what all was transitioned into your memories."

"No." I admit.

"And you're wondering if you lost something in that transition, something that stayed with the body you said they cremated."

I nod.

"And you've just realized that anyone who comes over after you will probably also lose whatever it was that was a part of our primeval heritage."

"More than that. What if there are structures in the unconscious mind that we consciously build upon to guide our behaviors, to recognize situations and react appropriately? What if we've lost the foundations upon which being human are constructed?"

Beth takes another sip of her wine to consider this conundrum.

"How did they transfer your memories?" Beth finally asks.

"A bulk loader is what they call it. Don't really know how it works. Thought there was such a limited need for such a device that there was no need to try to understand it."

"But you said you were going to test out transferring memories to another person or immortal."

I nod to not give any detail.

"So, you have reason to study the device in detail and figure out what comes over and what doesn't. Then you'll at least have a starting point to answer your question."

I realize I need to move up that little project on my priority list and send an email to Dr. Woodall asking if what I propose is possible, and if so, could he set it up? I think it and the email is gone. I look up at Beth who is staring at me. "What if this is just a rabbit trail? We don't know if it has any bearing at all. So, let's assume there's nothing there. How else do I attack the problem of ensuring that immortals are humane or at least consistent with human behaviors?"

"The fundamental question," Beth muses apparently deciding I've come up with a plan to attack the primeval structures. "Does it come back to the mind in another way?"

"Like what?"

"There have been theories that we only use a small part of our brains. If we could find a way to use more of it we would have super or supernatural powers."

"I thought most of them had been debunked."

Beth nods, "But just what if?" she looks at me with an intensity in her I've not seen since high school chemistry lab when she blew the place up.

"What are you thinking? The collective unconscious? No one has ever proven it exists."

"But all the commonalities in the human experience. Whether in literature, the same themes that come back across civilizations that were inaccessible to each other. There are more things about the brain that are unexplained than explained if I remember correctly."

I shake my head. "I need something I can replicate to make me more like you. What you're suggesting isn't something I can replicate because you can't replicate it in yourself since it's unexplained. I just don't see any way spending time on the unexplainable gets me any further towards my goal."

"What's your goal?" Beth pursues. "Being more like me, but if in order to be more like me you must replicate something you can't explain then all you need to know is how it operates. Something along the lines of Emergence."

"What's Emergence?" I have to ask, unfamiliar with it, but my mind quickly informs me.

A SMILE

MC happens into The Night club as I'm saying good-bye to Beth. I decide to see what she's up to as Beth ducks out the door.

"Crazy meeting you here." I look around. "Where's everyone else?"

MC looks embarrassed, "I'm not meeting them."

It suddenly becomes clear she is meeting A'zam. "In that case don't let me keep you."

MC looks around, "He may not show," she shakes her head. "Said he would try."

Sounds like A'zam. Always encouraging without committing. "Then let me buy you a glass of wine and if he arrives I'll disappear."

MC nods and we sit at the same table where I'd just been with Beth. The waiter arrives and brings MC her usual. An Argentinian Malbec.

"Why were you here?" MC finally asks.

"Meeting with a philosopher. Maybe you could help me understand something about the mind."

MC takes the glass from the waiter and takes a sip before she even sets it down. "Sure. What do you want to know?"

"Tell me about the subconscious."

"That's a big subject. Sure, you have enough time?"

"What role does it play in how we react to people and things?"

"Empirical evidence suggests that unconscious phenomena may include repressed feelings, automatic skills, subliminal perceptions, thoughts, habits, and automatic reactions. More tenuous from our observations are the possibility of complexes, phobias and desires." MC muses as she sips again.

"A major impact is the answer to my question," I consider each phenomena. "Repressed feelings would be feelings you experienced but have kept out of your conscious mind?"

MC nods.

"Automatic skills, subliminal perceptions, thoughts, habits and automatic responses are learned behaviors that your conscious mind doesn't control. Not necessarily wired into feelings, but may be."

"I'd say that was accurate."

"Complexes, phobias and desires are strong emotional reactions to some stimuli. Is that correct?"

MC nods. "What are you looking for?"

"I remember emotions, but I don't feel them."

"You've said that," MC doesn't need this step to follow my logic.

"So how do I operate if I don't have an unconscious mind?"

"You've talked about background processing. Isn't that the same?" MC asks.

"I don't think so. That's why I asked what goes on there. Can I develop a complex, or phobia or even have desires if there is no emotional underpinning for any of them other than a memory? And that memory would be one of how I or someone else may have acted in certain circumstances."

MC sips her wine as she contemplates my question, "I don't know the answer to your question, but it would seem to me that it would be difficult if not impossible to actually have a complex, phobia or experience desires as we know them. But I can see where you might exhibit the symptoms of any of those or hundreds of syndromes for that matter. All you would be doing is replicating observed behavior. If the psychologist didn't know you weren't like everyone else, and it's hard to tell, by the way, then a psychologist might well have difficulty in distinguishing the two."

"You're calling it the difference between actual behavior and replicated behavior."

MC nods, "That's one way you could describe it."

I actually take a sip of the glass of water that has been sitting before me since I arrived to meet Beth. Why am I doing this? Because some sensor in me tells me that my moisture tank is not full. Not empty either, but that I can add to its contents without having to deal with the overflow. But that raises a question for me, "What kind of sensors would a non-human need to be able to sense emotions?"

"In a human or another immortal?" MC clarifies.

"Either." I'm as pithy.

"Well, in a human it could be just observed behavior. Exactly what you did when you were like the rest of us. You made memories of how other people acted in social situations and you have those memories to draw on." MC takes a quick sip. "Someone who isn't a biologic entity? That's a little different in that you don't know what is causing the observed behavior if they don't react to emotional displays by humans"

"Other than through a limited set of memories they carry."

MC peers through her glass of wine. "You're still on the unconscious mind and what role it plays in how you see the world."

I nod.

"Without one I'd expect you to be very calm." MC muses. "Wouldn't see you getting upset about anything unless you have a memory of getting upset about something. Then you probably would in a similar circumstance. But is that so bad? As soon as the stimulus for your behavior is removed you'd calm right back down. What is it you're looking for? A hanging offense? What could cause a robot like you to go off the rails?"

"Robot like me?" I'm surprised at her characterization of me.

"Well, you told us you are, just not in so many words.

"I'm not a robot. I think for myself."

"Not what I'm hearing you say." MC sips again to let her observation sink in. "You're concerned because you don't react as a person would in any given situation. You react as you remember you or someone else did, back in the day. Not the same thing. That's what a robot does."

"Robots work from remembered behaviors?"

"Remembered, programmed. What's the difference?" I'm not sure why MC has gone off in this direction.

"There's a big difference. I decide what I will and won't do, not some programmer."

"But if the programmer only gives you a defined set of options as to how you should behave isn't that the same thing? You're not deciding except from a limited set of options she or he gives you?"

"I'm not a robot." I respond, calmly. Too calmly as a memory tells me I should be more upset, but I'm having difficulty figuring out how upset I should act.

"It's okay, Sage." MC smiles at me. "When the world is over run by robots like you all the rest of us are fucked anyway."

"What are you saying?" I'm not sure what she means by fucked, particularly since she's waiting for A'zam.

"We become slaves or a faceless sea of consumers. What's the difference? You run the world, we don't. And you're all just a bunch of super robots. Able to think faster and deeper than the rest of us. Living forever with access to massive databases so you'll never forget a thing. It's okay. We have it coming because we built you rather than taking responsibility to keep us alive like we are."

"I get the sense you're talking wider than the literal me and you."

"Doesn't make any difference. The result is all the same. The fact that you have a consciousness? That's all good. But I don't know as it will change anything. You don't see your own limitations. You only focus on what more you can do than the rest of us. And from where I'm sitting that seems to be mostly about speed. How fast you react to information. I don't know that your answers are any better, but you can certainly pick up on things much faster than I can. You know where a conversation is going before we get past the first few words. At least that was the case until I turned the tables on you just now and introduced a whole line of thought you weren't prepared for. But you opened the door. You asked the question."

"I did." I confirm. "But I don't have this pessimistic view of life you just depicted."

MC nods. "We're not there yet, but if I'm reading between the lines properly I'd have to give us less than a generation. Do you agree?"

"No." I look away to see who else is listening in on our conversation and to make sure A'zam isn't standing right next to me. "I have a whole different view of how the changes I represent will affect humanity. I think those like me can be a force for good. Make everyday life for the average person much better. But the problem will be getting the incentives aligned so that is the result. At the moment I don't know how we do that. But what I'm trying to do is to find out and make sure I do everything in my power to see that's what happens."

MC drains her glass and stands up. A'zam has just entered the building. At least he didn't hear what I just said, but I'll not be surprised if MC tells him in the midst of her orgasm.

"Sit for a minute. He'll wait for you at the bar. I have another question you can help me with."

MC looks dubious but A'zam apparently doesn't see us and goes to the bar. She sits back down.

"What?" she is clearly anxious to get to A'zam before he goes on to someone else.

"How do we perceive feelings in others? Is it all just sight and hearing or is there another level of perceptions we have?"

"What do you mean?" MC seems puzzled. "Like extra sensory perception? That in some cases you just know things?"

"I don't know. You tell me."

"We talked about the unconscious. People experience subliminal perceptions and automatic responses which is what I think makes up most of what people classify as extra sensory perceptions. What makes up a subliminal perception? Is it that their sensors pick up a wider range of cues? Do they filter things out of the environment differently? Or is it really just experience? Recognizing a cue you've seen before and seen the consequences of it? Most likely all of those situations occur in different people. There is no one answer to your question."

"But what about automatic responses?" I follow up since she identified it but didn't address it.

"Same kind of thing. It comes down to what kicks it off? What does the person perceive that they react without thinking, or at least thinking about it consciously? The major difference is that most automatic responses are the result of repetition. It's like in sports where you swing a golf club enough times, or throw a baseball or football, or kick a soccer ball. The more times you do it the easier it becomes and the more accurate you are. It's because you don't have to think it through, your body knows what to do. Your consciousness tells your body you need to swing at the baseball and experience tells you whether to swing high or low, how long to wait and whether to drive through the ball or just make contact. It may also tell you when to bunt, although if you do that at the wrong time the manager will probably get all pissy with you." MC ends smiling.

"You talked about sensors." I formulate another question. "You seem to think that our existing sensors are all we need, since you've pretty much said that extra sensory perception is really a myth."

"I didn't say it's a myth." MC doesn't want me putting words in her mouth, but I see her glance over at the bar so she's not going to stay put much longer. "But there's not a lot of evidence for it. Most of the studies I read are generally able to explain those situations that just seem to be beyond what we are normally able to do."

"But isn't that the issue? Finding a way to be able to do more than we can now?"

"A number of people and organizations have sunk a lot of time, money and resources to identify just that and so far the results have not been inspiring."

"That may be true, but if there is some way of creating new sensory capability through the use of fuzzy logic or machine learning or whatever the in-vogue approach is today, isn't that worth it?"

MC turns her attention to me fully for probably the first time since A'zam entered the room. "Is that where you're going? Wanting to figure out how to make yourself god-like?"

"Whoa. You didn't like it when I suggested you thought ESP was a myth. Saying I want to be god-like is in the same ballpark. Neither of us said it and neither of us are comfortable with the implications."

"Then why the interest in ESP?" MC looks at me with a hard expression.

"I'm still trying to figure out humanity." I confess. "Dr. Woodall loaded my memories when I transitioned, but I'm trying to figure out if there was more in there that I lost when I came over. Important things. Aspects of me that informed my perceptions, thoughts and insights that are gone. And if they are, what's the implication? Am I less likely to respond in a humanlike manner? Will I eventually become unable to bound my decisions by norms of behavior? Will I become an outlier and an outcast as a result?"

I fully have MC's attention now. "What made you worry about bounding your behavior?"

"Trying to understand my new self." I share with her. "It's clear I'm not exactly like I was before. I'm working from memory on a lot of things I shouldn't be, but that's all I have to hang onto. As more immortals result from transitions will their experiences be able to guide them as effectively as mine have? I don't know what to expect. And they won't know either until we better understand what we are creating and how it will work in the long run."

"Is this your problem?" MC seems genuinely surprised I'm even worrying about such deep issues. "I would have thought it was something for your doctor friend. What's his name?"

"Dr. Woodall." I confirm. "He may be working on it, I really don't know. But it's an immediate issue for me because I'm already over here."

"But outside your area of expertise." MC glances at the bar and sees A'zam looking over at us. He stands up. She finishes up. "I wouldn't worry about it. The doctors who designed your host body have to assume responsibility for not only what you can and can't do, but what you will and won't become."

"I don't think they've thought it through and someone has to."

MC rises and picks up her bag. "Then talk to them about it."

"Thanks, I kept you longer than I should have. You know me. I just want to make sure I know what I'm talking about before I go off and try to change something."

MC gives me a hug. "I don't think you need to change a thing. You look great."

"But looks can be deceiving."

MC hesitates, "Are you talking about A'zam or you?"

I smile, but don't respond to her question, hoping she understands my meaning.

THE FUTURE

I pay the bill and get all the way to the doorway when I find Windy getting out of a Googlecar. She turns around to see me looking at her. "Sage? What are you doing here?" Windy looks around like she's expecting to meet someone else. Then it clicks.

"A'zam's with MC. Did he call you?"

Windy can't look at me which tells me all I need to know. "Come on in and we can have a drink since you came all the way down here."

"I'm staying in town now." Windy finally looks at me. "Tom's staying at the ranch and I really don't have a desire to be there with him around."

Hearing the hesitation, I offer, "I'm buying."

"Well, in that case…" Windy scoots in the revolving door before me.

Once more I return to the same table where I've now talked with both Beth and MC. I take the same chair and notice that A'zam and MC are no longer at the bar. I glance at the door to see them ducking out. But before A'zam does he looks back at me to see who I'm with now. He nods, but I don't return it.

"So, what's the latest on the divorce front?" I open the discussion as Windy waits for a glass of white wine. Unusual for her. She's always been a red girl.

"Tom's playing hardball." This doesn't sound good. "Says he should get the ranch and the kids. Keep them together as a family since I'm the one who wants out."

"As I remember he doesn't come from money."

"Baseball scholarship is the only reason he got into college. Didn't have the grades."

I'm surprised at this revelation. "Always thought Tom was fairly intelligent."

"Lazy is the best word to describe him. If he'd have worked harder he could have gotten the grades, but he was always having too much fun to want to learn something."

"How'd he graduate then?"

"He graduated with a three-twelve batting average in the college world series."

"Still doesn't make any sense. He had to put the work in at some point."

Windy shakes her head. "Tutors spoon fed him the truth, the whole truth and nothing but the truth as required to pass any given course."

I have to consider this information for a moment. It certainly explains some things about Tom I'd never been able to figure out. Like how he got to where he did at the company where he works. Just has to talk to people and convince them to buy what he's selling. He's given a selling script. All he has to do is stay sober long enough to remember it when he's delivering it. "Did he know about your parents when you got together?"

"Everyone knew about my parents when I was in school. You even knew about them." And I did. They would come to visit on parent's weekend. Roll up in a Bentley. Her daddy always wore cowboy boots and hat with a big silver buckle. Her mother could have been a fashion model, always dressed, how would I put it? Expensively? They also insisted on taking all of her friends out to dinner somewhere expensive. I enjoyed their largesse, although I never really thought about how rich she was. Rocky wasn't and I was academic scholarship working my way through.

"So, Tom was shopping for just the right set of parents when he happened upon you?" I have to ask because we've never had this conversation before even though I thought we were best friends.

"Let's just say Tom wasn't interested in earning the material trappings of the upper class."

"If you saw what he was, why did you ever marry him?" I'm mystified.

"At the time he didn't give me much indication of what kind of person he was. College athletic hero and all that. Came up from nothing to be something. You know the whole story. You probably could have told a similar story if you'd wanted to."

"I was never the campus hero." I point out. "So, he's got one up on me there."

"But look at what you've done with yourself since. No contest as I look at it."

"When did you figure out he wasn't what you thought? You never said anything."

Windy thinks back, grimaces. "On our wedding night."

"Your wedding night? I don't understand."

"He'd already slept with three members of the wedding party that day and he couldn't get it up when we finally got to the hotel."

"There were only four…" I start and realize I was the only bridesmaid he didn't sleep with. "Really? He slept with Reese too?"

"That was before she met Jake and it was a hard time for her. I was getting married and she didn't have anyone."

"Is that why they all knew about the divorce before I did?"

Windy takes a long sip of her wine. "They all came to me individually to confess what happened. Guess they each thought I should forgive him for one transgression, but when Reese finally came to tell me, and I told her MC and Delilah had too. Well, at that point she told me it was time for him to go."

"Why didn't he come hit on me?" I'm curious if she has any insight here.

"I asked him that. He said you were just too formidable."

"Was that the term he used?" I'm suspicious.

"No, he had a different term, but when I pushed him it was clear he had no idea what the term meant. Typical of him."

"When did they tell you?" I can't believe she would have stayed with him, had all those kids if she knew he was this way on her wedding night.

"About a month ago when the word got out that Tom was screwing around. They each heard about it from different people. They came to me and asked if it was true and how I was handling it. That was when each one told me. I wish they hadn't waited. Would have saved me a whole lot of pain and bad choices I'll be dealing with for the rest of my life and my kid's lives."

I let her reflect on her last statement for a long moment before continuing. "When did you know?"

"There was always something missing. I just could never put my finger on it."

"How he treated you or the kids or your family?"

"It started in bed, I guess. It was always about him, never us."

"You mean never you." I challenge her statement.

"Well, there's that too. Foreplay was me getting him interested, never the other way around. Once he was big, well… it was over in a flash, so to speak."

"But you have three kids. You must have had an orgasm or two in there somewhere."

"We had to see a fertility specialist who had to explain the facts of fertilization to Tom before we conceived."

"Was he better after that?" I'm wondering why things didn't improve.

"For the two times I conceived after that, yes."

"So, in what? Twelve years of marriage you've only had three orgasms?"

"With him." Windy takes another long sip of her wine. I see a grimace in the corner of her mouth she is trying to hide from me.

"Were you sleeping together, or did that end too?"

"He had a healthy sex life. Mine wasn't so healthy. But he was getting his once or twice a week."

"And you lived with that degradation for more than a decade. Why would you do it?"

Windy tries to smile, but it's forced and not convincing. "Once we had kids it was like I can't take their father away from them. Can't send him away. And I can't leave and take them with me."

"Why not?" I push back.

"Really? I'm not a homewrecker."

"No one said you were." I'm curious. "Why would you use that term? A homewrecker is someone from the outside who comes in and breaks up an existing family. You're not outside."

"He made me feel like I was," is barely audible and comes just before another long sip.

"Then why was everything always sunny whenever we got together?" I'm still trying to understand why she never told me what was going on.

"I couldn't admit I was a failure as a mother and a wife. That I was undesirable to the college hero. The one guy all the girls looked up to. Even you said you wouldn't turn down a date with him before he asked me out. I remember that, even if you don't."

"No. I remember. But I was what? Eighteen then? I had no better idea what I was looking for than any of us did. I'm just sorry you won the lottery and have to deal with the consequences of the kind of man he really is. Flawed and with limitations that aren't worthy of you or your kids."

"Don't say that. My kids need to think their father is okay. Otherwise they won't think they're okay. Do you understand what I'm saying?"

"I do." I reassure, but have to ask this next question delicately. "How do you convince them that they aren't limited by what he's contributed to them?"

"What are you saying?"

"You said he only got in and out of college because of an athletic scholarship and a little help along the way from tutors. You don't want your kids to think that's the only way they'll get ahead in life. Do you?"

Windy was lifting her glass to her lips, but stops. Looks down for a moment before she looks back at me. "He's told that story so many times. They must think that's the Horatio Alger story everyone follows to fame and fortune."

"What do they know about your voyage through college and into a career?" I have to ask.

"I never talk about it." Windy admits.

"Maybe you need to start." I suggest. "And while you're at it, talk about the rest of us. How some of us got through on scholarships for academics and some of us got through because of great grades and some of us followed a passion that started young and we followed through on it. There are as many different paths to success as there are people following their dreams."

"Dreams?" Windy repeats.

"You had dreams. I know you did. We talked about them all the time when we were rooming together as undergrads."

"What? That I'd start my own advertising and public relations business?"

"You were a great graphics artist. You still are, but I haven't seen anything you've created in forever. You hire kids to do it for you. They're great with the graphics tools, but they don't have that whimsy you always had in the images you would hand draw. Do you remember that sunset you drew for me?"

"You had it hung in our room the rest of the time we were in college."

"And I still have it hung in my condo breakfast room. It's the last thing I look at before I leave to go to work. That sunset reminds me that every day is unpredictable. I can never be sure I know what will happen. And even though the image hasn't changed in more than a decade and a half, you created it in such a way that every time I look at it I find the unexpected."

Windy must be thinking about that image she created for me so long ago.

"You should." I suggest thinking I know what she's thinking.

"What? Teach myself the new tools so I can do some of the work myself?"

"If that's what it takes for you to rediscover your own creativity. That which sets you apart from everyone else. I'm sure you're a good business woman. You're paying your bills. But the reason you built the business in the first place was those hand drawn graphics that were so distinctive. They incorporated what is unique about you in the everyday world your customers saw but were used to not really looking at. The world is so familiar, and your graphics give them something different to look for, to look forward to seeing in a world of sameness."

"Why are you doing this?" Windy sounds suspicious.

"Doing what? I didn't even expect to see you tonight."

"You know what I'm talking about." Windy sounds annoyed, but not too annoyed. "Pumping me up. Making me get out of my funk about how life has cheated me."

"Life didn't cheat you. But unfortunately, you settled for too long."

Windy closes her eyes and grimaces before reopening her eyes and taking a last long sip of her wine. She places the empty glass on the table. "Settled. Yeah."

"You have to think of today as day one. The first day of my new life. Put all the negative stuff behind you."

"I can't. He'll never let me."

"You can. You just have to do it. You've been telling me he's just a mental midget in comparison to you. So why would you let him set the agenda?"

"He can be hurtful."

"Then kick him in the balls. What do you have to lose at this point? He's taken a decade from you. A time when you could have been incredibly productive. What were you doing? Damage control. Trying to keep him from doing more damage to you and your kids. That's over. You need to be spending your time on how you, not him, you can make your kids successful. And you know what?"

Windy looks at me unsure.

"You do that best by being an example. Show them you can be successful. Show them you can be incredibly creative. You can design graphics that are memorable and talked about the way they used to be, before you decided to be a big company rather than satisfy your customers."

"What do you know about that?" Windy laughs at me being the CEO at AppleCore Products.

"I know you can show your kids the way to their own success and I know you need to start on that today."

"You mean you won't hire my kids when they need jobs?" Windy is only half unserious.

But I change the whole tenor of the conversation, "To get hired at AppleCore your kids would have to transition and be like me."

Windy blinks repeatedly. "You're serious."

I nod.

Windy swallows hard. "You're telling me the world is about to change and I haven't given it any thought. Not only that, but the world you just gave me a glimpse of is the world my kids will need to negotiate to be successful."

I don't respond, letting her realization sink in.

"Sage. Tell me that's not the world my kids are about to inherit. How could it be? It doesn't exist. There are just two of you."

I shake my head, "There are more."

Windy motions for the waiter. "Scotch. Straight."

"You don't drink liquor." I point out.

Windy brushes my comment aside. "Do I need to become like you?"

"That will be your choice at some point. But the answer is only you can make that decision."

"I thought only dying people were transitioning. That's why I never gave it a thought."

I hesitate to respond knowing she will sleep with A'zam at the next opportunity. And he called her tonight. So, at some point they will be in bed together again. "That's not the future." I decide is the least harmful response I can give.

The scotch comes. Windy swallows half in the first gulp. "The future can't be as you've suggested. They can't possibly transition everyone. There are just too many of us."

Again, I don't answer hoping she will understand I'm agreeing with her observation.

Then her face falls in understanding. "That's the problem, isn't it? Not everyone will be able to transition. What does that mean for the rest of us, Sage?"

"Just as today, it means what you make of yourself will determine your future."

"That's bullshit Sage. You're already there. You don't have to worry. No kids. A top-level job at the biggest company in California. No kids to worry about, just yourself. Your future is made. Mine isn't."

"You're right. Both of our futures are set unless we work together to change that future."

TODAY

I stop at my condo and take a quick shower. After a change of clothes, I head back to my office. Spring dress and black leather is just what the doctor ordered to get my appearance in line with what I'm expecting for the day. It's a little after one am. No one waiting at my condo as it's way too late and past any deadlines anyone is working at the moment. No one at the AppleCore gate either, with the exception of the guard who waves me in.

Once in my office I find a message on my office phone.

"Hi Sage, It's Jackson, your friendly mayor. Just checking in to see if you're interested in getting together tonight. I know this is a last-minute call, but my evening just opened up and that doesn't seem to happen all that often anymore. Guess I need to start adding you to my calendar, if that's not too presumptuous. Call me back when you can. If not tonight, I still need to get you on the calendar. Bye."

The mayor of Cupertino. Who walks with me into work on some mornings since the company he owns happens to be on the way. My rose buddy. His mother knew roses and I'd set a goal of knowing all the kinds of roses planted along the way between my condo and work. That started the conversations and they have gone all the way to my bedroom, although never his. I wonder. He said he isn't married, but is he? My mind quickly googles him without even thinking I need to and his bio comes up. If the bio is current, he has never married and even better has no children from relationships whether short or long standing. How can such an appealing guy still be on the streets if he isn't gay? I haven't figured that part out, but for some reason he is. Maybe like Windy I won't figure out the answer to my question until long after it's too late. Why am I so skeptical that I can have a positive relationship with someone who may actually be as lonely as I am?

Interesting that Jackson has gotten the message that courting is not necessary with me. No dinners out, no movie or bowling or roller skating. No club, no concert, no sitting under the stars on a blanket in a park. None of the things that are taken for granted as the entry way to my pants.

I wonder what Jackson really thinks about me since he knows I'm an immortal. At least he knows that's how the media describes me. But what does that really mean? Is an immortal someone who lives two hundred years because that's longer than anyone else on earth? Or is it ten thousand years or a million? I've not seen anything in the media that has really defined immortal. In fact, what I've seen in the media is very shallow. It's designed to evoke a negative response on the part of the reader. That's not what I want. But how can I possibly convince the media to print what I want them to? They're not in business to tell my story as I would. They're in business to tell my story in such a manner that people will pay money to buy the blog or magazine or newspaper or whatever form the media is conveyed to learn what they want them to know. Not exactly a set of economic incentives designed to provide the truth to everyone. But that is the world we live in.

I visualize Jackson. See his craggy face and dark wild hair. It's not wild in the sense that it's just a tangled mess. But his hair is always askew. Windblown I guess is the term people would use for it. You can see what it would look like if it were properly combed, but it never is. Especially when he first gets out of bed having made love. Then it's a random tangle of black looking for order that once dictated its resting state. But that must wait a mirror to guide the comb back to the starting point as no number of hands running through it will restore it to the orderly state expected of it.

His strong back is the next image that comes to mind. He said he was once a weight lifter. Mostly in college. But he took it seriously and he worked on his upper body to give it the wide stance needed to lift heavy weights. He gave it the musculature needed to move heavy weights, whether in the form of bar-bells or heavy objects on the floor of his father's manufacturing company which he inherited upon the death of both of his parents. A strong back that belies a slim waist and similarly muscular legs. Jackson has a body that is highly desirable. That's about all I can say about it. Highly desirable. Purposely built in a gym hour after excruciating hour. For years.

There was a time that such a fantasy about a guy would result in a reaction in me. But not now. Thinking about him simply informs me of what he looks like, why he is a desirable bed mate and why I should want to make love with him again. But I don't feel it. Only think it because I'm thinking about what such a set of images should create in me. And that makes me remember arousal. I used to get aroused when a guy was good. But there were all too many who weren't. I'd end up faking it just so I could get the guy off me and move on. Way too many times. Is that why I stopped taking a chance on guys that weren't over the top? And did I miss a lot by adopting that stance? Probably. Subtlety is not associated with over the top. And yet some of the best orgasms I can remember were the result of a slow approach that carefully stimulated so many different places on my body that all my senses were awake and waiting for a release.

Now I don't even get close. I could as easily go through life ignoring cute guys or those who show their interest in me, because I'm not paying any attention. And even before I transitioned that was the case. Not really anything new. I am married to my job in so many respects. I've given up trying to form relationships. There isn't enough room in my life for everything that would be required by someone coming in, expecting things of me, wanting me home at reasonable hours to share time and thoughts and insights with. That was never me. Not even in the days when Rocky was willing to acknowledge that I was still living with him. Rocky never wanted to discuss anything that wasn't a requirement of being a parent. Report card? Check. School lunch money? Check. Parent teacher conference? Check. Rocky was so happy when I enrolled at college. No more silly meetings about my progress. That was no longer his responsibility. I was my responsibility now. I flunked out? Too bad. Go get a job as a hair dresser or Wal-Mart greeter. No dad. I'd rather be a chiropractor. At least I'd make enough money to live on. How many conversations did we have about the school of chiropractic even though neither of us for even one moment expected I'd ever end up there? But that was life with Rocky. An exercise in the futile as he waited for me to simply grow up and get on with my life, so he could get on with his.

Why did Jackson's call start me down this rabbit trail? I haven't thought about any of this in a while. So why tonight? Because I have time before the world awakens and finds I need to address some issue someone else has identified as critical to AppleCore or the case we are trying or the progress we are making moving our immortals through Dr. Woodall's hospital in Dallas. I've been lucky so far. When the judge agreed to hear the case, she did not impose an injunction. So, the transitions have continued. That was a clear indication to me that the judge decided it was incumbent upon the ACLU to prove their case than for us to prove ours. Don't interfere with commerce until you know there is injury. A totally different approach to the law than had been in place in the years before now under a different administration.

Timing is everything.

In a rush I remember that Jackson is making parts for A'zam. I wasn't happy to find out he was doing so. Making parts for the cadre of immortals A'zam is building to make AppleCore not only the preeminent company in California, but the preeminent company in the world. Incapable of being caught in the markets because of superior products, the result of hundreds and then thousands of immortals teams building things people don't even know they need. Yet. So why am I unhappy with Jackson? He's just trying to make money for his company. What I'm unhappy about is how A'zam keeps encircling me. He co-opts anyone who knows me, so I can only see everyone else in lockstep with him. No dissenting opinions. A clear march to a world of dominance. An undefeated team every year. Forever. Wouldn't that get boring if AppleCore was the only company capable of making a new product or feature set or whatever that meets a new need that we didn't even know we have?

But that's not the reason I'm chafing. I know the future can be different. I'm the reason it will be. But now that I've changed the trajectory, I need to find a way to change it once again so it becomes friendly fire and not unfriendly. I don't want the future to be one dominated by a single individual or company or country. We are a global society. We don't always agree. In fact, if anything we never agree. But that isn't the important point. We have the ability to improve existence for everyone. And yet that is nowhere on the agenda of things we need to address. Why is that? Why do we ignore the rest of the world and focus only on those who are closest to us? And why do those who have no proximity find means to co-opt the world's attention on things and issues that are of no consequence to the rest of the world, but gives them their fifteen seconds of fame. And then they are forgotten by the next individual who is seeking their fifteen seconds. To be succeeded by the next individual.

I don't care about fifteen seconds. I've had mine. I'd be just as content if they kept looking for the next person rather than circling back to me. I'd like to be done. Disappear in the annals of time to ensure a revolution no one pays any attention to but simply accepts as the way it is. That would be fine with me, but somehow, I don't see it as the way things are going to play out. A'zam is not going to let me slip into the twilight. He is going to hold me accountable at some point. And what he holds me accountable for has not yet been determined. For making immortals more humane? For enabling his supreme reign over the mortals and immortals for the rest of his existence? Both are feasible outcomes of the forces at play. And in fact, if I had to take a bet right now I'd go more towards the latter than the former. Don't bet against A'zam. He hasn't lost yet. And he's been able to shape the game. But only because I stood up. He saw what I'd become and what I could become. The fact he's had a month's head start on anyone else is important, but he would never give credit for it.

Is there an intersection between Jackson and A'zam? The David and the Goliath? They wouldn't see each other that way. A'zam would only see Jackson as a supplier and Jackson would only see A'zam as someone dealing with corporate governance issues that are way beyond anything he needs to deal with. Both would be right and wrong at the same time. Jackson has the ability to disrupt A'zam's march toward world dominance by simply not delivering parts. A'zam would sue and try to compel. But in the end, Jackson could disrupt A'zam's great plans. On the other hand, A'zam could force Jackson to find a way to greatly expand his capability to deliver parts by simply finding another incremental increase in the volumes of employees we are transitioning. That could happen. And I'm right in the middle of that analysis. Do I want to push more volume through Jackson's company? It would help him be more successful as he currently defines success. Increased sales. Increased profits. That makes him more successful, even though he's said that the city gives him more fulfillment than the company. He'd rather change the garbage pickup frequency than increase sales by ten percent. But that's Jackson. And that's Jackson at the moment. Will probably change as soon as his term as mayor is up. When is that anyway? Next year my mind quickly informs me. I think he told me that too.

Jermaine wanders into my office, probably suspecting I'd be here. "New dress? Don't think I've seen that one before."

"Mindi bought it for me. I don't have time to go shopping."

"Don't have to worry about your size changing anymore."

"That's true." I think for just a second, "What about your wife? Isn't she pissed you're not in bed with her at the moment?"

"We worked through all that." Jermaine sounds reluctant to discuss but I leave the hook out there for him. "As long as I'm there when she goes to sleep and when she gets up she doesn't give me any shit. Just means I've got to watch the time during the night time shift that I don't screw it up."

"And she sleeps…"

"Eight hours like clockwork. In bed at ten and up at six. So, I got time right now."

"What's on your mind?"

"First I want to say Oriana is doing great. She's been a tremendous help since she transitioned. As hard as it is for me to say that since she screwed me out of that job. You made the right choice."

"Happy to get something right once in a while." I retort.

"You feeling heat? You shouldn't be. We got things under control. And now that Oriana is working at our clock-speed? It's only gonna get better."

I cut to the chase. "I gave you two projects. You delivered one and it got great reviews. Our first immortal team project. Hopefully an indicator of how much things are going to ramp up as we get more and more teams over."

"We haven't hit our stride yet." Jermaine informs me. "Long way to go but every day we find a way to speed up, take a different approach, try a different process to deliver the improved results you're looking for."

"Oriana's job is filled." I state flatly so he knows flattery will not get him anywhere.

"I know, but as things start rolling I'd like you to consider giving me a wider portfolio. Think I'll be able to help the new teams spin up having been the first to walk that particular road."

I get up and walk to the window overlooking the coy pond. "I hear what you're saying." I stop and look back towards him before continuing. "But I need products in the market that will disrupt our competition. Sure, you can help the other teams come up faster, but I need those products today. And the first one I need is the one you still haven't delivered."

"Woody Allen's Orgasmatron."

"That's the one. The movie was Sleepers in case you'd forgotten the reference."

"The one with the time capsule containing a Volkswagen Beetle and things wrapped in tin foil. How could I forget?"

"Well, A'zam isn't looking for tin foil. He's looking for the Orgasmatron. Is it ready?"

"We're still making adjustments. You know how those things are. More art than science. I'll know it's ready when I have that great orgasm, which I haven't had as yet."

"What about your wife?"

"She's more than satisfied. But even she's starting to ask if there isn't something I can do to tweak it just a bit more. You know what I mean?"

I shake my head. "You've run out of time. What am I supposed to say to A'zam?"

"That we're close?"

"Are we playing horseshoes?"

Jermaine looks chastened. He shakes his head. "This has been so much harder than I ever imagined. Why didn't you tell me how hard this was going to be?"

"First of all, you didn't ask because you were arrogant enough, now that you're an immortal, you just thought your new super brain would easily be able to solve the hardest problems. Welcome to reality. Great to be able to process a lot more information. But the intractable problems are still intractable. No matter how much horsepower you apply the solutions will remain elusive, although a little less so than before."

"No bending the laws of physics."

"That would be a definite no." I wait a moment before continuing so he knows I'm changing the subject on him. "Tell me about Zara."

"Nothing to tell." He's playing with me. "She worked it out with her parents and she's ready for her own team. She will get them on Friday when the next group arrives from Dallas."

"And Moshe?"

Jermaine's expression changes. "Still a head case, but at least he's not being disruptive."

"What's your recommendation?"

"I'd transition him back, but I know you won't."

I shake my head.

"Then get him off my team and onto your special project. Today if possible."

RATTLE

I'm not prepared for what I find in A'zam's office. A portal into a different time and place. I see Anna Laura preparing dinner in our kitchen. Tabitha sits at the kitchen table where she sat so many days after school, doing her homework before dinner is ready. Why are they here? In this time and place. I know I should be having a reaction of some sort, but I've had no experience that informs me. What do I say? Am I angry A'zam has invaded my privacy, happy he's been sympathetic and willing to find my past to help me see those who I lost so long ago? I don't know what to do, so I do nothing. I just stand there looking at my lost family, glad that Rocky isn't here to see this. I'm not sure how he would react either.

"Aren't you happy to see your family?" A'zam finally asks, although I'm sure he's experiencing nothing akin to happiness either.

"Why?" Is all I can think of to say.

"Why what? Did I build a time machine? Did I select a time and place important to you. Did I choose to show you what you've lost?"

"An explanation for any of them would be an excellent place to start." I know this doesn't sound right but I suspect A'zam has no idea how it should sound either.

"Then I'll start at the beginning." A'zam lectures me. "You've been searching for something. Something you apparently think you've lost in transitioning. I understand. Although I don't think there's anything to be concerned about. So, I thought I'd show you what you had and let you decide for yourself."

"Where did this come from?" I wonder aloud.

"My fertile imagination." A'zam dismisses my question simplistically, which he knows will not satisfy me. "With a little help from our advanced products team."

"But this doesn't show up anywhere on the product roadmaps." I protest.

"I would be disappointed if it did. I commissioned it outside our normal processes, just as I have other products I don't intend to sell. There is no need to bother the media or shareholders with concepts and ideas."

"Is that where our special chips come from? Chips you never intend to sell?"

"Proof of concept design explorations." A'zam nods without further answering my question.

I now understand why I never see reports on certain activity of the advanced products lab. But at least I know who to ask about this work. I suspect, however, that A'zam has given them strict orders not to discuss any of his special work with anyone including me. "Why a time portal? It doesn't look like it could actually transport anyone."

"You're correct." A'zam runs his hand over the screen. "A portal. A window into another time, but not a door."

"And this is to give me understanding of what?" I ask uneasy about his motivation. "History? What happened, how it happened and maybe, if I'm lucky, why? I certainly can't experience it as it happened because that would involve feelings and emotions I can't access."

"No, but you can observe how others displayed their emotions. Learn the appropriate behaviors in any given situation. This is a living laboratory. Letting you gather the information and intelligence you need to better navigate a world without feelings and emotions."

"But what if we decide the only way we can act human is to be able to access emotions?" I push on his simplistic notion of how to address the problem.

"You have all immortality to seek the answer to your question." A'zam responds glibly. "But by the time you devise a plan to do so you will probably find it's no longer important."

"Then you wouldn't waste your time."

A'zam smiles. "I can't advise on how you should spend your immortality."

"What have you learned from your new toy?" I change the subject.

"That you come from a relatively ordinary background. Nothing extreme, challenging or remarkable from what I've observed. Although I've only had a few minutes to study it."

"What you've observed was very typical." I admit. "I can't tell you how many days I came home to find just this scene. Anna Laura multitasking. Preparing a meal for us and helping Tabitha with her homework. And all the time she was writing an article for one journal or another in her mind. That's the part you can't see in your portal. But if you let it run long enough you would see her write that article and then begin to check her sources as she wrote them from memory of something she'd read hours or days before in some instances."

"She could remember the quotes?" A'zam seems surprised such might be possible.

"Not exactly." I qualify his enthusiasm. "She would have to go back and confirm the exact language. But she always had the substance correct. She knew what it was she wanted to say and how to substantiate an argument from as many sources as needed to make it work."

"Would you say she was even more remarkable than your father? Who would calculate calculus equations long hand? Even did regression calculations as I remember."

I'm surprised A'zam knows anything about my father. "Rocky has a unique mind." Is all I'll give him.

"Ever the diplomat. I wonder what phrase you would use to describe me."

I elect not to take that particular bait, but look into the portal. Anna Laura is making a salad. One I recognize. I had that particular salad for dinner several nights a week for years. Lettuce broken into smaller bites, cherry tomatoes cut in half, cauliflower florets spread throughout, and chunks of cucumber, with a lemon vinaigrette dressing. Rocky liked it and therefore we liked it too by definition. I remember telling Anna Laura that I'd rather not have salad one night. She made me stay at the table until I finished it. No wasting food in our house. As big a sin as not taking a shower or passing up on washing my hair.

A'zam studies my face. "If nothing else I've succeeded in stimulating memories."

"That you have."

"Good or bad?" he asks simply. Unusual for him.

"Anything to do with my mother or sister is good."

"Is that because you lost them? As opposed to Rocky whose memories you're not so fond of?"

I look at him sharply. What does he know about Rocky? "Why is your question of importance?"

"Just trying to understand you better. We've worked together for a long time, and yet I really don't know you. Know you even less since you transitioned."

"Even after a hundred Kama Sutra positions? Twice?"

"That hardly informs me of much other than your dexterity." A'zam, of course belittles that shared experience.

"What about you? Have you used the portal to look back on your own life? To better understand yourself? What you really want to be when you grow up?"

"That's actually a very good suggestion. And the answer is not yet. But it might give me a chance to learn from my own mistakes."

"You didn't learn from your mistakes when you were younger?" I'm surprised he would admit he could have done some things better given the stature he has attained.

"Everyone has a chance to learn from the past. Even if you handled yourself correctly, there may have been a better way so that others were not so resentful of the outcome. Something that would have enabled greater success later in life."

"You're amazingly introspective today. Why?" I can't help but ask.

"My tool. I see an opportunity. I want to make sure I understand it and don't just use it as an amusement. I could you know. Just use it as an amusement. Give me a chance to study someone's formative years. Learn their weaknesses from how they handled past situations. That would give me forewarning of situations I need to be cautious of."

"Meaning?" is he threatening me?

"Meaning, hmmm. Let's use you as an example. You want to make sure I don't stray too far from the norms of humanity."

"Why me as an example?" I ask. "But I agree with the concern you point out. You push us away from human norms and behaviors everyone loses."

"Now who's coming on a bit strong?"

"My point exactly. Others back down and let you establish dominance because that is what you expect and that is what they have become used to having to do to stay in your good graces."

"Are you saying you no longer feel a need to stay in my good graces?" The threat is clear.

"Not at all." I react instantly to give him comfort. "I'm merely trying to establish with you that we have to work hard to stay within socially accepted limits of behavior. And that is hard when you've lost many of the inputs that we used before we transitioned to ensure we behave as expected."

"Why is it important to you to stay within those limits of behavior?" A'zam seems to have not considered this question before.

"We are two amongst nearly twelve billion inhabitants of this planet. You and I can be as rude to each other as we please because no one is going to get upset if it's just the two of us and we are talking at a speed no one else can follow."

"There are about a hundred of us now, including Dr. Woodall's team." A'zam reflects. "But I'll go along with your premise for the moment."

"We need to be able to interact with all those others more than we need to just interact with ourselves. And that's why it's important we look, act and sound like them. The more we separate ourselves, either by word, deed or speed, the more resistance we will create for ourselves. This lawsuit we're fighting at the moment? It's just the beginning. If you think we win this one and they'll go away? Think again. The resistance is there, and they have no basis for it other than what they imagine could happened as a result of our mere presence amongst them."

A'zam looks at me as if he had not considered the lawsuit anything more than a nuisance. "We have people and lawyers. People who are specialists at handling situations like that. Why should I be concerned?"

"Because the protesters won't stop until they stop us." I try to sound firm but not too harsh.

"Who are they? Civil liberties? Who cares about that? Just a bunch of lawyers looking for a paycheck paid for by the tax payers."

I shake my head, "Their lead attorney has never lost a case." I inform him.

"First time for everything." A'zam dismisses my concern.

"I said the same thing until I talked with Dietrich."

"Our general counsel? What did he have to say?" A'zam clearly hasn't spent any time with Dietrich.

"Under the best of circumstances, the only thing we have going for us is the law. Everything else is stacked against us."

"That should be enough." A'zam continues to be dismissive.

"Dietrich doesn't think so. Says our chances are no better than fifty-fifty and that's only if we are very lucky."

A'zam's eyes close partially. "You're saying no chance we just run over them and they go home with their tails between their legs."

"We prevail this once, through luck or whatever, they'll be back almost immediately using other tactics to tie us up as long as possible."

"But even if they succeed, we'll have several teams deployed and no one else will be able to do so. Your whole leadership team should be transitioned by the end of the week. At that point no one else could touch us even if it were shut down."

"Don't jump to conclusions." I warn him. "Others are working on similar techniques. Ones that may not make people into immortals, but will greatly extend their biologic lives and enhance their capabilities. They may not match us one for one, but they may be able to close the gap you think we've created. And don't forget the billions you've invested in the immortal's supply chain? No immortals and we may have to write off that entire investment."

A'zam spends more than a simple cycle considering the write off I've identified.

"You may think I'm off the reservation as you've defined it by being concerned by what you might see as immaterial concerns." I push again. "But since you're not considering them, and they could have a more than material impact on AppleCore as well as you and I…"

"Temporary blip in the road. But what do you mean impact on us?" A'zam sort of dismisses.

"That injunction would prohibit Dr. Woodall from upgrading us. It would also only permit him to maintain us as we are. No mechanical enhancements either. And that includes your Orgasmatron."

"Orgasmatron?"

"Woody Allen movie. Sorry for the obscure reference. That's what we taken to calling it."

"Can you update me with what you've got in case they do put down an injunction?" I've gotten through to him. He wouldn't want this upgrade now if he didn't realize the true situation.

"It's not ready," I push back waiting happily to see his dismay.

"Tell Jermaine to finish it today because I want it installed before the court hearing."

I've been able to rattle him and make him understand there's more at stake than he perceives.

TOGETHER

Time to go see Dr. Woodall. I'm finally understanding why he wanted me to try to find a way to ensure Immortals are humane. After my time portal meeting with A'zam it's clear he has no intention of being bound by such limits. Everything is focused on how to work around the current imposed restrictions and find a shorter path to becoming a deity.

As I enter Dr. Woodall's office, where I almost never meet with him, I notice he is eating a snack. Not what I would have thought a health-conscious doctor would be doing. He's eating pork rinds. In northern California bean sprouts maybe, although they've come and gone so many times I've lost count. They're still perceived as healthy anyway. But pork rinds?

Dr. Woodall pops another into his mouth and closes the bag, sliding it into a drawer. He wipes his hands on a towel before stepping forward to shake my hand. It only takes a moment before he swallows his treat and can finally talk to me. "Sure, you're not in for another upgrade? Seems that's about the only time you come in."

I sit down. He does the same. "I want to follow up on the discussion we had when I elected not to transition back."

Dr. Woodall puzzles on my comment before responding, "You know that's no longer an option."

"I do. You made some comments then I've been trying to sort out and I'm really not sure where it's leading me."

"About helping immortals remain humane?" he guesses, although that was clearly the lynchpin for much that has happened since. "And does this have anything to do with the lawsuit?"

"Not directly, at least not directly at the moment."

The doctor smiles as if he knows there was an answer in my response, but somehow, I disguised it so it wasn't evident. "I can tell."

Now I'm the one confused, "Tell what?"

"I can tell you've been spending time with attorneys." Dr. Woodall acknowledges. "You're sounding more and more like them."

"I'm sorry. You may be right." I have to admit. "But I'm really more concerned about what happens if..." and I don't finish that statement on purpose wanting to see how the doctor finishes it.

"Happens to who?"

"To you and to me," I say without emphasis, so he can still go in many different directions.

He hesitates a moment, purses his lips and then responds, "You win."

"Meaning you lose."

"That's generally what happens when someone wins." The resignation is clear.

"Why does it have to be that way?"

"Before the court case I never thought in those terms, but now." Dr. Woodall shakes his head. "It seems my lawyers are spending my money preparing me to lose."

"You won't lose." I try to sound reassuring since he is clearly in a funk. "The worst that will happen is you will have to do some things differently. I'll probably have to do some things differently. But a court case can't outlaw saving people's lives."

Dr. Woodall perks up, "Is that how you're spinning things? That this is a precedent? One that could make it difficult for doctors to save lives?"

"In part." I confirm for him. "It's a complex case. There are layers of defense and we try to build those layers such that the judge or jury, if she seats one, won't be able to separate them. If we're successful, the precedent would be so damaging that other courts would quickly seek to overturn it."

"Live to fight another day if it goes badly in this round." Dr. Woodall muses.

"We always have a backup plan," I try to reassure him. "Although we always go for a knockout in the first round as well. Try to suck the air out of the room so no one wants to go in there after us."

"You certainly are mixing your metaphors today," Dr. Woodall notes.

"A pure metaphor you would probably forget in five minutes. When I mix them, you have to think about them more and there's a greater chance you'll remember it. Particularly if the mix is incongruous in itself."

"So you're messing with me on purpose." Dr. Woodall notes, although not angrily.

"I'm trying to get you to focus on the question I came with."

"Making immortals humane." Dr. Woodall lets me know I've not sidetracked him at all.

I nod encouraging him to speak his mind without direction from me.

"That's probably the most important thing to do. And yet I don't see any signs anyone has taken responsibility to make it a universal tenet of orientation, or a common trait exhibited by all of the immortals as they come through the process."

"Why didn't you?" I have to ask him since he was in a position to do so early on.

"How do you know I didn't?" He asks as if testing me.

"I would know." I respond

"You seem to be behaving ethically," he observes. "Not so different than anyone else."

"I brought that with me. But I'm not seeing it universally practiced."

Dr. Woodall shakes his head, "Those who you're not seeing ethical behavior in are those who brought something else with them. It's not so much that it's not there, it's that not everyone who is transitioning brought it over with them. But from where I'm sitting that's because it wasn't a strong trait in them before they transitioned."

"So, if it's not coming over with them, how do we instill it in the transition? The person may not be inclined to behave that way no matter what we do in orientation, or chip design."

"You're not so different from a young child in many ways," Dr. Woodall begins. "We have to socialize our children otherwise they would be like wild animals."

"Socialize?" I'm surprised at the direction he seems to be taking. "You think we can socialize immortals to act as society wants them to when in many respects they are the closest thing we've ever seen to a real god?"

Dr. Woodall looks at me sharply, "You're not a god." He shakes his head. "You can be destroyed. In fact, without charging or periodic maintenance you'll die in all the same respects as the rest of us."

This is a blinding flash of insight I'd not had before. Never considered what would happen to me if I didn't recharge. "Is that why you were reluctant to use the term immortal?"

"I think we have to stop using that term." Dr. Woodall seems determined. "It's creating a false set of expectations. And here you're falling into the trap. While yes, it is theoretically possible you could live forever, or at least a very long time, there's no guarantee you will. And you could at any time decide to put an end to your own life. You simply don't recharge."

"I'm not like a car whose battery runs down? You change out the battery and I'm as good as new."

"If you are without any power for a prolonged period your consciousness will fade and ultimately disappear."

"Why didn't you tell me that before?" I'm surprised at this revelation. "None of the others know that do they?"

"Life is fragile. While I may have enabled you to survive a disease, there is no life form that can live without that which powers it one way or another."

"So, we are more human than we think." I observe.

"You have human failings of many different sorts, but it really is up to you to discover what they are. And you may find failings we have not predicted and not have some we expect. That's why I think socialization is a good way to think about what needs to be done to ensure a continuation of civil society."

"But does it need to be civil?" I push to see where he goes with my question.

"Of course. The alternative is chaos."

"Or dictatorship or even a religion."

Dr. Woodall's head snaps up at the mention of religion. Apparently, he'd not thought a religion might result from his breakthrough. He grimaces as he considers my new insight. "No. I don't think you would see a religion. There will be too many of you for anyone to gain that kind of centralized power that men would worship one person."

"Think about it." I challenge him. "If someone devises a means of always having a chipset that is at least one generation ahead of all other immortals and he has a trap door in the mind of every other immortal where he can over-ride their thoughts and desires. Why not a religion?"

Dr. Woodall considers my scenario, knowing exactly who I'm talking about. "Is that what this is all about? Why you didn't want the trapdoor in your configuration."

"How do I know he hasn't introduced it through the upgrades you didn't create?" I point out.

A shake of his head means to me that Dr. Woodall doesn't know if A'zam limited the trap door to the software system the doctor delivered or if A'zam discovered the modifications I'd made from the specification. "You're painting a disturbing picture."

"I don't think either one of us has any idea what A'zam is capable of becoming or doing."

Dr. Woodall loses some of the color from his face. "Are you saying I could live to regret what the result of my proudest achievement may become? An enslavement of humanity?"

"I don't know what may or may not happen as a result of what you've brought into this world. What I do know is that we are at a point where it is still possible to shape things. It will only become much harder when there are a thousand or a million immortals. We have to find a means of making it not only impossible for A'zam to dictate what will happen, but impossible for any one person or even small group of individuals to dictate how we develop."

Dr. Woodall nods, "A different problem than I was focused on."

"Maybe it wouldn't be such a bad thing to lose the first round of this lawsuit."

Dr. Woodall looks at me like I'm crazy.

"It might slow A'zam's efforts enough to give us time to find a means of broadening responsibility and authority." I clarify. "To involve more people in the discussion about what humankind will become when there are more than just one kind of us roaming the earth."

"Like with Neanderthals?" Dr. Woodall leaps to the comparison. "That's not a promising comparison since Homo sapiens wiped them out."

"At the moment it's more likely that those of us who have transitioned could be wiped out by the sheer number of mortals in the world who may not take kindly to the thought of a super human race pushing them aside and keeping the wealth and knowledge to themselves."

"Is that what you think could happen?" Dr. Woodall apparently hadn't considered such an outcome.

"Anything's possible. And when Homo sapiens appeared, there weren't all that many Neanderthals to deal with, and yet it was probably thousands of years for the transition to take place."

"We weren't as good at killing then." Dr. Woodall puts a different spin on my observation.

"But we are talking about a similar period in history, so what we're seeing isn't unprecedented. And we have a lot of history about how that played out that can inform us of how to avoid the same mistakes."

"What mistakes?" Dr. Woodall seems surprised I'd use that term. "The good guys won. The smarter beings inherited the earth and created a society Neanderthals never could have devised. That historical fact is what has made all that we know as modern civilization possible. I certainly wouldn't have wanted it to have turned out any other way."

"Then given that immortals will be able to advance the state of knowledge, evolve new constructs of civilization, and continue to enhance what we devise as the means of organizing ourselves, won't that fit the same criteria you just used? A superior society as seen in retrospect from one of those who benefitted from that society? But what of all those who won't benefit? Who might be enslaved if only in the fact that their freedoms of choice will be limited, that the society will be structured to favor the immortals probably at the expense of mortals. Won't that by definition mean that it would have been better for the Neanderthals to have won? Because then modern man would never have organized in such a way as to have created a civilization capable of destroying itself?"

Dr. Woodall shakes his head, "No. It's different. We aren't inferior beings. We're just equipped with different sensibilities."

"Different organizing principles I think is how it will evolve over time."

"I prefer to think sensibilities because at the moment your sensibilities are limited to your memories." Dr. Woodall muses. "And in time I hope to expand your ability to sense emotions and feelings in others. To find a way that you will share the sensibilities we all have."

"I hope so too." I affirm. "But do you have a path forward? Do you know how to go about doing that?"

Dr. Woodall looks glum, "Not as yet. But it's early. We haven't been at this even six months yet. Give me a little time, more experience in developing upgrades. Finding new approaches and solutions. It's not hopeless, it just needs time."

"And that's the one thing A'zam is dedicated to not giving you. He's rushing his army into the field to ensure you're not the one building the primary systems. That there will be a range of chips creating different levels of cognition, different levels of senses, if not sensibilities. A'zam doesn't want you to be able to succeed with the dream you had. He wants to hijack immortality and make it his own."

"We can't let him." Dr. Woodall responds simply as if he and I can simply say 'no'.

"He has a head start over any other party that might want to change the nature of the game. And right now you and I are his biggest enablers. You assemble the bodies and I bring you the people who are transitioning. Neither one of us can sabotage that process because there are human lives at stake. So, we have to find a way to change the nature of the game without harming those who are changing according to the rules as they've been written."

"That's an almost impossible handicap to overcome," Dr. Woodall realizes aloud.

"But that's what you and I have to do together."

LET US GO

I'm back in my office, thinking about the conversation with Dr. Woodall. Suddenly the portal that A'zam built pops in my mind. Why did he really build it? There's more to that story than he told me. Was he spying on me? Seeing what I was like when I was still a child to get insights as to how he can control me? It was just such a surprise. He'd never mentioned any interest in building a time portal. Never expressed an interest in time or history or anything prior to the day he is living. So where did it come from? Probably someone in his private labs had an idea and built it on his own time. When it was done, then he showed it to A'zam who instantly had an idea how he could use it for his own purposes. Just like when he figured out I was an immortal he seized on what I'd become to bend it to his own purposes.

How can I change the game on him? I'm going to have to think about how he can use it to play mind games. I'll also need to decide how to defend against them. He's going to remind me of things about Anna Laura and Tabitha I've long forgotten. Remind me of them to establish the power of more perfect knowledge of my past than I have myself. He's watched it in the last twenty minutes and I haven't even thought about it in twenty years. And what I do recall is imperfect and incomplete. Now A'zam actually has a better image of what Anna Laura looks like than I do, even though I lived with her for more than a dozen years and he's seen her for ten minutes.

What do I do when he starts on me? Telling me that I'm not the person I think I am because he's seen the real me. What I was like in my formative years. He understands what drives me from having witnessed the events that caused me to become what I am. Could he see the accident I never did? The accident that changed my life? That I've played in my head from angles I never could have seen, because my mind created them to fill in the gaps from what I was told, what we saw when we got there and the accounts the police and others recited for us. And yet few of them saw it either. Maybe I could actually witness that which has preoccupied me in reverie for so many years. Provoked more speculation on my part than anything else in my life, including technical solutions I've spent days concentrating on.

Do I dare tell Rocky about the portal? He would want to see Anna Laura and Tabitha, but I don't know if A'zam would let him. Better not to mention it as it would just drive Rocky crazy that such a device exists and yet he doesn't have access to it. I'm not even sure I'll ever see it again. Most likely A'zam will move it somewhere no one else will have access to it. Why did he have it in his office in the first place? Kind of reinforces my thoughts about one of the people in his private lab built it on his own time and brought it in to show A'zam. That would make sense given what I saw. It looked to me like A'zam was checking it out and used me as the guinea pig. Probably was surprised to find I had a sister I never talk about

But that makes me wonder. If A'zam keeps it in his office even for a short time would there be an opportunity to get in there when his admin, Brit, isn't guarding the door? Use it to learn more about A'zam. He never talks about himself. Never brings up the lessons he learned as a child that shaped what he has become. Could it be turned around? Give me an opportunity to know more about him than he knows himself. Bring things up to him about himself that will test his memory. That could be entertaining, but would it actually have any impact on him? Would it make him question something he believes? Make him reconsider his plan to become the supreme being on earth and all others mere supplicants to his grand plans. I doubt it. And that's why I'm having difficulty understanding how it will keep me off balance. I'm probably making much more out of the portal than is really there. But maybe that's exactly what A'zam wants me to do. Obsess about what he intends to do and overlook something he's doing.

I can think more on A'zam's time portal later. Right now, I need to think about my conversation with Dr. Woodall. It seems every conversation comes back to the same thing. How to ensure immortals are humane when we don't even know what that means. The discussion of the Neanderthals reinforced it in my mind. Neanderthals developed a society that took advantage of their capabilities, established a set of norms they lived within. When Homo sapiens came along suddenly the norms changed. The Neanderthal limits on social organization were quickly breeched by the Homo sapiens. This did not occur because of anything the Neanderthals did overtly, it was a result of new abilities in the Homo sapiens. And it will be the same with Immortals. We will be able to do things mortals will not. We can do things mortals cannot now and the rate of capability change will only accelerate. The longer we exist the greater the distance that will arise between us.

It occurs to me that we could see forbidden cities built around the world. Just like in Beijing where the Emperor lived in a great warren of buildings and rooms, in the middle of, but apart from the larger society over which those who lived in the Forbidden City ruled. Because Immortals think faster, communicate faster and act faster and longer than mortals who must rest and sleep will we set ourselves apart? Will we only wish to interact with those who communicate at our speeds and bandwidth? Am I making too much out of the whole concept of humanity? Maybe it won't be necessary for us to be like mortals. We aren't the same, just as Homo sapiens weren't the same as Neanderthals. If we set ourselves apart we won't need to slow down our processing and communications to interact with mortals. We simply send the communications and let the mortals process what we have to say at their own speed. Mediated communications. We've already set that expectation in society, so why should it be an issue for it to be the way Immortals and Mortals interact?

However, if such a separation were to occur it plays directly into the kind of society A'zam has foreseen and begun to create. A society with a powerful elite and everyone else. The only difference from today is who the elite are. Instead of families and entrepreneurs it becomes those who are in a position to transition into a higher capability body.

But will the original vision Dr. Woodall had of a universal approach to save the lives of those whose body has contracted an incurable disease or otherwise come to the end of its ability to sustain a life disappear? Will the reason I became an immortal no longer be available to others because being an immortal is reserved for those the new elite wish to have join them from the ranks of mortals? But if we are mediated, how will immortals know who amongst the mortals should join us?

The more I try to understand the potential futures the more I become pessimistic that any future will create a fairer or more just society. I've always thought that was an objective of a humane society. The issues we have wrestled with for hundreds of years will simply be seen as something for those directly involved to address as they see fit. Immortals will have problems of their own to solve. Whether minorities of any type are discriminated against, kept from the full expression of their abilities by a set of expectations that pervade the society will not be a concern of those who are neither limited in any way, nor concerned about individual rights. Particularly if it ends up that we are simply an extension of A'zam's consciousness. Limited by him and what he decides.

For some reason I suddenly have an image of Anna Laura appear in my mind. She is the one who established boundaries for me when I was young. She was the one who communicated a set of expectations that I inculcated and have used as a north star for my voyage through life. Why is what A'zam is trying to do any different than what Anna Laura did? It's not, other than Anna Laura had a societal expectation to set the boundaries for Tabitha and me. That was her role as a mother. Rocky was supposed to help her do that, but he pretty much abdicated that role to her early on. Anyway, society conferred that role on Anna Laura. It has not conferred that role on A'zam. And maybe that's what has me seeing his whole effort as illegitimate. No one conferred anything on A'zam. He just took it upon himself. But is that any different than so many religious leaders? They step up and take it upon themselves to establish their link between the great unwashed masses and the lord their god. And then based upon the reading they have done of holy scriptures and the interpretations that other men have made of those scriptures, the religious leader feels empowered by the lord to be an interpreter. To bring the unknowable lord to its people. But how can something that is unknowable be interpreted by just another human being who has no special two-way radio to the lord?

The more I think about it, A'zam is not unique. He is only doing what so many others have done before him. Seize upon a moment of change to establish himself in a position of power. And all good will flow to him as a result. So why should I care? I'm in the same position. I have the same opportunity to try to sway things in a direction I would prefer. But maybe the difference between us is that I have no grand illusions about being more than I am. I wasn't a CEO before my transition. Sure, I had an important role at AppleCore, but I wasn't any more important than the people who were on my team. If I had died, one of them would have stepped up into my role and probably done as good, if not a better job at it than I was. Would it have been Oriana or Jermaine? I don't know. A'zam would have had the authority to hire the new person. As I remember, Julia who was the Chief Operating Officer when I transitioned, had apparently already interviewed for my replacement and had made a recommendation to A'zam. It was a done deal that I was gone. Only I upset those plans and now Julia is gone.

Something brings me back to Anna Laura. A'zam has his time portal to give him insights for some undefined purpose. What if I were to create a robotic version of Anna Laura? Someone who I could instill with all the memories needed to be a moral guide for me? Someone who I could consult when my memories aren't enough to guide my behavior in a humane way? A counter weight to A'zam who will want to claim that role for himself. It would probably be easier to establish this moral guide in just software and load it in a partition of my memory. Something I could consult without an external dialog, but somehow that just doesn't seem as satisfying to me. With society going further and further out the mediated communications structure, the idea of someone you consult just has a certain appeal. Could we make a robotic parent for every mortal as well as immortal? Yes, it could be a product, but let's not get ahead of myself here. I need to prove it out first. Build a prototype and perfect it before I show it to anyone. But I don't have a personal team working projects just for me that aren't on the company development table like A'zam. I certainly wouldn't use them. So who could build such a device for me? Of course, the most logical person is Rocky. He knew her better than anyone, although I'm not sure his memory is all that good at this point. He has idealized her to the point I'm not sure she could ever go swimming again because she would walk across any body of water.

But how would Rocky feel about recreating his one true love, although he's made noises that this new woman might eventually get to that same status. But I'm not sure I believe he really thinks that. He's still rebounding from my taking Anna Laura's eyes away from him. He's made it very clear I had no right to do that to him. He'd made a safe haven for himself with my occasional appearances reinforcing the fiction of his continuing life with her even though she left us two decades ago.

The more I think about it, though, Rocky probably wouldn't want any part of such a… what would I even call it? Moral guide? He would tell me I should forget about the whole thing. Would probably think I'm only wanting to create such a device as a way to convince him he doesn't need to get remarried after all this time. I only need the robotic Anna Laura to talk to, to gain comfort from, to laugh with, and to commiserate with. No. Rocky would not be happy with the thought of a substitute Anna Laura. But I will need his help if I want to go forward with this idea. Only he has memories of her that I would need. And the more I think about it, Rocky probably could build her if he wanted to. Of course, he'd need some help, but all the expertise he would need resides at AppleCore. I'd just need to get them temporarily reassigned without drawing attention to what I'm doing. After watching A'zam doing exactly the same thing, the path forward to getting this done should be relatively straight forward. And there is plenty of precedent.

In fact, I could probably get Jackson's company to fabricate some of the parts I'll need. He probably, with a little help, could fabricate most everything I'd need except the items we would custom build inside. Most of them could be dual use items. Things we build for other products and the only thing that really changes is the software. And I can write that software. The more I think about a robotic Anna Laura the more I realize it is readily doable. The most difficult part will be getting Rocky on board with the idea.

My mind starts assembling a parts list. I push that task into the background. I don't want that to be the primary subject of my thoughts at the moment. It gives me a sense of accomplishment that I've devised a counter to at least one of A'zam's initiatives to keep me off balance. And it will be nice to have conversations with Anna Laura again since I never had the chance to say good-bye to her or Tabitha. I wasn't ready for her to be ripped from my life like that. I'm still not. Maybe that's why I've come up with this crazy idea. And it is crazy. Who would want to listen to a robot telling them what they should or shouldn't do? People grow up with adults telling them things and when they become adults they expect they are beyond that need. But we always listen to our grandparents. Why is that? Because they represent wisdom? A set of experiences that helped them navigate a long life that has seen many dramatic changes just as we are seeing dramatic changes. We listen to our grandparents because we love them. They represent the continuity of who we are. The generations that made a life for a family that continues through children of children. A robotic Anna Laura may have that same wisdom residing in its memory. Probably will have more wisdom than the actual Anna Laura. But the robot won't represent the family generations in the same way. That means people will react to the robot differently. Won't have the same deference to it that a parent or grandparent brings. So maybe there really isn't a market for my moral guide. And that's all right. If I'm the only person on earth who wants such a device, then at least I'll be satisfied I met my need.

Then I think about Jackson. The mayor of Cupertino. Owns a small machine shop that can fabricate the parts I need for my Anna Laura. I'll have to produce the part drawings he'll need. And he will want official

AppleCore part numbers assigned to them, so I'll have to work that back through engineering at the company. List the parts under prototype development, only then the engineering folks will ask why we don't simply produce the small quantities we want using 3D printing at the company. We could. Probably even makes the most sense since we have to produce the drawings and mechanical files anyway. But I don't want to keep this entirely inside. I want to involve Jackson. Get him to do something for me and not just A'zam. Balance his allegiances.

My mind presents me with two alternative approaches to a part design. I don't want to deal with this right now and am about to send it back when a particular detail catches my attention. Of course, I scanned the two proposed documents. When my mind works as fast as it does now it really doesn't take any longer to scan and make decisions than it does to simply scan to understand the issue my mind is presenting to me. What has caught my attention is that one approach would limit the short-term memory. This means that the new Anna Laura would not be able to remember my last question when I bring up a new one. I don't want that. I want Anna Laura to remember me and what I asked before. I want her to be able to learn. To consider the many questions I ask and draw inferences from them. Is there a pattern? And if there is if I adopt an approach to similar problems will I generally be right? I want to be able to learn from this Anna Laura the same way I did from the first Anna Laura.

That makes me stop and think about what do I really want this Anna Laura for? Am I seeing that immortals need a mother to help them socialize as Dr. Woodall described it? An Indian guide who can lead us through the wilderness that is so different and strange to us, but one that they have transited many times and know like the back of their own hand? But no one has been here before. As much as the Homo sapiens encountered a similar situation, it really wasn't the same. They inhabited a much more primitive world. The nature of dangers were well known. Generally hungry animals looking for their next meal, poisonous plants and reptiles that could kill you, precarious land forms such as cliffs and sand pits that could also take your life if you were ignorant or careless. The weather could also be a danger. Too cold without warm furs and one could freeze to death. Too much sun and one could die from sunburns or from dehydration. And still Homo sapiens had mothers and fathers to guide them. Extended family members to hunt with and be warned of dangers the family members encountered on previous trips into the unknown.

For those of us now embarking on the new frontier of immortality the dangers are completely unknown. I was surprised when Dr. Woodall mentioned that immortal is not a good term for us since we can die if we are either ignorant or careless about staying charged. Just like the early Homo sapiens could die if they were ignorant or careless, but from very different causes. What is most concerning to me is how little I know about what will happen. And I know I shouldn't be concerned about the future since I really need to navigate today better than I am. But I'm too close. I see how the future is being pulled in different directions. Any one of which could succeed for reasons I can't begin to see and I'm in the vortex, the eye of the storm. Is that the problem? In the eye I'm being whipped around so fast I can't possibly get my bearings and decide how to change the direction of the future. Does the future have a direction? I don't know as I've never thought about it in these terms before. What I do know is that I'm struggling to get a foot on the ground. Plant it so I can stop spinning and see where I am.

And that's why I need Anna Laura. I need someone who can reach into the eye of the storm and pluck me out. Grab hold and not let go. Look into my eyes and say everything will be all right. Make me believe it because I believe in her. And at the end of the day, I need someone who has her feet planted when she reaches into the storm. Someone braced to take on the storm, knowing she too could be carried away, but is not concerned because she knows she is right. Knows that the future was not constructed such that either of us would not be a part of it. Anna Laura welcomed the opportunity to look death in the eye and smile, knowing that to do so would confuse death and he would let us go.

WORKING LATE

Rocky surprises me when I tell him of my Anna Laura plan. "You'll never get the eyes right."

Does this mean he thinks it's a good idea? The answer to that question doesn't take long.

"Why you need to bring her back now?"

It's clear Rocky is still processing the notion. If I wait a little longer I'm sure I'll get the feature length version.

"Are you doing this to make sure I don't get married again?" the accusation is what I actually thought he would start with. Shows I don't know him as well as I thought. "Bring back Anna Laura so I'll realize my new lady friend isn't what I think? You've got an evil mind, there young one. You think because you're a robot that maybe all I really need in my old age is a robot too? That's not how it works. A robot's not going to keep me warm and toasty in bed at night."

"Could if I built her that way."

"I've read about those comfort robots." Rocky shakes his head as if to say he's not interested.

"Rocky." I interrupt him. "I'm not considering this robot for you, I'm looking for someone who can give me guidance when things get hazy. Do you know what I mean? I don't feel emotions. You do something that should get me mad, I don't feel anger. I may have a memory that I was angry once before when you did something, and I react as I remember I reacted then. That may be the right reaction, but it may be way off the mark. So, I'm looking to create something that can help me in those situations where I don't feel something and my reaction would get me into trouble."

"Why don't you fix the problem rather than doing this whole work around?"

"The problem?" I ask not sure what problem he's identified.

"Figure out how to have emotional reactions." Rocky responds simply. "I can see that memories would be an easy fix for the short term, but it's not for the long term. You need to sit down with your doctor friend and come up with a sympathetic nervous system for you and all the others of you that you're gonna make."

"Sympathetic nervous system?" I'm not sure I'm following him.

"The part of someone that releases adrenaline in a fight or flight situation. It's the part of you that reacts most strongly to emotional stimuli."

"Didn't know you knew anything about physiology."

"There's lots you don't know about me. And if you ever cared to learn more I'd never tell you anyway. So you need to go talk with your doc. There's got to be a way of creating a nervous system that would allow you to experience feelings. Then you wouldn't need your robot of Anna Laura."

"Since you've been hiding your brilliance under a bushel all these years, how would you do it?"

"I'm not a medical doc. That's not my area of expertise."

"But we're not talking about a human body, we're talking robotics. And you are an expert in robotics."

"Big difference between a few circuits and a whole robot," Rocky tries to bail on me.

"Not so much as you'd have me think. I'll bet you could build this Anna Laura for me. In fact, you'd probably do a much better job of it than I could because you remember her better than I do." Not likely he will take the bait, but I have to try.

"You're on your own on this one. You want an Anna Laura that's your business. I got me a new lady. Nothing you're gonna do is going to keep me from marrying her. I need someone who's gonna take care of me when I get old someday." Rocky hesitates, playing with me now. "When I get old. You know. Not now. I'm way too young to need a lady just to wheel me around in a wheel chair. That's when I get old and decrepit. You know. Like an old person."

"So then why do you need a new lady when you're so young and virile? Bet you went out dancing again last night, didn't you? Probably closed the place down like you did when you and Anna Laura were dating."

Rocky looks at me surprised.

"You didn't know I knew that did you? Anna Laura told me. Said you were a good dancer. Light on your feet and on hers too, she said."

"I did step on her feet more than once." Rocky remembers with chagrin.

"Anna Laura said I could do a lot worse than finding a guy like you."

Rocky considers Anna Laura's advice to me, and then his expression hardens. "But I'm not gonna build you an Anna Laura, so just get that thought out of your head. I've moved on. I don't need her anymore, even if you think you do. So, the answer is no. Let's move on to something else."

"What's her name?" I follow his direction, but with a purpose of circling back.

"Who?"

"Your lady friend, since that's how you're still referring to her. She must have a name unless she's just an imaginary friend. And if that's the case a robotic Anna Laura would have to be better than someone you can only see in your dreams."

"My lady friend has a name. She's not just in my dreams. What difference does it make any how?"

"I'm just trying to understand how serious this is, really."

"Like I said, I'll need someone to take care of me when I'm old and gray."

"You most certainly are gray." I point to his hair. "And you're no spring chicken."

"All right. So maybe I'll need her to take care of me earlier than I'd like. I still got some time here I can do some damage before she's rolling me around to doctor appointments."

"Or you could let me put you in for the immortals program at AppleCore. As an engineering fellow you would qualify."

"I told you before, I'm not interested in living forever." Rocky cuts it off there.

"But if you transitioned you'd never be wheeled to doctor appointments."

"The answer is still no. I'm not gonna let you turn me into you."

That sets me back a moment. He doesn't want to be like me, even though I'm just like him. "Then help me with the Anna Laura project," I decide to wait to see what he says now.

"Why do you call it a project?" Aha, he's weakening. Maybe his lady friend really is in his head.

"Because if she does what I need, there may be a market for others like her. Not the same. Not Anna Laura. But someone else's mother or wife or grandmother. Whatever fills the need for immortals who have lost their emotional compass."

"Why didn't you tell me this part before?" Rocky seems to be softening, but there's some edge there he doesn't want me to hear, but I do.

"We're at the prototype phase. Proof of concept. I have no idea where this will go. It may be a one-shot deal. Build Anna Laura and she doesn't serve the purpose. If that's what happens, then we disassemble her and use the parts on another project. And even if it does, whether that works for other immortals I can't predict with any kind of accuracy. Does this help?"

"It does. So, what you're asking me to do is help you define a new product that will be part of what you're calling the 'support' market."

"Yes, and you've already agreed to help A'zam with his design. This would just be an extension of what you're already doing. Only in this case I'm your customer and not A'zam."

"I'll bet A'zam pays better."

"I'll bet he doesn't." I come right back knowing A'zam will pay Rocky whatever it takes to ensure I know Rocky is working for A'zam. Part of the campaign to keep me in line.

"I still won't help you. You want to do this I certainly am in no position to stop you, but I won't help you. And if you do build it? Never bring it here."

What caused the switch? One moment he seemed to be coming around the next he wants absolutely nothing to do with it. I have to take a different tack.

"Do you remember that last Sunday before the accident?"

Rocky seems to freeze. Only his eyes move to look at me. "What about it?"

"At dinner we talked about going on vacation as a family. Do you know how long it had been since we had been on vacation together as a family?"

"We never went on vacation as a family."

"That's what I remember too. So why had you and Anna Laura decided we had the money to go on vacation together when we had never had the money to do so before?"

"Money wasn't the issue," Rocky reveals.

"We had gone on day trips as a family, but we never stayed anywhere overnight."

"I don't remember that." Selective memory now.

"Why then?" I push. "Why did you decide to take our first family vacation together then?"

Rocky gets to his feet and walks away from me, but stops in the doorway leading to his shop. "I didn't. Anna Laura decided we needed to take that vacation. I went along with her idea, because I always went along with what she thought the family needed. And she thought we needed the time away. Time to be together. Just have fun together."

"That's not how I remember it." I challenge his memory. "She told you she was going to take us on a vacation to Yosemite and either you could come with us or stay at home. It was your choice. You hemmed and hawed, as I remember, but you finally came around and said you would come but it couldn't be more than a long weekend. Not the week-long trip she proposed."

"Not how I remember it."

"Not how you choose to remember it." Now the question I've sat on for twenty years bubbles up. "Was she going to leave you and take us with her?"

"No," come flat and strong as if he doesn't want to admit something he's blocked for a long time.

"Then why can't you bear the thought of seeing her again?"

Rocky turns back to his lab, but doesn't move. He looks down the hallway for a long moment. He then finally turns back to me. "I was supposed to pick up Tabitha that night, not her. I ran late so she took the longer drive so we could all get home about the same time. I should have been in the car with Tabitha, not her. Don't you see? I killed Anna Laura because I insisted on working late that night."

APPLESEED

Dr. Woodall returns a call I made to him. I wanted to follow up on something he avoided talking about in our last meeting. I'm in my office at AppleCore when the call comes in. "Hi, Sage. What's on your mind?"

"Software."

"Which software?" he responds cautiously.

"Have you delivered any new software since I rewrote the update?"

"Yes." Comes without hesitation although a little guilt can be heard. "A'zam asked for a series of new capabilities your version didn't provide."

"Did he discuss why he needed the new capabilities, since they evidently weren't anything you saw as important?"

"Why do you want to know?" Dr. Woodall apparently doesn't really want to get into specifics.

"Because he's using you to lay the foundation of his control over the immortals, don't you see that?"

"Not really, no." Cautious response. There's fire here. "How could he control the immortals through my software update?"

"Tell me about the new features. What are they?" I have no specifics but A'zam has been too quiet so he's definitely up to something.

"It's really an attempt to create the socialization we talked about. At least that's how I see it."

"Socialization." I repeat now seeing where that whole conversation came from in the first place. "Socialization like instilling a set of expectations we have to respect? Would that be a good way of describing what you've written?"

"I hope to get to respect at some point. But now we have to be a little more blunt in how we administer socialization. I'd have to describe it as more like a car speed limiter. You can do anything up to a point, but you can't go faster than a limit we put in place."

"I'm certainly glad A'zam wasn't involved when you transitioned me, or I'd be very different than I am. Limited. Unable to make independent decisions. Forced to conform to someone else's expectations. And I take it that someone else is A'zam?"

"We're using his template at the moment, although I have the authority to change it as needed based on feedback from those transitioning."

"Authority. Immortals are the result of your brilliance and hard work and A'zam is giving you the authority to change your invention?" I try to make him realize he's abdicated authority that is his.

"He's paying for these modifications."

"But you're transitioning people, not pets."

Dr. Woodall doesn't have a response to my observation.

"I thought we had an understanding about the danger any one person with too much control over immortals poses." I try to measure my words carefully.

"We discussed that, yes."

"So why are you simply rolling over to A'zam?"

"I'm not… rolling over. But he's funding an acceleration of our work. The fact he's sending people through has enabled us to scale up our operations, transition the staff so they can work faster, learn the lessons quicker, make adjustments on the fly and then incorporate new capability faster. This is a dream come true. I never could have foreseen all this happening so fast. I didn't even expect to have transitioned the first person yet. Wouldn't have if you hadn't been presented. Don't you see, A'zam may have ulterior motives, but the fact there are now over one-hundred transitioned people in the world is giving me a rich environment to study the effects of transitioning. We're learning so much now. Your experience is much better and that of every person who goes through now is so much better. No. I'm not rolling over. I'm embracing the opportunity A'zam has given me and my team."

"A Faustian bargain." I suggest. "What about all your stated concerns about humane immortals?"

He ignores my observation about Faust. "I am concerned, but I've given that task to you. You're in a much better position than I am to make a difference there."

"So humane immortals is a nice to have for you." I try to state it as bluntly as I can since he's waxed eloquently about all the good things A'zam has done for him.

"I wouldn't put it that way. But we have time to work it in."

"Work it in." I repeat totally deflated. I made this journey in large part because Dr. Woodall had challenged me to save humanity from inhumane immortals. And now I find he simply outsourced a minor task he'd identified.

"You don't have any time pressures." Dr. Woodall observes. "It's not like the world will come to an end if you don't find a solution in the next two weeks."

I'm still working through the revelation and don't respond to Dr. Woodall, which apparently unsettles him.

"Why are you unhappy about this discussion?" he asks.

I set my thoughts aside about humane immortals and return to my original question. "Tell me how the new software works? How does it limit behavior?"

"It essentially establishes a deference to authority."

"Hard coded in."

"Yes." Dr. Woodall answers simply.

"So, the individual finds she or he must obey an authority figure."

"That's right."

"And how do you define authority figure?" I am suspicious.

"According to roles assigned by society. Policemen, Judges, government officials…"

"Hold on." I stop him right here. "Policemen and judges, I understand. They're part of our judiciary and law enforcement branch of government. Government officials for the most part are public servants. They should be taking instructions from us, not the other way around."

"If the President asked you to do something you wouldn't?" Woodall asks.

"The President has no legal authority over me. She or he can't tell me to do anything. The President can sign a bill into law after approval by both houses of Congress that would compel me to do something, but it would then be up to law enforcement to ensure that I do, not the President."

"What about your boss at work?" Dr. Woodall comes down a level.

"I wondered how long it was going to take you to go here. The answer is still no. I am employed by a company to do something for them. The supervisor is responsible for assigning the work to me that must be performed, to ensure I'm adequately trained to perform it and given the resources including time to do so. The supervisor then has the responsibility to check my work to ensure I'm performing to standard. But the supervisor is not an authority figure in the sense of law enforcement. If I repeatedly fail to perform my work according to established standards, and all attempts to help me reach those levels of performance fail, the only recourse may be to terminate my employment, not put me in jail."

"Who said anything about jail?" Dr. Woodall seems genuinely surprised I would bring up jail.

"You're talking about limiting behavior. Jail limits behavior externally."

"But I'm doing it internally."

"No, you've removed the freedom of choice. Jail limits freedom of choice. Just like with the example of the employee. The employee can make choices. Those choices may end up in termination from their job, but it is still their choice. You're hard coding has eliminated that freedom to fail. It's the same as an external control, even though you've written it in."

"I don't see it the same way you do." Dr. Woodall finally concedes I may have a point he'd not considered, although he's not stated that specifically.

"You see it the way A'zam wants you to because he's paying you to see it his way."

"No. I disagree. A'zam didn't walk me though what we just discussed. This is how I see it."

"Rationalization for selling out." I push back.

"I'm not selling out." Dr. Woodall sounds unconvinced himself.

"No. You already did."

"I didn't remove your override capability." He offers as a concession to my anger.

"So, I haven't lost my freedom of choice in the updates since I wrote the first version." I seek to confirm.

"You haven't lost anything. You've only gained additional capability."

"But what about the other immortals coming through?" I suspect I know the answer.

"They have the same override capability, only they don't know how to use it."

Dr. Woodall continues to walk the tight rope between A'zam and me. He can't afford to piss off either of us so he complies with what each of us wants without telling the other. I'm going to have to go back to square one on how to achieve my goal of humane immortals. But then I wonder. Has Dr. Woodall programmed in my quest so that I really have no choice? He could have inserted code to that effect in one of my updates and I wouldn't know.

"What other proscriptive code have you inserted in your updates?"

"What do you mean?" Dr. Woodall apparently was hoping I'd not ask this very question.

"Since you're writing code to limit our behaviors, have you written code that compels others?"

"Can you give me a for instance?"

"Code that compels me to recharge when my batteries fall below a ten percent state of charge?"

"You have autonomous code if that's what you're asking. Code that automatically performs certain tasks so that your body and processors will do all the things necessary for you to function and stay alive."

"Is it possible to create a sympathetic nervous system equivalent?"

Dr. Woodall puzzles on my question. "What brought this on?"

"Is it possible?"

"Yes, but not necessary the way you are constructed." He defends his design.

"I disagree. I think you need to start down the design path towards a nervous system equivalent that can inform our decision making. It's the only way for us to achieve humane behavior. We have to have emotions. Humans are emotional beings. Without feelings we are only approximations of the beings we were when we had them. So rather than writing limiting and compelling code, you should be focused on how to create a nervous system that enables emotions."

Dr. Woodall considers my recommendation. After a long silence he looks at me again, "I'll have to give that some thought. Not an easy retrofit. Would be better to design it in from the beginning, but we're well down the road now without it."

"You said yourself you're learning lessons from those of us who are out in the wild. The most important lesson I've learned is that without emotions I'm going to drift further and further away from human behaviors. That will be to the detriment of those of you who elect not to transition."

"You're back to A'zam who you think has already drifted further away than you have, I take it."

I don't answer as he is stating the obvious. I need to find a way of convincing him that he has to take more responsibility for the future of his invention. He seems to believe anything that accelerates getting more and more of us out there is good for him. It gives him more data to work with, greater understanding of how we navigate in the wider world, what are our limitations and what should be our limitations, but only because A'zam has pushed him in that direction. When I came through limitations were not part of the software design. This is all new since A'zam.

"Are you going to make any changes to the software as a result of our conversation?"

"About who authority figures are?"

I nod.

"You've made points I'd not considered. I'll have to talk it through with some of the members of the design team."

"Did you do that before you plunged ahead this last time?" I suspect an answer.

Dr. Woodall shakes his head. "A'zam gave us the specification. We built it to the specification."

"Tell me how your design team works now versus how it worked before A'zam showed up."

"We are very collaborative. Talk through everything and come to consensus. That's how your functionality was decided. It wasn't always perfect, but we knew that going in."

"And now?"

"We still work the same way on those projects we are working for the core model. But A'zam has all this customization he wants done. So, we have what we call the Appleseed model. That incorporates the changes he wants off the core."

"Seeds from the AppleCore. I get it." But then another thought occurs to me. "Did you transition your team to the core model and not incorporate Appleseed functionality?"

"A'zam insisted we transition the team with Appleseed functionality."

"And all of the Appleseed updates including deference to authority limitations."

"He insisted." Dr. Woodall responds as if trying to make me understand how persuasive A'zam can be.

"But you didn't." I surmise.

Dr. Woodall looks at me, but doesn't answer the question.

"I'm not going to tell him." I reassure the doctor. "But you've just confirmed what he's doing is making you and your team as uncomfortable as it makes me. And that's why I need you to keep a more open mind about what he's asking you to do. Find ways of ensuring freedom that A'zam is trying to remove from the immortals. Ensure there is always a way for the individual to chart a path different from authority figures. That may get them into trouble with law enforcement, but let them. It's not your choice. It should be theirs. And in the end, they should be able to select their own god, if they want one."

ESSENTIAL

Petra, my bone thin but always perky CFO, wanders into my office, closes the door behind herself and takes a seat. She is expressionless, which always describes Petra. "The good news is the judge threw out the injunction."

"I see you've been in with Dietrich. So, we continue as we are." I seek confirmation.

Petra nods, "But the bad news is she's going to conduct a hearing to give both sides an opportunity to discuss the merits of the case more fully."

As I feared. It's circus time. The judge sees a lot of interest in this case which will lead to notoriety for her. I suspect it will be like the OJ murder trial. People who are complete unknowns will become household names for the duration of their fifteen minutes of fame. But that fifteen minutes will completely disrupt the proceedings.

"Each person who testifies will make it seem like you shoot death rays from your eyes and leap tall buildings at a single bound," Petra continues.

"I don't?" I ask trying to sound surprised.

"Not while I've been around."

"And lucky for us they won't know you're an immortal as well." I point out.

"We certainly don't want to go there." Petra agrees.

"Does Dietrich have a time frame for the hearing?" I ask, wondering how far along with the deployment plan we will get before attention really becomes an issue.

"He thought she will want to stage it properly, so it could be weeks or months. More likely months."

"Enough time for the media to build it up into a major event." I surmise.

Petra nods as if lost in thought. "We will need to coordinate your media appearances to be sure we are setting the right tone. We need to humanize you as much as possible. Would your father do an interview with you where he confirms you're still very much the daughter he raised?"

"Probably not a good idea." I try not to sound an alarm. "Rocky's not so happy with me. I'm sure that would come up somewhere in an interview."

"Pointing out you're not the same." Petra concludes. "What about those gal pals you hang with? Would they be credible?"

"Most of them are sleeping with A'zam."

"As are we." Petra reminds me and instantly I remember Jermaine was supposed to upgrade his Orgasmatron software and yet I've not been called upon to help him test it out. Curious. I wonder who got that call.

"I'll have to give it some thought. No one I can think of would be credible and beyond reproach. I'm afraid what would come across is that I wasn't all that warm and cuddly before I transitioned and that's not what you want. The impression should be I'm no different than anyone else. And if you append to that, 'who's risen to become CEO of a consumer products company', you might get a few other CEOs to agree, but no one who walks to work in the morning."

"You still doing that?" Petra is reminded that I do.

"When the media isn't laying in ambush. I still have to be careful. Come and go at odd times, things like that."

"Easier for you to do since you don't have anyone at home waiting for you."

"How is that working out for you and your husband?" I suddenly realize she has a different set of restraints on her than I do.

"He thinks he's married to a twenty-year-old again. Still waiting for him to get tired of every night, but so far he's hung in there."

"It's only been a week." I point out.

"But when you're only used to doing it once a month, that's a lot. If A'zam would leave me alone It wouldn't be so bad, but fitting them both in on the same night… well."

Guess I know who A'zam's been calling. "He say anything to you about the last upgrade?"

"Your team did something to make him adjust to be a better fit. Creates a lot more friction and that means it doesn't take long to get off."

"That mean you're having more orgasms since you don't get as sore?" I have to ask.

"Isn't that how it's working for you?"

I nod now understanding the situation and deliberately causing her to think I'm agreeing with her question, even though I'm not. "But did he say how it was for him? He complained previously."

"Dissatisfied customers are never a good thing." Petra notes, but doesn't give me the answer I am looking for. "And speaking of customers, I understand there's a request for another media conference.

Only this time they've asked A'zam to participate."

"I've been waiting for him to make a statement." I confirm my thoughts for her. "It must be killing him I'm getting the press and he isn't."

"He made you the CEO of the products company knowing it would raise your profile and also bring positive media attention to the company. I don't think he's upset you're taking the arrows at the moment."

Petra's insight on that front would be as good as anyone's. "Do you think he will… join the conference?"

"Dietrich advised him not to with the lawsuit pending and the fact we are mounting the defense." Petra lets me know I should expect to remain out there by myself. She rises and glances at the door. "Just a word of advice, run everything you would ever consider saying to the media past Suzette in communications. If she has any question, she'll consult with Dietrich. But at the moment she seems to have a pretty good idea of how he thinks we're going to have to play it, at least through the hearing."

Petra looks back at me for a long moment, thinks something she doesn't share and heads for the door.

As the door closes my phone rings. Mindi is on the line, "Windy for you."

A click and Windy is breathless, "They threw out that lawsuit against you."

"Not exactly." I respond to temper her enthusiasm.

"It was on the news. Said the judge didn't grant the injunction the ACLU sought."

"She didn't. But there's more."

"Oh." Windy sounds deflated. "I thought I was going to bring you good news, but you already know more than I heard."

"Petra came in and briefed me."

"She's not your lawyer." Windy isn't following.

"No, but she was apparently in with Dietrich when the word came in."

"He wasn't in court for the decision?"

"We have outside counsel representing us for this one." I inform Windy. A General Counsel usually wouldn't appear on behalf of his client if outside counsel had been retained.

"Can you come out and play? Everyone's dying to hear what's going on."

"You probably know more than I do."

"About A'zam?" Windy hesitates before continuing. "We probably do, although we've been sharing a lot more than we used to. He's playing games but we're getting better at catching him. I think he's not happy with any of us at the moment."

Explains why Petra is getting the call. "Where are you?" I don't want to commit if no one can get some place until later.

"We're all together in a Googlecar outside your office building, waiting for you."

"Guess you aren't going to take no for an answer."

"You don't come down, we come up." Windy affirms my expectation.

Within a half hour we are all at The Night club. Wine all around, even for me, although I get no buzz from the alcohol. I just expect that if my posse has been giving A'zam a hard time and Petra's husband is wanting quality time with his wife that I'll be getting a call soon.

"It feels like a balloon when he's inside," Delilah explains to the rest of us. "He fills the space so it's nice and snug. It means we have to be wetter than usual, or the friction can be fierce."

"It's also quicker." Windy advises us. With more friction it doesn't take long."

"For you or for him?" Reese asks, even though she's the only one of us who hasn't slept with A'zam. At least not yet. Or at least she hasn't told us if she has.

"Both of us." Windy admits.

"So, Reese, what's the story with you and him? He gotten to you yet?"

Reese smiles with an unusual smile for her. "He's trying his best."

"So, you're still an A'zam virgin." MC observes. "You really ought to try it so when we talk about the experience you'll understand better."

Reese continues her smile, "You are all being wonderfully descriptive. Don't think I'm missing much."

MC turns to me, "What's happening with your quest? To understand what it means to be human? We've been giving you some ammunition about the sexual side of humanity. What else do you need?"

"A lot more." I respond immediately. "There's just so much I don't know. How different is it for different people? We see one side of humanity here, but it's a decidedly western idea. Modern, secular, very commercial. Happiness is mediated by artificial intelligence. In other parts of the world it's very different. Ancient civilizations, theocratic, bereft of commercial goods and services. If you don't grow it or kill it, you don't eat it. Happiness is mediated by a religious figure, as is most of your knowledge and literacy skills and experience. And then there's everywhere in between."

"You raise an interesting question," MC continues. "How much of humanity is dictated by the society in which you live?

"I think there are core values or attributes that go across societies or cultures or whatever you want to call it." Reese contributes to the discussion. "I took all those courses as an undergrad. Anthropology and sociology and psychology. All the 'ologies, that someone told me meant the study of someone, whether it's old groups, new groups or just one person. They all seemed to come back to a set of core beliefs, if you will."

"Do you remember what they were?" I have to ask.

"Not exactly, but there seems to be a core that includes, love. The ability to care about and for others. Whether that person is your nuclear family, your extended family or your own family. Love of family I guess is one way I'd modify that."

"People form bonds with others they don't know when they find out they are related somehow." Delilah adds.

"Form bonds," I stop the discussion for a moment. "Like emotional bonds."

Head nods all around. My conversation with Dr. Woodall about a central nervous system is coming back making even more sense now.

"Being human means providing for others, whether your family members or friends or neighbors, who can't provide for themselves." Windy suggests.

"It means contributing to the community in which you live."

Reese suggests. "Like all the times a parent will help another parent by shuttling the other's kids around with your own. To soccer practice, or ballet recital, or school band, or football games. Raising money so the team their child is on can get new uniforms or take a team trip to a tournament. Being human means pulling together and helping others out."

"Being human means being vulnerable at times." Delilah contributes to the discussion. "Listening to criticism of you or something you've done, and acting on it to make yourself a better person."

"It means being there for someone who is sick or dying." Windy suggests. "I'm not talking just about your own kids or family. But a friend gets sick or has surgery, friends and neighbors stop by to see how they're doing. They bring food so the family doesn't have to prepare a meal that night." Windy hesitates before going on, but she does. "And when someone is dying? It means staying with them until the end. Comforting them. Letting that person know you're there and you care about them."

"You all seem to be coming at it from a similar perspective," I point out. "Is there something particularly human about how we organize ourselves? The fact we establish farms and grow what we and our families need, or live in cities and make things to sell to others?"

"What about bees or ants?" MC chimes in. "They live in colonies which is a lot like living in a city."

"But does any other animal plant seeds to grow crops or raise animals it then harvests and eats?"

"Not that I can think of." Delilah responds.

"Then what about socialization?" I have to ask since it's been on my mind since Dr. Woodall raised it.

"Tell me more." MC puts her head into her hands and rubs her temples.

"You talked about what parents do for others to help out and all." I try to frame my question as non-threatening as possible. But you didn't talk at all about what a parent does to prepare her or his kids to function in society. What are the expectations that society has of an individual? You know, like you will go to school and learn to read and write and do math. You'll follow the law and do as a policeman or judge instructs you. When you deal with adults you will be respectful and listen to what they have to say and do what they ask if it is reasonable. Things like that."

"Are you asking if it's human to socialize your kids, or are you asking if it's human to have been socialized by your parents and act accordingly?" Reese is all over this question.

"Both, maybe." I try to open up space for a range of answers. "Tell me what you think."

"I think the problem is what is socialized is all over the place." Windy notes, as the one who has lived all over the world. "As you said before, what is part of socialization in the west is very different from most parts of Africa or the Arctic."

"But is it an essential part of what makes us human?" I have to know the answer.

TRANSITIONS

Suzette sits next to me and Dr. Woodall on the other side. We are meeting with the media at Dr. Woodall's Spartan office in Cupertino. This is his personal office and not the site where he performs updates. No lab or operating rooms here for reporters to ask to see. Just offices of doctors, engineers and bioethicists. The latter is a recent addition to Dr. Woodall's staff. The 30ish Nate Salisbury was an academic at UCLA until a week ago. And now he's trying to parse the theory he has been writing about his whole life. He now sits in the back of the room hoping to remain inconspicuous, but learn from the nature of the questions the media will ask.

The room is crowded. More showed up than were expected. Suzette starts things off, "Welcome everyone. As requested we are making Dr. Bart Woodall and Dr. Sage Washington available for your questions. Neither has a prepared statement as there has been nothing of note to report to you since the last press conference. We are prepared to take your questions now.

All clamor for recognition. I nod to a young woman in the front row who hardly looks old enough to be out of school, but I quickly come up with her name and affiliation, "Miss Scott of the New York Times. I hope you didn't come all the way out here just for the opportunity to ask me a question."

The young woman smiles, "I didn't. I came all the way out here to ask Dr. Woodall a question."

Dr. Woodall nods and she proceeds, "Dr. Woodall, there are reports that you have not accepted any further medical cases for review as you did in Dr. Washington's case. Why is that?"

Dr. Woodall smiles at Miss Scott although I see his hands shake slightly as he adjusts his posture in his chair. "Miss Scott, I can't discuss individual cases we are reviewing, but let me say we are reviewing cases for transition." His voice is a little shaky.

"But there are no reports you have accepted any." Miss Scott continues.

"Nor will there be." Dr. Woodall's voice firms. "You get reports when public officials are hospitalized because of their official duties. If they are going to be incapacitated for an extended period someone may need to act in their absence. When Mrs. Smith down the street goes into the hospital no media is notified. She has no official role that may require someone acting in her stead on behalf of the people."

"That's not the point, Doctor." Miss Scott is getting annoyed.

"Privacy isn't the point, Miss Scott? Should we tell everyone in this room that you have a severe medical condition that could be life threatening? That you are going to undergo an extreme and unproven medical procedure to try to save your life? And do you have any idea how many people are in exactly that situation every day? You members of the media have not chosen to report on any one of them. So why someone who has been referred to my procedure? From the perspective of the patient and from the perspective of society it should be all the same."

"But it isn't the same." Miss Scott continues. "No other procedure results in someone who is dying suddenly living forever."

"A supposition on your part, Miss Scott."

"What? That those you transition will live forever? That was clearly articulated at your first press conference."

"Nothing about my procedure guarantees that the individual who transitions will live a day, a week or a million years. There are many unknowns about the procedure. And while it is theoretically possible that someone who transitions could live as long as the universe continues to exist, there are literally thousands of conditions that could result in that life prematurely terminating."

"That's not what was reported at the first press conference." Miss Scott continues.

"The confusion is a result of my remarks, not Dr. Woodall's," I insert myself into the discussion. "I made several points that day as a way of calling attention to the fact that I am not a robot, which was an assumption made and discussed at that time. I am very much a living person. Like you in all respects except one. Instead of biological parts, my body is made of electronic and mechanical systems. But my consciousness is identical to that before the transition."

"And thus, you won't die like everyone else because as parts wear out they can be replaced." Miss Scott is following my explanation.

"Correct. But the other thing you have to consider is that I won't age the way a person does. You won't see my hair color change with dies to make you think I'm younger than I am. I will look the same, only the clothes and hair styles will change with the times."

The other reporters are tired of waiting so every hand goes up and everyone calls to be recognized. "Mr. Badu from the Dallas Morning News. Welcome to California. I thought Texans didn't make it out to the coast all that often. Something about an aversion to the politics out here." I again try to set a direction for the questioning.

"I too have a question for Dr. Woodall. My offices are downtown. Every day on my way into work I drive right past the medical district where you transitioned Dr. Washington. I've noticed that there is a new hospital under construction there. But there have been no reports as to who is building a new hospital. So as a good reporter I have asked questions in the tax office and the city building permit office. What I learned was surprising to me. I learned that the hospital is being built by a new corporation you own along with the other doctors in your practice. Not an unusual practice. Many doctors have built clinics for their practice. But this hospital appears to be a special purpose surgical hospital. Designed to house twenty-five surgical suites. Is what I've learned so far accurate, doctor?"

"Yes." Dr. Woodall responds softly.

"Twenty-five surgical suites. That's a lot of transitioning patients, particularly when you only acknowledge one successful transition to date."

Dr. Woodall does not respond, but rather waits for a question. Mr. Badu realizes the doctor is not going to volunteer anything.

"Why would you build so many surgical suites, doctor?"

"If you had attended my first press conference you would remember that this procedure was developed to address all those incurable diseases where no known treatment or cure exists. All the diseases and conditions that have populations too small to attract large scale research grants."

"Are you saying there are a large number of patients, who, for the first time have a chance at survival? And you expect a large number of them to seek to transition?"

"At the moment, the only place an individual can transition is in Dallas at UT Southwestern Medical Center. Once the new hospital is complete next year we expect to have the procedure well established. The new hospital will give us a place where we will be able to address fatal illnesses and conditions early rather than losing patients who have no other options."

"And who is financing this new facility?"

"Private investors have committed to the project."

"Is AppleCore one of those investors?" Mr. Badu has had his ear to the ground.

"I am bound by non-disclosure provisions of the investment agreement, so unfortunately I can't respond to your question."

"And there are no public filings of your financing agreement?" Mr. Badu pushes.

"None that I am aware of." Dr. Woodall looks for another questioner.

I recognize a woman in her forties, hair tied back in a ponytail. Streaks of grey amongst the jet black. "Mrs. Walters from the Chicago Tribune. Didn't anyone from San Francisco come out today?" I ask. Three people in the back row raise their hands. "I'll get to you next."

"Dr. Woodall. I've been given copies of emails indicating parts and subassemblies for a large number of bodies for your transitioning patients have been shipped to Dallas. The email indicates the shipments are continuing. Do you have any comment on this?"

"Yes, we are receiving materials to build up an inventory of bodies. It takes time to assemble each one, because as you can see from Dr. Washington, there is a bit of custom work to make the individual look like the person who is transitioning."

"How long does it take to prepare a new body?" Mrs. Walters continues her line of questions.

"In the case of Dr. Washington, it took almost a year."

"And now?"

"We are in the midst of a learning curve. We are learning new ways every day to prepare faster, to minimize rework, to do things right the first time. I really can't give you an estimate."

"Do you have a target?" Mrs. Walters seems to be running out of things to ask about her question since she didn't get a smoking gun answer. "Like a week or a day at some point?"

"We are talking about people, Mrs. Walters. This is your name?" A head nod from the reporter. "So, efficiency is a relative thing. We are getting better at bringing the basic components together and integrating them, but it's all the finish work. That's what takes time, but it's what everyone notices. And did I mention we are continuing to develop new capabilities. We are doing upgrades for Dr. Washington, to ensure they perform as expected. But they are becoming the new baseline configuration."

No further questions from the Chicago Tribune, so I recognize, "Mr. Cardinale from the San Francisco Examiner."

"Yes, Dr. Washington. I have a question for you. Would you make the same decision again, to transition like you have knowing what you know now?"

I don't hesitate, "Mr. Cardinale, that's an easy question. I was hoping for something hard, you know? I have this big brain now and all. The answer to your question is yes, I would make the same decision I did. I have survived terminal diseases. I actually had a combination of syndromes, either one of which would have killed me in time. Together, the inevitable was sped up considerably. So just the fact that I am alive is justification for the procedure I underwent. Medical outcomes I think is the term the professionals use."

Dr. Woodall jumps in, "I think it's important to recognize that Dr. Washington's body survived for only thirty days after her transition. Part of that is because her consciousness was removed from it. But had she not transitioned, she would not be with us this morning."

"What happened to her body?" Mr. Cardinale continues the line of questioning.

"It was cremated after she elected to remain in her new condition."

"You consider her new state a condition?" Mr. Cardinale again.

"Yes."

"But she's super human, if I could use that term to describe her." Mr. Cardinale thinks there's something worth writing about and none of the prior questions gave him anything.

"In some respects, you're right. But if you stop to think about it there are athletes, who play professional sports, or participate in the Olympic Games that are super human in some respect. Albert Einstein, or Stephen Hawking were super human in a way that is very similar to Dr. Washington. She has the ability to look at problems and solve them in a way that is very different from you or me. The ability to do that is unremarkable in and of itself. What is remarkable is what she does with that ability. People remember Einstein not because of his big brain, but because of the theories he developed. Stephen Hawking is remembered for his ability to describe astronomical premises and how that might explain natural phenomenon astronomers were observing."

"English doc?" Mr. Cardinale jokes. "No, I get what you're saying, but you're making my job harder. I must use a fifth-grade word to explain what you said in an eleventh-grade word. That's not always so easy. So, if you could speak in plain English we would all appreciate it."

"I'll do my best." Dr. Woodall responds.

"Okay. So, the doc here is not Wonder Woman. She's just real smart and she may or may not live a lot longer than me. Is that the story you're trying to give us?"

"Yes." Dr. Woodall responds before I can.

"That's not so much a story as a sales pitch, since the alternative is she would be dead."

"I hope that is the story, because I want people with incurable diseases to know there is an alternative to dying."

"You're like Cracker Jack. Not only does your patient get the popcorn she or he came looking for in the procedure you offer, but the patient who is dying also gets a prize, which is to be much smarter and to live longer than they ever expected."

"I've not heard that comparison before, but in some ways it's apt." Dr. Woodall responds with a smile.

"One last questioner?" I ask to move towards conclusion. I look around the room and spot, "Miss Mojazza from the Des Moines Register."

"Thank you for taking our questions. I think everyone who came today was hopeful we would gain insights that will help us understand what is going to be discussed in the upcoming hearing. The way you have explained the situation today would make it seem there really is nothing for people to be afraid of. Quite the contrary. Parents should want their children to contract life threatening diseases because then they have an opportunity to become the smartest kid in their class at school."

"No parent should want that for their child." Dr. Woodall responds. "Treating children with life threatening diseases is one of the hardest medical practices. Your heart is broken daily. And it has to be much harder on each parent than it is on the doctor who seeks to provide a cure."

"Is that why you have not married, doctor?" Miss Mojazza is following a different path.

"In part." Dr. Woodall responds honestly. "It would devastate me to be unable to save the life of my own child if it were to contract a disease. And that's the world I see every day. The world that drove me to try a different path to curing those many diseases. Ones that until now gave the patient no hope." He turns slightly to glance at me. "Dr. Woodall would be dead now if my procedure wasn't there for her when her need became life threatening. I want to be able to do the same for any other patient in similar circumstances."

"You speak eloquently about the need for your procedure to cure incurable disease, but there are reports that you are transitioning people without diseased bodies. Is that true?" Miss Mojazza has gone for the jugular after a feint toward the personal.

"I am not aware of such reports." Dr. Woodall glances at me and back at Miss Mojazza. "What is your source?"

"As a journalist I'm not permitted to reveal my sources if they chose not to be cited."

"As a physician I'm not permitted to talk about patients unless they chose to be discussed in public and not many do."

Miss Mojazza looks at me. "The reports indicate that at least some of those who have transitioned are AppleCore employees. Can you confirm that AppleCore employees are not transitioning even without medical conditions that would require such a procedure?"

"As you know," I begin. "Federal privacy laws do not permit me to know about individual employee medical conditions, procedures or company expenditures for their medical treatments..."

ANNA LAURA'S EYES

Of course A'zam is sitting in my office waiting for me when I return from the press conference.

"I understand the media is picking up the scent," he informs me without even looking around.

"People are noticing things. And even though each person has signed a non-disclosure and agreed not to discuss their transition the word is getting out."

"Probably telling their spouses and the kids hear things and talk at school." A'zam sounds resigned to the reality. "You remember how that all works."

I take my seat behind my desk. "Would explain it."

"But how did a reporter in Des Moines get hold of the story when the major papers including the bay area papers haven't?"

"She probably knows someone's neighbor here. Impossible to tell, really. But you can be sure they will all put the pieces together and we will be reading all about it, probably before the hearing."

"Ah yes, the hearing." A'zam changes direction. "How are we playing that?"

"Dr. Woodall did a great job of demystifying immortality. Weakened the ACLU's case, although they now have time to build other arguments. And they will. Dietrich thinks the story will morph during the hearings, but that's why we have to be rock solid consistent."

"I agree with you on the basic strategy, but I'm worried about how the media is going to play it. You both seem to have mastered answers that are truthful, but not directly answering the question. That will probably come back to haunt you in the stories that will be appearing in the next few days."

"We can't be seen as hiding anything." I insist. "That just sends the media into a frenzy. All kinds of facts, fiction and everything in between starts to show up. There is just so much garbage that appears people can't decide what's fact and what's not."

"But that is a basic assumption of the media. Big companies are always hiding something. And it's just a fact of life that big companies are conservative. People don't get ahead if they are not risk averse. The worst thing is to make a million dollars for the company one day and lose three the next."

"I understand that. But why has the media made the assumption that the company is always wrong, or doing something that is not in the best interests of the consumer or the public?"

"Because companies make profits." A'zam has a ready answer. "And the media hates to see anyone make money off of the public or consumers. I don't know if it's jealousy or something else. Maybe the reporters all wish they worked at the companies that make all the profits because then maybe they would get paid more. The media is notorious for low pay until you get to the very top."

"Maybe. But I understand they wanted you at the press conference. I see you chose not to attend."

"Of course, they wanted me there." A'zam sounds slighted I'd not assumed the media would want him to answer questions. "But it's better they ask Woodall. He sounds innocent and besides he's a doc. And docs are supposed to be the good guys, even though most of them are as greedy as the next person."

"Dr. Woodall did a good job. But how long do you think it will be before their requests become more insistent. Particularly when they get confirmations about AppleCore employees transitioning?"

"You'll handle it." His response is dismissive.

I nod, knowing I've just been thrown under the bus. "Guidance?" I'm trying to get his fingerprints on the media strategy since they are all over the contracts underlying the whole effort.

"You're more than capable of navigating these waters."

"Then why did you come to visit?" I need to understand his objective.

"A couple of things. First, the upgrade for what did you call it? The Woody Allen thing?"

"The Orgasmatron."

"Yes, that. It's a big improvement. Still not phenomenal, but Jermaine and his team should be commended for advancing the state of the art."

"And you want the next upgrade when?" I ask almost disinterested.

"As soon as it is ready. Since there was no injunction I don't have to worry about not getting further upgrades. And while I think it's theoretically possible we could end up with some legal restrictions coming out of the hearings, from what Dietrich told me, it appears unlikely."

"I would agree. The judge ruled in our favor on the request for injunction. That would indicate Jane Williams and the ACLU did not establish sufficient damage to warrant a cease and desist. They have the higher burden of proof now and that's all good for us and Dr. Woodall."

"And there is one more thing I wanted to discuss. I understand you wish to build a single prototype of a new device. Something outside our normal product areas."

Boy word got around fast on that. Where did he get the information? I nod but don't comment.

"Why do you think there may be a market for such a device?" A'zam pursues.

"Why do you think there may be a market for your portal?" I come right back at him.

"I'm not sure there is. Only time will tell. But since there has been such a fascination with time travel for centuries, I think it a reasonable investment to investigate whether the portal may be a suitable approach."

"You could say the same for my little experiment," I hide behind his response.

"Why only one?"

"Proof of concept." I confirm. "I'm not sure if what I have in mind is even feasible. Much like the one portal you had built. When the first one was designed and built, it was not a given it would actually work."

"True, but I think it would have been prudent to build a few of them, try them out in different configurations. See what works and what doesn't rather than stop when you have one version which might have fatal flaws, but flaws that could be overcome with a different approach."

"Why are you so interested in my little project?"

"You described it as something that might have a similar size market to the immortals market. Why?"

Now I know where he got his information. Jackson. The Mayor of Cupertino. He's the only one I used that description with. Why would he tell A'zam about it? I'll have to pursue that further. Tells me I can't completely trust Jackson. But then again, I wasn't explicit about not saying anything about it to AppleCore folks. Lesson learned. "Just a frame of reference as to why we would spend time and money on a new product that's so dissimilar, as you pointed out, from our traditional products."

"It doesn't have anything to do with what your device is going to look like?"

He must have seen the mock up I gave Jackson. He would have recognized Anna Laura having seen her in the time portal. "You're the reason for that little conceit on my part. You showed me Anna Laura in your time portal. That was probably still on my mind when I did the design."

"And why did you do the design rather than hand it off to your teams?"

"I like to keep my hand in design work. It's important I stay current with the tools and processes so when a request comes in for us to invest a ton of money on something I at least have an appreciation for what we are buying or replacing."

"You've become quite proficient at it haven't you?" A'zam stares at me.

"What?"

"Only giving part of the truth. I don't think I can believe anything you say without putting it together with something else you've said. Why is that? Don't you trust me?"

"I've learned my behavior at the feet of the master," I throw right back at him.

"Understandable. I've not always been completely up front with you. Couldn't really. If you have too much information you could make things difficult. Not that you'd want to. But there's just so much no one understands about the changes we are creating."

"Why can't you trust me?" I let him know I disagree with his assessment.

"You're going to say I trusted you with the company. I trusted you for ten years developing one solution after another. I trusted you to reposition us every time we got ourselves down a blind. And now that you can do more for me than ever before, I don't trust you."

"Is it because for the first time I'm your equal in every way?" I test a theory.

A'zam hesitates. Bingo. "Equal? No. We are different in our abilities. You may be able to handle the same level of complexity I can, but we have such different experiences. No, we're not equal, nor will we ever be."

"Then why?" I don't believe his denial, but am willing to see how he explains himself out of this corner.

"Bandwidth."

I look at him thinking he's either kidding or making this up as he goes. "You think there's too much to do, even with all the new capability we both have acquired."

"Don't you remember the bargain when I promoted you?"

"I do, but what does that have to do with trust?"

"I trust you to keep the wheels on the cash flow, to grow our scope, markets and leadership in our industry while I position us in a whole new industry. What I do feeds your ability to feed what I do. Together we will create a juggernaut that will be the most influential enterprise in history and for as long as either of us can imagine."

"We talked about that." I confirm. "And I bought in despite my reservations about where it would all go, since I can't see how fundamental decisions that will affect me and every other being on this planet are being made. It almost seems you are making arbitrary decisions for the world. I'm not sure any one person should have that much influence over the lives of all the billions there are of us."

"I understand your reservations." There is something in the tone of his voice. An attempt to hide something, or so it seems to me. To be agreeable when he's not at all. "In fact, if the roles were reversed I'd probably have similar reservations about the direction you would want to take not only the world, but our company as well."

"Then why did you promote me?" I push harder now. "If you don't agree with my leadership and you don't think I have a vision for the very long future we both share now, why put me in the position you have? Why not Julia who wanted to be your clone?"

"Why not Julia?" A'zam almost laughs. "Julia was there to demonstrate to the board what they would lose if anything happened to me. She was never my second, I never trusted her with any meaningful decision. And when she stepped in when I transitioned, she screwed up nearly everything she touched. I surrounded myself with second tier people, so no one would ever rise to the attention of the board as a legitimate threat."

"Thanks for letting me know just how inadequate I am." I respond, knowing I should be hurt by the estimation, but realizing he never thought that about me. If he had, he never would have let me have the run I did, working essentially independently, delivering results year after year with no direction from him or anyone else for that matter. Even when I was dying, he never stepped in, but simply sought to hire a replacement who could deliver like I had.

"You know, this is one of those moments." I grin at him after completing my assessment of what is really going on.

"Moments?" A'zam really hasn't understood what he just did.

"When the table turns." I try to remain stoic.

A'zam is clearly unsure of where I am going so he says nothing.

"You had only one person on your team you could trust, and that was me. I am the only person you ever let alone to do her job. Even when I was dying and struggling, you still left the fate of the company in my hands. It created some problems, but I always saved your bacon."

"Not how I remember the last ten years."

"You can remember anything you'd like, but the facts are you can't succeed with your new strategy if I don't keep the lights on and the cash flowing. You have no one else who could do that and manage the transition to an immortal fueled development team. No one. So, you need to trust me with what you're doing."

"But you don't trust me." A'zam tries to use as an excuse.

"You wouldn't trust you if you treated you the way you're treating me."

He hesitates for just a moment, trying to follow my logic. "How do we always end up in the same place?" A'zam asks as if he has no idea.

"Because you can't admit I'm your equal." I put it right back out there. "You demand respect from me, but you don't return it. You note I never said I was superior to you even when I had transitioned and you hadn't. The fact you couldn't wait to transition, threw all kinds of money at Dr. Woodall to make sure you were next in line, even though you met none of the criteria, says it all. You couldn't stand being number two, even though you still had the number one job."

"But you would have taken it when it became clear what you had become," A'zam's voice becomes harder, as if he remembers an unpleasant situation.

"It never entered my mind." I inform him. "I never wanted your job. It's not as much fun as creating new products, engaging young minds in solving the insolvable, delivering novel solutions to life's problems and delighting customers every day."

"You would rather go back to software?" A'zam apparently never considered I might have a different future for myself in mind. "But I gave you the best job in the world."

"You put me into the best job to help you do your job without any consideration of what I might want to do." I set the record straight as far as I am concerned. "I know I'm in this job because I could accelerate your plans. It would take anyone else you wanted to do this job months or years to transition, learn the job and deliver results. I had already transitioned, know the products, the markets and what it takes to get them into customer's hands. You're at least six months further down the path right now because of the decision you made than any other course you could have taken. So, don't blow smoke at me."

"Is that why you almost decided dying was preferable to working in this role with me?" A'zam hasn't gotten over the decision I had to make.

"Didn't think you even noticed," I respond truthfully.

"When you left that morning without telling anyone what you had decided I was amazed. It was such an obvious choice, and yet you struggled to make it. I actually went to see Rocky to understand what you were going through. He was the one who told me about Anna Laura's eyes."

CONFORMANCE

I had asked Mindi to set up a panel of academic experts. The organizing question was: what does it mean to be human? Mindi decided to take a short cut. Rather than research experts in various disciplines, she sent out an announcement to a select group of universities and requested any published experts in this area should attend our meeting, not to present papers, but to discuss the topic. We had to move the meeting from the auditorium at AppleCore to a much larger one at Stanford University.

I look around the room at the sea of faces. My mind starts bringing up bios on various people in the audience and I quickly review their publications record. I decide this is how I'm going to have to find the right experts.

"Dr. Rose. I see you are an expert in societal formation in the anthropology department at Cambridge University, London. Your primary work has been in regards to the transition from hunter-gatherer social formations to agricultural division of labor. Very impressive work from my limited understanding of the field. Have you given thought to our framing question?"

"I have, Dr. Washington. In fact, it underlies all of the research and writings of my professional career. I am honored that of all of my esteemed colleagues here in attendance that you would select me to go first."

I am already wondering if I made a mistake with this approach. It may have been better to just have them submit papers I could scan quickly and move on. But I thought a discussion would clarify nuances I might completely miss by reading a paper. I nod to the professor to continue.

"Being human means the ability to communicate both concrete and abstract thoughts in such a manner that novel, at least to that individual, solutions are proposed and tested either by the individual or groups of individuals."

"Are you suggesting the scientific method is core to being human?" I'm surprised at this definition since it appears nowhere in the articles he wrote that I quickly scanned. "In which case no one prior to the sixteenth century would have been considered human."

"Seventeenth century to be exact," Dr. Rose responds with a chuckle. "No. I'm not suggesting early man wasn't human. And I need to be precise that when I say man, I'm referring to both men and women. In any event. As a species, we have always relied on trial and error to learn. Is that the scientific method? Yes and no. The scientific method would have us postulate the expected results of an experiment. We validate the postulation and create another to validate. Trial and error may not have a postulation about what should happen. A monkey that hangs from a tree just above a tiger thinks that she or he is quick enough to avoid being caught. The monkey postulates an outcome and then tests it. So, the scientific method is not limited just to man. But what is different is the communication to others of the postulation based on both concrete and abstract reasoning and concepts."

"But monkeys communicate to other monkeys. Do we know they don't communicate abstract concepts and reasoning?" I question. The more I think about his definition, the less agreement I have with it.

"We have not been able to ascertain either abstract or complex reasoning in monkeys."

"Dr. N'Cube. I see you are an expert in linguistics from the University of the Swaziland, with degrees from McGill University in Montreal, Canada. Would you like to offer an opinion of what makes us human?"

"Thank you, Dr. Washington. I will try to give you original thoughts on the matter." Dr. N'Cube stands to address me. "Dr. Rose has the conception half right. Humanity is the result of our ability to communicate linguistically, meaning not with gestures or with gestures that accompany sounds which are not meaningful in and of themselves. Because our minds are so much more developed than other species we are able to communicate the levels of complexity that we can imagine more precisely and completely than the other species."

"Do we communicate emotions differently than other species?" I ask wanting more than what I perceive to be a simplistic conception.

"If your question is do we communicate emotions in a unique manner, apart from all other species? The answer is no. Are there other species that communicate in a manner that is completely different than we communicate emotions, the answer is yes. But no species we have observed communicates emotions in a totally unique manner."

"What I think you just said is that we haven't observed a totally unique manner of communicating emotions. Communication of emotions is shared, to one extent or another, across all species."

"Approximately. There are rituals that are unique, like the mating dance of the honeybee. No other species does a dance quite like it. But there are other mating dances in other species. In fact, a dance is a tradition in many human wedding ceremonies."

"So, you would say that a wedding dance is not something that makes us human." I try to clarify.

"A wedding dance could be a human tradition, but it is not an inborn trait that every human engages in on their wedding night."

"Is it easier to say what being human is not?" I wonder aloud.

"If you were to ask me to list ten things being human entails and ten things it does not, that might be a useful exercise, but I am not sure it would provide you with the information you seek. Maybe if you were to explain to us exactly what you are hoping to obtain from this discussion we could be more precise in our answers."

"Didn't the invitation explain the purpose?" I'm surprised. I thought I'd seen the notice before it went out.

"Just what the framing question was to be and that it relates to the struggles individuals such as yourself have once you transition into your new form."

"That's a start." I respond surprised I need to go back to square one with this group of distinguished scholars. "My body is more than 99% electronics and mechanical systems. The only part of me that is the same as my former self is my consciousness. It is the consciousness that informs my memories as to the desired actions I will take. But when the biological self is gone, those like me are no longer constrained by a delicate and fragile body. I can do things I could not before. I conceptualize much more data and can assess more information than any human has been able to until now. All this permits me to do things we have not considered previously. And as I begin to do different things and do things differently I'm attempting to understand, where do I cross the line such that I am no longer human, but something else?"

"You will never be a rhinoceros." Dr. N'Cube offers in response. "Nor a giraffe, for that matter. You may become something other than you are today, but we all do. You are born a child. A child has almost no capabilities and is completely dependent upon others in order to survive. And yet we have survived as babies and children for millions of years in one form or another. The same is true when you age. When you are old, you are different than when you were a baby. You have immensely greater ability to reason and discuss art, history, science and even contemplate the future. You have evolved from when you were a baby. You are a different being. But you are both human."

"What is it about both of us, other than the number of chromosomes in our DNA that makes us human?"

"That may be the only thing you have in common." Dr. Roberts from UCLA offers.

"You are a molecular biologist, Dr. Roberts." I recognize him. "Why do you not think there is some core to humanity? A core that enables familiar patterns to occur in any being with those core elements if you will?"

"Elements? Not a good choice of words." Dr. Roberts responds. "I understand what you're trying to get at. The building blocks of humanity as the elements are the building blocks of the universe. You can look at traits of humans. You can look at values. How humans organize themselves. You can even go into the emotional life a human experiences as a defining characteristic. Maybe that's the term you're looking for. Characteristic. We can talk about human characteristics. But as Dr. N'Cube so succinctly put it, there is often more difference between a baby human and an adult human than there is between a baby monkey and a human baby. If you go down the trait path, there is a huge variability in human traits. To a great extent I think socialization has a massive impact on traits, and we haven't even discussed how we mold ourselves to be social animals. For your task, socialization may be a greater determinant of how to keep the human characteristics you desire. Am I answering your question?"

"You are raising definitional issues that are essential to getting to the answer I'm seeking." I respond, while I try to decide where I want to go next. I'm not through with Dr. Roberts. He has raised a number of points along with Dr. N'Cube that have made me completely reconsider what it is I'm trying to achieve. And somehow, I'm surprised it has come back to socialization after I'd dismissed that as an A'zam ploy to indoctrinate all immortals. Or did A'zam get to Dr. Roberts and plant him in this audience? If he was aware of the invitation that would have been easy to do.

"What is the role of socialization?" Dr. Robert continues, apparently believing I've asked him to do so. "Where do the common themes of such socialization come from? Do parents make them up, different ones for each and every child? Is it simply the memory of the lessons their parents communicated to them when they were children themselves? If that were the case, how do new life lessons get incorporated? Where do they come from? Does the young first-time parent remember what they were taught or told? Is that all there is? Or does that first-time parent think about the lessons they were taught and decide how they wish to change those lessons for their children? Modify bad experiences they had so their children will not have the same adverse reactions they had to a certain set of circumstances? Does the means of socialization change over time? Through bedtime stories, family trips, or sitting together as a parent and child milk a cow together? There are many different ways socialization takes place. One of the complaints that have been heard in urban and suburban communities is that parents have abandoned the socialization role. They expect the schools to do it. Why? Because it's hard? Because it relies on principles that the parent may not have fully embraced themselves? Socialization is a slippery slope, Dr. Washington. It is not uniform, it is not always grounded in principles, and many of those who are charged with the responsibility to perform it have abandoned that role to others."

"I disagree with some of your points," Dr. Rose of Cambridge University London rises to his feet. "Socialization has been a part of humanity since the first father took his son our hunting and the first mother took her daughter out to gather fruits, vegetables, nuts and grain. While there is a great deal of variability in the specifics of the process, it has some time-tested commonalities that are important to the question you have asked. First, socialization is generally started by the parents of a child. Grandparents and siblings become the second layer of socialization because those are the individuals the new child spends the most time with when very young. As the child grows older, peer socializers join the list. Their socialization lessons are often at odds with those of the immediate family and starts the period of social rebellion. The influence of the peer socializers grows as the child moves from adolescence to teenage years and even beyond. For many the peers of high school and college, who are their primary socializers during those periods become life-long friends. They continue to reinforce the importance of those behavioral norms. For young men, sports may dominate their leisure hours, or drugs, or social media. For young women it is more likely to be social media, clothes and boys. Not necessarily in that order. The boys may sneak in ahead of the clothes, but then the clothes draw up to be of equal importance to be able to attract the boys. And so it goes. Are these social rituals what it means to be human? I think it has a significant influence on what we think of as human characteristics. And I would hate to see the rite of passage become a thing of the past. But from what's been described about you, it would seem that the family elements fall away. You transition living beings into being like you, but you do not produce new beings like you. And that is a significant human characteristic that you will not be able to retain regardless of your efforts overall."

"It does not seem that you have significantly disagreed with me." Dr. Roberts rises since this seems to be the means of gaining attention. Dr. N'Cube started it and everyone else has decided is appropriate. "If anything, I believe you have done an excellent amplification of the concepts I introduced. I happen to agree wholeheartedly with your points, but I think there is a component of socialization that we have not addressed but is important to Dr. Washington's task. That is the socialization of emotion."

"Please explain further." Dr. N'Cube requests.

"Children are taught not to cry." Dr. Roberts begins his new line of reasoning. "It is important for both boys and girls to pick themselves up when they fall or are hurt in some manner. Crying is not permitted as an emotional release. This is not a good practice because it makes for inhibited individuals who have difficulty expressing their feelings and emotions. Think about the popular culture. The movie 'A League of their Own.' The phrase everyone remembers is 'There's no crying in baseball.' The character in the movie was referring to a woman baseball player, but he went on to tell the women that when he was playing his manager called him awful names, but there was no crying about it. Our society has confused emotional expression with weakness. It takes a very strong person to be able to express how one feels about another or a situation when the individual who is receiving that information is hostile to it. In my opinion, we would be creating a more humane society by making the expression of emotion more acceptable and expected."

Dr. Kawasaki from the Tokyo Institute of Humanities clears his throat. "Honorable Doctor Washington. If I may interject a point for your consideration. If you look at the literary themes over the millennia you will find the defining characteristics you seek. It is not so much how smart you are, or how dedicated you are to your family that defines your humanity. It is the decisions you make. Literature recounts the situations and the decisions we make when under stress. Those are the defining moments that tell us who we really are. Those are the characteristics you seek to retain as more like you are unmoored from the shackles of a biologic existence. Selflessness. Sacrifice. They are generally opposed to someone who is self-centered or living off the largess of others. Both are human characteristics and yet they are diametrically opposites. That is why it is very difficult to accomplish the task you have set out. You may encounter individuals who are only concerned about their own well-being. That may well be something that you do not believe in, but that does not make them any less human. If those who are like you become evil as commonly perceived as evil that does not make them any less human."

"Thank you, Dr. Kawasaki. Those are excellent points for consideration. But tell me, if literature is the repository of all characteristics of humanity, and those characteristics have been recorded in civilization after civilization, hundreds or thousands of years apart and in some instances half a world away, does that mean there is some sort of collective unconscious where these themes that have emerged from our primitive origins have resided for the millennia?"

"You have asked a question that has been theorized about for decades." Dr. Kawasaki responds firmly. "The collective unconscious is a pet theory many researchers have sought to prove, but there is no direct evidence it exists. It does explain such physiological constructs as our nervous system and such mechanisms as our fight or flight triggers. We react to situations almost instinctively, although again we have not been able to prove instincts exist in humans. We theorize they exist in animals, but we have no proof. How else do we explain our knowledge of situations we have never seen before, an understanding of how to do something we have never done before, having almost the same thoughts or using very similar words to describe something we and another have seen for the first time. Some researchers ascribe it to coincidence and probability. I am not so sure of their explanations. However, neither am I convinced a collective unconscious exists. If it did, how would we access it? How is the collective communicated? There seems to be no biological mechanism to enable this collective unconscious."

"But what if there were?" I ask. "How could such a thing work?"

Dr. Ned Hawthorne, Professor of Comparative Religion at the Southern Methodist Divinity School rises. "You have moved from the physical to the metaphysical realm. Just as we do not know God in the physical sense, we see his evidence all about us. The collective unconscious is a repository of past lives experiences that we all recognize as motifs and unconscious reactions. We fear things we do not understand because as a hunter-gatherer, what you did not see or understand often killed you. That lesson became an ingrained part of socialization across the millennia. What I think you are seeking is what is known as Emergence, where the collective consciousness of humanity focuses on one thing that is common to all and by doing so raises the awareness and conformance of all."

START

I'm on my way to Dr. Woodall's lab. Time for my next upgrade. Only he didn't bother to tell me what he is doing to me. If it were just software, he could have updated me over the air. But he said I had to come in. I wonder if A'zam has already had this update. Of course, he has. Why would I think I would be upgraded ahead of the guy who is paying Dr. Woodall's bills?

Every time I talk to someone else I get a head full of new ideas about what it means to be human. The socialization approach seems to be gaining support from new quarters, but I'm intrigued by Professor Hawthorne's discussion about metaphysics. Is there something to the human psyche that we can't explain? Something that explains the metaphysical, or paranormal experiences or even extra sensory perceptions? I let one of my processors start working that in the background while I continue pursuing other approaches such as socialization. The heart burn I have with socialization is that someone has to be responsible for the socialization content. At the moment, A'zam seems to think he has the right to provide that content. That makes me real uncomfortable, but I don't know who should be responsible.

I only wait in the lab for a few minutes before Dr. Woodall joins me along with an assistant, Jordy, I think is his name. "Afternoon," the doctor greets me. "Jordy is going to do the installation today."

"And just what is it you're installing?"

"New sensors." Dr. Woodall informs me. "Ones that should help you react to some situations better. Not near what you're used to, but at least a step in the right direction."

"What prompted this?" I have to ask.

"Our continuing discussions. We had these under development when we transitioned you, but they weren't even close to prime time then. Still not sure they're ready. But I want to see how you react to them before I try them out on anyone else."

"Not even A'zam?" I push.

Dr. Woodall shakes his head, but doesn't respond.

"Where do these sensors go?" I'm curious now, but not sure he just told me the truth about A'zam.

"Torso. We install them next to the power supplies you access during your recharge procedure."

"Do they work when I'm recharging?" I'm not following the reference to my power supplies.

"Actually, they work when someone else reacts. If you see someone else's eyes dilate, and pick up the electrical signals that their muscles are tensing it informs you they are preparing to react physically to something. If someone is angry it might help you avoid a physical conflict."

"Sounds primitive and advanced at the same time. Primitive in that it only gives a gross level sense of what's about to happen, but advanced in that humans aren't able to access electrical impulses in muscles and tie it to pupil dilation. Well, that's an indication we might be able to get to the point where we can at least better respond to some cues people or other immortals are giving us."

I take off my blouse so Jordy can access my torso panel to install the new sensors. He shows them to me. They are very small, and he doesn't have to take me offline to make the installation, which I find refreshing. I don't much care for the off-line periods since I have no idea what is happening to me. Am I getting protective of my control over myself? Maybe. Where does that come from? A preference I'd not thought much about the first months of being an immortal. Dr. Woodall accesses what he needs to in order to upgrade me. But maybe I'm getting more concerned that A'zam may slip something in an update that will give him control over me. And I certainly don't want that. He has enough positional power over me as it is.

"Why Jordy? Why didn't you do this yourself?" I ask Dr. Woodall.

"Jordy will be installing the others if we get a good reaction from you. Just easier than showing different people how to do the same thing." Again, what should be a simple explanation seems to be more convoluted than it needs to be. Is there something going on or am I reading too much into the situation?

The installation goes quickly and in only a moment I'm picking up sensory readings of Dr. Woodall shifting his weight from one foot to the other. "I think you've set it too high, or I'm going to have to get used to discerning which electrical impulses I need to pay attention to and those I don't."

"Give it a few minutes. I think you'll get the hang of it quickly." Dr. Woodall responds as Jordy closes up the panel and comes around to look at my reaction with Dr. Woodall. I pull my blouse back on and button it up. The two men are standing still now so I'm not picking up electrical impulses, but I am picking up information about the size of their pupil dilation, which has now also gone back to normal as they are waiting to see what I'll do next. But then Dr. Woodall steps towards me and I pull back away.

"It works as I expected," he notes.

Jordy turns away. His movement doesn't result in a reaction from me, apparently because his eyes didn't dilate prior to or at the same time as his movement. Jordy stops near the door to the lab and looks at Dr. Woodall. "You good or do you want to remove them?"

Dr. Woodall looks at me expectantly.

"Let me play with them for a bit." I respond. "How do I shut them down if it gets to be too much?"

"Send me a text and I can disable them." Jordy responds.

I shake my head, "I need to be able to control anything you put into me. I'm not going to wait for you to get to a control device if I need to shut it down. So, what's the magic password?"

Jordy looks to Dr. Woodall who nods to him. "If you visualize the device and think 'inhibit', that will take it off line."

"Does that work for anything else I might want to take off line?" I respond.

Again, Jordy looks at Dr. Woodall, who answers for him. "Yes. I don't know why you would want to inhibit any functionality, but that is a standard approach to take any subsystem off line."

"Thanks, Jordy." I let him know I want to talk to Dr. Woodall in private.

When the door is closed I study Dr. Woodall for a moment. "How long have you been working on this little addition?"

"Like I said it was in a rudimentary form when you transitioned. What we just don't know is whether it will do what you want it to do."

"Anything that lets me react to people from what they do rather than from a memory of a similar situation will be an improvement."

"Then we're on the right track," Dr. Woodall seems satisfied.

"Can this be tied into the Orgasmatron?" I ask seriously.

"Orgasma??" Dr. Woodall breaks out in a wide smile. "Are you asking what I think you're asking?"

"You saw the Woody Allen movie. You had to."

"Dr. Woodall shrugs."

"Whatever. This sensor picks up muscle responses and eye dilation. Could it be used to sense when someone is peaking for a release?"

"An immortal?" he asks.

"I was thinking mortals."

"Are you sleeping with mortals?"

"There are a lot more to choose from." I inform him.

"You have a point. Guess I wasn't thinking you'd be attracted to a mortal when the immortals will be more proficient from what Jermaine has told me."

"Yeah, well, Jermaine is singing his own praises now that he's transitioned and built the last update."

"Have you been able to compare?" Dr. Woodall surprises me with his curiosity.

"I have, but neither has been anything to write home about yet." I hesitate, not sure what I want to say next but I plunge on ahead. "We've been more focused on the male experience so far. A'zam has insisted. But we will get back to the female experience since so many of those you are transitioning are women now. If I don't do something soon, they'll probably take the whole thing into their own hands and then I'll have ten different versions to deal with."

"Maybe you should let them all come up with a different version. Could be like open software. Let users improve the baseline. Would introduce new variation you might find both entertaining and interesting."

"Are you getting a little kinky in your advancing years, there Doc?"

"It's been a successful strategy in the past," is his weak response. I'm starting to see the doctor in a different light.

"I didn't think you wanted people playing with your code."

"You do regularly. And now A'zam has his own development team in there too. So I lost control of the baseline a while ago."

He's right and I am the first one who changed his baseline with the first orgasm software, even though it was pretty crude. "Think it will be important to get control of it again. If you don't you'll have differences between immortals that make the racial differences today look tame by comparison. And the battles between the different groups will make today seem like a tame society."

"Why are you Dr. Doom and Gloom today?" Dr. Woodall asks me.

"We talked about socialization last time I was by to see you. But I have a question I didn't think about then. Who decides what gets socialized?"

"The parents," Dr. Woodall doesn't hesitate, but then he thinks better of his answer. "But that's the very problem, isn't it? When we transition people, the parents are seldom involved, at least at the moment."

"When you get back to transitioning terminal patients you will have some children. And that in and of itself creates a bit of a problem for you. Do you transition a child knowing it will remain a child for eternity? Or do you transition a child into an adult body, in essence robbing it of childhood and time to inculcate the socialization we have just been discussing."

"We have actually talked about the situation you pose." Dr. Woodall confides. "Luckily, we haven't had to deal with it yet, but we will. And what we've discussed is an annual transition until they reach a twenty-year-old body. We would stop there. We should be able to recycle the younger bodies, changing the external appearance so no one would know the body has been occupied by another previously."

"So, in those situations the parents continue to play the socialization role as will peers when the child gets old enough." I remark. "Nothing different than what we have known. But for the immortal who transitions as an adult, there is no external authority to educate or enforce a set of norms."

"But why is that any different? The norms should survive in the immortal's memories. The imperative of parental authority should remain just as it does today for most people."

"But only as a memory." I insist." And as an immortal retains more and more memories those that date back to the formative years will lose immediacy and impact, if you know what I mean. The immortal will have to shift through so much data to get back to those early memories. It won't reside in flash memory or even short-term memory where the immortal lives for the most part. What then?"

"This is the very situation you've been afraid of since the beginning." Dr. Woodall notes. "How do we keep socialization memories immediate, so they will be accessible when needed? Not stored in long term memory where they're seldom consulted. And if stored only in long term memory that would give the immortal a free hand to improvise behaviors that may not resemble those we have come to expect because of the way we socialize our children."

I nod pleased he is finally understanding my concerns.

"So, if we create a behavioral cache memory that every situation is screened through, wouldn't that resolve your concerns?" Dr. Woodall muses.

"But how do we update your cache when we encounter new or novel situations?" I counter. "Particularly if we don't react appropriately and the results are not favorable for either party? What I'd like to be able to get to is something that avoids those awkward moments and inappropriate behaviors. The cache approach does much to address concerns, but not all concerns."

"I'd still like to get a team to look at it as one approach." Dr. Woodall suggests. "It would be just like the sensor we installed today. Another step along the path to something better. A minor improvement that may not have a big impact, but it might help us find a bigger and better approach that will."

"Let me ask you what you may think is a strange question." I change the subject completely.

Dr. Woodall engages me with his eyes, clearly searching to decipher what I might be chasing.

"Do you think there may be something to the metaphysical?"

Dr. Woodall leans against a surgical table to consider my question. "Metaphysical. Meaning something we observe or sense, but have no explanation for."

I nod.

"As a scientist I'm not sure how I could reproduce what you're describing in you or other immortals. That's the problem with something we can't explain. We can't duplicate it either."

"I know, but what if there is something to it. The collective unconscious was one of those things that started me down this path. What if there are deeply embedded memories that we all have from primitive times that guide our behavior unconsciously?"

"That's different. We absolutely could implant deep memories that are subconscious but could guide general behavior. Is that where you're going with the whole discussion of who decides about what gets socialized?"

"It's a different approach." I suggest.

"Might be a damn good approach." Dr. Woodall seems to embrace the concept.

"It still has the same governance issue." I point out. "Who decides what those deep memories are that guide behaviors?"

Dr. Woodall nods understanding we are at the same place, even with what might be a better approach.

"Is there any research about what the collective unconscious might be? What it might contain?"

Dr. Woodall appears to puzzle over my question. "I remember a few papers on the subject, but I think they were considered highly speculative. Not something that would be peer accepted."

As I start reviewing a series of papers in my mind, I respond, "Got to start somewhere."

TRIANGULATION

As I come into my office, Mindi is waiting for me. "Oriana says you've been ignoring her requests to meet."

"Not ignoring…" I start to respond, but realize there is no reason to tell Mindi what's on my mind right now. "Tell her to come on up." I say in a weary tone, even though I don't physically feel tired, but realize I haven't charged recently and one of the software updates was to provide a signal that charging is needed soon. That update was to replicate a slowdown of reactions. Guess it's working.

Oriana must have been close by because she appears quicker than she could have if she had been either on the floor with her teams or in her office. "Do I have leprosy?" she starts the conversation.

I don't answer the question that doesn't deserve an answer. "I don't have the answer you're looking for."

"I didn't expect you would, but I still want to talk to you about it," she informs me.

"You have three minutes." I frame the discussion as we can communicate at Immortal speed and that should be about all she will need.

"Marketing can't keep up with the rate of changes we can deliver. You need to put some of them through the transition so we can synch up our efforts."

"The problem isn't in marketing," I inform her.

"Has to be. We're delivering the products. It's their job to sell them."

"You're half right. It's their job, but they have to find a way to step up the rate of acceptance and that goes back to the mortals we are selling all these wonderful innovations to. They're having trouble keeping up with the rate of change. What's happened is exactly the opposite of what we wanted. Because so much is coming so fast, people are slowing down what they buy, waiting to see if the next one will have something special it's worth waiting for."

"That's not my problem." Oriana insists.

"No, it's everyone's problem. We have to work together to find a way for people to get excited about every release. We haven't done that."

"You're saying that's my job?" Oriana clearly doesn't believe it is.

"It's your job to define feature sets that sell. That means you have to listen to what the marketing folks are hearing in the stores from customers. That means maybe you don't build the next upgrade until you can leap frog to something better. Maybe you slow down on a product and work on something entirely new. But that means you have to spend even more time with marketing to make sure the brainstorm you've had actually has a market. It's all right to do a small pilot to prove what you think is true, but before you roll out millions of items that are going to sit on shelves because no one wants them. The technical part is only part of your job now. I have no doubts about your ability to innovate and put product on shelves. But what you haven't shown me yet is the ability to adjust to the customer. Lead where you can, but not get so far out in front that you turn around and find the customer has gone over to Symbol Ventures because you've missed something."

"That hasn't happened." Oriana sounds defensive and confused.

"Yet," I try to refocus her. "It happened to me on more than one occasion. Symbol is a very good technology company. They have excellent marketing folks, who work very hard trying to discover what we've missed. You can't think that just because you can think faster and more broadly than they can at the moment you can out think them. You can't. For the most part you can reach conclusions faster and some of your teams can innovate quicker to realize the solutions you want to put in the field. But most of your teams are no faster or better than theirs. Ours are just used to winning the wars because as a complete company we have found the right solutions at the right time."

"I'm not here for the sermon." Oriana is losing patience since I only gave her three minutes and I've used up a big chunk of them. "I actually need you to do something."

I wait for her to continue.

"You have to rein in Moshe."

I'd put him out of my mind after I restored his speech and sent him off to do my special project. "What's the problem?"

"He's doing the market research you asked him to take on, but he keeps enlarging the scope of the project, bringing in more people and quite frankly pissing off more and more of them because he is doing exactly what you just did."

"Explain the situation?" I ask, thinking that was what I'd been doing.

"No. Preaching. He's trying to sell solutions he's come up with rather than listening to what the customers really would like to have."

"And you know this because…"

"I know some of the people who have been invited to his focus groups and been surveyed by the outside firm. Did you know he dumped the firm we usually use for surveys because they insisted on developing the instrument rather than just taking what he gave them?"

"No, I didn't." I'm wondering why Landon Bannerjee, the head of marketing, let Moshe get away with changing firms and why Landon wasn't involved in developing the instrument and conducting the focus groups. Both are his responsibility. I send a note to Landon asking him to come by and see me.

"Time's nearly up. If I do something, as you've asked, what else did you want to talk about?"

"Cognitive dissonance."

Not a term I expected to hear, "Tell me more."

"The teams that have transitioned? Well, they're not functioning like teams. We talked about the fact all immortals will be processing at the same clock speed. That should get everyone on the same page faster. That should keep everyone working in close coordination. But it doesn't work that way. If anything, the individual differences between world views seems to be accentuated in the immortals. They actually have to take longer to work through disagreements or differences of opinion about the best way forward. Because everyone has gone further down their individual paths before they coordinate, they tend to get more entrenched in their approach or solution. It's a much more difficult process to get everyone to the same point."

"First I've heard of this." I admit. "What needs to be done?"

"I don't know just yet. I'm talking with the team leads and they're trying different approaches, but so far nothing we've tried has had much effect."

"It's early, but keep close to it and don't stop trying different approaches just because you find one thing that works. I expect this will not be a one size fits all issue."

"No recommendations?" Oriana is fishing.

"Like I said, this is the first I've heard of it."

"What are you seeing with the leadership team?" Oriana goes to the point. "How are you keeping us all aligned?"

"We're communicating constantly rather than waiting for the weekly or monthly ops reviews. Everyone is empowered to work directly with another team member to work through any issue that cuts across functional areas."

"The team leads have tried something like that."

I wonder based on her imprecise response what the teams actually are doing. "Do you have more than one team member working a product aspect?"

"In most instances I think they have a lead and a backup working each area."

"Is that where the issues are coming out?" I wonder aloud.

"I don't know for sure. I'll have to do some talking to find out."

"My guess is the immortals teams will need to have only one person working an aspect, then they will need to work together to coordinate solutions across aspects, but again, one lead with one lead. I think if they start talking early and are constantly coordinating the dissonance may get better."

"See, I knew you'd have something to recommend even if you hadn't thought about it yet."

"Why hadn't you come up with something yet?" I want to know. I'm afraid she's become dependent on me to give her direction and that can't be the situation as I'm just not going to have the bandwidth to address everything in her area and keep up with my own responsibilities.

"I did, but I wanted to compare with what you thought before I just went off and found I needed to change direction."

"Why would you need to change direction after talking with me?"

"Why wouldn't I?"

"Because your ideas are every bit as good as mine." I want to make sure she understands the situation.

"I know that." Oriana admits. "But just as you pull ideas from everyone, I'm trying to do the same."

"So, what was your solution?"

"Pretty close to yours. I'm having them start out with a joint planning session where we talk about the product and approaches. We try to narrow the scope and solution sets at that first get together. After that it's almost exactly what you've suggested."

"Then you should go with your approach." I insist, hoping to reinforce her self-confidence.

"I am, but it hasn't solved everything yet. I think it's getting better, but we need a few complete product cycles on it to know where we really are."

"And a few more teams using it to see if there are team dynamics on some teams and not others that affect your results." I suggest.

"See? Even after telling me to go with my approach, you're still adding value to the solution as you see it."

"Okay. Are we done yet?" The three minutes are just about up, but I'm not going to kick her out at 180 seconds and she knows it.

"No." She sounds tentative. "There's one other thing I want to do, but I need your concurrence since it's a personnel matter and involves a senior person in my organization."

I nod for her to proceed.

"I want to move Jermaine off to do a special project."

I'm not expecting this request since she relies heavily on Jermaine. "What's the special project?"

"I want to put him in charge of transitioning all the teams. I need someone who can spot the team dynamics issues earlier than we are. Someone who has the respect of the entire organization. Someone who can make a change, or take an action that won't be second guessed for weeks or months."

"Like what I did with Moshe?" I guess.

"If anyone else had done that, the whole organization would have been in an uproar. But everyone knew you did it for the good of the team and not as a punishment."

"Why couldn't you do it?"

"I can, and I will, if needed." Oriana begins to explain. "But I will be second guessed. There is a perception that if A'zam goes off somewhere else that you will bring me up here in your current job, just like you did when you came here. You held it for me for weeks. That didn't go down so well."

"I was aware of the chatter. But it was the right decision for the organization and for you. In that order. That has to be the way it is."

"Oh, I know that. I'm trying to be like you in that regard. But it's the perception thing again."

"Do you think if Jermaine takes on this different role that will get you out of the line of fire?" I have to understand her thoughts on this.

"Not why I'd like to do it. I think Jermaine can settle things down faster than I'll be able to. And the main thing about immortals is how fast everything goes, just like this conversation."

"I'm going to make a suggestion you need to think about and not just react to."

Oriana knows she isn't going to get the simple concurrence she came looking for.

"I'm going to suggest you formally make Jermaine the Deputy for Software. Make it official that he's in charge when you're away, he's the one team leads go to first to get a lay of the land before coming up to bother you with issues that might be better handled elsewhere. You're still swimming with everything on your plate. We started this conversation talking about the role you have to play that is beyond what you are used to doing. The success of the enterprise is in your hands to a great extent. You also need to listen to Jermaine more. He has insights I use all the time. You need to tap into them as well."

"You're preaching again." Oriana informs me as her way of saying she got the message about not reacting to my recommendation regarding Jermaine.

"Message received. But preaching is about all I can do in this role. You're responsible for what I used to do. The rest of the team is far more expert in their areas than I am. I have to find a way to keep everyone focused on results and making the decisions that will enable us to blow the doors off our markets as we start solving the very issues we've been talking about."

"Why are you concerned?" Oriana seems surprised.

"That's the nature of this job. To question everything. To never be satisfied we are doing all we can to ensure success."

"Doesn't sound like you're enjoying it all that much."

"It's a challenge. Just like the ones I've put you in charge of addressing. We're both learning as we go. And we'll only minimize the mistakes if we are constantly talking, asking questions and gaining insights from our teams."

"Nothing you and I weren't doing before, just on a different scale."

"Now I have a question for you." I change the subject one more time. "How do you create a capability from the triangulation of other capabilities, none of which do what you want to do?"

"I don't understand."

"That's okay. Just think about the question and come back and tell me how we might be able to do it. At the moment I don't think we can, but I've been talking with people who tell me that it may be possible. We just need to figure out how."

CHILDREN

Mindi comes in and sits down across from me as soon as Oriana leaves. She looks chastened. I don't understand why. So, I ask, "What's the matter?"

"Landon," is all she will say as if that is enough to tell me all I need to know.

"He hasn't proposed?" I ask as the only thing I can think of that would put her into this kind of funk.

"The numbers," oh, oh. That is the one thing that could easily put an end to the romance. And if Landon doesn't have Mindi keeping him organized who knows what will happen to my entire marketing effort.

"I thought the numbers were favorable," I look for clarification since I'd had one bit of information when her parents performed the ceremony.

"They were not strongly favorable. And now Landon's parents have insisted he look for a better match."

"And he's giving in to their demands?" knowing Landon I see he would go in whichever direction he is pointed by someone of authority like his parents.

"He hasn't agreed, but he hasn't told them he loves me and doesn't care what the numbers suggest."

"Explain to me how the not strongly favorable result works."

Mindi shakes her head, "That would take too long. But what I will tell you is if the numbers were strongly against the match it would never happen. In this case the numbers were not the strong endorsement Landon's parents expected for their only son. They think he can do better and should wait for someone the numbers indicate is more suitable."

I nod in understanding, although the idea that numbers determine your fate seems beyond my comprehension. "What are you going to do about the situation?"

"What can I do?" she is almost pleading for me to do something, but I don't know what will help.

"You will have to tell me. In this situation you know much more about how the whole numbers thing works than I do."

"But you are so wise." Mindi almost seems panic stricken by my response. "I can do nothing, but you could appeal to Landon. Make him see why it is so important that he has me to make him successful. He will listen to you."

I don't like the undertone, "Are you saying you want me to tell Landon he could lose his job if he doesn't marry you?"

Mindi demurs, "Not in so many words, although you might have to use words such that he would actually understand what you are telling him." She apparently thinks more about how Landon is likely to respond.

"I can't do that," I respond. "It would be mere speculation on my part. I have no idea how Landon would get through a day without you, but there may be someone else who..."

Mindi cuts me off, "No. There is not another that could do for Landon what I do. Impossible."

"I hear what you're saying. But think about it for a moment. Do you want Landon to marry you because he loves you and appreciates you, or because he was afraid he'd lose his job if he didn't? I've always thought relationships last because of shared feelings of respect. If Landon doesn't share your feelings, being forced to marry you won't improve them."

"Landon loves me, but I admit there are times when he probably doesn't realize it."

I shake my head. This is a no-win situation for me. "I'll talk to Landon. I need to on another matter anyway. Now I don't want you to call him. I'll talk to him, but not just now."

"But this cannot wait. If he decides to end the relationship, he will never come back. Landon is very stubborn. He would see it as a weakness to have to say he is wrong about me to me."

"I don't understand, nor do I want to." I hold up my hand because Mindi is about to launch into another explanation of why I absolutely must help her save her not quite yet marriage. "I'll get his side of things and see if I can determine what he intends to do. I'm not going to threaten him or give him any reason to reconsider what the numbers mean to him or his parents. That's the best I can do."

Mindi looks glum. She was hoping I was going to solve her problem. I rise and follow her out of my office. Mindi turns to look at me, "You're going down to see him. Aren't you?"

I shake my head and just keep going, not wanting to give her enough time to work Landon before I can get there.

Since his office is only down one flight of stairs I'm there in short order. When I peek into Landon's office he is on the phone, to Mindi I am sure.

"She's here now, got to go." Landon hangs up embarrassed.

I come in and sit down, "Mindi?"

Landon smiles a wan smile. It's the one he always gives me when I guess something he doesn't want to discuss.

"I need to talk with you about Moshe."

Landon looks completely surprised, rolls his eyes as if trying to remember what Moshe might have done or not done that Landon is now in the middle of. He doesn't say anything, so I continue.

"As I understand it, and please correct me if I am wrong, Moshe has been conducting market research for me on leapfrog preferences."

"You call it leapfrog. I call it advanced." Landon clarifies.

"Are you directly involved with what he's doing?" I try to sound neutral, not sure I am from Landon's expression.

"Let me say I am aware."

"Of what?" I push.

"Of the effort Moshe is making to better understand preferences for products that do not exist, but might if we can devise a means of creating them."

"Who is working with him from your team?"

Landon looks puzzled. "My team?"

"He is supposed to be working with marketing. Who is he working with?"

"This is the first I have heard about him working with members of my department."

Score one for Oriana. She identified a problem no one else had addressed. "You were aware of the project."

"Yes. Moshe came to see me. Said he'd been given complete authority to produce the research. Said if he needed any help he'd be in touch. That was the last I've heard."

"And you didn't think to check up on what he was doing, given it is squarely in your area of responsibility?"

"No." Landon looks blank. "He said he had complete authority. Even you said he is doing it for you. Why should I question what you wish to do?"

"Maybe you should check back with me, make sure you understand what I want you to do in support of the effort, and by the way, ensure Moshe isn't bullshitting you."

"Moshe would bullshit me?" Landon seems completely surprised at the thought.

"He evidently did." I point out.

"You are angry with me."

"Not angry, but disappointed." I let that sink in for a moment. "What I need you to do to redeem yourself, is to call Moshe and inform him you learned he's supposed to be working with and through your team. You want him to come brief you about what he's done so far and to lay out a plan on how he and you will complete the assignment together." Knowing Landon doesn't like confrontation I know this will be hard for him, so I have to push him. "And I need that done before you do anything else today. I understand Moshe is creating some turbulence with our customers. Trying to convince them of certain products or solutions he has in mind rather than what the customer might like."

"That would make the research invalid." Landon realizes.

"Yes. And if we start building things Moshe likes but bomb in the market, that will reflect poorly on you as the head of marketing."

"But I am not responsible…"

I cut him off, "Are you not the Vice President of Marketing?"

Landon swallows hard. "Yes," comes across barely perceptibly.

"Then you are responsible."

Now that I have Landon backed into a corner I change the subject. "Mindi tells me you have been discussing your future together."

Landon loses all color to his face. "Mindi and I talk of many things."

I wait for Landon to say more. He waits a long time, becoming more and more uncomfortable.

"What is it you wish me to say?" Landon finally continues.

"I'm sure you know Mindi is unhappy at the moment."

I see Landon trying to decide what to say. He apparently knows I will continue pushing him until I get him to tell me what I want to know. "I thought personal situations were private and not to be discussed."

"Obviously Mindi has discussed the situation with me. So much for privacy."

"She told you about the numbers."

I nod.

"And that they did not suggest an auspicious future."

"Do the numbers always suggest an auspicious future?" I inquire.

"Not always."

"And do those who do not get auspicious numbers ever marry anyway?"

Landon nods half to himself seeing where I'm going.

"And are any of those couples who do not get auspicious numbers ever happy or successful?"

The corner of Landon's mouth twitches, but he does not answer.

"Does this mean you don't know, or you do but wish not to confirm my suspicions?"

"My parents did not get auspicious numbers and they married."

"And produced you and your sister. Two phenomenal people. What's wrong here?"

"They hate each other," Landon grimaces. "If she hadn't been pregnant they never would have married."

"So, you are the reason they married and have hated every day since," I surmise.

"That is how my mother would describe her life. My father? Well, he would say he got the better end of the deal. He has a son who is successful. My mother? She has a daughter who is never going to amount to anything. She waits for the numbers to tell her who will make her happy. So far no man has ever made her happy including my father."

"Sounds like you don't believe in the numbers," I suggest.

"It is very hard to disagree with your parents. They expect so much and always say I am living the life they could not. I must fulfill their dreams and expectations just as I must plan that my children will fulfill mine."

"Wasn't your father a successful doctor and your mother is an artist of some renown?"

"Yes. They are very successful."

I put up my hand, "Wait. You said the numbers weren't

auspicious for them."

"They weren't."

"But they are both very successful. They have a successful son, and a daughter who is creating her own success by waiting for it."

"Yes."

"So, what am I missing?" I have to ask, completely confused now.

"That tradition and belief dictate what they must do."

"Even though they are living proof that tradition and belief can be wrong?"

"My mother would not agree she is living proof." Landon shudders." She would point to the fact that she hates my father and he hates her. That is all the evidence she needs to support her belief."

"What would your father say?"

"That he may have been happier with someone else; or maybe not," Landon almost imitates how his father would react.

"And Mindi?"

Landon stops to reflect. "She is very unhappy with me that I haven't told my parents it is my decision and I'm marrying Mindi."

"So, you are listening." I note for his benefit. "She's afraid you aren't."

Landon looks down at his hands, "I know. It is very hard on her. She was so happy. Smiles all the time, even when I came out in the morning and she had to completely redress me. But I think she likes dressing me, making me presentable. Listening to my hopes and dreams. She wants so much to marry and have children. That is all we talked about before the numbers ceremony."

"Do you?"

IMPOSSIBLE TASK

The commotion in Mindi's office could only be one thing. "Send Moshe in." I call out. The argument stops and in only a moment Moshe bursts into my office and flings himself in the chair across from my desk. "What the fuck?"

"Careful, you lost your tongue once already."

"You shitting me?" Moshe gives me one of those looks like I'm purposefully making his life hell.

"Neither one of us is capable of doing that anymore." I point out.

"What's the deal?" he shakes his head as if in disbelief. "Landon? Really?"

"You were instructed to work with and through Landon," I go right to the chase.

"You put me in charge."

"With instructions you ignored," I point out.

"How do you know?" he's trying to sound dismissive, but not doing a particularly good job of it.

"I asked."

"Who? Landon?"

I nod. "It might surprise you that I do talk with the people who are responsible for results."

"You don't talk to me."

"Is your report done?" I have to ask knowing the answer.

"No."

"Then it wasn't time for me to waste my time on you," I'm pretty much done with him.

"You've got an attitude about me. How do you get past that?" Now I am.

"Mindi."

Moshe looks confused. Turns around to look at Mindi as she comes to my door.

"Call security. Have them come pick up Moshe and hold him for transport to Dallas. He's being transitioned out of the immortals program."

Mindi nods and is gone to her desk.

"You can't do that. You just gave me this assignment."

"Which you flunked." I inform him. "The first rule of management is to know when to cut your losses."

"What if I just get up and leave?"

"Be my guest," I look him directly in the eye.

Moshe is very uncomfortable right now. "What do you know that I don't?"

"That if you walk out of here and can no longer recharge you'll cease to exist in a week."

Moshe displays an 'oh shit' look. "Can't we start over again? How about I get up and go out in the hallway? I'll come in all nice and calm. Peaceful. You know? Then maybe we can work this out."

Two security officers appear in the door. I nod to Moshe who refuses to look behind him.

"C'mon, Sage. You discovered me. Promoted me. Gave me my first chance. And I came through for you, didn't I? You can't waste an immortal procedure on sending me back. That's a two times loss on your investment."

"Don't expect to get another job in tech." I inform Moshe.

"You're going to black ball me? That's illegal."

"Don't have to. The word will get out. After all you were the subject of the story that appeared about your team. When you show up looking for work, people will want to know why. That's all it will take."

Another 'oh shit' look as the security guards help Moshe out of the chair and my office. "I'm calling my lawyer."

"Mindi." She appears in my door. "Please make the arrangements."

"Of course," she remains in my door. "What did Landon say?"

"About?"

"You know." She's annoyed with me for not giving her the straight answer. "What's he going to do?"

"He didn't tell me that. You'll have to ask him."

"What did you talk about then?" Mindi seems exasperated with me.

"Mostly Moshe. That's why this whole scene took place."

Mindi looks out after Moshe, "But Moshe doesn't work for Landon."

"Actually, he was working a project in Landon's area and didn't involve Landon or his team."

She looks surprised, "You made Landon confront Moshe?"

"I suggested that if Landon is responsible for marketing he would be held responsible for the results of marketing efforts even if he wasn't directly involved in them."

"That's cold."

I look up at her confused by her choice of terms.

"You were hard on Landon." Mindi realizes aloud. "You've not been hard on him before. Why now?"

"I take it you've not been hard on him?"

"Oh. I've been hard on him." Mindi seems to be thinking about my remark.

"In a loving and kidding way." I suggest. "Let's wear matching socks, Landon."

"What are you suggesting?"

"That if you love him, you'll be hard on him." I suggest without any specifics.

"What does that mean?" She's either not listening or wants me to spell it out.

"You've told me how much you love him and how much he means to you, but have you told him?"

"Of course," Mindi responds, but somehow it seems hollow.

"Then it's time to be hard on him."

"You're not going to tell me what I should do?"

I shake my head slowly.

"You're being hard on me now. Aren't you?" She guesses.

"Make the calls on Moshe." I end the conversation.

As Mindi steps out into her office Jermaine appears. "You have a minute? I promise, that's all I need."

"One." I respond.

"Why did you tell Oriana to move me?"

"I didn't. It was her idea."

"But you told her she could," Jermaine confirms.

"I suggested she should think about a few things."

"Are you willing to share what they were?"

"No."

"What is it with you and Oriana? Some special girl's only club?"

I shake my head hoping he gets the message not to push his frustration on me.

"I'm sorry, that was uncalled for."

I just look at him to see where he goes next.

"Could I express a preference?"

"To her."

"You're not going to intervene on my behalf."

I shake my head. "Minute's almost up."

"Have I peaked somehow?" Jermaine sounds bewildered.

"No, you're still the best technologist I have on the teams. You could end up here if you do the right things and they produce the kinds of results that get you accolades."

"This new assignment just doesn't smell right."

"Have you screwed up?" I put it to him straight.

"Not that I'm aware of." Jermaine is remembering everything since he transitioned.

"Then why would Oriana ask you to do something else unless that's where she has decided you can do the most to help us achieve our business goals?"

"That's what doesn't smell right. You said I'm the best technologist, but she has me coordinating the immortals as they come back. Get them onto teams and working with them until the teams are well integrated and firing on all cylinders."

"That's probably the most important job in software right now," I suggest.

"But anyone could do that," Jermaine isn't comfortable it plays to his strengths.

"Only one person could do it, so we leverage results to the maximum. And that's the person who successfully transitioned the first team back. You've spent more time with immortal teams than anyone we have. You were the one who noted the clock speed discontinuity."

"The what?" Jermaine isn't following me.

"The fact that immortals weren't coordinating well because we assumed when everyone is working at the same clock speed everyone would be solving problems at the same rate. And you were the one who discovered that wasn't the case."

"So?"

"Having had the most time to consider the problem, I think Oriana expects you to devise a solution."

"You don't know?" Jermaine still thinks it was my idea.

"I didn't know Oriana had even spoken to you about the change."

"And here I thought you knew everything," Jermaine is kidding me now.

"I'm lucky," I respond.

"How so?"

"I got to move into this role after becoming so much more capable than any of my predecessors. I actually know much more than any of them did about what goes on in the company. I'm flooded with information and spend much of my time trying to understand the implications of it all. So, I'm in a much better position, I'm much better informed, and for that reason hopefully I'm making better decisions."

"Why you telling me this?" Jermaine wonders aloud.

"I hope you feel lucky too."

"How am I supposed to do that when I don't feel anything?"

"Do you think you're fortunate, then? More fortunate than most?"

"Don't know why you're going there, but yes. I know I'm fortunate in a lot of ways. Got a great wife, super kids, good job and friends. I get to create things for lots of people. Hell yes, I'm fortunate. But is that because of some mystical set of circumstances, or just hard work and good judgment. You know. Being in the right place at the right time."

"Isn't that being lucky?" I ask.

"I don't know. Haven't given it all that much thought."

"Do you think there are unexplained things in this world?"

"Absolutely." Jermaine looks puzzled again. "I don't know where you're going with this discussion, but there are probably more unexplained things in this world than explained things. You know it seems every time I turn around there is another theory that's shot down or confirmed. About the universe, about time travel, what have you. But if you can ever figure out my wife, you tell me."

I smile at his concession to marital mystery. "How do you think the unexplained affects you and me, since we are almost entirely electronics and mechanical systems?"

"Doesn't." Jermaine is definite in his response.

"Are you sure?" I hesitate before continuing. "Don't you think we need to understand the unexplained and try to figure out how we replicate that in immortals?"

"Whoa. Have you just tied this discussion back to what Oriana wants me to do?"

"She hasn't moved you then? She just talked with you about it?"

"She hasn't put out an org chart showing the move, but I think it's a done deal as far as she's concerned."

"So, think about it. How do we fill in all those sensations, experiences, and thoughts we can't explain? Instincts, if you will. All the things we do without thinking about them."

"We got that covered with background processing," Jermaine informs me.

"We're just breaking up tasks into partitioned parts of our processor. It's not the same. And I want to go further than just have deep memories that guide behaviors. That's no different than the conscious memories we use to guide our behaviors now."

"Sounds like you're giving me an impossible task."

APPROACHABLE

It's the middle of the night. I'm walking back to my condo. The discussion with Moshe reminded me I'm in need of a recharge. The only time it seems safe to go home is about one am. It's a little later than that now. The moon is full and bright in a cloudless sky. I look closer at the various craters I can see on the bright side of the moon. I think about all the space junk we have left there since the first landings so long ago. And yet we have never colonized the planet. We've brought samples of various minerals, but that's about all of value we've retrieved.

Ancient peoples looked up at the moon since the beginnings of intelligent life on this planet. Millions of years. In the beginning we did not understand what the moon was or why it was there. It just was. And now we've been there. We've taken the mystery out of it. Explained a lot. And yet we still know very little about it because we just have not had the interest to continue our visits in a way so as to establish a continuing presence. To explore and learn all that we can about it. Why are we so uninterested in something that has been a part of our existence since the beginning?

I see and recognize each of the roses along the way. A fun exercise when I did it the first few times, but now it's familiar. That takes away the novelty. So, I return to my thoughts about humanity. A number of ideas flood my thoughts. I've come back to Delilah talking about life was never intended to be easy. That's how we got the blues in our music. Life is hard and then you die. It is for a lot of people. Most people probably. Those who actually enjoy life are probably a small minority although most people probably enjoy parts of life. They enjoy their families, and friends. Lots of people enjoy the work they do, but not everyone. A lot of people work because they need the money and it's the best job they can get with the skill set they have. People enjoy moments with nature, like I enjoyed my exercise of identifying every rose between the office and my condo. People enjoy a good movie or book or story someone tells them. They enjoy jokes, sports, or a documentary movie about some historical or scientific events. People like to learn. But is that the same as enjoying learning? Do people enjoy learning something new? Some people do, I think. How does joy tie to enjoy? Is joy what results from enjoyment? And is joy just another word for happiness?

I am not happy. But I'm not unhappy. Is the absence of happiness and unhappiness contentment? Am I content with my life and being an immortal since I can't feel anything including happy or sad. But maybe content really means mildly happy. If you're content, you clearly aren't unhappy. But if you're content maybe you are happy, just not laughing out loud happy. So that would mean I'm not content. Maybe I'm just accepting. I've accepted how things are. I'm neither happy nor unhappy about my circumstances. Yes, that makes the most sense to me. I'm just accepting of how things are. If I was unhappy I'd be motivated to change something. But I am motivated to change the future I see, but not the present circumstances. If I were unhappy I'd tell A'zam to go run his own company. Upgrade the immortals and create his new religion if that's where he's going. I'll just go off into the wilderness with my recharging bed and a solar panel to keep me going forever. Alone with my non-stop thoughts. But I have no intention of doing that so I'm not unhappy. All of the nuances to language makes it difficult to know exactly what I should be thinking or doing.

I reach the condo and enter through the back door. I came home once and entered through the front door and the Cupertino police showed up shortly thereafter wanting to know if I was breaking into my own house. I leave the lights out as that also would attract attention. But my night vision is sufficient that I have no issues navigating back to the bedroom, dropping garments along the way until I rest naked on the recharge bed. I feel the warmth and hear the hum as it begins the process of re-energizing me, filling my moisture tanks and checking my diagnostics.

Rocky pops into my mind. Just like always, random thoughts come to me when I'm charging. Must have something to do with the near field magnetics involved in the energy transfer. Rocky is looking at me the way he did when I first came home, having transitioned. He was shocked and disappointed and disoriented all at the same time. I understand why now, but I didn't then. I thought he was disappointed in me. As I thought he was disappointed in me so many times after Anna Laura died. I was all he had left and that was the problem. I wasn't up to the task of being all the family he had left. He couldn't count on me to do what Anna Laura did, even though I tried for a while. But Rocky was always pointing out I wasn't doing something right. That's not the way Anna Laura would want it. Not the way she would have done it. Why didn't I learn what I needed to know when Anna Laura was still with us? Rocky never seemed to understand I had no warning, no expectation that I didn't have a lifetime to learn Anna Laura's lessons. Never thought he would expect me to do the things she did. Be like her in time, maybe. But actually, do what she did? Just never occurred to me. That wasn't an expectation until she wasn't with us anymore.

Now I'm in bed with Raoul. Why Raoul? I never really liked him all that much. And that reminds me, I haven't heard from him, even with all the stories about my transition. How could he not know? Did he guess there was something different about me that last time? If he did, he didn't say anything. But then it wasn't good for me either. I should think if I wasn't feeling it I probably wasn't making it good for him. But Raoul was only about himself. Never about me. Would I have slept with him that last time if I wasn't curious about what it would be like now that I had transitioned? Probably not. I don't get horny. Nothing drives me to want to crawl into bed with a guy, although when they make it evident they are interested I react, but only because I remember that's what I should do. What does sex have to do with love when you can't reproduce? If you didn't have the memory you probably wouldn't want to have sex. Is that why A'zam was trying to make me believe he didn't remember doing the whole Kama Sutra twice? It didn't have any feelings attached? It was just something to put me into a place where he could show his dominance of me? Probably. That's certainly the message I took away from that experience, particularly since it appears he's sleeping with Petra now and I've fallen off his sexual conquest list. After two hundred times I guess it's not such a mystery anymore.

Suddenly Reese pops into my mind. She's telling me about what it means to her to be a mother, to care for someone else more than you care about yourself. Selflessness is the term she uses. That she would instantly sacrifice her own happiness for that of her husband and children. Do what is necessary for them before she would do something just for herself. She reminds me of the instructions on airplanes before you take off where they say if the facemasks drop down, put the mask on yourself first, but only because you need to be conscious to help your children or relatives with theirs. As a mother she has to be told why she should take care of herself first rather than just doing what is instinctive. But is it instinctive? It's not something we do because we make a conscious decision. We do it consciously but because of an unconscious decision. And how many other unconscious decisions do mothers and fathers make when it comes to their children. If a child is in a burning building either or both parents have been known to rush back in to get their kids out to safety. At peril to their own lives.

What does it mean to do something instinctively? I've heard people describe someone as instinctive. That person makes decisions instinctively, which means without a lot of data to support it. The individuals who are good are respected even though others cannot fathom why they are right so often. Generally, I've always thought instinctive decisions come from experience. Seeing and observing how things happen so as to be able to predict probable outcomes. It's like the baseball player who sees enough balls pitched to him or her. After a point patterns are set in the mind and when something about the release of the ball, or the early flight looks the same as hundreds of earlier pitches, the batter lets his muscles respond as they have before in swinging at that ball. The batter swings automatically the way he or she has made contact with the ball most frequently. All in the blink of an eye because the ball may be approaching the batter at over one hundred miles an hour. I don't even like baseball, so why am I thinking about it as an example of instinct? I don't hear people talking about so and so as being an instinctive baseball player. But maybe that's because they all are, and we just take it for granted.

A new image comes to me. Mrs. Walker, my fifth-grade teacher. She is short and overweight, big chested with long brown hair. She has a peculiar smell, at least it's peculiar to me. I remember that smell because Mrs. Walker was a hugger. She always made contact with you when she was talking with you whether it was a good or bad talk. There was something reassuring about that contact. She was letting me know that despite whatever it was we were talking about she accepted me for who I am. We have a connection. An ease and familiarity that enabled our discussion, regardless of the topic. Mrs. Walker taught me how to cook. Anna Laura taught me basics, but Mrs. Walker taught me how to interpret recipes, what the different measures meant, and the difference between dry and wet volumes, about onions and garlic and olive oil. I showed Anna Laura what I'd learned from Mrs. Walker. She was pleased and let me make dinner once a week, so I could practice my new skills. Anna Laura would show me something new and I'd ask Mrs. Walker about it. Mrs. Walker would always touch my arm as we talked, she always told me I should learn as much as I can from Anna Laura, and not just about cooking, but about life and a woman's role in the world. I don't think of her as a feminist, but she always reinforced that a woman could do or be anything a man could, we just had to work harder to achieve it. I asked her what working harder meant. She would always smile at me and say I'd find that out when I decided what it was I would be passionate about. I asked her what she was passionate about and she would always smile and say her students, because each of us was an opportunity for her to shape a future. She loved for us to come back and see her after we had gone on, whether it was to the next grade or after graduating from college. She was still in that same classroom all those years later, having shaped another thirty or so futures every year in some fashion that she could only imagine.

Tabitha is suddenly pulling my hair from behind. She did that a lot, or at least I thought she did. It was her way of getting my attention. Tabitha was two years younger than me and maybe that explains why she always seemed to think she should do everything I did. As far as she was concerned we were the same age and we should do the same things. But I was the older sister. I was supposed to be the role model for her, at least that's what Anna Laura would always say to me when Tabitha did something wrong and somehow, I was to blame. That also seemed to happen a lot. Tabitha liked to play videogames, but she didn't like playing against the machine. She liked the ones where she would compete against me. Always trying to show that she could beat me, although it was a rare occasion when she actually did. Somehow that was the goal. To show she could do something better than I could. There is no question, at least to me, that she would have been a better athlete than I was. She had the build of a runner. Lean, strong legs and a will to keep going no matter what. She probably would have been a distance runner. And she was learning tennis as well. She actually had a great two-handed backhand. She could hit the ball hard and drop it nearly anywhere she wanted. I know since I was her usual opponent in long practices. We didn't keep score, much to her disappointment. It was practice. We were both trying to get better, not see who could beat who. At least I wasn't. When we started out I didn't want to discourage her by always winning. That was why we only practiced. But as she got better and better she started wanting to keep score. Occasionally I would agree, but only occasionally. And shortly before she passed on, we were having very close matches that could go either way. She would always want to play a match on Fridays, but I seldom gave in to her insistence. I probably should have more than I did.

Now it's Windy, lying across my dorm room bed in just her underwear like she did so often. We would talk late into the night and sleep in. Somehow, we would usually make class, but I showered and got dressed first while Windy would continue on discussing whatever it was we had decided was the topic d'jour. Generally, it was an attempt to demystify one guy or another, but we also got into deep discussions about family. Since mine had been truncated at an early age and she was an only child, I think we were drawn to each other as the sister she never had and the sister I lost. Although Windy was nothing like Tabitha since I never remember her pulling my hair or trying to compete with me. It was always a free flow between us. We recognized a kindred spirit in the other. Someone trying to navigate a world that didn't make much sense to either of us. We thought we could talk our experiences through and eventually the world would come into focus for both of us. It did in many respects, although I think I must have failed her when it came to Tom. I should have been more vocal about my reservations. Should have warned her that it would not end up with a Hollywood ending. I knew that back then, why didn't she? What is it about sexual attraction? In Windy's case I think that was what overcame her usual good sense. Tom had something that attracted women. And he worked hard at keeping a mystique about him. Star athlete, he would either become a professional, which didn't happen, or because of his exploits on the field of play, some company would want him to help sell their products, which he did. Tom knew who he was going to be. His future was assured, and because it was, he was assured in his relationships with women. Windy got caught up in being the one who married the big man on campus. Was that a competitive thing for her? The number of women who were ready to sleep with him on any night was large. It increased as his exploits with a football also became legendary, at least on our campus. From all accounts he seldom turned down an opportunity. Windy knew that because I did, and we talked about it. A lot. Tom was a continuing topic of discussion in our senior year. I knew she was fascinated with him, but she had deliberately chosen not to go out with him or even let him know she was interested. I think she was afraid if she made a move too soon, he would get bored with her as he did every other woman he went out with. She wanted to be alluring, but also become someone he couldn't have unless he was willing to commit to her. The strategy worked, too well. She won the prize only to come to regret it. I should have been more insistent. Maybe convinced her to at least go out with him once in our junior year. Even if she didn't sleep with him. That would have ended the allure for Tom, I'm sure. But it might have backfired in that she might have become more obsessive about him. Not that she wasn't. But she did it in a controlled way. Incremental steps. Planned well in advance. Be at a certain party with so and so. Go to the homecoming dance with one of his team mates. Never sleep with anyone Tom knew so as to ensure he never got a report on her performance in bed. She had to be this complete mystery to Tom if she was going to win him in the end. I don't think I could have been as disciplined as she was, but then again, I really didn't have much interest in guys since I wasn't looking to become Mrs. Anybody in school. I was there to become something more.

Delilah has always been an enigma to me. Even though we hung out in college, we were never close like Windy and me. She was always there, with us through thick and thin. And always the one to go home from any party or campus event with a different guy. I couldn't keep up with her grading system. She evaluated guys on a scale that made no sense to me at all, but it worked for her. Anyway, she made it a rule never to sleep with the same guy twice. Said the guy was always trying his hardest the first time to make it good for her. The second time was all about making it good for him. So, she never intended to do it a second time because it would never be as good. She never told us what happened that she made that rule, but I had and still have the sense that some guy got really rough with her the second time. Don't know if she ended up in the emergency room or what. But I suspect it was nearly that bad if not that bad. So Delilah was the campus queen or campus tramp depending on your perspective. She could give you a run down on any guy without even having to think about it. Photographic memory when it came to how big they were. It was like fishing stories. 'It was this big' and she would hold her hands apart. She would crack all of us up when she would show her hands only a couple inches apart and say, 'and he was this big'. I'm surprised that Windy didn't heed Delilah's advice about Tom. She admitted he was one of the bigger dicks on campus, but she put it just that way. Said Tom wasn't very good in bed. In a hurry and seemed to only want relief. Foreplay was short and not very gentile. Delilah said she didn't have an orgasm and was glad to get out of bed with Tom. Why Windy didn't listen to the voice of experience I can't say. Other women on campus talked about

Tom as just this god-like experience. I think either they were just so in awe of the guy's reputation that they didn't want to be seen as having a contrary opinion or experience. Others were probably only trying to make themselves look better because they had slept with the big man on campus, at least size-wise. Delilah was funny in college. She would come up to me and ask who I was interested in. My usual answer was Newton, if I was studying physics or Faraday if electronics. She'd always tell me I needed to broaden my interests. After all, sex drugs and rock and roll are there for a reason. When I'd ask what that reason was, she would say that we are trying to cram way too much information into our heads and that we need the release that sex, drugs and rock and roll provide in order to find room to stuff more knowledge in there. An interesting thought, but not one I really subscribed to. If that were accurate, it would explain why Delilah stayed an undergrad a full year after the rest of us left. She was setting campus records. I envy Delilah. She knew exactly what she wanted, she went after it with gusto and she has had a range of experiences, sexual and otherwise that even A'zam and I with our twice through the Kama Sutra can't approach. She said she can tell in the first twenty seconds if a guy is going to be good in bed or not. Is that instinct or just experience? I'd have to say experience, but someone who didn't know Delilah's background might think of it as instinct.

I've got to decide what to do with the idea Dr. Woodall has about the flash memory as a means of guiding behavior, providing the memories on a constantly loaded basis needed to negotiate life.

The buzzer goes off. I'm fully recharged. Time to shower and dress. What do I want to wear today? Something nice. I'm feeling more feminine is needed for the day. Why is that? Instinct or just experience? Either way I'm going to look frilly, soft, and approachable. Am I also going to emulate Mrs. Walker and be a hugger today? Maybe I ought to think about doing that as a rule. Might make me more approachable. That's the word for the day. Don't know what's going to happen, but with so many things up in the air, it could be any one. And if any one does come down I need to be ready for it.

THE WHOLE WORLD

I'm approaching the AppleCore building still lost in thought when I see A'zam come out of the front door. It's about 2:00 am. Why would he be out walking around? The time of night isn't an issue since he doesn't sleep either. What's curious is that he's out here, and now I see he's coming directly towards me. I check the cameras on the building. Yes, we are clearly in view so security can see us. Probably the only reason he would come outside.

"Morning," he greets me.

I nod and wait until he reaches me, surprised that he takes my arm and turns me around to keep walking in the direction he was going. "What's the matter?" I ask when we are walking in lockstep.

"I've decided I have to be unpredictable."

The tone of his voice tells me nothing, nor does his expression. "Any particular reason?"

"We're entering a delicate time. I don't want anyone to bug my office, or intercept communications or anything that could make others aware of our plans."

"Anything make you think someone has?"

"No. But I can't be too careful. Neither can you." A'zam looks at me to gauge my reaction." Like walking to your place. It's routine for you. Now I know you're doing it in the middle of the night and changing the time and all that. But it's still routine. You should install a charging bed in your office, or even use mine."

"Don't think that would be a good idea. Walking around naked in your office, even if it is to recharge." I inform him.

"Who's going to see you?"

"Security. Don't think I want those tapes playing throughout the building during lunch hour."

"I'm sure I could get agreement to limit it to the night shift." A'zam displays his devious smile.

"Don't worry, I'll make it work the way I'm doing it."

"I gave you fair warning." A'zam concludes that discussion and moves on to the next. "Do you have another upgrade ready for me?"

"Jermaine hasn't been in touch?" I ask already knowing the answer.

"Not since the last time."

"That was last week." I remind him.

"Plenty of time to make real progress."

"On what aspect of the experience? I understand we've enhanced the physical side of things. I really don't know what more could be done for you there."

"He promised to make it more explosive," A'zam informs me.

"Explosive?" I echo. "Is that what you really want? Or would it be a better experience if it varied. Sometimes long lasting. Others explosive. And still others erupting in a series of releases all triggered by the same stimulation?"

A'zam has to think about my question. "How is it supposed to be?"

"Different people experience orgasm differently. But why shouldn't you have variety? Experience the range rather than just what you were used to? You're going to be around for a long time. Doing it the same way and experiencing it the same way will get old quickly."

"That's why they invented the Kama Sutra." A'zam reminds me.

"Right. But that's only the position. How you experience the release the positions cause can and should be different. And it should vary even when you do it in the same position. Go for infinite variations for the infinite times you are going to do it."

"Is that what you told Jermaine to do?" A'zam is wondering if I gave different instructions than he did. Got to be careful here.

"You worked out your version with Jermaine. If you just want explosive I'm sure that's what he will deliver when he's figured out how to get to the ultimate explosion. But I also asked him to start working on an infinitely variable version. If nothing else immortals will be able to select what they're used to if they don't want to change. Or they can explore new worlds all at the change of a setting. And the user can configure it right up to the climax."

"Will your configurable version include the explosive option just as I requested it?"

I nod rather than answer since I haven't spoken to Jermaine about any of this.

"How much longer will it take to deliver your version?"

"I don't know. Oriana just gave him a new assignment and it's going to take a lot of his time."

A'zam frowns. "You mean he's not just working my project?"

"He's going to be responsible for ramping up the transitions with Dr. Woodall and our teams."

"Why would you have him working that? Anyone could do it."

"Because the teams aren't playing nicely together."

A'zam stops walking. "Really? Why haven't I heard about this before now?'

"Not on your side of the dividing line." I inform him.

"Oh, that's right."

We walk on in silence. I suspect he is waiting for me to give him the details, but I don't.

"What's happening with Symbol Ventures? Have you put the offer on the table to them yet?"

I shake my head.

"Good. "

"And why is that?"

A'zam walks on in silence.

"You set the rules." I remind him. "I run the shop, you focus on everything else."

A'zam doesn't respond.

"Just for your information, the proposal is done. I've been sitting on it trying to get to a fair valuation."

"That's the problem," A'zam states as if he knew.

"The valuation?" I'm surprised he would know. "I have three different merchant banks working on it, but this is such a huge acquisition they're having difficulty valuing the IP."

"Tell them to stop."

"Why?" I am surprised, but still don't have enough information to know what to do.

A'zam doesn't respond.

"Oh, that's right. You're not answering questions."

Now it's my turn to walk along in silence.

"When we start flooding the market with new products…"

"Not going to happen." I inform him.

"I'm sure there is a reason the person who is responsible for our core business is not trying to maximize the value of the firm." A'zam states to see what reaction he gets.

"I'm sure the value of the firm will be maximized in time."

"I'm sure you won't be here to see it." Simple, straightforward threat.

"In which case neither will you since it won't happen under the approach you would have us hand jam. You have thought of everyone except the customer."

"The customer is king." A'zam responds reflexively. "Everyone knows that."

"Except you."

"I disagree."

"Pleased you think so, but it ain't so," I inform him.

"I can't think of an example of what you are referring to."

"The average product replacement cycle is sixteen months." I begin and check to make sure he is following me. "We have convinced our customers to upgrade to new functionality every six months or so. That means we get two replacement cycles of software updates for each hardware replacement."

"I am aware of those statistics."

"Only because you're looking at them right now." I point out. "The issue is if we up the rate of new product introductions, our customers will get confused about what and when they should update. Preliminary market research Landon has shown me indicates a new product blitz has had the opposite effect of what we desire. Our customer, on average only updates once in a year and replaces hardware once every two years, on average."

"Why would they do that?" A'zam truly sounds surprised.

"I'm going to break the rules of our little game here, since you did first by asking the question. New feature fatigue, is what I call it. They have so many choices they wait for the next big thing to come out. Something that is totally different. Opens new channels of communication. Makes it even easier to reach out and touch people they want to touch while making sure those who they don't want to touch them can't."

"All right. I do have another question. How long have you known about this market research?"

"About a week. I actually assigned Moshe to validate it using a totally different approach. But I had to pull the plug on it and him, quite literally."

"You terminated Moshe?" A'zam sound surprised. "Now things are getting interesting. I take it we will never find the body since you can't go to jail."

"Moshe is transitioning back. He simply would not adapt to what was expected of him. Thought as an immortal he could do no wrong. Thought we had too much invested in him and need immortals too badly. Found out he was wrong."

"Impressive." A'zam observes. "I didn't think you had it in you to do the hard things."

"I haven't begun to do the truly hard things yet. But I suspect they may be starting today."

"Let's see." A'zam begins to recount the schedule. "We have the first hearing on the ACLU suit. That should be a piece of cake. Your budget plan is due for review, which should define our research efforts for the next year. There must be other things, but I don't know what."

"The first class of twenty immortals arrive today."

"Woodall has his team up to four a day?" A'zam asks as if surprised, but I'm sure he already knows this.

"I believe the contract is for a time period, not a set number of transitions."

"Correct."

"So, no matter how many transitions per day he performs, he still does so for twelve months."

"The more he transitions in a day the more we will have transitioned when the period of exclusivity runs out." A'zam fills me in. "But there's more."

I wait for him to continue since he still isn't responding to questions. I don't know why he insists on playing this silly game.

"The last contract was signed yesterday."

"So, we now have exclusive rights for all components in the immortals body that are supplied to Dr. Woodall's team?" I seek to confirm.

"We also have the exclusive right to buy each and every one. It's only a right because we want the ability to change suppliers if new and better vendors show up."

"Supply chain is tracking the technology suppliers to identify emerging alternatives for each part and also for potentially more effective subsystems." I inform him.

"My team is doing the same on competitive solution providers." A'zam hesitates. Why would he do that? "You know it's tough to convince technical supply chain folks to look at medical procedures and try to understand who could do something like what Dr. Woodall's team is doing. They've never had to look at anything other than hardware or software. A procedure was really hard for them to wrap their minds around."

"Understandable." I concur. "We're breaking new ground here. Breaking new ground with our teams as well."

"But at least they're still doing what they knew how to do." A'zam muses.

We walk on in silence for a bit. I've now told him what he wanted to know, all through a silly game he wants to play. I guess it makes sense that when you can communicate at such high rates of speed, it makes sense to make the communications more challenging, more amusing. At the same time that makes precision more challenging.

"I need to start back as I have a senior team meeting starting shortly." I inform A'zam who has also been deep in thought.

He nods, and we turn around, now seeing the AppleCore headquarters lights illuminating the night.

"I never get used to seeing it this way." A'zam marvels. "It's a symbol to the world of innovation, thought leaders and changing the dynamics of human interaction."

"But the world never sees it like this." I realize aloud.

"And that's why I took this walk. The last time I was out at this time of night walking around our campus was the first week I worked here. That was over ten years ago. I had spent my whole life working for that day. And it came and went so fast I never had an opportunity to appreciate it. I went through that first day of meetings both with the media and our senior teams. And I was still here at midnight, reading and trying to understand what I'd just been made responsible for. So, I came out here and walked all the way around the building, looking at it from every angle. I knew I was going to have to look at the management issues that way so I might as well start with the building itself."

"That was also the day I first met you, on that walk," I remind him.

"I don't remember meeting you until later that week, when you came in to interview for the SVP role."

"I was sitting on a bench on the other side of the building. It was a little past midnight, but I worked late regularly. I had my condo down the street, so it was only a short distance to get home."

"That was you? It was dark, I guess that's why I didn't recognize you when you came in."

"You asked me why I was working so late, do you remember what I said to you?"

"That if you love what you do, it isn't work." A'zam nods. "And you said you only get one chance to change the world. AppleCore is the one place where it can be the whole world."

CHANGE

Shortly after sunrise I look up to find Mindi staring at me as I sit at my desk. I had heard her come in, but she usually just goes to her desk and starts to work. Not today. "What's the matter?" I ask.

"It's Landon."

"Of course. What is it now?"

"He was notified," she says emphatically as if I should know what she's talking about.

"They ended the draft a long time ago. Is this the Indian Army?"

"Jermaine sent him the date to report."

"Jermaine? Our Jermaine? Report for what?" but then it's all too clear.

"To go to Dallas…transition into an immortal. If he goes, we will never have children. This couldn't happen at a worse time."

I decide to try out my new approachability technique. I reach across my desk and touch Mindi's hand. She looks at me surprised, but she doesn't move her hand from under mine. "Back up for a minute if you would. What happened with his parents?"

"Landon said he grew a pair of balls." Mindi smiles but then blushes. "He told them if he can be as successful as they have been he was willing to be miserable with me."

"What did his mother have to say to that?"

"She said it wasn't fair to me."

"Glad to know she has your best interests in mind." I note.

"Now that we can be married, he will be an immortal and we can't have children."

"Does Landon wish to delay the transition?"

"No." Mindi admits although she clearly would prefer it were otherwise. "He's afraid this may be his only chance, since we are putting only a few non-engineers into the program. He says it's an incredible honor that a creative person may have the ability to imagine beyond anything that has been imagined before."

"We need his skills to manage the transition." I reply, wondering how she will react.

"That's not what I wanted to hear," Mindy responds glumly. But then she looks determined instead. "I want to go through with him."

"Wait a minute." I slow her down. "You told me, and Landon told me all you talk about is children. Having a family. Are you telling me you're ready to walk away from ever having a family? Children of your own?"

"If I can't have children with Landon Bannerjee, I don't want any children," she announces.

"No. I can't put you into the program because you're just reacting now."

"I'm not. I know my heart and Landon is all I want. Now and forever."

"You need to talk with Landon. There are alternatives you've not considered. I won't enable a decision you will regret later." I try to sound as firm as possible, so she won't challenge me.

"Why are you being horrible to me after all I do for you?" And Mindi doesn't wait for an answer, returning to her desk to sulk.

I'm feeling whiplashed. No matter what I do, I find more and more diametrically opposed results hitting me. My priorities don't align with the team, or the employees. If A'zam gets his way, they may not align with what the whole world wants.

Dietrich calls, "You have a minute?"

"As many as you need. I take it we have feedback from the first day of hearings?"

"See you shortly."

Dietrich doesn't waste time reaching my office. He closes the door behind him, so he doesn't even want Mindi to hear this discussion. He looks out to the coy pond beyond my desk for a moment as if he is trying to put what he is about to discuss with me into perspective. Then he collapses into the chair across from me, slouching rather than sitting straight as he told me his mother often reminded him to do. "It isn't going well."

"I could have guessed," based on his behavior.

"There are over a hundred intervenor parties who wish to provide testimony."

"Are any friendly?" I'm trying to understand who is showing up.

"Can't be sure of everyone, but the vast majority have established their nexus with the proceeding as related to advocacy for one or another human rights organization."

"Are they representing my rights?" I ask already knowing the answer.

"Only if you're a contributor." Dietrich puts the whole dynamic on the table.

"Maybe I should start contributing," I respond deadpan, "You want to give me a list?"

"You're serious?" Dietrich isn't sure he knows how to read my comment. "Can't be company funds or it would just blow up."

"Would give me standing to contest their advocacy positions if they are anti me in any way."

Dietrich mulls my strategy. "It would, but since the vast majority of their members would probably support the 'anti' positions, I doubt it would have any effect." Dietrich summarizes his expert opinion.

"I'm not looking to change their position, but rather to just lob some hand-grenades over their heads." I explain. "Might give them some pause while they try to figure out whether it's better to oppose immortals or be early supporters, if in fact immortals end up in power positions."

"You just might earn your title." Dietrich admits as a backhanded compliment. "But that won't help us in the short term. The judge intends to let each have as much time as they wish, which means this circus will go on for weeks. Let's say each intervenor talks on average one hour. That would be over one hundred hours or two and a half weeks of testimony alone. Add thirty minutes of cross examination and we have another fifty hours. So, we are approaching a month. Then probably a month for the judge to review the testimony and decide what she wants to do. Figure two months, one of which is the circus and two months from now we will be dealing with her ruling."

"Two months." I muse. "We get up to eighty transitions a week we will be nearing seven hundred and fifty immortals, including the entire leadership of AppleCore."

"Over seventy-product teams and you have an immortal team working every product area." Dietrich muses. "Two in the most important."

"Before the competition can field even one." I point out. "But it's not all cruise control from there on. We have significant challenges to making this transition work."

I must catch Dietrich unawares. His facial expression changes to one of concern. "Challenges?"

"Put the ten smartest lawyers you know in a room and ask them to draft an opinion, what happens?"

"I see your point." Evidently Dietrich can visualize the problem.

"But how do you get lawyers to work together?" I ask. "There may be a kernel there that might help us get to faster productivity."

"First of all, we would never put ten partners in a room and expect them to decide on anything other than partnership shares."

"Good point."

"We always have one partner who will review what the younger associates propose. We have a senior associate who is trying to make partner leading the discussion, shaping the direction of the legal research, and proposing the key and most salient arguments, which the younger associates will then draft and rewrite endlessly until the senior associate is happy. It then goes to the partner who will rewrite again and give it back to the senior associate to polish, who in turn gives it to one or more junior associates to draft alternative language and it goes up the chain one more time."

"Doesn't sound very efficient." I note.

"It's not, but it's all about how we train junior associates, give our senior associates an opportunity to prove they are worthy of a partnership and everyone is happy because the billable hours are enough to keep everyone busy and happy at the end of the year when partnership profits are divided out."

"So, tell me, why did you ever decide to come over to the corporate side of law?"

"I get to keep all my old partners fully engaged." Dietrich admits.

"But we don't do that? Do we?" I have to ask.

"Not quite that, but we still have junior and senior associates who are hoping to become general counsel at some point."

"If I can take the key point from your description it would be to establish teams that have senior and junior members. Establish different levels of authority based on seniority rather than expertise."

Dietrich shakes his head. "What works for lawyers is different. We have the same skill sets, just different domain expertise. For your product teams you have different domain expertise and different skill sets from what I can tell."

"Yes and no." I visualize the team structure. "We have multiple engineers who are all designers, but specialize in different areas of the product. The problem has been to get that group on the same page because they all want to run ahead to a solution and not wait for others to make a decision."

"Now that's different than what I thought was the problem." Dietrich muses. "Do you have a team lead who is also your chief engineer?"

"Not always. Depends on the team."

"That may be your problem. The senior person should be the senior design person as well. Aligned authority if you see what I'm suggesting. The person who kicks your butt for being behind schedule is also the same person who kicks your butt for going off the reservation on the design."

"Maybe you should be working with Jermaine in putting the

teams together." I suggest half in jest, but not entirely.

"I have enough to do to keep you out of jail or worse places." Dietrich responds apparently bringing me back to the immortals trial.

"Worse places?" I follow up not understanding the comment.

"If they go where I think they intend, the intervenors may ask that you be transitioned back and that no future immortals can be created." Dietrich is very serious. Evidently already part of the conversation.

"How likely is that outcome?" I'd not considered the court could require me to be terminated as an immortal since I have no human body to go back to.

"You weren't listening." Dietrich is emphatic. "Anything could come out of this process. Reason and logic aren't permitted into the court room. It's all about spectacle and glitz. Who will be the most controversial? Who will introduce a wrinkle no one saw coming? Who will be the surprise star witness? I'll even go so far as to say they will subpoena your friend Dr. Woodall and grill him until he is well done on both sides."

That would not be good as there is no telling what the doctor might say with a global audience. "What you're saying is that since the entire leadership of AppleCore has transitioned, the court actually has the power to force a complete turnover of our management without even realizing they are doing so."

Dietrich nods slowly. He apparently came to this conclusion a while ago.

"Do we have a schedule of who is testifying and in what order?"

"Probably in the next few days, but not yet." Dietrich has asked the same question, I am sure. "We will have an opportunity to discuss the calendar with the judge before it is officially released, but I don't expect she will give us any deference. If anything, she will want to make it look like she is sticking it to us to appease all the liberal members of the legislature who want her replaced with someone who will be more activist in her rulings. She's actually been relatively even handed thus far."

"What should we expect?" I'm about out of questions since so little is known and there are so many directions the whole proceeding could go.

"Lots of people all suggesting you are the devil incarnate."

"Are you suggesting I'm not?" I respond in mock surprise. "I always thought AppleCore was the friend of the technophile. Since I've been responsible for most of the products those people have purchased, how could I be anything other than someone who is trying to separate them from their money all while linking them closer and closer to their social reference group."

"This isn't about you, Sage." Dietrich announces. "It's about all of us now. We are in this boat together, pulling to get to the same place. You don't have to carry the whole burden anymore, even though I know you think you do. You need to relax. Bring the rest of us into the discussion. Confide what we all can do to help you and A'zam succeed and lead the revolution in consumer technology."

Dietrich has raised an issue I've not considered before. "Is that what you think this is all about? Consumer technology?"

Dietrich frowns, "That's our business. What else would it be about?"

"You're going to live forever. That's more than a minor change in civilization and human history. We are going to change more than just what device people carry and what it does."

AMBUSHED

MC wants to have drinks. MC never meets with me alone, so I have my antenna up when I get the call. And what is even stranger, at least to me, she doesn't want to meet where the posse meets. I've never been to this place. Evocation. A club I've only heard about. Mostly younger crowd. Never see the power elites here. Just the wannabes.

When I walk in the lights are low, even though it is late afternoon, but before the crowds start drifting in. Nothing unusual about the bar. Long and polished to a gloss. Dark wood and chrome with the usual racks of glasses hanging upside down so the bartender can quickly fill a drink. The alcohol is set out on the back shelf in alphabetical order by type rather than by producer. So, all the gins are together and all the scotch or bourbon. Easy for a bartender to find.

MC is sitting at the bar with a glass of red wine. She sees me come in, swings around in her swivel chair and waits for me to come give her a hug. Not a Mrs. Walker hug, but the posse hug I've given out since I was an undergrad. Why were they always deserving of hugs, but not Mindi or Oriana or the other members of my team? Probably because I didn't want to seem too physical with people at work. Not a good thing even if you mean only to improve your communications.

"You doing wine or water today?" MC asks.

"A white wine is fine," I respond as I take a seat next to her.

"Gruner Veltliner for my friend." MC orders for me and points to a table in a corner. I follow her, and the glass of wine is delivered even before I am seated with my back to the corner.

"What's the occasion?" I have to ask since she gave me no clue on the call asking to get together. "Are the others joining us?"

"The occasion is I want to ask you something. And I know you're going to be surprised I would ask, but I've given this a lot of thought and I need to do this now."

MC is the most deliberate in our group. So, something important must have happened that she would want to come talk to me one-on-one. "How can I help?"

"I want to transition. To be like you."

She catches me totally by surprise, but I don't react. "I have to admit, you're the last person I would think would want to transition," comes out of my mouth faster than I can stop myself. I have to recover, "So what's up you're feeling the need?"

"When you first told us about what happened to you I accepted it at face value. You know? Would have died so extreme treatment procedure to save your life. But now that I've had a chance to watch you for a while, I've come to the conclusion this is more than just a lifesaving procedure. This is a fundamental shift in humanity."

"You've been reading the ACLU propaganda." I suggest.

"I have been a life-long member, but that's not what's behind my realization. I look at you and I look at A'zam. I don't know two people who could be more different, and yet somehow the two of you have been responsible for building an amazing company that touches nearly everyone in the world."

"You're giving us a lot of credit I don't think is deserved."

"The issue is I can't ignore that the world is changing. It's changed an incredible amount just in the last few years. But you represent a fundamental shift from the world we have known. And I can either sit on the sideline or jump in and be there when immortals become the dominant cultural force in our society."

"Jump in, like transition yourself?"

MC nods.

"But why should you transition? I mean I was transitioned because I had an incurable disease. Why should Dr. Woodall transition you? If he were to do that it would open the floodgates and there would be no constraints on who transitions or why. The first in line I would expect to be the government, wanting soldiers to go fight wars who can fight anywhere."

"Why should I transition?" MC has clearly given this considerable thought. "Who better to help those who transition make the adjustment from a short-term visitor on this planet to a longer term one?"

"I hear you." I hesitate, trying to formulate the appropriate response. "But psychologist, teacher, physician, engineer, clergyman. Where does it start and where does it end? Who gets to choose and why? What becomes the criteria? How many of each? Who specifically? I don't know how you make the decisions about who and when and why."

"A'zam told me you're transitioning AppleCore employees. Why should they have preference over me, for example?"

"Did A'zam tell you he negotiated a contract to establish that, right? And that contract is costing AppleCore billions of dollars?"

"That contract doesn't limit the transitions to people who have incurable diseases. Take A'zam as an example. He didn't have a physical problem that was going to cause him to die like you did, and he was able to transition."

"He did, but that doesn't say he should have. Do you have trillions of dollars at your disposal to throw at a problem? A'zam did."

"Look." MC evidently sees she's not going to win this discussion. "You and I have been friends forever. Something unexpected happened to you and it has opened up a whole new world for mankind. I see the value and the struggles that are going to come along with the changes that are coming. I just want to be on the side of those who are leading those transitions."

I understand what she's saying and why she, in particular, would want to be involved in the emerging society. "You are one of the few people who has been able to see the future. Through me and through your involvement with A'zam. That's a portal that if opened wider would cause a stampede of people wanting to force the doors open wider so they could squeeze through and be part of the revolution. I understand. If I were in your position I'd probably want the same. But that doesn't mean I can rewrite the rules to help you and Windy and Delilah and Reese to all transition, if you all wanted to. And at the same time, if I open up the admissions for you I would have to for them and a whole host of others."

"None of them want to." MC informs me. "I've asked."

"I can see that. But think about it. If all of a sudden you transition don't you think that would cause them to rethink it?"

"No. Reese has no interest. She's the earth mother. She lives for her kids and frankly when they've grown and are gone I think she's going to have difficulty redefining herself. Delilah is the opposite. She defines herself by the last relationship and the lessons she's learned about what she doesn't want to do again. And Windy? She's at sea at the moment. She doesn't know what she wants or have any idea what she will become. Transitioning to an immortal? That's about the last thing on her mind."

I nod. "I understand your perspective. But not why you have this urge to become immortal. It just seems so far from anything you've ever expressed an interest in."

"Why me?" MC confirms the question. "The challenge. In my current role I help people make adjustments in their lives. Something changes, and they try to keep doing what they've always done. It doesn't work for them anymore. So, I spend a lot of time helping them to understand what changed, often why it changed, and what they have to do differently now that a new reality confronts them."

"Why isn't that enough for you?" I have to ask. "You always wanted to understand people and help them understand themselves. At least that was your frame of reference when we were all in school together."

"I think about the change a person has to make when they are no longer bound by time. You now have all the time in the world. If you don't do something today there will be millions of days when you can. For the rest of us there are only a few days when you can. We are in a hurry, rushing to the gravesites where we will be for the rest of our existence. You aren't. The gravesite has no bearing on your future. Your life today could well resemble your life a hundred thousand or a million years from now. That's a whole different perspective. It carries a whole different set of motivators. You may deliberately decide not to do something today that you normally would in order to save something for you to do tomorrow. Where most of us today, have to make decisions about things we will never do because there just isn't enough time in our busy lives to ever get to it."

"I haven't seen that yet." I dispute her expectation of what it's like to be on this side of immortality. "If anything, I'm finding I'm trying to squeeze even more things into a day than I did before. Sure, I have all day and all night to get things done. But I'm filling up those nights with analysis of problems I tend to address the next day. I'm just more thorough and more deliberate in the decisions I'm making, but if anything, I'm making more decisions in a day with a lot more analysis behind them than I could get to before."

"Is that just a reflection of your job?"

She has a good point. "I don't know. Would you do the same thing? Would you spend your nights thinking about your patients and how to best help them or would you spend the night watching old movies? That would be your choice. Everyone would be different in that regard."

MC sips her wine, thinking about what I've had to say. Apparently looking for another argument that would sway me to help her. "You're transitioning people with no support. If I'm correct, I think A'zam made mention that a condition of their transition is that they can't talk about it outside the company. If that's the case then you may have all these head cases running around, about to explode and no support for any of them because they can't talk about it and you have no one inside who they can turn to for help."

Another good point. "They come to me. I've been the one they come talk to. We've had a few who experienced difficulty. So far only one has not been able to be successful."

"And what happened to that one?" MC pursues me, and I have to be careful about what I say to her.

"He will eventually transition back to his biologic body." I decide is safe to say.

"Back to a state where he had previously been successful." MC summarizes.

I nod.

"How many have there been? Does he represent twenty-five percent or one percent?"

"Neither." She wants too much information. She admitted she's an ACLU member. Even though she's been a close friend forever, by turning down her request I can't be sure what she would do with such detailed information. "We're tracking things carefully. It's not a problem at this time. The one instance was more a reflection of violating our own selection criteria than any real issue we haven't already identified. I can't tell you anything more about that one instance without violating privacy. I originally denied the request for transition for all the right reasons, but then changed my mind to give the individual the benefit of the doubt. Unfortunately, all of my worst fears were realized."

"If I transitioned, I could help you with cases like that. Probably save you the cost and problems you will encounter by transitioning that person back."

"What do you mean? Problems we will encounter?" I have to ask.

"Once you transition to your side, psychologically you assume a new mind set. You have to in order to deal with the differences in your existence. The new-found powers and capabilities, the limitations in the things you used to do autonomically that are no longer required. And from what A'zam has told me, the aspects of your existence that no longer measure up to that which you knew when you were mortal."

I'm surprised she's gone to this length of thinking through the differences between her and me.

"But if you decide to transition someone back, against their will, which is what it sounds like is the case in this instance, you create dissonance. Today I'm a superman, and tomorrow I'm not. That could create severe depression. Maybe even suicidal thoughts. In the worst instance possible suicidal tendencies that may not be mitigated. Particularly if that individual is not able to find a role with similar challenges in their mortal life. If the person encounters the certainty that life is limited once again with death a certainty and no possible intervention, what hope is there for the future?"

"Why didn't you tell me this when I was contemplating transitioning back?"

"Because I didn't understand enough then. I've learned a lot more by talking with you and A'zam. Watching you both. Just thinking about the situation. When you transitioned I thought you were going to be the only one of your kind for a long time. I didn't realize how quickly others would follow. And frankly given the numbers that seem to be in the works now, putting me into line wouldn't seem to affect your plans. With my skills, I might even be able to accelerate them."

She's come up with exactly the one approach that might make sense.

"Why you? Why not our staff psychologist?"

"You don't have one. I asked A'zam." She's apparently discussed this at length with him. I'm surprised he hasn't said something to me. But then he's probably waiting to see what I do based on her coming to me. He probably even knows she's here talking to me today. Damn. A'zam has his foot on my throat every minute of every day.

"But if we did. Why would I go to someone outside the company to play that role? Particularly someone with no corporate experience?"

"What you're really looking for is cover. A reason to explain to A'zam or Windy or your HR person why you put me, a psychologist in private practice, through the transition as opposed to any other psychologist."

"That would be helpful." I admit, but isn't the motivation for my question.

"Because I took the time to try to understand the issues and problems that individuals who transition might encounter. I thought there would be individuals who would experience dissonance. You confirmed it. I've thought it through even more than you have. And if you don't do something you're going to be overwhelmed by individuals. Truth be known, I bet you have a number of individuals you've already transitioned who are struggling. I could help them, but only if I'm on the inside since those of us outside aren't permitted to know anything about what you're doing. And since they have signed non-disclosures they can't come seek help from me or anyone else outside the company."

"That would include you if I agreed. You couldn't even tell Reese or Windy or Delilah because they're not AppleCore employees and you would have to become one."

MC seems to think about that for a long moment. "Leave my practice."

"Yes."

"I hadn't considered that." MC admits. "You're saying I'd have to give up my current patients."

I nod.

"Could I negotiate to wind down my practice over time? After all, I can't believe you would require my services full time until you have substantially more immortals than you have now, but perhaps I could offer my services to your non-immortals team as well. As a corporate benefit like your company physician."

I'm not happy about being ambushed in the first place, but I need to consider this more. "We're not negotiating since I have a lot of other factors to consider before we may get to that point."

SHIT

"Mr. Badu on the line for you." Mindi calls out from her office as I'm sitting in mine working through a replan on a new product line we are trying to accelerate.

"Who?"

"Dallas Morning News. He was at the last press conference." Mindi clarifies.

"Can I call him back?" I don't want to talk to the media right now. Too many moving parts and I don't want to get snared.

"Says he has a major story about AppleCore and will go to press with what he has if we don't give him attributable responses.

"Have Suzette join me." Just in case I trip up.

"Mr. Badu, yes, nice to chat again," I pick up the call.

"Dr. Washington. As I explained to your assistant we have pieced together a major story regarding AppleCore and we're looking for comment from you."

"I'm happy to share whatever is not competition sensitive," I respond so he understands there are some things I won't discuss.

"Of course. Let me get right to the point."

Suzette comes into my office listening to the voice on the line.

"Mr. Badu, just for your information, Suzette Bain of our External Affairs office has just joined me."

"Miss Bain? Weren't you at the press conference?"

"I was, Mr. Badu. I remember your questions." She doesn't comment on them further.

"Of course. Dr. Washington, the information we have obtained is that AppleCore has been sending employees to Dr. Woodall's clinic at UT Southwestern on a regular basis. It would appear they are transitioning to immortals. Do you have any comment on that?"

"Mr. Badu." I respond firmly. "First of all, we do not respond to rumors, let alone confirm them. Second, we are not permitted to comment on our employees since they are protected by privacy laws. Third, any relationship with Dr. Woodall's clinic by the company would be of a contractual relationship generally protected by non-disclosures because of competitive implications."

"So, you are saying there are three reasons why you can't comment on what we have learned."

"I would take exception to how you are characterizing the information you claim to possess. You have apparently been informed of rumors. Since there are no facts to hang such accusations on it would appear someone is trying to garner attention in advance of the legal proceedings that are beginning next week out here. Create controversy to draw attention. Since I understand there are now more than one hundred intervenors who wish to be heard, I can understand it will be difficult to be noticed amongst the many who would want their voice heard above all the rest. A rumor such as you have described would be the kind of attention-grabbing headline whether there were anything to it or not. Do you see where I think this whole inquiry is heading? If you would be so kind as to determine whether your source is intending to participate in the hearings out here, I would hope that would put your quest to rest."

"Too bad I can't use that quote." Mr. Badu remarks. "Quest to rest is the kind of statement people remember."

"Could I ask you a question, Mr. Badu?" I turn the tables.

"Of course. What could I help you with?"

"It appears you are following the ACLU suit. What do you think? I'm looking for your personal opinion, not necessarily a newspaper position. What do you think is the reason so many intervenors wish to speak to the subject of immortals amongst us?"

"That's an interesting way of putting it. Immortals amongst us. Do you mind if I quote you as using that phrase?"

"Since I did, then you are certainly within your rights to quote me as long as it's an accurate quotation and in context."

"All right. Then as to your question. Why are so many groups wanting to go on record about immortals? My personal perception is you caught us all by surprise. Not many were talking or writing about immortality as anything other than a spiritual concept. And then one day Dr. Woodall has a press conference and introduces us to you as a fait accomplis. We didn't have time to prepare for you. As you know we like to discuss things endlessly. To understand not only what is happening, but why and what does it mean in the larger context. We didn't have that opportunity in your case. As you look back in history time after time organizations grew rapidly with very little regulation. And inevitably we were surprised in some way that they were either doing something we would have preferred they not, or were not doing something we thought they were, like protecting our personal information or not."

"You're saying you think these intervening organizations are hoping to get on record early to ensure immortals can't do something mortals can't simply by virtue of their longevity or lack of biological limits?"

"That's one way of thinking about it."

"Do you think there's something in particular these organizations may be worried about?"

"You're asking if there is something you've done that has people spooked?" Mr. Badu considers my question.

"Yes."

"What has people spooked is they don't know what you represent. You've gone out of your way to appear to be just like anyone else. But we suspect you're not. You and Dr. Woodall have said over and over you're not. You've taken the consciousness of a person and imprisoned it in a mechanical body that will live forever, even though no one is even sure if you're alive. How can you be alive if you're a machine?"

"But I'm not a machine." I thought I'd settled this discussion a long time ago. "How much of your body can be replaced before you're not human? I think the answer to that is you're always human as long as your consciousness remains, no matter how little or much of your body is replaced. In my case I'm just someone with the maximum number of body part replacements."

"You replaced your entire brain with computers. No one has ever replaced a brain with a computer."

"But we have had man machine interfaces for a long time. We've had direct implants into the brain that have allowed people to interface with computers, to move prosthetic arms and legs by simply thinking about the prosthetic moving. This may be a step further than we've gone before. But it's only a small step. What has people spooked, if I may venture a guess, is that I'm all of those things rolled into one. No one is quite ready to accept we have moved to this state."

"You may be right, so why did you ask me if you already have your answer to your question?"

"I don't have any answers, Mr. Badu. I only have questions and want to compare theories others may have. Personally, I'm hopeful. Hopeful we will be able to do some things sooner than we would have been able to otherwise. Mostly in the area of saving the lives of individuals with incurable diseases."

"And not in the realm of developing the next generation of personal computing products?"

Mr. Badu has returned to his question. I have to be careful how I answer this one too. "I've been on the job with my new capabilities for a couple months now. I'm working harder than I did before, but mostly because I was very ill and couldn't even do a normal day's work. Now I'm making up for that lost time and pushing my teams. I'm able to move AppleCore in certain directions because of my reasoning bandwidth that now far exceeds what I used to be able to do. And I work longer hours because I don't need to break for meals or sleep. So, am I having an effect on AppleCore? I hope so and I hope it's positive to our performance."

"Are you taking full responsibility for the blizzard of new products and apps your company has released in the last few weeks?"

"Responsibility in that as the CEO of the products company I am ultimately responsible for everything we do. But our teams have stepped up to the challenges I've given them. Everything you have seen in the recent days was in work before I transitioned."

"What you're trying to do is show me there is a plausible explanation as to why you have been so prolific with new products without them being the result of teams of immortals designing them through the night at AppleCore." Mr. Badu summarizes.

"What is Dr. Woodall saying?" I change the direction thinking I know this answer.

"That he is building a new hospital to enable transitions but that is more than a year away from completion."

"And I take it he tells you he is monitoring my progress closely. I'm his prototype test bed. The lessons he's learning from me will show up in future versions."

"I see you've been monitoring what he's been saying as well."

"Yes, Mr. Badu. I'm dependent on refinements and updates and new functionality Dr. Woodall and his team are developing. They will be the determinants of whether I become even more like you or less. Technology will be as much a determinant of that as are Dr. Woodall's skills. I'm along for the ride because the alternative was that I wouldn't be along at all."

"You keep coming back to your medical condition. But Dr. Woodall hasn't discussed other patients with similar terminal conditions who have been transitioned or are in line for such a procedure. Why is that?"

"You would have to ask Dr. Woodall. He hasn't discussed his plans for further terminal patient transitions. And he shouldn't. If you think about it, would you want your doctor discussing your condition with a previous patient who had a similar illness? That would be a violation of a bunch of patient privacy laws. So, I'm not surprised I have no insight into his work or plans in that regard."

"I have it on good authority AppleCore is a major contributor to Dr. Woodall's new hospital. Do you wish to comment on that?"

"Since you asked the question I'm reviewing our charitable contributions as we speak. And the answer to your question is that AppleCore has not made a charitable contribution to Dr. Woodall, his clinic, his hospital project or the University of Texas Southwest Medical Center. We have made a significant contribution to health care charities, but all of them are in California."

"Do you have any contractual relationships with any of those entities?"

"If we did, it would be considered competition sensitive. We routinely decline to comment on any of our suppliers as all of our contractual relationships are protected by non-disclosure requirements."

"With your reluctance to give me anything that would confirm or refute the reports we are getting, what story would you be chasing?"

"I would be doing stories on the patients who may be helped by this procedure. The backstory kind of thing. What the illness is, what the other treatments are, and what the prognosis is without transitioning? That may be outside your purview. But you might suggest it to your editors. I think people would be appalled by how few other options exist."

"I'll consider that." Mr. Baidu offers. "But what about a business story? Would you suggest I talk with the suppliers to Dr. Woodall? Learn about the technologies that make up your replacement body as you like to describe it?"

"I think there have been stories out about the component parts for decades." I observe. "Replacement heart valves, prosthetic limbs, bionic eyes and ears. Not sure your readers would be all that interested in stories that rehash what has already been out there. But what might be interesting is how all this technology has been integrated to make a complete replacement body."

"And that's Dr. Woodall and his team."

"They are the only one's I'm aware of doing it." I confirm.

"I already went down that road." Mr. Badu explains. "He declined to discuss it with me."

I briefly consider Dr. Woodall's response, but decide to give him something. "I think Dr. Woodall is being prudent in ensuring he has not only the procedure down, but also the systems perfected that will be the home to the consciousness of people who otherwise will perish. If I were him I wouldn't want to lose a patient because I was still learning about how the procedure and supporting systems will work long term.

You've talked about immortals. I'm probably as much as anyone responsible for that term being used. But the truth is no one knows how long this body will last. Sure, we can replace parts easily. And that may be the long-term solution that enables me to live a very long life. But I could have major system failure tomorrow. That could cause me to perish. No one knows. At the moment I hold the record for surviving transitioned patient. I hope I will continue to hold that record and keep extending it one more day each and every day. No one knows for sure and Dr. Woodall will tell you the same, because this is what he told me the day before I transitioned."

"Last question, I promise. Thank you, by the way for being so patient. I thought this was going to be a very short interview. But my last question is, when will A'zam confirm he has transitioned and is just like you?"

I decide to laugh, not to be rude but to give a plausibility to my response. "I'm afraid I can't, and no employee can comment on any other employee because of privacy laws."

When Mr. Badu finally hangs up Suzette lets out a big breath. "Shit."

THE DIAGRAM

I enter Rocky's house as usual, with the security system still not sure it's me since I don't have fingerprints and my iris isn't recognized either. The logic of the system is I have to pass two of three identifiers. All I can pass is the facial recognition. As usual Rocky has to override to let me in. Maybe that's just his way of making sure I can't surprise him.

Rocky is in his workshop as usual. The sounds of him moving around are unmistakable, even though he usually is sitting at his workbench viewing his microscope screen working on a circuit that is virtually invisible to the naked eye. "Hey," I call out.

As I come into the workshop I stop short. Anna Laura is seated at Rocky's worktable, looking at me as she so often did, only she is expressionless. I don't think I ever saw her without a smile or frown. After only a moment I remember I sent this version of her over to Rocky. Had her specially made. But she doesn't have a consciousness. That is Rocky's job. Develop a control system that will sort through the recommendations her processor makes and determine what memory should drive her behavior in response to the situation she is facing. Make decisions the way my consciousness does for me in my similar body.

"Is this what's inside you?" Rocky asks almost as if annoyed.

"Pretty close." I admit.

"I'd send me back if I was you. Not an elegant design, not even a classic design. In fact, it's down-right pedestrian. Hell. With a little time and couple of techs I probably could have done better."

"I'm sure you could have." I agree, even though I've not really taken the time to study my schematics and system design, although I probably should have by now. "Have you downloaded your memories yet?"

"This morning." Rocky shakes his head, "All those memories and it only took an hour."

"What about the master controller?" I'm not really sure what to call this unit's version, since it's not an immortal, and in fact will really just be an android robot that looks like Anna Laura.

"Working on it." Rocky hesitates as if trying to decide what to say next. "Hard problem is what you gave me. Why me and not one of your young whiz kids? The ones who make all the systems you sell?"

"I want her to be just for you and me. If I had the lab design and build it, we'd be seeing Anna Laura's everywhere we go."

"They didn't build the body?" Rocky is surprised.

"I had a subcontractor assemble the parts and do the body sculpture." I inform him. "Someone who won't necessarily see this as an opportunity to go into business against me."

"Who's that?" Rocky doesn't believe me. "Someone who's deaf, dumb and blind?"

"No, just a good friend." And I let it go at that.

"Well, if your good friend has half a brain she or he will be able to figure out the missing control system and then what? Anna Laura cleaning ladies?"

I don't answer his question, "What do you need from me to finish her?"

"Your memories of her, for starters."

"I can do that now, if it's all right with you." I look at the skull cap neural net Rocky used, but instead I pick up a cable and plug into her port behind her left ear and under her long brown hair, and then mine. Direct link should be much faster download. I sit down in the chair next to her. It's strange. My memory of her is exact and here she is. My mind tells me she isn't Anna Laura and yet my memories tell me she is. I'm trying to overcome the conflicting messages my processor is receiving. I'm surprised at how powerful the memory is when my logic tells me she's a robot. My memory tells me I should tell her things. All those things I wanted to tell her in the days after she died in the accident. The things I think of even now that I wish I could tell her. All the questions I've had in the last twenty years only a mother could answer for me. But then I realize she will get all of that as part of the upload. The question is whether she will try to answer any or all of them for me over time. Probably only if Rocky or I program her to do so. And then the answers will only be from Anna Laura as Rocky and I knew her. Who knows how different that would be from who she really was?

Rocky turns and looks at the cable between Anna Laura and me. He evidently thinks something about it but doesn't share. Instead he asks, "Think you can do two things at once?"

"Sure. What do you need?" I respond pushing the download into the background.

"Take a look at my design. For her command module. That's what I call it, but you probably have a different name. I don't know if it will even work. I know so little about the systems they've integrated here. Almost seems like someone raided a used humanoid shop and just took what was on the shelf."

"You may be right." I humor him.

"The person who built her must not have liked you very much."

"Why do you say that?"

"I basically had to disassemble her and put everything back together again. Only I did it right. Everything works now. Didn't when they delivered her."

"Don't give me that shit. You would have taken a battleship apart if one was delivered to your door, just so you could completely understand how it works. You had to do that in order to come up with a master controller design. I expected no less from you."

Rocky shakes his head, annoyed at my pushing back on him. "I had to design it in layers or levels or whatever you want to call it. Each different layer deals with a subsystem and yet shares control with the next layer to integrate. The higher up the messaging goes the greater the degree of integrated understanding."

"Is it hierarchical?" I'm not sure I'm following his description.

"Yes and no. The levels share data or information across different layers at different touch points that connect at different layers. It permits a sort of parallel processing with continuous and multi-point integration." Rocky hands me a diagram so I can see what he has described.

I study the diagram and have one fundamental question, "Why did you come up with this approach?"

"No one has been able to describe to me what consciousness is. I know your doctor Woodall has that figured out. But he seems to be about the only one. So, I did some reading. Everyone from biologists, bio-ethicists, theologians, paranormal psychologists and even the Hare Krishna. No one seems to understand. But the one thing I picked up is that it isn't a simple and straightforward kind of thing. It has to be elegant, unusual, but highly functional. Able to massively parallel process and yet have a design that enables rapid and direct communications between data nodes. I slept on it for a couple of days and discarded everything I came up with as infeasible."

He wants me to ask the obvious question, but I decide not to, knowing he will tell me in time as he is just too proud of the design not to tell me. "Looks like as good an approach as any other."

"What? Are you blind? It's elegant, it's simple it's functional in a way few would have ever considered."

"I'd agree." I respond without looking at him.

"This is a bigger breakthrough than the angstrom length circuit I won the fucking award for." Rocky is getting worked up now.

"Are you going to submit it for an award?" I inquire as if only mildly interested.

"You'd never let me." Rocky puts it right back on me. "It's the secret sauce that makes her into what she is. The closest thing to Anna Laura that isn't Anna Laura."

"Good. I'm glad that's settled." I respond and then glance up at him. He's fuming. I reach out and touch his arm. "You're misreading me. It's not that I don't want you to get recognition for what you've come up with. I just don't want still another group of near humans running around confusing the situation more than all of us are going to."

"You think people would want their own Anna Laura?" Rocky responds, surprised.

"Not an Anna Laura, but an android of their mother or father or dead wife or husband. Maybe even a child that has died. I don't know. But the fact we are creating her tells me there are others out there like us who may well want to do the same thing if they saw Anna Laura and realized what she is."

"What is she?" Rocky asks, apparently unsure how I see her.

"Comfort." I respond.

Rocky thinks about my response for a long moment. Shakes his head. "She's not going to be comfort for you or me. She's going to be a reminder we don't know everything. That there should be a different perspective in the room and we need to consider it. She's going to question us. Make us give things a second thought. She's going to be the pain in the ass Anna Laura was to both of us. Only we needed that pain in the ass then. I'm not sure we do now."

"I need her," I respond simply.

Rocky hangs his head. "I'm sorry you had to grow up without her."

"It wasn't your fault." I squeeze his arm. "If it had been you then I would have grown up without you. In that case I wouldn't be me. I'd have been a teacher or salesperson. Hospital administrator, maybe. Not what I am today. And that's not to say that Anna Laura wouldn't have pushed me the way you did. But I never would have gotten the breaks at AppleCore because I never would have gotten that first internship without you there."

Rocky looks at my hand on his arm. I can't remember the last time I touched him, gave him a hug or showed any physical affection for him. He comes and stands behind my chair and puts his hand on my shoulder. Just the way he did when Anna Laura would give him a hug and he'd pull me into the four-way hug with Tabitha. "Why did you do this to me?"

"What?" I ask although I suspect I know the question he is really asking.

"Bring Anna Laura back into our lives."

"She's always been here. I feel her spirit, see her ghost, and hear her laughter every time I come into this house. I suspect you still do, even before our friend arrived."

Rocky doesn't respond, in effect telling me I'm right. I would get up and give him that hug, but I'd have to disconnect the cable and I haven't transferred everything yet. So, I continue sitting and just hold onto Rocky's arm.

"Could you do a Tabitha?" Rocky finally asks. I hear his loneliness.

I nod.

"How would she look today?" Rocky wonders aloud.

"There's software that can age a face, I'm sure I could locate and download it if that's what you think you really want. Why wouldn't you want to pick up the next day? The day after they died?"

"Because then you wouldn't fit. Neither would I." Rocky explains. "If Tabitha was the age she would be today you and she would always have each other because you would both stop aging at the same point in time."

I'd not thought about Anna Laura always being mid-thirties in this android version, but Tabitha and I will always look twentyish. And Rocky? He still doesn't plan to be here. "You know when they deliver Tabitha and we get her up and running, you'll have the family back. Are you sure you won't transition so we can be together always?"

Rocky looks at Anna Laura. Moves a lock of her hair the way he always did. Trying to make her look perfect. As she always did. "They'll come live with you. Your place is much nicer than mine."

"It has nothing to do with place, Rocky. It's all about where they're needed. I need Anna Laura as a mother. But she was your wife. A husband and wife are supposed to be together. The kids are supposed to grow up and go off on their own. You need that time with her you never had."

"I knew it." Rocky moves away from me, breaking contact. "You did this just to make sure I don't get remarried."

"Get remarried." I try to make it sound like it's no big deal, although to me it is. "You want a flesh and blood wife? That's your business. But this is a full-service android. Can fulfill your needs and your fantasies while being the sounding board I need for what I have to do."

"Why are you messing with my life now? I've been on my own for twenty years. You don't pay any attention to me all those years. And now that I've got a chance to start over, you suddenly reappear with an Anna Laura doll to keep me distracted."

Why is he so resistant to having his family when he's the one who asked for Tabitha? "All right. Hand me the drawings of the master controller. I'll take it from here. I don't need you to get distracted from your new life. From your new wife. You don't need the satisfaction that you took your concept and made it real. You've already downloaded your memories of Anna Laura, so I guess I don't need you anymore either."

Rocky looks at me puzzling what my end game must be. After a minute he picks up the drawing and hands it to me. He continues to look at me.

"Can't leave just yet." I inform him. "Have to complete the download first."

Rocky nods in understanding, but still he doesn't move. I'm not sure if he's looking at me or Anna Laura. He's thinking something, but he's not sharing.

"It won't be long now. Maybe five minutes." I inform him.

I sit there waiting for the download to complete. Rocky doesn't move, just continues to stare at me and Anna Laura. I glance over at her, wondering if she can walk on her own or how I'm supposed to get her out of here. The download completes. I remove the cable and stand. "Do you have a remote?"

Rocky takes the diagram from my hand, and just stares at me.

WHITE RABBIT

"Do you remember that little project you gave me?" Oriana asks as we walk down the hallway towards the new lab I asked her to set up with Jermaine taking over the team selection and integration tasks.

"I haven't given you any little projects." I correct her.

"All right. You didn't give it to me, I gave it to myself after we had that discussion about not being able to find enough customers for all the products we can devise now."

"Now that I remember," I confirm for her.

"I knew what you were doing." Oriana clarifies for me. "You were framing the strategic situation and wanted to see how I would go about addressing it without specific guidance from you."

"If you say so." I don't look at her afraid she would see the faint smile I can't hide.

"Well you basically said we were going down a rat hole. If we don't do something differently we will induce feature fatigue in our customers. They'd stop buying. And it would be my fault because I'm not delivering what the customers wants."

"And that is?"

"Don't laugh," Oriana can't believe what she's about to tell me. "Unconscious awareness."

She's watching me closely trying to gauge my reaction. I look at her as I consider her concept. "How would you achieve it?" I ask as neutrally as possible, so I don't signal either approval or disapproval until she's had a chance to tell me more.

"I thought about how we developed all those systems to track what a shopper looks at when they go into a store. If they look at something longer than other things we note it and present information about it and then information about similar items."

"I remember," I want to encourage a full explanation.

"And I thought about the capability you have to process all that kind of information in your head. Then it just hit me. What if… what if we put the two things together? Moved the ability to track things into your head? But track your thoughts. So, when you pause on something that your mind is screening we have a background processor go deeper into that subject. Let it present concepts, ideas, facts, what have you for your consideration. All without you having to consciously think about it until it's presented to you."

I walk along for a moment as my mind pulls up all the literature I can find on alternative approaches. None are particularly promising, although with enough time and money some could eventually produce an approach that in my judgment might work. "How do you make it an internal system without surgery? In my mind that's a bridge too far at the moment."

Oriana finally stops me to have a conversation now. "I agree. Surgery isn't an acceptable means at the moment because we haven't figured out how to heal faster. I've had the whole team working independent approaches and then we had an exploration day."

"What do you mean? Exploration day."

"I told the team that they should bring their ideas to an all-day session. We talked through each and every approach, non-judgmentally. No comments about this is stupid or that will never work. Everyone, and I mean everyone was told to find the limitations to the approach and propose solutions. That was it. We explored each and every concept. Everyone had a chance to ask clarifying questions and point out limitations. But they were instructed once they pointed out a limitation, they had to propose a workable solution. None of this we could… bullshit. Always, if we did such and such the probable result would be such and such and we could address any shortfalls by doing x."

"Sounds like a good approach." I want her to know I approve but I'm still waiting to hear the result.

"We had some just amazing discussions. I mean I couldn't believe some of the concepts they came up with. Approaches I'd have never considered until they were put into context and explained and then everyone built upon each one, so we could see what we were looking at and what we might do with it."

"You're going to make me ask, aren't you?" I finally have to break down and put the question out there without asking directly.

"No, I was just going to show you what we decided to try first."

"You didn't make the decision?"

"Consensus." Oriana clarifies. "There were three strong contenders. We talked them through in terms of who could see a viable approach to quick implementation. We went with the one everyone agreed had the highest probability of being feasible and achieving the desired performance."

I decide not to ask any further questions about what I'm going to see until I get there, so instead I ask, "How's the adjustment?"

"Adjustment?" Oriana isn't following my change of direction.

"To being immortal."

"Oh. That." Oriana takes a moment to decide how to answer me. I know she can't say anything negative because it would cause me to probe further, and she can't say it's wonderful because I just went down that path and know it's not. Hard question, I know.

"I'm just looking for ways to make it easier for you if I can." I relieve her discomfort.

"You know how it is." She finally settles on. "Good days and bad days, just like being a mortal. Only when they're good, they're really good. Like I can't believe what I just did. And when they're bad, it's like oh shit. What do I do now?"

"Just like before, only the highs and the lows are exaggerated."

"That's a good way of putting it." She glances at me. "Is that what you said to A'zam?"

"No. He was never interested in knowing how I was doing," I put the situation into context.

"Here we are." Oriana leads me into the lab where I come face to face with A'zam.

"Understand this is the best show in town." He greets us. "Today, anyway."

"Most days," I correct him. A'zam glances at me with a look of curiosity as if he is wondering how much I influenced what we are about to see. I won't give him any indication and won't even through the questioning that will follow.

Oriana leads me to the screen where we will see the demonstration. A'zam falls in behind us. I wonder if he's looking at my ass. Suddenly I'm self-conscious about it. But I know there's nothing I can do. It's about the perfect size and shape anyway, so why am I worried about it?

A'zam comes up to stand next to me when we get to the display area.

Oriana goes to the front. "This idea is a product of the entire team vetting and working with an original concept Shondra pitched to us. Since she is the originator I've asked her to explain it and show you the visualization."

Shondra is surprisingly short. Not even five feet. All I can think of is we should have been able to transition two her size for the same cost as A'zam who is about six foot six.

"The problem is how we embed a platform in the brain of a living being?" she turns to point to a visualization of a human brain on the screen behind her. "The objective was to deliver a platform inside that can engage the neural cortex and the visual preceptors at the same time. We want the customer to not only be able to process the information and store metadata tags in the neural cortex, so retrieval will be accelerated, but also to be able to visualize what is being presented for consideration."

"So you have to embed your platform elements in two different locations of the brain and at the same time link them such that data can transmit at high rates of speed between them," I summarize. A'zam glances at me, but I continue anyway. "And it all has to be upgradable as more speed and more bandwidth is required." I complete the thought.

"We're not quite there yet." Shondra clarifies. "But we have an approach to the upgrades and we are running experiments as we speak to determine whether they will work."

A'zam nods in agreement with the approach.

Shondra continues, "We spent a lot of time with nanotechnology types. Spent even more time on nanobots that can work at the molecular level as assemblers inside the body."

"Sounds like atomic scale to achieve molecular sized systems that when connected leverage sufficient scale to produce the platform capability while working off piezoelectric power levels."

Shondra shakes her head, "Actually piezoelectric isn't feasible in these circumstances. We have found a method that lets us tap into the electrical impulses between nerve cells without impeding the information transfer within the nervous system. It's amazing how little power it actually takes to run this platform."

"Are you using the native capacity of the brain to do most of the processing such that the platform simply speeds up the rate of processing and directs it in a more efficient manner?"

"Again, you're very close, but there are some differences we've adopted. Rather than spend a lot of time trying to answer your many questions, why don't we show you what we've been able to do and then we can answer all your questions."

A'zam nods, clearly tiring of not being the focal point of the discussion.

The image comes up of thousands or millions of tiny particles entering the blood stream. They move to cluster into two groups and separate. Somewhat larger particles can be seen in each cluster.

"Are those the nanobots?" I ask pointing to them.

"The larger particles?" Shondra asks in response. "Yes."

I nod with the confirmation.

The two groups of particles move off in different directions in the blood stream. The image pulls back, and we can now see them both in two different veins moving to their intended spots. "We were able to magnetically repel those that were not part of the subassembly, so they would separate. You can see the visual system taking this path and the neocortex system taking this one. We want to implant close together, so the link doesn't need much power to communicate. It has to be two way so that makes it even more difficult."

We watch as the groups arrive at their destinations. "How do they know when they are where they need to be?" I ask although I see A'zam was probably thinking the same question.

"The customer is wearing a hat with markers that transmit a location to the bots in each group. They home in on it and herd their particle systems in that direction. When they get at the designated site, they move out to the end of a vein and establish that as their new home."

"Didn't realize the molecular assemblers were that sophisticated," A'zam has to get a comment in here.

"They're even more sophisticated than we needed for this particular task. But we leave them in place when we're done in case we have to go in and do a repair later."

"Or upgrade." I suggest.

Oriana answers now, "We discussed that as an option, but we haven't settled on an approach as yet."

We watch as the molecular assemblers, also known as nanobots, begin to arrange the particles into subassemblies and connect them together. A fascinating process that has been sped up for us as we would not have wanted to stay here all day waiting for this to complete. A couple of times Oriana points out how a subassembly is complete and the nanobots are moving on to assemble the next subassembly.

Soon the final components are brought together on the visualization assembly which is now complete. We have to wait for the neocortex system to come together as it is a bigger and more complex system than the visualization module.

"Fascinating." I declare as both systems appear before us. "What happens now?"

"This image shows us the increases in data and information processing the customer is now experiencing. You can see we are bringing her up slowly, although this demo film is sped up so you don't have to wait while they adjust."

"Did you learn the lessons from your own transition about how to handle the disorientation that results?" I ask.

"Jermaine did that work for us as he was doing something similar for the immortals transitioning."

"And it seems to be working?" A'zam again.

"Yes," Oriana defends her best friend, even though she won't admit it.

"How wide a trial have you put this through?" I ask.

"The usual for a platform, random sample of one-thousand, globally."

"Insertion mechanism?" I ask knowing that if there had been any issues in the trials they would not have brought it forward to us.

Shondra holds up a blue pill. "One pill makes you stronger."

"And you call this the White Rabbit?" I guess.

"It was either that or Alice." Shondra responds confirming my guess. "But we didn't think as many would understand Alice."

"Why didn't you make the pill white then?" A'zam asks apparently trying to catch up to the discussion about Alice in Wonderland and the song by Jefferson Airplane.

"We wanted to reference the movie the Matrix as well." Oriana answers. "That was the discussion. Which should it be? Most thought the name of the submarine would be too obscure from the Matrix, so we took elements from each."

"What did Landon Bannerjee have to say about this marketing

conundrum?" I ask, realizing how hard it's going to be to get people to swallow this tale, let alone a pill that embeds a data platform in their brain at two preselected locations. And worse yet they have to take the pill at the store where they buy it, so they can use the hat that helps steer the bots to the right locations.

"He was actually number one-thousand and one." Shondra responds. "We finally came to the conclusion he would have to experience it in order to be able to market it. And once he came on line it wasn't all that hard to explain the whole concept to him."

"You haven't answered my question." I point out.

Oriana changes the image on the screen to our advertisement. Multiple images of users and Alice in Wonderland, the white rabbit and the Matrix, ending with "Enter a Whole New World."

"When does this go on sale?" A'zam asks.

"You can place your order now and schedule your installation appointment." Oriana beams.

FOR WHO?

"Beth Allison from Symbol Ventures is on the phone," Mindi calls to me as I sit at my desk going through sales figures. The White Rabbit from AppleCore has set global records for first day adoption. We are asking for a deposit with the order and the cash is just rolling in. Those first day deposits alone will more than pay for the entire development costs and initial production run.

I answer the call still reviewing the numbers, trying to understand why some markets are seeing much greater penetration than others. "Beth?"

"Where did the White Rabbit come from?" Not the question I expected.

"A twenty-six-year-old systems engineer's mind." I answer as cryptically and intriguingly as I can.

"Not from yours?"

"I don't have time to do design work anymore." I answer truthfully.

"Can we lure her away then?"

"No." I answer firmly. "She has a bright future here, and I'm not about to give you her name."

"Not a problem." Beth sounds non-chalant. "My spies will eventually find out and then she'll be designing for us."

While I know she's serious, she's just reminding me we are in a war for talent. Whoever has it wins that particular round. Only I've been winning consistently now for a while. The White Rabbit has just established a new distance between our two organizations. That, of course, will only make her more desperate to lure talent from us, making her stronger and me weaker at the same time. It's the only way to close the distance quickly. "How are you?"

"I was gaining ground on you until this," she sounds exasperated.

"I know." I respond softly knowing she will accept that better than any other response I could give.

"I don't understand how you got here. It's just such a radical departure from anything we've had in the developmental pipeline. There's absolutely nothing in the conference proceedings or technical symposiums or papers that would suggest this path."

"It came from a twenty-six-year-old, Beth. Someone not encumbered with all those technical papers and conferences suggesting the Holy Grail can only be found where Christ lived."

"Why did you use that simile?" Beth challenges me.

"Sometimes true believers are your worst enemy." I respond, not quite sure why, but something my subconscious has been toying with brought it to my mind.

"Don't I know that," Beth exclaims, which surprises me.

"What's the issue?"

"I don't have the ability to get past the guardians of our culture and way of life."

I hear what she's saying, "I respectfully disagree. You have the ability. You apparently don't have the organizational interest or the support from Fisher."

"Interest is not the problem." Beth assures me, leaving me to conclude her CEO, Fisher, isn't willing to pay the price to break the logjam of tradition to embrace a less known world of innovation.

"Looking at the numbers I'm seeing, you don't have much time." I point out as gently as I can.

"I'm sure I'm looking at the same numbers." Beth sounds depressed. "How do I recover from this? Your proprietary platform is going to be in nearly every being on earth in a month at the rate you're taking orders."

"Only you can answer that." I respond and wait a moment for her to realize the truth to my statement. "I don't know what's in your pipeline or how close you are to your next big platform release. That's probably what it will take to even the playing field."

Beth can't tell me her situation and I'd not expect her to. I'm just trying to get her to concentrate on the right things, so she can right her sinking ship.

"Is this why you held up submitting your indicative offer to buy us?" Beth accuses me. "Waiting for us to crash and burn so you can pick us up for pennies on the dollar?"

"No." I'm trying to be honest. A'zam wanted me to wait, but he wasn't the reason it took so long. "I couldn't get the board to agree to a price based on an incomplete integration plan."

"I don't understand. You couldn't figure out how you would integrate us into your product lines?" Beth seems incredulous.

"As you can see, we're shifting our focus into a whole different approach to the market. I haven't been able to put together an accretive plan for integrating your technologies into our new market direction."

"Except at a low-ball price for our assets." Beth come right back, angry with what I'm saying.

"Hold on Beth. Put yourself in my place. You come up with a

market shifting innovation. While you're going through your testing and market validation you're looking at AppleCore and trying to figure out how you integrate us into a totally different offering. You have to ask yourself, what will our customers and their customers do? Especially when the two customer sets are nearly identical but invested in different operating systems. Some of my customers migrate to your new platform. You have to ask yourself, is it not better to let AppleCore continue with their obsolete platform and any marginal improvements they can make than try to buy them, migrate their customers to the new Symbol Ventures platform and figure out how to derive value from a massive organization that no longer has a market or products the customer demands?"

"Then why did you approach us?" Beth demands to know what she thinks is a hole in my logic.

"From a traditional market view our two companies together have to be stronger than either alone."

"I would still agree with that."

"I may, but I won't know until I see what kind of legs White Rabbit has. If we're a one day wonder and everyone goes back to sleep tomorrow, then I'll be working that valuation validation and go to our board again. But if it does have legs, then it's a matter of if I can still see synergies that are accretive to our stock value."

"But you haven't answered my question." Beth is getting annoyed with me. I don't want her to. She's a good friend and I want to be open with her as much as I can. But in my current role that gets to be real hard.

"Why did we approach you when we knew we had White Rabbit in the works?"

"It doesn't make sense." Beth responds and she's right.

"Because at that point White Rabbit was far from a baked product we could put any reliance on. There were technical challenges that could have easily made the whole thing impractical. In fact, for a long time that appeared to be the probable outcome. We were just very fortunate."

"That's bullshit, and you know it. Companies make their luck in this industry. You took an approach where you had a collection of expertise that could make it work. You don't waste people's time and money on something that you don't think has a reasonable chance of success. You brought in the expertise you needed and built an innovation team. We don't have anything that can match what you've done. And frankly I don't even know where to begin. So it all comes back to you and the advantage you represent for AppleCore. We can't catch up as long as you put your company one step ahead of us all the way."

"I disagree, as I've told you before. I don't represent anything. Sure, I'm different now. But I have as many new limitations as I have new capabilities. This new direction came from Oriana and her teams. If I'd stayed in the other role would we have come up with this approach? I don't know. It would have depended on whether I was open to listening to a twenty-six-year-old rather than those who have always delivered results for me in the past. My move out of development is probably more of a determinant of this than anything." I'm trying to reassure her, but I'm also hearing echoes of the ACLU suit and wonder if Symbol Ventures is one of the intervenors. Are they looking for something to use against me? Get me out of AppleCore so they can recover position? Maybe I'm getting paranoid because I'm not responding emotionally, but only logically. And I've tended to look at everything through the lens of friendship in the past. Now I'm no longer sure what friendship even means because it's no longer an emotional bond for me, but a memory that I like someone and want to be their friend.

"Either way you're responsible for White Rabbit." Beth continues to go back to the same theme. "If you'd stayed as SVP…"

"If I'd stayed as SVP I'd probably be dead now." I try to reframe the attack. "Oriana would have moved up and White Rabbit would have resulted from her move into the software leadership role. That's what I'm trying to tell you. I may have enabled it by my tenure as SVP. Just as you've enabled almost all of Symbol Ventures' successes since you've been there. But White Rabbit would have come out of our labs in any event."

"Tell me this. Did your engineers reverse engineer you?"

I have to laugh, "You mean take me apart to see how I'm built and then make our own design?" I can't believe she asked such a question. "No. But now that you've suggested it maybe we should."

"You're saying you really aren't responsible for the change in architectural direction for your main product line and you're the CEO?"

I'm hearing testimony at the ACLU trial or an unfair trade practices suit from Symbol against AppleCore, so I need to be very clear. "As CEO did I approve moving forward with funding the development of this project? Yes. Did I support the marketing of a whole new product platform? Yes. Did I design it? No. Was I involved in reviews of the design? No. Did I have details of it until we were ready to move forward with production? Only at a very high level. So, did I influence it applying anything that is the result of my transition? Only indirectly."

"I guess we will have to wait to see if it's as ground breaking as it seems to be." Beth reflects. "I just get these vibes that it's going to be like the iPod moment all those years ago, where a failing company makes a complete turn and grows to be the largest market cap company in the country and one of the largest in the world."

"Obviously from where I'm sitting I hope you're right, but I don't feel that vibe." I respond hoping to put her more at ease since she seems to be getting more and more worked up. "I'm hoping it just has legs for a few weeks. Beyond that we'll see."

Beth knows this conversation is over. She is quiet for a long time and then changes the subject. "What's going on with your ACLU lawsuit?"

Mentally I shoot a note to Dietrich asking the same question so hopefully I'll have more current information before this conversation is over. "Haven't been all that close to it. Dietrich Zellers is handling it for us. We're really only tangentially involved because the suit is against the doctor who is performing the procedures. We only got pulled in because I work at AppleCore."

"You see, that's where you lose me." Beth is still not happy with me. "Why are you involved at all? If the suit is against the doctor why is AppleCore a party?"

"Because we don't want me to have to transition back, which by the way is impossible since my body was cremated."

"That should be you personally, not the company." Beth pushes.

"We are interested because we are watching what happens, just as I'm sure you are. If there is going to be a large number of terminally ill transitioning, will that create a new market for our technology? Obviously White Rabbit wouldn't be applicable, but the delivery of content to an immortal is different than for everyone else. We're looking at how we might have to change our platform approaches to serve a new niche if one develops. And that's really what the whole trial is all about, in my opinion. Will a niche market happen, or will we ban transitions?"

"But you just said you've not reverse engineered yourself." Beth is still looking to poke holes through my arguments.

"We haven't, but we generally understand the approach Dr. Woodall's team took. How serving content to me is different than to you. When you get down to the technical level do we have an approach worked out? No. But if the trial comes out as I personally hope, then we will go take a closer look at how we would serve a growing number of us."

Dietrich's response comes in. I quickly scan it. "Since you asked about the trial, I sent a note to Dietrich who just responded. Says the judge is dealing with a number of potential intervenors who missed the deadline and have now requested to be granted late admission to submit testimony."

"How many have been included?"

"Over a hundred." I remember. "But the judge was concerned that once the testimony starts if she hadn't shut it down there would be new people wanting fifteen minutes of fame by testifying even if they really don't have anything of relevance to say."

"That's right, we are talking California, aren't we?" Beth seems to relax a bit now. Not sure if she got what she was looking for or if she's trying to convince me Symbol Ventures isn't involved in the case.

"So, is Symbol one of the intervenors?" I put it right out there.

"No," comes almost too quickly as if she was expecting this question.

"What I'm hearing is a bunch of folks don't want to be listed but have been working with one of the Non-government organizations that have signed up. Feeding them questions to ask, and information to use in cross examination. I'm sure Symbol Ventures wouldn't do that. Just like AppleCore wouldn't work behind the scenes to influence outcomes."

"Jane Williams of the ACLU has been meeting with our outside counsel. I don't have any of the details since Fisher is working it directly, but we're there, just as you knew we would be."

"Is any of what I've just told you going to end up in Jane Williams' list of questions?"

"As I said, Fisher is working that directly, so I'm not involved." Beth hesitates but plunges on. "What you're really asking is has this whole conversation been to take advantage of our friendship, so we can derail you in court? What would you do? You asked earlier for me to consider the shoe on the other foot. What would you do?"

"This is an interesting question because without emotions I should be completely dispassionate about taking advantage of our friendship. But that's the odd part of it. Because friendship is a memory for me that I use to guide my current behavior, I'm probably less willing to deviate from what friendship meant to me before than you would be. So, the flat answer is no. If the shoe were on the other foot, I would not use anything from this conversation in court without having told you that was my objective up front, so you could judge what to tell me and what not to tell me."

I wait, but Beth doesn't say anything, apparently not having expected this answer.

"I'm really no different than the person you knew in high school chemistry." I finally continue. "I depended on you in that class, so we could both get a grade and move on to graduation. I depend on you now to help enforce the norms of our industry, so it will be a humane experience for us, our companies and our customers. And I really do want you as part of the AppleCore team, but only if it makes sense."

"For who?" Beth comes back immediately.

RECONCILING

The note from A'zam to get my upgrade comes out of the blue. I'm not even sure what upgrade he is referring to since I'd just seen Dr. Woodall. "Jermaine. You have an upgrade for me?"

"A'zam said he'd ask you to come in when I upgraded him." Jermaine confirms.

"So, this is the Orgasmatron?" I'm reminded.

Jermaine laughs, "I still can't get over you calling it that. But, yes."

"Who did the work? I'm not sure I'm ready for whatever you might have in store for me."

Jermaine laughs again, "Who's the sexiest person you know?"

"Delilah." I answer without even thinking. "If she gave you the input parameters I'd be good."

"And Oriana worked with the coders directly. Not sure that was a good thing or not since I've never slept with her, but I tested my version out on my old lady. She was more than satisfied."

You said she was more than satisfied when you came back from your transition with no upgrades and I know how crude that was."

"I wasn't going to go there." Jermaine laughs although somewhat hollowly.

"How long?"

"I can do it over the air. It's all software."

"Push it to me then. A'zam is waiting."

The Googlecar drops me at A'zam's apartment. I see reporters down the street. Evidently, he got a restraining order to keep them far enough away so as not to impede his access to his own apartment. But now I'm sure there will be mention of me coming to see him here. And those who imagine the worst will unfortunately be correct.

He greets me at the door with nothing on and a full erection. I reach out and squeeze his full member until it starts to shrink. A'zam looks down and laughs. "You trying to tell me not to get my expectations up?"

I enter his apartment and A'zam immediately begins to remove my clothes. Since he has nothing on there is nothing for me to do except wait for him to remove mine. Guess this will be a record short foreplay. When he has me down to my shoes, I kick them off and he picks me up and carries me to his bedroom, lays me across the bed and then lays on top of me, tongue in my mouth before I can even say a word.

I kick up my processor speed because he clearly has. Now the explorations of my body with his hands seem more like what I've been used to. I feel the over the air updates occurring at the same time A'zam is trying to get me turned on. It's working because I can feel myself getting moist. My nipples are standing out and A'zam is kissing them, licking them, pinching them to get an even taughter experience.

Another level of secretion. Now I'm probably wet enough he could come in and I'd not be too dry for him or me, for that matter. He's working the tongue in my mouth, and then he's kissing me in all the turn on spots. Only I have no idea if whoever programmed these changes knew what the turn on spots are. Are they causing me to react? I think so. Is it more than last time? I'm feeling what I'd have previously called interested. Not where I'd normally be at this stage of foreplay, but it's clearly further along than I remember last time at the climax.

Definitely an improvement.

A'zam has his finger up me and is simulating copulation. Slow. Not the rush I remember him being in the last time. He's more interested in getting me interested in what he intends to do next, which is refreshing. I'm not used to A'zam caring at all what my side of the experience is like. That was clear during the two tours of the Kama Sutra.

Now he's inside with his very firm member. Only it's not the same size as before. I remember Windy talking about him filling her up. He has done that for me this time. Even though he did not before. Jermaine said something about expanding the size when inside. I wonder how he did that, but I'll have to wait to ask him. Don't want to be sending out emails in the middle of the experience. Not something A'zam would want to learn after the fact. And I never know what he's going to learn, after the fact.

I feel the build. Quicker than before. Something about this level of friction. He's getting to me quicker and I'm responding even without thinking about it. I feel the tension in my midsection, tightening of my buttocks. And then I feel the first wave of contractions rising within and exploding across me. Continuing. Increasing in their intensity and speed. Is it because of how perfectly he fits me now? Is that what's made this release so much better than before? I don't know but it overtakes me, and I just let it go.

I feel A'zam's release. Intense. Explosive as much as mine. It almost seems like he's staggered by the intensity of the release. And it continues on. Much longer than before. He's actually contracting longer than I am, and this is the longest contraction I can remember, although I've not kept track of exact lengths of time.

And then he lies across me, still inside. Still moving slowly. I don't know if he's planning on withdrawing or if he's waiting to catch his breath for a second go at it. I can feel he's not as hard as before, but he's also not come out. He's waiting to see if he can come back for dessert.

I wonder if Petra has been this good for him, since she was at an earlier release version. She apparently didn't get the same updates I did, so no matter how good it was for her, it was better for me this time around.

A'zam rises up, looks down at me. His expression is one of contentment. Not an expression I think I've ever seen before. And now he's filling me up again. I feel the friction and involuntarily I feel the rising tension within me. I'm responding to him. Even though I'm not thinking about being turned on or particularly interested in wanting a reprise. My body responds to him even though I'm not willing it to. Is that what the new software design was intended to do? Make me more human like in that someone inside me can overcome my conscious thoughts about it?

I feel the rising tension. Higher. Higher. My buttocks push me up into his thrusts even without me directing them to. And the thrusts become stronger. More directed to my release trigger and then I can feel it take me to the peak. I stay there for I don't know how long. It's an experience I don't' think I can remember ever having before. Not this long. Not this high. And then it all comes crashing down as the orgasm overtakes me, contraction after contraction. On and on.

A'zam starts to slow. Evidently his orgasm is over, although mine continues in dribs and drabs. He pulls out even though I could continue if he stayed inside and kept moving. But this is A'zam. I couldn't expect him to even think about something other than his own orgasm. If this is what Windy experienced, then I understand why she's enthralled.

Is this the best orgasm I've ever had? I don't know how to compare them since they're so far removed from each other. But this is clearly the best I've had in a long, long time. Damn. Oriana is making it tough for me to hate A'zam when he can bring this out in me. And this is the second orgasm.

A'zam lays down next to me. He clearly wants me to lie across his chest as they always do in the Hollywood movies, but I'm not about to give him that satisfaction. I roll over and lay next to him, pressed up against him, but not on top of him. We're equals in this experience. He's not in control, even though he seems to think he should be. Not going to give him that satisfaction.

"Better than last time?" he finally asks.

"Yes. You?"

"Explosive, just like I asked for. How does he make it any better?" A'zam is wondering aloud.

"Maybe you should give Jermaine feedback that this is enough until he can come up with an entirely different paradigm."

"What do you mean?"

"You may have had the ultimate orgasm."

"I doubt that, but it's clearly better than anything I've experienced before."

That tells me what I wanted to know about his engagement with Petra. "Then be satisfied. Don't push the boundaries now. Let your expectations catch up to the reality of the experience. When you can give him direction on how it might be better for you, then it will make sense. But just to push the boundaries when you have no direction to give him will probably cause you to have an experience you'll regret the next time because it will be different in a way you don't appreciate."

A'zam doesn't respond. I'm surprised. He always has a response to everything I suggest. He turns on his side and starts to circle my nipples with his finger, pinching them, leaning over me and kissing my nipples. He's seeing if he can keep me turned on even though we've already done it twice. I feel the nipples responding to him and standing out, firm. That's apparently what he wants. Is he planning a third assault on me? I wonder if he could take me even higher. But he seems amused at keeping my nipple taught.

"What are you thinking?" I finally ask, wondering what's next.

"Why I never appreciated you more."

"It's Jermaine's software, not me." I bail on him.

"I don't agree. I've been sleeping with… I don't even know how many different women. You were the best the last time and you're even better this time. What is it about you that touches this place in me no one else gets to?"

"I have no idea." I answer as best I can, surprised he would make this proclamation. What's his end game? He has to have one. He never shows a moment of weakness. This could be construed as being one.

"Do you remember when I told you I was going to promote you to CEO?"

I nod, but don't answer.

"When I did that I thought you had me in a corner. That I had to offer you an opportunity to be a partner because you could go off and partner with someone else and I'd be out in the cold. I felt I had to make that offer or I'd lose everything I'd worked for. I was actually surprised you agreed."

This is all news to me.

"Maybe because Julia had convinced me you were done I'd dismissed you. Thought you'd never be able to be a player in our future. Clearly, I was wrong. You're not only a player, you're the driver of the whole immortals… I'm not even sure what to call it. Subculture?"

"I'm not." I respond to him. "I'm one of many, but I'm not the driver. Look at what you're doing. I'm trying the best I can to keep the company focused on the transition it has to make to own the future, but you're creating it with the work you're doing to own the inputs to immortality."

What the fuck am I doing? Why am I sucking up to this bastard whom I hate?

A'zam leans over and kisses me, long, languorous. "That's what I mean. You see things more clearly than anyone. You're putting us where we need to be to own the future. And that's what it will take to be the leaders, to create the future civilization that will emerge from the ashes of what was once a dysfunctional attempt to organize human existence on this planet."

"You've been spending too much time with Elon Musk's avatar." I proclaim.

"He's still there, somewhere behind the scenes." A'zam informs me. "He just doesn't want people to see him as an old man. Even though he is. You know he's a perfect candidate for a transition. Would you contact him and offer him one of our slots if he would serve as an advisor to us?"

"If I can get through his people." I note. "They're fanatics."

"True believers is the term I think you've used in the past."

Holy shit, he listened in on the whole conversation with Beth. Why am I not surprised? Damn. I have to understand he's monitoring everything I say or do. What is he so afraid of? Hell. He just told me. He thinks I'm the driver of the immortals subculture, whatever that is. But clearly, he has defined it in some fashion. So where do I fit into the whole hierarchy of influencers in his ecosystem of key contributors to the evolving society, dominated by immortals, under his influence? Clearly, he thinks he can influence me by the orgasms he induces in me. I need to look forward to more of these intimate experiences.

I decide to push back. What do I have to lose since he said I'd just given him the best orgasm of his life? "Why are you listening in on my conversations? I take it you don't trust we have the same interests."

A'zam pushes down a little harder as he circles my nipples. Then he sucks on them to pull them up to their maximum stiffness. "You represent a particular vulnerability for me."

"How is that possible?" I respond, taking his member in my hand and softly squeezing it to get it hard again.

"You're the only one to have transitioned before me. That gives you legitimacy I can never claim. You were also dying. A particular heartstring you can pull any time, I can't. You have established a rapport with our development teams I've never even attempted to foster. You could easily do what I struggle to do, and you seem to be quite unaware of your unique position."

I start massaging his member as it stiffens. Run my other hand down his thigh to activate the sensors that inhabit that area of his body. Knowing they will stimulate his thoughts towards another orgasm. "I'm not unaware, A'zam. I'm just not interested."

A'zam lays back and lets me stimulate his interest with my long slow stokes and squeezing of the head. I feel him responding. Increase the pressure, but only slightly. Increase the tempo. But only slightly. I feel the response in his body. I wonder if it is as involuntary as mine was. He has no interest in sharing this experience. Probably waits for me to take his firm member in my mouth, but I have no interest in that. This will be a mechanical release, not one I aid by my organs.

He rises as his buttocks tighten. Higher. Higher. I see him raise his chin towards the ceiling as the explosive first release overtakes his body. He holds it as long as he can, but then I see the contractions overcome him. He gives in to them and rides the crest of the wave. As long as they will let him. And then I see him begin the process of relaxing. Letting go of the force that has overcome him. Relieved him of his own senses and control. Letting him ride the wave of sensation his mind has released as a result of the orgasm.

When A'zam finally relaxes, he looks at me. "Why has it taken so long for me to appreciate you?"

"Maybe because I was focused on making you successful." What the fuck am I saying this for?

"And you." He reminds me.

"If you're successful, I'm successful. Learned that lesson a long time ago." I continue to stroke him even though he's gone limp. Not sure how long it will take him to come back, but I'm sure he will. I want him distracted as we continue this discussion.

"How do we reconcile our different visions for the future?" he asks unexpectedly.

"Do we need to?" I squeeze a little harder to get him stiff.

"Most decidedly." A'zam tenses in response.

READY

Windy is the next of my posse to call wanting to talk. She's always been my best friend, or so it seems. We only met in college, so I didn't even know her in high school. But still she's been my best friend forever.

We meet at the usual place, The Night club. Usual corner. The waiter brings our drinks without even coming by to ask. Is it a problem when you're that well known?

"MC says you're working on getting her a slot to transition."

"As an AppleCore employee." I point out. "She's helping us with the psychological issues our immortals are dealing with as they transition."

"I thought you were the only one." Windy reminds me I'm talking with someone outside the company and I have to be careful.

"I don't know what MC told you, but I have very little influence in this whole thing."

"Not what she told me. Said you have slots in the near term and everyone else is waiting a decade or more."

Not how I would have put it, but be it as it may, "If you're looking for me to give you slots for you and your kids, I'm assuming you don't want Tom to transition, but that's an assumption on my part, I really can't help you."

Windy takes a long sip of her red wine. "You're telling me you'll help MC but you won't help me and my kids."

"I told MC this would happen," and I know Reese and Delilah

have to be thinking the same things.

"What? That your best friends would expect you to stand by them?"

"This has nothing to do with standing by anyone," I protest.

"That's where you have your head up your butt." Windy responds without a moment of thought. "You did something miraculous. Only way I can describe it. And that has put you in a unique position. None of us could have ever thought about being where you are. But now that you're there, you're our only hope."

"Of what?"

"Of surviving." Windy summarizes. "Do you know the waiting list is already a decade? We're locked out. No way can we transition. That means some people will have a decade head start on my kids. That's just not acceptable."

"First of all, that assumes the economy will never grow and there won't be opportunities for people who transition as time goes on. I think the recent history shows that's not accurate. Apple, Facebook, Amazon, Baidu, Ten Cent, Alibaba. Where were they ten years before anyone heard of them? They were there, but just much smaller and proving out their marketing strategies."

"You're giving me a lesson about how the economy works?" Windy is surprised.

"Since you're claiming the only way your kids can compete is to transition early, I think you're making assumptions the recent history doesn't support."

"You're a freaking nerd." Windy points out. "What do you know about the economy?"

"More than you'd apparently want to give me credit for." I push back.

"Okay." Windy isn't happy with the direction of this discussion. "What will it take to convince you?"

"You don't need to do anything to convince me." I respond. "I see where things are going and why you would think you need to use my connections for your kids and yourself. I'd probably come to the same conclusion if I were in your position. But the truth is nothing you assume is true."

Windy takes a long sip of her wine before reengaging me on this one. "Can you give me an explanation? Sounds too much like the Matrix to make me comfortable."

"What do your kids want to do when they grow up?" I challenge her.

"They have no idea. Jobs come and go so quickly it's hard to think about a career."

"I'm not thinking of career, but are they wanting to be technical geeks, like me or more on the marketing and support areas like you?"

Windy gazes off in the distance as she considers my question and finally reengages me. "They have no idea. My guess, although I'm probably wrong is they would tend towards the non-technical side of life."

"The absolute worst place to be." I inform her.

"Why?"

"Anyone can fill those jobs." I inform her. "You want technical skills for your kids so only a few people can do what they do. Good for job security." I inform her.

"The technical folks, as you refer to them have always been expendable. We can always find someone who can do what they do for a whole lot less, whether on the Moon, Mars or on a space station." Windy tries to set the stage for me, but I'm not buying it.

"That's the popular conception." I reflect. "Some companies actually try to work that way. But I can tell you from our perspective, the longer a team works together the greater the results. And I would assume you've seen much the same."

"I have. That's not the issue." Windy ties to decide what tact will work on me. "I have three kids. I know you don't have any and maybe this is a stretch for you. But as their mother I've got to find a way to ensure they can be successful. At least as successful as Tom and I've been."

"Even though Tom is now officially on the outs." I point out.

"Yes, but. Tom is a yardstick that will tell them if they're being successful or not. Despite his many shortcomings as a father and husband, he was relatively successful in the economic parts of our lives. He brought in enough money to pay the bills. Have a nice home for us all to live in. I can't fault him there."

"Then where do you fault him?"

"For not knowing what he wanted." Windy reflects. "The ability to transfer a hunger to his kids. A hunger to be something more than they are today. None of our kids have that hunger. They're only concerned with whether one or another friend is going to have a date since they've never talked with an actual live guy other than through a chat or blog."

"How do you make that connection?" I ask Windy.

"I wish I knew the answer as I'd be in a much better position with my kids."

"So making connections isn't as easy as texting someone. You have to be willing to follow up the opening text and actually stare some guy or girl in the eye and have something intelligent to say to them that isn't just pop culture?"

"I don't think so." Windy responds.

"What I'm hearing you say is you're scared for your kids. That they won't be able to compete in the world evolving before us. The rules are changing, and you don't know how to encourage them to follow a career path that will give them a good chance of success regardless of what happens."

Windy reflects on my question. "I don't think any parent is ever comfortable their children will be as successful, or more successful than they have been. We look at them as they're growing up. They seem so naïve. So unprepared for life in the real world. I've not sent any out to test whether I've done a good job of preparing them or not. I hope I have, but I have no track record either way. And because I don't have any objective evidence I can offer you, I'm asking you to help them. Give them the advantage of being one of the first in the new world. The opportunity to fight for a place, rather than arriving in this brave new world after all opportunity has been claimed by someone else. That's what I'm asking and I'm sure Reese will be too, once she understands what's at stake."

I know she's right. Reese will want the same for her kids. But how do I intervene in a changing world order on behalf of my friends and at the expense of the families of all the AppleCore employees who have worked so long and so hard to ensure our success? What happens when the first kid goes through? Will that open up a flood of requests? Right now everyone sees their peers and only their peers going through. There are no questions because each knows when they come out the other side everyone coming out will be on a product team at AppleCore. But if I change that expectation with even one non-AppleCore employee I'm going to get the Mindi effect. If Landon transitions she must transition. And then I'm no longer creating advantage for AppleCore. I'm choosing the winners and losers in the new economy.

"You were there with me when I underwent my transition." I point out to Windy. "You're the one person I could turn to in the whole world when mine was seemingly coming to an end. The one person I knew I could count on to do whatever would need to be done if the transition didn't work. You knew my situation and yet you were there for me through it all. Now you're asking me to show that I'm that one friend who will stand up and take care of you and your kids when no one else can."

Windy looks at me hopefully, apparently never having thought of the situation in these terms.

"The difference is you're asking me to commit and use company funds to transition you and your kids. I have no right to do that. And we're talking a half million dollars each. So for you and your three kids I have to commit two million dollars. That's not an inconsequential amount. And I can't spend company money on you all. So, help me here. I didn't ask you to spend your money or your company's money when I transitioned. How do I put you on the list without involving a cost to the company that would be illegal?"

"Two million?" Windy responds as if I'd taken the wind out of her sails. "I had no idea."

"It would be two and a half for Reese, her kids and her husband, because she would want him transitioned as well." I point out knowing Windy and Reese will talk about this at some point.

"That payment would go directly to Dr. Woodall's team?" Windy clarifies.

"All I could do is give you a slot we've reserved, but then all costs would have to be borne by you."

Windy nods in understanding, "Do it."

I'll have to figure out a way to isolate them from the rest of the AppleCore teams in Dallas. Maybe Dr. Woodall can help me with that.

"When can you all be ready? It's going to take about a week."

Windy nods, "I remember."

She looks lost in thought as if she's trying to convince herself now that I've given her what she asked for is it really what she wants. I give her a few moments to consider the magnitude of the decision before continuing the discussion.

Windy returns before I interrupt her thoughts. "The sooner the better."

"You realize that once your kids transition that's the age body they will always have."

Windy shakes her head, "What do you mean?"

"How old is your oldest?"

"Ten."

"He will always have a ten-year old's body until he can upgrade to a new body. And that's a half million each time, at least that's the cost today. It may go down in the future, but I can't guarantee that."

"That doesn't work. You have to put them in a twenty-year old's body."

"Now?" I ask.

Windy is suddenly conflicted knowing she may not be able to update their bodies as they mature. That's why she thinks it makes sense to put them in their permanent body now. "You'll be robbing them of their childhood to give them immortality." I inform her.

"How could I do that?" Windy wonders aloud. "Take away their childhood to guarantee their future."

"You basically have to home school, let them engage others

through social media without a video portal and keep them home until their twentieth birthdays. Given where you live, that seems possible, but I thought you'd moved into the city because Tom was still at the ranch."

Windy suddenly looks wide-eyed. "He is, but I can't let that continue."

"It sounds to me like you have a few things you need to take care of at your end before I can schedule you. And you really need to reflect on whether you want to go through with it given all the unanticipated consequences of your decision."

Windy takes a long sip of her red wine, puts the glass back down on the table. "Why isn't anything easy?"

I change the topic, "What's going on with you and A'zam?"

"Who?" She looks at me ironically. "That guy who loved me and left me? I haven't heard from him since that one night."

"So, you blew up your marriage over a one night stand."

"I can't say you didn't try to warn me. But Tom and I were over. All A'zam did was make me see there are other fish in the sea."

"You're not upset about the way he's treated you?"

Windy finishes her glass of wine, even though the glass is still half full. "I know how the game is played," she shakes her head apparently remembering dating in college.

"What are you going to do? Once you transition life becomes very different. I'm not sure either of us can see how different. Relationships will change, particularly since all of your kids will appear to be your age. While that's an issue in the short run, it won't be longer term. But anyone you bring home will find it… strange."

"I don't need to work. The wind farms are humming along, and the money just keeps blowing my way. I can live even if I never find another job. But from what you've said that probably won't be an issue. I'll be a lot smarter than I am now. I can't imagine how many companies will want what I bring."

"You'll land on your feet as will your kids. But I have to warn you, there are a lot of things that will be a problem. Like the fact you'll no longer have feelings about anything including your kids. You'll only remember the affection you hold for them and it will be the same for them. Are you ready for that?"

EVERYTHING UNDER THE SUN

Dietrich asks me to come to his office to watch the hearing proceedings. The jury room is full, cameras everywhere. The Judge comes in and is seated and begins to hear the testimony. The first party up is Jane Williams and the ACLU. She is to frame the argument for prohibiting human transitions.

"You may proceed Ms. Williams." The judge intones.

"Thank you, your honor. The American Civil Liberties Union is dedicated to ensuring that every individual has the opportunity and ability to enjoy the full spectrum of rights guaranteed under the constitution and following laws not only of this great nation, but each and every governmental subdivision within this county. And for that reason, we have brought suit to stop, forever, the bifurcation of our society. A medical procedure that would establish a group of individuals with rights and abilities far greater than the rest."

"Stop right there, Miss Williams." The judge interrupts. "We are not here to discuss abilities. There is nothing codified in any federal, state or local laws that addresses ability."

"A poor choice of words on my behalf, your honor." Jane Williams pulls back.

Dietrich glances at me, "That was intentional. She was trying to get it into the record. If she had succeeded our chances would have been slim and none."

"Miss Williams. You are one of the most experienced attorneys on staff at your esteemed organization. I know you know the law. If you try to insert editorialization again in my court I will terminate your testimony and have whatever you've submitted stricken. Is that understood?"

Dietrich slaps his knee, "Good for her. Didn't think I'd see her push back even with such an egregious crossing of the line."

"Yes, your honor." Jane Williams sounds like she was expecting this response. I wonder if it wasn't planned to give us hope. Maybe miscalculate the reception we are going to receive.

Jane Williams continues, "We at the ACLU do not wish to establish a precedent under law that enables individuals the right to transform themselves into a super human race living within our society. A group of individuals able to live forever, to use their own terms, while everyone else lives a normal human lifespan. A group of individuals capable of supplanting a number of individuals in work assignments, thereby reducing access to economic liberty and a fair living. What the defendant's procedure does is change the fundamental nature of being human in a manner that no one who does not transition can compete. Our nation was founded on the idea that all citizens are equal under the law and yet this change is so fundamental that equality will cease to exist as a concept within our communities and within the law. These are our brief opening comments. We request the right to provide testimony again at the end of this proceeding to address the varied assertions that will be made by all parties."

"So, noted, Miss Williams. And I thank you for being brief. I pray that those who follow are as respectful of the time of this court. Next."

The judge recognizes the next to provide testimony, "Mr. Richardson. On behalf of Dr. Bart Woodall and his Life Extension Clinic, the defendants in this case."

"Your honor. Thank you for your reasoned dismissal of the injunction and the opportunity to provide further testimony in response to the claims of the American Civil Liberties Union and Miss Williams. The procedure performed at the Life Extension Clinic is not a threat to anyone's civil liberties. In fact, the procedure ensures that the civil liberties of the patients undergoing this procedure are protected under the law. Everyone is guaranteed a right to Life, liberty and the pursuit of happiness. What the clinic does is to ensure that its patients have the right to a full and complete life in the face of debilitating and life-threatening disease. My client is mystified that Miss Williams, her employer and the more than one hundred intervenors to this case have not recognized this fundamental right. In the brief filed by Miss Williams on behalf of her employer, she makes over two hundred allegations with none supported by facts. I would like to file with the court at this time our response brief to those allegations, supported by facts, where facts exist. And that is part of the problem this court will need to address. Few facts have been established and the court is being asked to make a ruling based on hysteria, demonization and showmanship rather than fact. My client is a talented physician, who sought a procedure to extend the life of patients for whom there was no alternatives. He has now shown the level of his talent and innovative spirit. He has achieved an ability to treat a wide range of terminal disease, although the long term prognosis is still to be determined. As an example of the speculative nature of Miss Williams's case, the first individual to transition did so only a little more than one hundred and twenty days ago. Yet she alleges this individual will live forever. While Dr. Woodall is hopeful she will have a long life, we simply do not know what the limitations of this procedure are. She could pass on tomorrow for all we know. We pray the court will find that every individual has the right to seek treatments and procedures that will enable them to enjoy the constitutionally guaranteed right to life that disease seeks to take from them. Thank you, your honor."

"Thank you, Mister Richardson. I appreciate your brevity, but I'm not so sure I'm going to enjoy wading through your rebuttal brief since it is what? Five hundred pages or more?"

Mr. Richardson nods to the judge and rises from the witness table.

Dietrich turns to me, "I wonder who the next will be to provide testimony."

The judge answers his question, "Miss Anthony of Americans Against Immortality. You have no more than fifteen minutes."

A short woman dressed entirely in black with a high neck dress and her hair in a bun at the back of her head approaches the microphone, seats herself and lays out her briefing which she commences to read. "Judge Hobart, thank you for this opportunity for Americans Against Immortality to state the reasons we believe immortality is a threat to our judicial system and legal structure." She clears her throat and takes a sip of water before continuing. "In considering the facts of this matter, despite Mr. Richardson's assertion that there aren't many as yet, I believe we can establish that individuals who will live forever will not regard the law in quite the same fashion as an individual who has a finite lifetime. Are we as a society prepared to put to death an individual who we would not want to be released into society in a hundred or a thousand years? The reason I ask this question is that a hundred or a thousand years for an individual who will live forever is like a sentence of a year or three years for an individual with a hundred-year lifespan. This is what is meant by the remark that an immortal will not regard the law in quite the same fashion as someone with a finite lifespan. Furthermore, a person is bound by emotions and norms we have established over thousands of years. An immortal will not be bound by either as they are incapable of emotions, having no biological body, and the norms of society are not important because they were established to accommodate the bodily needs of the human race. When bodily needs are no longer a factor the immortal no longer exercises care when around others because there is no need for them to safeguard themselves in a similar fashion. An example is we currently limit the number of hours a pilot or truck driver may fly or drive to ensure they are adequately rested and alert to avoid accidents. An immortal no longer requires sleep, does not need to rest and will assert that they should not be limited by such laws. They do not pertain to their physiological structure. Would we exempt immortals from the laws that we have established to protect the well-being of all citizens? I could cite hundreds of examples where an immortal will create inconsistencies in how we apply our laws, creating openings that may jeopardize the health and well-being of the greater citizenry. I have provided a few such examples in my written brief, which I herewith file with the court, and ask that this proceeding result in a ban on procedures that transition individuals into beings that are immortal. Thank you, your honor."

"Thank you, Miss Anthony. Bailiff, who is our next witness?"

Dietrich turns off the monitor. "Just thought you'd like to get a flavor for the attacks against you."

"Your best guess is this will continue for another month or more?" I ask, not sure what I should take away from the opening arguments.

"The testimony, yes. And another month for the Judge to render her decision. Today won't mean anything because as you saw both sides kept it high level and reserved the right for a final rebuttal after all testimony has been filed."

"And in the meantime?" I wonder aloud.

"In the meantime, we continue transitioning AppleCore employees and further distinguishing ourselves from the competition."

"I was meaning to ask you about that." I change the direction of the discussion. "I had a conversation with Beth Allison at Symbol Ventures. I think they may be considering a suit against us for anti-competitive practices."

"For White Rabbit?" Dietrich guesses.

I nod. "Not sure what the basis of their claim will be, other than she seemed to be trying to asset that I'm able to drive our performance in a manner that limits competition."

I watch Dietrich reviewing case law in his mind. It takes only a few moments and he looks back at me. "No precedent for such a filing. But there is no precedent for the ACLU filing."

"Which reminds me. Beth admitted that Symbol's outside counsel has been discussing the case with Jane Williams. So, they are providing inputs without being listed as an intervenor."

"We would probably do the same if this wasn't such an important case for us." Dietrich admits.

"So, nothing we need to do with that information?"

Dietrich shakes his head. "I assumed they were in there somewhere and several of the others we compete with probably are too. We've factored that in to our testimony. I'm not concerned at this point. But at least it's helpful to know where they are. We can look for the arguments they have inserted and see if we can establish what they hope to gain."

I nod agreement and am about to rise, when Dietrich holds up his hand to stop me. "I have something else I wanted to ask you."

I sit back down.

"What's A'zam up to? I assume you know more than the rest of us."

"What's your concern?" I'm not sure why Dietrich would have one.

"He took my best contracts person. I've tried to find out from her what she's working on and she will only tell me A'zam asked her not to provide any details back to us."

Given everything else A'zam has been doing I'm not surprised. "The only things I'm aware of are the immortals project and the Symbol Ventures acquisition. But there's no reason you shouldn't be aware of contracts he's entering into on behalf of the corporation. You need to be reviewing what he's committing us to."

"That's what I was afraid of." Dietrich is clearly not happy. "He's up to something he's not sharing with anyone. Acting without board approval. Now if it's just contracts for piece parts related to the immortals project that's one thing. But why wouldn't he permit us to know what those contracts are?"

"I think you need to call your contracts person in and let her know despite A'zam's direction she works for you and not him. She needs to keep you fully in the loop. Now I have a different problem. I work for the board and he's the Chairman, so I can't make such demands on him. He can withhold information from me and there's really nothing I can do about it."

"I thought you were sleeping with him." Dietrich goes right to the heart of the matter.

"Petra too." I advise him.

"Really? Didn't know about Petra. At least he's keeping it all in the family, so to speak."

"Actually, he's not. That's part of the problem. He made reference to sleeping with someone most nights, but I've only found a few who he's slept with more than once."

"I'd certainly advise him against continuing that behavior."

"I'll let him know," I chuckle since we both know A'zam wouldn't take that advice.

"He's not said anything to you in your one-on-ones?"

"Nor any other venue." I confirm. "I don't like the sounds of what your contracts person told you. Petra made a similar comment about him having her write very large checks that haven't been flowing through the corporate statements."

"What?" Dietrich is alarmed. "That could constitute all kinds of SEC violations."

"Suggest you may want to stop by and have a casual conversation with Petra, but I wouldn't bring up the part about her sleeping with A'zam. I'm not sure how many know about that."

"Would you like me to begin a formal investigation of what A'zam is doing since it could be exposing the company to considerable liability?"

I consider his question for only a moment, but I review a number of documents in that short time frame. "Informal only at this point. Fact finding more than investigation. Let's assume he's following the law and all corporate policies for the moment."

"Even though we have already established he is not at least on the contracts side and probably on the finance side as well." Dietrich points out.

"Fact finding. May want to present those facts to the appropriate board committee at the appropriate time."

"Understood." Dietrich is reflective for a moment. "You know where this could go?"

"A disciplinary action by the board." I acknowledge.

Dietrich considers my comment, apparently considering the personalities on the board and their relationship to A'zam. "You're probably right." Apparently, he was thinking more removal than discipline.

"Coming back to the real reason you invited me down to your office..."

"Are you sure you know why I invited you down?" Dietrich advises I probably shouldn't be making an assumption.

"The proceeding?"

"Not a good assumption, but what's your question." Dietrich smiles knowing he's told me why without having to tell me.

"What should we expect now?"

"Lots of stories in the newspaper. My advice is we simply don't respond to anything that is asserted. If someone defames you, I'll evaluate whether you should sue and give you my best advice. It would have to be a private suit as the company would not get involved unless the party is incautious and makes us party to the defamation."

"You would recommend someone to handle that for me?"

"Of course. We're a full-service legal department." Dietrich smiles again. "How are you holding up through all this scrutiny?"

"No issues."

Dietrich studies my face and my posture. "You know it's going to get a lot rougher. It's going to get personal. Expect stories about your liaisons with A'zam. They will call you everything under the sun."

CARING

The call from Rocky caught me off guard. I could have asked why he wants to see me now, but I have a pretty good idea as I step out of the Googlecar and walk up to his door, which curiously I find open. This is by far the strangest visit I've made to him here.

I push the door open and listen for the usual Rocky sounds. And while I've almost always found him in his lab, this time the sounds are coming from the kitchen. It sounds like he's attempting to cook something. As I come through the doorway I see my mistake. The Anna Laura android is trying to cook something, and Rocky is correcting her. I guess that means when Rocky downloaded his memories of her that did not include her recipes. Of course not. Rocky never spent any time helping Anna Laura cook, so how would he know? What I'm surprised about is that she did show me how to cook and apparently those recipes didn't come across either.

"What are you making?"

"She's trying to make eggs for me, but she can't remember how I like them. I'm trying to explain it, but either we don't have the ingredients, or she can't remember how to prepare them. Anyway, we're on our tenth iteration and nothing edible had come about as a result."

"Anna Laura?" I call out. The android turns and looks at me for just a moment.

"Good morning, Sage. Do you remember how Rocky likes his eggs? I seem to have forgotten."

"Let me help you." I approach the android and it seems like I'm twelve again, helping Anna Laura in the kitchen. "He likes them scrambled with a little cream cheese and chives. That's probably what you're lacking." I check the cooler and as I suspect Rocky got her eggs but not much more. "Need a touch of milk too."

"How much is a little?"

"For two eggs I'd add an ounce and one chive chopped."

"And a touch? How much is that?"

"Maybe a quarter of an ounce. If they're still firm, I'd add another touch to make it a half ounce. They should be slightly creamy. At least that's the way you… the way Rocky likes them."

"How do we get the other ingredients?" the android asks.

"I've ordered them. They should be here soon."

"Okay. I'll tidy up."

I look at Rocky who seems frazzled. "Not even a phenomenal job from you? What is it? You just expect me to do miraculous things every day? Yesterday I had an idea for an architecture no one had ever tried. Today she's walking and talking and trying to make eggs. How great is that?"

I remember Mrs. Walker and give Rocky a hug. He freezes, probably thinking I'm going to give him a Heimlich maneuver or something. But once he realizes I'm showing him affection he slowly and gently gives me a hug back.

"Tidy up?" I ask with a grin.

"She used to say that all the time." Rocky responds in his own defense. "Used to do it too. If your friend here starts cleaning up around here I'll never find anything I need."

"Tell her to leave the lab alone. You'll tidy up in there. She'll do what you ask."

"Why would she? Anna Laura never did." Rocky points out a difference in expectations.

"I beg to disagree. You asked Anna Laura for two children. She gave you two. You asked her to love you, she did every day you were together. You asked her to trust that you would get us through the hard times. She never left you even when we didn't have enough to eat."

"You remember all that?" Rocky genuinely seems surprised.

"And more." I nod towards the living room, "C'mon. Let's go see what she'd doing." Rocky reluctantly follows me into the other room. There we find Anna Laura dusting the furniture with a rag that was probably white when she started but is now completely gray. The android must either hear us or sense our presence. "When was the last time this was cleaned, Rocky?"

"I don't know. A month ago? We have a house keeper who does all that."

"Not any longer. She doesn't do a good job. I'll take care of it now. We're going to have a clean house. One where you won't look like a museum piece after each time you sit in a chair."

"Where did she get that?" Rocky asks me.

"Must have been from you. I certainly wouldn't have come up with it." I poke Rocky in the side.

"When was the last time you sat in here?" Anna Laura asks Rocky.

"I don't remember. A while. Why?"

Anna Laura pulls a Ding Dong wrapper out of a chair cushion, holds it up for us to see. "Mold. It's been there a while. New rule, Rocky. No eating in the living room. You eat in the kitchen and throw out your waste. I don't ever want to find half eaten food, wrappers or mold anywhere in this house."

"Does that include the lab?" Rocky almost seems to be negotiating with the android.

"The lab is your space." Anna Laura responds. "You've made that quite clear. What you do in there is up to you. But I ask that you just not blow this place up because you don't make enough to replace it."

As the Anna Laura android carries the wrapper towards the kitchen, she passes us, stops to give Rocky a kiss and me a wink before heading out to dispose of the garbage. Rocky seems to be in a dream.

"That the first kiss she's given you?" I have to ask.

Rocky nods, still comparing it to what he knew. It must be very close because he seems completely overwhelmed.

I hear the doorbell and retrieve the groceries I ordered, bringing them into the kitchen where Anna Laura joins me. I hold up the cream cheese and say, "Cream cheese. Let's use just an ounce. That would be marked on the label as this much." Anna Laura looks over my shoulder. I set the cream cheese down and pull out the chives. "One stalk, like this." I pull one stalk out and hold it up. "Chop it into rings about an eighth of an inch. Like this." I pick up a knife, set the chive stalk down on the chopping block next to his sink and show her how to chop it. "And this is the milk. Just a touch."

Anna Laura nods to me, "Got it," and begins to make Rocky's eggs.

"She can learn that way?" Rocky asks from the doorway.

"She learns just like you and I do. If you show her what you want her to do and talk her through it she'll do just fine. You'll see."

"The proof will be in the eggs. If she makes eggs like she kisses I'm in big trouble."

I smile at Rocky and point to the table where Anna Laura, I presume, has already set out his plate and utensils. "No coffee this morning?" I look around but don't see his usual cup.

Rocky shakes his head. "Never got to it. I was going to make it but then we got going on the eggs."

"You want Anna Laura to make it for you?"

"That would be wonderful." Rocky beams. "She always used to you know. Been so long since I've had real coffee I'm not sure I would recognize it."

"What's different when you make it?" I ask, not sure why he characterized it the way he did.

"Care, probably. I just put the grounds in the filter and add water to the brewer. A few minutes later the beeper tells me I have coffee. I never watched Anna Laura make it. So I don't know. I just followed the directions on the label."

I replay that last morning with Anna Laura. We were in the kitchen and I watch in my memory what she did. A much younger looking Rocky comes in, goes up to her and kisses her on his way to the table. She delivers the eggs to him on his plate. His special plate. One he got when we visited the Kennedy Space Center when I was about six. He always ate his eggs from that plate. He used to say if he could only contribute something to the knowledge of mankind the way the space program engineers did he would die a contented man. So the plate was a reminder that he had a special purpose every day. I look around and see Anna Laura go to the coffee brewer and I ask, "How do you make coffee?" Anna Laura reaches out and pulls me in close to her. I smell her soapy smells and the detergent she washed our clothes in. A clean smell. At least that was what I remember clean smelling like. Anna Laura shows me she has two different coffee cans out. "I use half of one and half of the other. It gives the coffee a different flavor your father likes." "What kinds are they?" I ask. "One is a French roast and the other is Columbian. Your father said he likes to build bridges between worlds, so that's what I try to do with his coffee. Build a taste bridge between the old and new worlds."

I'm back in the present and look around for his cupboard. I open the door and find only a can from Indonesia. No wonder Rocky can't tell if it's real coffee, it's neither old nor new world. Must be he just went into a store and bought the cheapest kind on the shelf. I send in an order for coffee knowing it will be delivered in a while, but Rocky won't get Anna Laura coffee with his Anna Laura eggs. He'll live.

Anna Laura android puts the eggs on Rocky's special plate. At least she got that from his download. She carries them over and places them on the table before him just like my mother did. I see Rocky looking up at her appreciatively apparently smelling the Anna Laura egg smell he loved. I watch his expression as the first fork full enters his mouth. He closes his eyes and the corners of his mouth arch up in a contented smile. She nailed the recipe, carrying Rocky back to his happy days when Anna Laura completed him and enabled him to do his work. Rocky reaches out and squeezes the android's hand, just like he used to do when she did something he liked.

"You're going to have to be patient with her." I point out as I sit down across from him at the table.

"What do you mean?" Rocky continues to enjoy his favorite breakfast.

"You will have to show her things you'll think she should just remember. Tell her what you like and what you don't. She'll remember some things, but anything you and I don't because Anna Laura just did them without talking about it? She won't know to do it."

"Like?"

"Your coffee," I suggest as the doorbell rings. Another delivery. I rise and retrieve the two kinds of coffee, bring them in and touch Anna Laura's arm, like I used to do to get her attention.

"Rocky likes you to make a blend for him. Half French," I hold up the French coffee can. "And half Columbian." I hold up that can. I then show her how to use the coffee brewer, where to add the water, how much of each type and turn it on.

"There are services that will deliver it prepackaged." Anna Laura tells me. "It's much easier."

"I know, but this is how Rocky likes it." I give her a hug, because that's what I used to do when we would have these sharing sessions where she would show me something and I'd tell her what I'd learned at school or from my friends or from a book I was reading. Anna Laura hugs me back, just like she used to.

When the coffee brewer dings that it is complete, Anna Laura draws a cup and carries it over to Rocky. She places it before him with the milk carton, so he can add a touch of milk, which is how he likes it. But Rocky always added the milk himself. Not sure why, but that's just what he always did. He stirs it as Anna Laura sits down where I had been sitting to watch Rocky's reaction. He inhales the aroma and nods that it smells like he remembers, blows across it and then takes a sip of the hot brew. The nod tells me all I need to know. This is the coffee blend he remembers Anna Laura delivering to him every morning before he'd go off to AppleCore. Now wide awake. Now focused for the day and ready to complete the project he was working.

"I'm glad you approve. Sage showed me how you like it."

Rocky winks at me, a wink that only Anna Laura used to give to Tabitha and me. I never saw her wink at Rocky. Not sure why. It just seemed that winks were reserved for us kids, and it was a special way of communicating just between us women. Of course, Rocky wouldn't understand that, but I'm appreciating that he's trying to recreate that happy time in our lives. I'm glad he is accepting the android as it tries to recreate the presence of Anna Laura. There's no question Rocky knows what I'm trying to do, and his initial reaction was so negative I was afraid he would never even give the android a chance. Guess I was wrong.

"Did you call me just to show Anna Laura how to make your breakfast?" I push Rocky now that he has finished his eggs and is sipping his steaming coffee.

"No, I called you because I wanted you to thank me for completing your project."

"Thank you, but she's not complete."

"Oh?"

"She has a lot to learn and she needs your help in learning all that I need her to know to help me understand aspects of my transition that are essential."

"That's right." Rocky sounds like he doesn't believe me. "You created her, so you can learn from her. It had nothing at all to do with me and my pending marriage."

"You want me to take her home with me? It will slow down the project because I can't be the source of the knowledge I'm expecting her to share with me. It's knowledge you have tucked away in your memory from the time you were together."

"I already downloaded all that." Rocky is trying to understand my need for his continued involvement, although I don't for a minute believe he will let me walk out of here with Anna Laura.

"But you need to inform those memories with how you made decisions together, how you divided responsibilities, how you communicated and how you loved each other. Without you adding context and texture memories are only partial guides. I've come to completely understand that."

Rocky takes another sip of his coffee before he will answer me. "I guess I can work with her for a bit longer. But this doesn't change my plans. I will marry and maybe even have more kids."

Now I know he's just jerking my chain. "The son you never had?"

"I'm too old to teach a kid sports now."

"I have a question I'd like to ask Anna Laura to see whether she will be able to help me on my journey."

"Be my guest." Rocky looks at Anna Laura who is rinsing the breakfast dishes and has her back to us.

"Anna Laura?" She turns to look at me. "What does it mean to be human?"

Anna Laura looks at Rocky, "It means caring for someone else more than yourself."

NEW REALITY

I come down to the lab at AppleCore at Oriana's invitation. Actually, it was more than an invitation. She left the message while I was with Rocky that she is ready to release the second phase of White Rabbit and would like to show me before it hits the stores.

A'zam is not here this time, so apparently Oriana picked up on the fact I wasn't happy to see him here last time. Probably going to do separate but equal demos for us.

"What is phase two?" I ask as I enter the room and see on the monitor what looks like a neural net placed directly on the neocortex of a patient in a cutaway image.

Oriana comes over and I touch her arm just to make contact. Thank you, Mrs. Walker. Oriana smiles and leads me towards the monitor. An engineer comes forward for the brief. This is not Shondra, so I'm pleased that Oriana is giving opportunities to a number of her engineers to lead segments of the project. "This is Mohammed Khan. His mother is a Pakistani Muslim and his father an Indian Hindu. He has learned both world views and practices aspects of both religions. This has given Mohammed a very different view of the world. He's also the oldest member of our development teams at seventy-seven. He is an Engineering Fellow but asked to be just a member of a development team like our youngest engineers. That's why I gave him the challenge you discussed with me after the White Rabbit demo and release."

Instantly I understand what I'm looking at, even though I thought it was something different initially. "Please explain it to me, Mohammed."

"We took the same Nanotechnology approach we used for White

Rabbit. We create building blocks at nano scale and introduce them into the body the same way, this pill." Mohammed hands me a red pill.

"Back to The Matrix I see." I smile at Oriana. "The blue pill or the red pill."

She nods in return also with a smile.

"In this case it is the blue pill and the red pill." Mohammed continues. They are two parts of the same platform. White Rabbit is the leverage of your senses, Mad Hatter is the antenna and connector that feeds the platform, but at the same time speeds communications across the brain hemispheres and sectors while both receiving and sending signals to others."

Instantly I realize Oriana and the team have delivered the capability we had discussed after the White Rabbit demo. I'd kept the discussion very high level and recognized White Rabbit as a building block thinking we were still some time away from the integrated solution. But here it is.

"Tell me Mohammed, as an engineering fellow, would this capability have been possible if we had not transitioned you and the team?"

"Maybe in time. But I cannot tell you how much time. Not soon, of that I am sure. We are on the brink of enabling the collective unconscious and the collective conscious if we chose."

"What's missing to get us to that capability?"

"What I would call the concentrator." Mohammed has thought this part through. "We have the ability now to collect impulses of each individual through a mesh network. We can organize those impulses, put them in buckets if you will. We can then prioritize them and register back what the will of the majority is. Everyone will know what the norm is and how strong is it. This creates a reinforcement of the collective unconscious. Everyone will know what the unconscious norm is, but it will remain unconscious."

"The flight or fight impulse." I suggest as an example.

"Correct. Everyone will now understand what is the norm of all humanity that is connected through the Mad Hatter and White Rabbit."

"So where does the concentrator you suggested come in?"

"Awareness is one thing. Reacting is another. The concentrator will enable everyone to react the same way if they chose. The impulse will be strong and uniform across all humanity."

"Let me ask a hypothetical."

Mohammed nods for me to proceed.

"Could the concentrated impulse be strong enough that it could override an external order given by someone of authority to an immortal?"

Mohammed hesitates only a few seconds as he clearly has reviewed something in his head. Then he looks at Oriana before responding. "Theoretically yes. You are bridging the collective unconscious with the conscious and seeking an unconscious override of a conscious response to an external authority. Theoretically, the answer is yes. It is possible. I am in need of some research, some reflection time and some sharing with my peers to arrive at an effective approach."

Oriana responds, "You have the time, Mohammed and the authority to take a solution to prototype. I assume there will be an immortals component to your solution so you have the authority to work that as well."

Mohammed gives a slight bow and withdraws from us with an expression of concentration. He is already well along in organizing his thoughts.

"When do you brief A'zam?" I ask Oriana when Mohammed is

out of earshot.

"None is scheduled. I wasn't sure where you were going with this concept. Now that I am, I don't think we want to give him a briefing, just the new product summary along with all the others."

"How will you handle it when he wants one?"

"Same as I always do. Bring him down, describe the product and how it complements the White Rabbit with peer to peer connectivity and speeds signal acquisition. That's where the discussion will end. We will not discuss what is next. If he asks, it will be focused on content."

"Do you feel like a conspirator?" I'm trying to understand her comfort in the role.

"You said A'zam has not been forthcoming about what he's doing. We're just taking our cues from him."

"What are your thoughts about the scenario I just painted for you?" I look about to see who can hear us. No one appears to be in range or paying attention to us from what I can see.

"You've been privy to a lot I'm not aware of." Oriana responds deferentially. "I have to believe you think there is cause to be worried about such a scenario. If we can facilitate freedom in any form I think that's a good thing. Does that answer your question?"

"It does, and I hope you understand why I'm being cautious." I lower my voice, so it is hard even for me to hear myself. "We are creating a whole new society. That in and of itself is nothing new. We've done it periodically throughout history. What is different this time is the radical departure from the past in a very short time frame. And what I hope evolves is a stronger society with shared norms that bubble up from the people and cannot be shoved down their throats by a few who seek power and glory for themselves at the expense of everyone else."

"There is a danger." Oriana responds. "You are working from the collective unconscious. That's appropriate for the society you are trying to create. But when you cross over to the collective conscious, you are subject to manipulation by small groups who seek to impose a view on the larger society through demagoguery. And if collective conscious is enabled by Mad Hatter we may actually be worse off than we are today."

I nod in understanding her concern. Oriana is growing in her ability to see the larger picture much quicker than I anticipated, which is all good. "We don't discuss the two-way capability of Mad Hatter. We talk about it being a receiving antenna and hemisphere express bus that enables quicker reception and processing of the White Rabbit capability. We don't talk about its other capabilities."

"But is that ethical?" Oriana pushes back. "We're hooking people up to each other in a way they never anticipated. We in essence make them superhuman from the perspective of where we are today and where we've been. And we will enable collective will to enforce global norms. Is this the death of cultural differences? Will everyone be alike because the global norm over rides the local differences? I'm not sure we've thought this all the way through."

"Follow me." I motion towards the lab door. We walk the halls in silence as I continue to process my thoughts about the issue Oriana has raised. We enter my office, nodding to Mindi as we go through hers and close the door behind us. I push open the door to the atrium. No one ever goes out there except the maintenance crews that change out pond water and feed the fish. No one out here today. We go over to one of the ponds.

"This is so sensitive I can't take the chance of someone listening. I know A'zam has been listening in on my external calls. The issue comes down to this: we are at a point where an individual or very small group of individuals can and will attempt to control not only immortals, but all people through the immortals. You mentioned freedom downstairs. It is under attack in a way it has never been before. We are rushing into that world so fast that only a few people anywhere have any idea what can and most likely will happen given what we are putting in place. A'zam has placed freedom limiting chips in us. White Rabbit and Mad Hatter will enable a similar capability in anyone who has swallowed those pills. We have to find and deploy a means of overcoming the control A'zam and others he may be working with are seeking. And the only way I see that working is if the collective will of the people can overcome a directive from those who seek to limit us."

"Emergence." Oriana responds.

"I've heard a number of people use that term. What does it mean to you?"

"Exactly what you're describing. If I look to the official definition it's a noun that goes back to the Latin root *emergere,* meaning 'bring to light.' It came into English in the 17th century. Just as something comes to light or shows up where there was darkness or nothing before, an emergence happens. In this case we are enabling people to bring to light the collective norms of the people and a mechanism to see that those norms are enforced through the will of the people. You're suggesting that an individual or small group wish to establish new norms that everyone must follow through control systems in immortals and with our help, everyone else. All you are trying to do is ensure those new norms are very hard or impossible to impose. And the mechanism to do that is through technology."

I nod. Oriana understands what I'm trying to do. She will be able to deploy what is needed as long as A'zam doesn't understand how we have altered his plans. At least the plans we are aware of. And what sticks in the back of my mind is that he's up to something he's not sharing. I assume it has something to do with his grand plan for humanity, but since I know so little about it I really can't tell.

"Why don't you come out here more often?" Oriana asks. "It's really quite tranquil."

"The floor to ceiling windows lets each of us experience the tranquility without spoiling it with our presence. Besides if we were to come out here very often it would probably not be tranquil for long because it would just be another meeting place."

"How do you see this whole scenario playing out?" Oriana is wondering if I have the chess moves all planned to checkmate.

"There are a number of ways. About half preserve what I think is important in a humane society. The rest do not. I'm doing all I can to increase the odds in my favor, but I can't tell if I'm succeeding. What you're doing with White Rabbit and Mad Hatter is essential. Without them, from what I can see, I have no chance. And from what Dietrich is telling me, those I'm trying to protect are working to destroy me. The world is all upside down at the moment. I can't tell how it will all end, because it will never end, just evolve into something else altogether that we've not imagined to this point."

"You're sounding more and more philosophical." Oriana responds. "Not like you at all. You used to only focus on the technical solution and then the schedules and budgets to get it into the hands of our users. I rarely hear you talking about those now. It's like you've morphed into someone who's larger than life, trying to balance impossible demands while tying your shoes."

"Did I tell you I built an Anna Laura?" I suddenly have a desire to change the topic.

"What do you mean?" Oriana isn't following.

"I had an immortals body built that looks just like Anna Laura. But since her consciousness isn't available, I asked Rocky to build a control system to make her into an android."

"I take it he's succeeded?" Oriana is cautious about this information, probably because of the rest of the discussion.

"He has." I hesitate about how to continue this discussion, what is it I want to tell her. "He called me. Asked me to come over."

"What did you find?"

"Actually, he wanted me to show Anna Laura how to make his breakfast. We downloaded our memories of Anna Laura, but they didn't include the recipes. So, I showed her how to make Rocky happy, at least following the old adage that the way to a man's heart is through his stomach."

"Why would you do this?" Oriana still is surprised by my actions. "Are you trying to find a way to re-establish the family you never had after the accident?"

"Not for me. The original idea was that I could create a mother advisor, someone who I could bounce ideas, thoughts, and theories off and get a response from the point of view of Anna Laura. You know, a mother's response. I've been trying to get the perspectives of all kinds of people about what it means to be human. But that's a perspective I can't get without recreating Anna Laura. When I told Rocky of my plan he was so negative I knew it could also help him with his loneliness. And apparently I was right."

"Could this be a whole new product area for us? Bringing back deceased family members as companions?"

"Maybe. I want to see how this works out with Rocky first." I hesitate, but then decide I want her reaction to the other part of it. "Rocky asked me to create a Tabitha as well."

"You would be recreating the family he lost."

"As we talked about it I told him I wouldn't want to bring her back at age ten, which is when she died, but rather what she would be like now, if she'd lived. Rocky wasn't keen on that idea. What do you think?"

"I can see both sides of that. What you're thinking is that you would freeze Tabitha as a child and Rocky wouldn't let her evolve beyond that."

"She would grow in mental capability but be trapped in the body of a child. Even though the android isn't aware of what's happening, Rocky would see it and not be able to do anything about it. But if she were today's age, she would be able to function both as part of his family and within society normally."

"What's normal about any part of what you're describing?" Oriana takes exception to my use of terms, knowing that's lazy thinking on my part.

"If you think about it, what we're describing may well become the new normal. A world with an immortals class, a mortals class and an androids class, all interacting, all taking on new roles in relation to each other and within themselves. With Androids we are no longer a bifurcated society. We are now looking forwards and backwards simultaneously. Time takes on a very different meaning. For some it never ends, for others it is short, and the third group lets you live in the past, the present or the future."

SOMETIMES

Jermaine stops me in the hallway as I'm heading down to the lab to see what Mohammed's thoughts have led him to. "Hey Sage. You remember me?"

I play along, "Aren't you that guy who built the Orgasmatron? Could I have your autograph? You must be nearly as famous as Woody Allen."

"Who?"

"What's the issue with your wife?" I ask to see what he really wants.

"No issue, but she thinks I must be doing research to figure out the ultimate orgasm and she's afraid it's not just with her."

"You said she's never been as satisfied as she's been since you transitioned."

"That's true, but she just wants to keep me in line," Jermaine confides his suspicion.

"Okay. So, what's really on your mind?"

"Time off for good behavior."

"I take it you're not fulfilled by your current assignment."

"Hell, Sage. I'm an inventor of technology solutions, not a god-damn personnel agency. People are a much harder nut to crack than coming up with a novel idea or solution to a hard problem. I'm sitting here on the sidelines watching Oriana go to town. Two revolutionary solutions just since I took on this job."

"You telling me you were the roadblock?"

"Hell no. But I'm feeling on the outside, you know? I used to be the main man on all the hard projects and now I'm not even in the room."

"I hear what you're saying, but that's just part of what life is going to be like here now that we have all these big brains coming together on the teams you're transitioning and standing up. The pace and number of revolutionary products is only going to accelerate, and you can't be in every room. There will be no one team that does all the main projects. There will be too many of them. Where you are now you at least have a hand in enabling every single project by deciding who gets transitioned, who else will be on the teams with them and assembling expertise in a way we can do things no one else has the talent to even explore. What you're doing now is core, Jermaine. Even more than what Oriana is doing, because she's pushing projects to the teams and if you haven't stood them up right, they won't be able to produce diddly let alone something that transforms."

"You can stop blowing smoke at me now." Jermaine isn't happy. "You know me as well as I know you. I'm a products guy. HR is for weenies who can't code. I can code. Remember?"

"You have always been one of our best coders, if not our best coder, until we started growing the immortals corps. There are a whole bunch of folks here now who are even better than you because they're using their new capabilities in ways you haven't thought of. That's not a knock on you. It's just an observation."

"You saying I've lost the touch? Put me back on a project team. I'll show you I haven't lost a step."

"I don't put anyone on product teams." I remind him. "You do."

"Then you have a problem if I put myself on a team?"

"That's between you and your team lead."

"Oriana." Jermaine realizes. "Why's it always come back to her?"

"She's your best friend."

"She also took me off what I love to do and made me a bureaucrat like all those other useless people around here."

"I've just told you what you're doing is more important to the long-term success of this company than what Oriana is doing at the moment."

"In the long run we're all dead." Jermaine responds, and then adds, "That's a famous quote. Don't remember who said it, but I guess it's not accurate anymore. But you know what I meant. I don't want to wait a thousand years to get back into the middle of the action. I want to be there today. What I hear Mohammed's working on just has me all spun up. I have ideas. Approaches that might get us there quicker. You know what I bring."

"Nothing's stopping you from having lunch with Mohammed and sharing your insights."

"Not the same," Jermaine is frustrated. "You're not going to intervene on my behalf, are you?"

"If you were in Oriana's role and someone you put into an important job went over your head to me, would you want me intervening on behalf of your team member?"

Jermaine sees the logic but is still not happy. "What can I do to be more central to what we're doing here?"

"You think you're not central?" I let my response settle in for a moment. "You're the lynchpin of everything good that's going to happen here in the next million years. How is that not central?"

"Did you put Oriana up to moving me into this job?"

"No. I wouldn't do that, and if I had, I doubt she would have followed through, not understanding the logic of it."

"But you didn't question her decision."

"Actually, I did." I try to dispel his notion of what happened. "But when she explained her logic and her understanding of the importance that her best person needed to do this job, then I was supportive. Although all I did was not tell her it was a stupid idea, because it wasn't. She has responsibility to deliver results. She has to put people where they can deliver the greatest value to the company. She thought where you are is where you can have the greatest impact. Think about it. Your technical insights may have put White Rabbit on the shelves a month earlier. But where you are will put new capability on the shelves years and decades earlier. A thousand years from now who will be remembered more? You who have enabled our continued success or Shondra, who enabled a fork in the road that influenced product architecture for a generation?"

"That's easy. Shondra. We talk about the iPod changing corporate fortunes. People remember those who enabled that product. They don't talk about the person who put that team together."

"Name one." I challenge him.

"One what?"

"One person who was on that team."

Jermaine doesn't come up with a single name.

"Who put the team together?"

Jermaine shrugs.

"Steve Jobs. He put the team together."

"No, no. That doesn't work. That would be like saying you put the team together. You didn't. You were just in charge when it was put together."

"But Jobs decided who would put them together, just like Oriana decided you would put the teams together knowing that was the crucial decision."

Jermaine looks away, shakes his head. "Bottom line you're not going to do anything to help me."

"If you believe that then I have seriously misjudged your character." I push back.

Jermaine's shoulders drop, and he shakes his head. "How is it you always know exactly what to say that makes it impossible for me to blame you for anything?"

"Blame me for everything." I respond. "For you being at AppleCore, for you being our number one team leader, for you being promoted to deputy Senior Vice President."

"Wait, whoa. What was that about deputy Senior Vice President?"

"Didn't Oriana inform you when she promoted you?"

"I don't remember anything about a promotion."

"I signed the paperwork. Maybe you were just so unhappy you weren't listening."

"What are you telling me?"

"That you're Oriana's deputy. Clear line of succession. You should be taking advantage of that time with her to influence her, as well as that pay change. Didn't you notice that either?"

Jermaine is distracted, "My wife said something about it being more money than before, but I didn't really pay any attention to it."

"You're beginning to piss me off." I warn him I'm losing patience with his petulance.

Apparently, that got his attention. "I'm Oriana's deputy?"

"And if you get your head out of your ass and start really contributing to our success from where you are, not where you would rather be, you will be the next SVP of Software."

"She's not going anywhere."

"Neither was I." I point out. "Stop finding excuses and start finding solutions. I don't have time to make you feel better or intervene on your behalf. You want to go back to leading a team, then whoever takes your current job will be deputy to Oriana. Pick your poison and get on with life."

"You've certainly become a hard ass."

"Next time I see you, all I better be hearing is about how the teams you put together are enabling our success."

Jermaine shakes his head. I leave him standing in the hallway.

Five minutes later I'm in the lab with Muhammed and Oriana. "What can you tell me?"

Muhammed posts an image for my consideration. "A concentrator must be able to amplify the strength of the signal from all the disparate collection points. I think it best that it be distributed. That means there is no single concentrator. Instead, there is a dispersed capability that when aggregated results in a much stronger signal than from any one collection point."

"And how do you propose to do that?" I inquire.

"There are multiple ways. Our team was not of one mind as to which was the best, but we finally agreed that a simple module that attaches to the base of the Mad Hatter net is most likely to leverage the range, strength and redundancy of the system as a whole."

"Does it fit your architecture?"

"We're still looking at that." Muhammed responds. "We think the modifications will not affect any other parts of the deployed system. But we have not completed that verification."

"In summary you have an approach but are still verifying various aspects of the integrated system."

"That is a fair summary."

"When will you know for sure?"

"Few days. Two or three maybe if the stars align and the fatted lamb dies quietly."

I hesitate until I remember Oriana's introduction of his mixed Muslim and Hindu background. "The sooner the better, but no shortcuts. We need to get this right the first time." I respond.

I shake Muhammed's hand and turn away from the display screen. Oriana is at my side, "What do you think?" I ask.

"Muhammed is confident he can produce something."

"Do you have an alternative working?"

"Three actually." She proudly informs me. "Although none are superior to this approach. One might get to a verified state a day sooner."

"Ride them all hard. We need a solution before many more get through the transition. Retrofitting is much harder than original installation."

"Understood." Oriana glances over at an engineer who has his head down on his desk, lifting it up and dropping it as if hitting his head against a wall. "Excuse me." I watch as she approaches the young engineer. She touches his shoulder and he looks up, startled. She kneels down to be closer. They have a conversation I can't decipher. Oriana uses gestures that I also can't decipher. She gets up and retraces her steps with a reflective image on her face.

"What was that all about?" I have to ask.

"Transitioned last week. Said if he knew then what he knows now he never would have done it. Too much isn't defined. He's not sure what to expect. Just all too loosey goosey."

"That's Jermaine's fault. He was in charge last week." I point out.

"I had Jermaine working the paperwork last week. Not his fault he wasn't down here with the troops as they came back from Dallas."

I hear her culpability statement, but I don't hear how she's going to fix it. "So, what's next for him?"

"Counseling. We have a psychologist on retainer. Call her when we need something."

"Do I need to call Jermaine to find out what we're doing to prevent this happening again?"

Oriana shakes her head. "No need. You know Jermaine. Get past me once and it will never happen again."

"I know Jermaine and his record, but you have him outside his comfort zone. Are you effectively using him as your deputy? Consulting him on what you're doing, what you're deciding, on the new product strategies or are you just leaving him to his current task?"

"We talk," Is her response which tells me she recognizes she isn't using him to the best advantage and she hasn't done anything about it.

"When you look at my decisions can you see who provided input and where?" I push her.

"Sometimes."

LEVERAGE

When Bart Woodall asked Mindi to have me stop by to see him, it was all very vague. Is this another upgrade or what? As I step out of the Googlecar a horde of reporters swarm around me.

"Miss Washington, are you here for another upgrade? If so will you be able to fly?"

"Miss Washington, are you sleeping with Dr. Woodall?"

"Miss Washington, are you here to consult with the Doctor about the trial and what it could mean long term?"

"Dr. Washington. Is it true that AppleCore now owns the IP around immortality?" I look to see who asked that question but with so many crowding around me I can't tell.

"Miss Washington, what will you do if you lose the case and the court orders you to revert back to non-immortality?"

"Miss Washington. I understand Hollywood is going to make a movie of your life story. Will you play yourself? And if not, who would you want to play you?"

"Sage! Your fans would like a few words from you. What should they be doing to help you retain the rights you've fought so hard to win?"

I stop to make a simple statement, "No questions please. I can't answer them all particularly with a trial in progress. But let me say just one thing. I appreciate the support of those who understand my circumstance and wish to make this procedure available to all who need it. To those who oppose my very being, understand those things about me you oppose are not the reason I exist. They are a means to an end, which is the preservation of a threatened life. I'm sure if you were in my position you too would want the right to survive to be the result of medical expertise of a doctor rather than a court with no immediate stake in the outcome."

"Sage! Have you been following the testimony?"

"Sage! Have you given any thought to who comes next?"

"Sage! You're missing the larger picture. There are societal implications of this trial. Big implications."

"Sage! You can't just dismiss a court action. Everyone has a right to their day in court."

"Sage! Are you and Dr. Woodall getting married? There are rumors you're pregnant."

The doors to the clinic close behind me and the sea of questions closes and rolls away from me. Apparently, Dr. Woodall got a restraining order to keep them out of his clinic. A wise decision. I ride the elevator to the top floor where I find Dr. Woodall in a conference room overlooking the sea of reporters and media vehicles below. "Understand you wanted to chat."

Dr. Woodall looks back at me. He has been looking out the window. A monitor is on in a corner tuned to a station with a reporter in the square below. He has apparently heard my discussion with the assembled media. "Good statement. Measured, reasonable and focused."

"I notice you've never given one." I respond.

"Nor will I. I'm a doctor. I talk with patients not the media."

"That why you put me out front at the first press conference?"

Dr. Woodall nods, although I remember he did make a statement about his procedure. I guess the stakes have risen since then. "How are you feeling?"

"I don't feel anything." I remind him.

"Of course, you don't, but you have formed an opinion about the state of your condition. Is that positive or negative?"

"As you know from looking at the monitoring logs, everything is functioning within range. I should feel normal if there is such a thing for an immortal. If you're wondering how I'm reacting to the continual circus and the calls I should give up my new-found capabilities, never quite saying I should be put to death, knowing the court would not make that ruling, but could make it an outcome of having to give up my new body. Well, that's an interesting unanticipated circumstance."

Dr. Woodall turns back to look out the window. "What other unanticipated circumstances are you dealing with?"

"There are so many. Where do I begin?"

"A'zam for instance," Dr. Woodall suggests.

"Would take too long. You don't have enough hours left in the day for that discussion."

"Then his request to me and my team."

"Which is?"

"New software," Dr. Woodall doesn't sound happy about the request.

"Which does?"

"Inhibits charging."

"Why would he want software to do that?" I haven't heard of this request previously.

"I hoped you could give me a plausible reason to comply, knowing if I don't he will find someone else who will. It's not a complicated routine. In fact, I suspect he's already built it. And if that's the case then his sole purpose is to see what I do with the request. Do I talk to anyone about it or just simply deliver what he ordered? Am I trust worthy or will I lose the ability to produce any software for his patients?"

"That's only the next year." I point out.

"The carrot and stick. He's already presented me with an extension. Exclusivity for an additional four years with incentive clauses for ramping up production."

"Sounds like he intends to make you a very rich man."

"Or insure that none of his competitors can have even one immortal on their staff for five years. An eternity in the immortals world as you well know."

"And the recharge inhibitor would make it impossible for anyone to challenge his authority."

"Apparently you made mention of that vulnerability to him or someone he talks with regularly."

I remember doing so, "Guilty."

"He is systematically closing every avenue of attack upon his supremacy."

I shake my head in disgust that I gave him one more avenue to attack me. "How do I prevent this software from killing me if he wants to?"

"Push of a button." Dr. Woodall responds. "If he pushes this software there is nothing you can do to stop it other than to block all updates before he sends it. That would be less than a week."

"At that point I am me for all eternity. Immortals advance I won't."

Dr. Woodall nods. "As far as I can tell."

"If I block the over the air updates, can you still do manual ones here in your lab?"

"Yes, but once it's embedded in the core software code you're asking for trouble with a non-standard configuration. Most likely he will have his developers write in conditional execution files that require it to do the next task."

"I'm surprised as a doctor you have that level of software understanding. That's my area of expertise."

Dr. Woodall blushes, "I'm a geek. I'll admit it. I want to know what I'm doing to people before I do it. And I spent a long time with my developers to understand the range of implications, so I didn't just go blindly where no man has gone before."

"Nice parody of Star Trek." I respond.

"You know how it is. Weren't you into all that when you were a kid?"

"I was," I admit. "Probably the reason I am what I am."

Dr. Woodall smiles in remembrance of better times, when the world wasn't attacking his life's work. "So, I have to propose to do A'zam's software. Can you give me one ray of hope to be able to comply without giving him a lethal tool? To make him the sole arbiter of who lives and who dies amongst the immortals?"

"Write your code and send it to me this time. I'll look at it and see if I can find a means of defeating the functionality once it's pushed. He's just making this harder and harder." I muse.

"Wearing us down. A war of attrition. At some point we will

conclude it just isn't worth all the work to try to stay a step ahead and then he wins."

"He thinks he already has." I suggest.

"What makes him think that?"

"He already has his controls in every immortal except him and me and he doesn't know about me."

"As far as you know." Dr. Woodall reminds me I probably shouldn't assume as much as I am.

"You're right. He may have figured that out or overwritten it with an update I wasn't aware of." I acknowledge, but then another thought hits me. "From an architecture point of view, he's now asked you for just two features. Simple code basically in both instances. Code he could have easily written himself, except you have to push it in your updates. What do you make of two disparate control features in your basic control platform?"

"Really haven't given it much thought." Dr. Woodall responds. "Should I have?"

I play through scenarios in my head. "Do you know his functionality is in the code you've been loading in the new immortals?"

"I assume it is." Dr. Woodall responds.

"But you haven't checked it."

Dr. Woodall shakes his head.

"Have one of your people do a thorough review of the code you're loading. Do a file compare and see what's original, what your updates are and what has come from A'zam, since nothing has come from AppleCore."

Dr. Woodall touches a button on the conference table. "Harry

Porter. This is Woodall. Do a file compare of the current software configuration and the Life Extension Clinic baseline. I want to know what's different, if anything, and what specific functionality is affected and how." Dr. Woodall looks up to me. "Harry is probably the brightest doc on my team. He transitioned so it shouldn't take him long to get back with an answer."

"How are you holding up through the circus?" I ask noting he has big circles under his eyes I'd not noticed before and his hair is not as neat as usual.

"I spend way too much time with lawyers, and as you know they aren't exactly my favorite people to have idle chats with. Richardson just drives me crazy. He's so precise and so rigid. He looks for nuance in words I never would have paid any attention to. And yet he has an excellent record in trial. I don't understand that world. I could never make a living parsing words and seeking out obscure meanings upon which to hang a legal argument. There's too much at stake. If the lawyer loses all he loses is his fees. And in most instances not even that. While the party to the suit may lose everything including professional licenses. If the court chose it could take my medical license and I'd never be able to practice ever again. That just doesn't seem right."

I decide I have to distract him from his morose condition. "Let me ask you a question I don't expect to be the outcome, but as you've gone to extremes in your thinking this through, I probably need to do the same. What if the court determines that transitions aren't to be permitted? Should the court decide all who have transitioned must go back, how could we do that given most of the bodies have been cremated?"

Dr. Woodall frowns. "That can't be an outcome. Medically you have nowhere to go. You have no host other than a mechanical one. I just don't see the court going there."

"But it is possible, so let's talk about an alternative. A'zam wants inhibitors and charging blockers. Why couldn't you insert code that simply doesn't permit charging after a certain number of years? A hundred, two hundred. It doesn't matter. But if you were to do that it would take the immortality issue off the table."

"It would, but it's a remnant of a biological system that has no bearing on the new host system. There is no reason to do that."

"Other than to appease groups that will never be satisfied." I point out.

"There's that. If you're asking is it feasible? Absolutely. Is it moral? I think questionable at best. Is it something I would volunteer to do? Absolutely not."

"The problem is that once the court rules, you won't be given a chance to propose an alternative. I'm not saying you should instruct Richardson to offer it, but it might be something that you work into the testimony if things look bad. Just as a way of giving the court an option they may not consider otherwise."

"I'm not good at maneuvering in courts. If you want to talk with Richardson about it be my guest, but I'm certainly not going to propose or even bring it up."

I go back to an unanswered question. "Are you going to sign A'zam's extension?"

Dr. Woodall glances at me, apparently hoping he'd escaped having to discuss that further. "I don't know. It would certainly solve some big issues I have to deal with. But it also pushes back the time when I'll be able to help the patients this procedure was developed for. I've already told him there would have to be some provision to permit me to either treat life threatening circumstances at the new clinic or set up a separate one where I can train new docs in the procedure and work the thousands of terminally ill patients who have already submitted their paperwork. I never should have signed the exclusive agreement even for the first year. I've been looking at some of the cases we can't handle. It breaks my heart. If you were to come to me today as you were six months ago, I couldn't take you for ten months. You wouldn't have made it ten months."

"Then why would you even consider it?" I have to ask.

"He has my entire supply chain under contract. He can set the prices of components and subassemblies. He controls their R&D budgets. He can set delivery schedules. I'm totally at his mercy. And if I don't sign he can basically shut me down and deliver my bodies to any other physician who thinks they can perform this procedure. It would just be a disaster."

"He? Are you talking about A'zam or AppleCore?" I wonder aloud.

"What's the difference?" Dr. Woodall seems surprised by my question.

"The amount of leverage that can be brought to bear."

TAPPING IN

In my office I call the Mayor of Cupertino on my cell phone remembering A'zam is monitoring my office phone calls. "Jackson, Sage."

"Didn't think I'd be hearing from you anytime soon after our last attempt to get together didn't work out."

I decide to cut through all the clutter. "I'm calling to ask if you have a rapid prototyping capability."

"So, this isn't an official call as Mayor?"

"Nor an invitation to visit me at my condo because I won't be going home. But I need a favor and I need it tonight."

"I could extend an invitation to my place if that would make it easier for you."

"Would be harder because then the media would have one more data point about my loose character. I'm going to send over prints for something I need one prototype of to see if it will do what I need it to do. If it won't then there would be no further on orders, but if it does, it could become a significant part of your business going forward."

"Is this for AppleCore or New Visions?" The question stops me right there. So A'zam has another company called New Visions. I have to recover quickly.

"AppleCore."

"Well the work A'zam is sending through New Visions is eating up most of my capacity at the moment, although he won't give me more than a week of firm orders. Says there are a number of things in play that could interrupt his deploying the parts in his new project."

Is he retrofitting all of the AppleCore immortals? To do what? What's he up to? "I'm looking for one part. If it's a problem for you I'd be happy to bring my files over and run it on your machines."

"You have to have the same machines I do at AppleCore. Why don't you have one of your employees do it for you?" Jackson seems confused.

"The same reason A'zam isn't having his parts made here."

"He said it's a capacity issue." Although Jackson is now getting the sense he may not have been told the whole story.

"I'm sorry I asked." I change my approach. "I'll get it made somewhere else."

"No, no! Don't hang up on me." Jackson is almost in a panic. "I've been waiting a week or more to talk with you again and now that I have you on the line I'm not going to let you get away. Send your files to me and I'll hand make it myself. If you want to come visit with me at the shop while I do that I would be grateful for the company. If not could I bring it over to your condo later? Say ten?"

"Unfortunately, as I said I'll not be going home tonight. I don't most nights now."

"You living with someone?" Jackson leaps to the usual explanation for such a circumstance.

"No. If I go home the media is waiting for me and I can't get into a protracted discussion when we're in the middle of a hearing on whether people like me should be outlawed."

"People like you..." Jackson is acting like he's confused.

"Have you forgotten I'm an immortal?"

"Oh, the trial. I thought something else was going on. I thought the trial involves the doctor who transitioned you. Are you involved in that?"

"You apparently haven't been watching the news. Yes, I am involved and AppleCore is a party to the defense in the suit. Since I'm exhibit A, everyone wants to better understand how a whole bunch of people like me might threaten individual civil liberties."

"I'm not following that logic, but maybe that's why I turn metal parts and try to keep the garbage picked up in the city."

"Whatever. I can't go home because they're there every night waiting for me with a thousand questions I don't have the time to answer and if I did my answers would be misconstrued by those who want fifteen minutes of fame at the hearing."

"You sound a little jaded. You need to relax. How about a hotel? I know a discrete one…"

"Yeah, I probably do need to relax, thanks for the offer, but no, I can't go there right now. If I get you the drawings in the next hour when could you have the part ready for me?"

"I take it the prototype has to be metal?" Jackson asks.

"Yes."

"Depends on how big."

"The size of six quarter dollars stacked one on top of the other." I quickly visualize.

"Give me three hours. How do I get it to you?"

"I'll come to your shop." I'm already working the logistics in my mind.

"I'm waiting for your file."

"Thanks Jackson. Lot going on right now and I'll try to make it up to you. And I'd appreciate it if you don't mention anything about this to A'zam or any of his people you might be dealing with."

"No other people. Just the man himself. I'm surprised he's working the details like he is. Almost seems like he doesn't trust anyone on this project. Even his contracts lady has no idea what I'm making as she sent over a frame agreement with the terms and conditions and each schedule calls for a part by number only. No drawings attached to the schedule. Just a part number, quantity, price and delivery date and location. Strangest thing I've ever seen."

"She's on loan just for this project. She's really one of our best contracts people."

"You know who I'm talking about then. She keeps asking me about the parts but A'zam made it clear I'm not to provide any details to anyone else in the company including you."

Great. "And that didn't seem strange to you?" I have to ask.

"Well, this conversation has confirmed my concerns that the left hand doesn't know what the right hand is doing over there. Only it seems to be by design. I suppose you have a good reason for it."

"I'll be in your shop in about four hours. I have to get a file ready for you."

I set my cell phone down. I close the door to my office and begin the drawings in my mind. No AppleCore machines involved in this part. Got to keep it out of A'zam's reach.

An hour later after a series of calls to Dr. Woodall's office, I send the file to Jackson's personal e-address. Within minutes I get a call back from him on my cell, thank goodness. "This what I think it is?"

"What do you think it is?"

"An antenna, tuner and energizer. It's very close to another part I'm making, also in limited quantities."

Apparently A'zam has hit on the same solution to communicating directly with immortals, only he's using it to send control messages to them and I'm trying to establish two-way communications with both immortals and mortals using White Rabbit and Mad Hatter. I'll have to figure out a way to take advantage of his approach, but after I get Jackson building my prototype. "I can't confirm anything for you at the moment, but are there any of the others in your shop that just might be laying around when I get there?"

"You come earlier, probably since they're in a production run right now. You come later my team will have gone home and probably locked them up for the night."

"That part of your contract?" I inquire suspecting it is not part of the standard terms and conditions. Only processors require that kind of special handling.

"No, but it was a request A'zam made. Said the parts are proprietary."

"And since I'm paying for them it shouldn't be a problem for me to see them," I assert hoping he will accept it.

"Then come earlier."

"See you in a bit."

I step out in the hall and walk down to the lab. On the way I call Jordy at Dr. Woodall's office.

"Can you meet me at Precision Machining on the south side in about three hours? Will need you to insert a new part on my spine. Yes? Great, see you then."

Next is Oriana. I walk into her office where she is meeting with her team in the small conference room. I wave at her through the glass wall and she comes out.

"What do you need?" she asks immediately.

"I need you to bring Jermaine and meet me at Precision Machining over on the south side in three hours."

"Why? What's up?'

"We're going to find out if mankind can preserve itself or not." I announce.

"What? I don't understand."

"Just bring Jermaine and be there in three hours." I don't have time to explain it all now.

"Where is this place?"

"I'll send you a text with the address," and I leave her to return to her meeting.

About two and a half hours later I walk into Jackson's shop, ask where I would find him and the machinist who stops me points down the hall. "He's in the work area to the right." I follow directions and just before I make the right turn I see the components on a tray to my left. I move closer to inspect them, without touching. Exactly what I thought. Antenna, tuner and energizer. Apparently A'zam hasn't considered the need to use this mechanism for automated communications since the individual is already receiving internet service. I let my processor measure and store the dimensions and visible characteristics of A'zam's device. My processor compares to my design and it is extremely close.

"That you Sage?" I hear Jackson's voice.

Rather than respond I simply walk into the prototyping area. Jackson is dressed in blue jeans and a shop apron. He is wearing safety glasses and steel toed shoes. That reminds me I am in a machine shop. He is watching the 3D printer forming my part according to my specification directly from the code files that drive his machine. No human intervention between the file and the part so it will be exact. Even though the build-up is going on behind a glass window, Jackson still needs to be dressed appropriately. I am not, so I can't get too close. This reminds me of the days I used to go down to the shop floor at AppleCore with Rocky. I loved the burning smell of the turning metal, the lubricating oils and smoky haze in the air. Not now. With this process none of those are required. The powdered metal is melted and injected into a mold cut by a laser to the exact dimensions. When the metal cools it is a solid piece ready to be installed.

Jackson looks around, comes up next to me and gives me a bump with his hips. "Thanks for sending this my way."

"I'm sorry I've not been responsive to you," I remember I have to recognize my behavior has not been what he wants.

"You were very responsive the last time."

"I don't mean that."

"Apology accepted, but you have no more excuses. We are going to have an evening alone even if it has to be in your office."

"I could have Mindy bring in an Inn and Out Burger for you."

"Animal style?"

"However you'd like it."

I see the printer shut down. "Is it ready?"

"Needs to cool for a bit and then it will be."

Jordy arrives, I approach him and have a quick conversation about what I need him to do. Dr. Woodall arrives a moment later. "Didn't expect you to come out," I acknowledge him.

"When Jordy advised me of your request I thought I needed to see what's going on."

"Dr. Woodall, this is Jackson, your Mayor and owner of this shop. He's just fabricated a device I need Jordy to install in me." They shake hands.

"You've become your own test bed?" Dr. Woodall asks, but I don't respond.

Oriana and Jermaine arrive next.

"This is Oriana, our SVP of software development and Jermaine, her deputy and our most innovative technologist." I see the introduction pleases Jermaine. "Did Landon take the red pill?" I ask Oriana,

She nods, "About two hours ago, should be deployed by now."

"Jackson would you give the part to Jordy?" I turn to Jordy as he receives the part. "You need to insert it to clamp onto my spine at the base of my skull. It should turn my spinal column into an ultra-high frequency antenna."

"What are you trying to accomplish?" Dr. Woodall wants to know.

I don't answer but rather turn my back to Jordy, who accesses my spinal column, clamps the device into place, connects it to the power supply, tunes the antenna to the frequency I'd given him and reseals me.

"That's freaky.' Jackson remarks. "Never seen anything like it."

"Oriana, would you retrieve one of the devices on that tray across the hall and give it to Jordy?"

She does and when Jordy has it, I continue, "Would you insert this unit into Jermaine at the same point as where you inserted mine? Same frequency."

Jordy does as I ask although Dr. Woodall is still waiting for his answer.

I close my eyes and concentrate on an image I'd once seen with a slight modification, as if I am seeing it live.

Jermaine looks at me hoping I will give him some clue as to what he is supposed to do, but I keep my eyes closed. I concentrate, open to any signal, image, something that might be an indication I should do something or not.

Jermaine asks me, "Anything?"

I shake my head with my eyes still closed. Nothing. I open my eyes and look at Jordy. "Are you sure you set it to the right frequency?"

Jordy responds. "Both of you are set at exactly the frequency you asked for. About the only thing I can suggest is that maybe you need to run a series of experiments in the lab to see if there is another frequency that delivers what you're looking for."

"Think of a situation, Jermaine." I suggest instead. "Don't tell us what it is. Let me see if you pick up a response."

Jermaine closes his eyes. He concentrates just as I did. I can see him straining to hear something. No matter how faint or distant. Something in response to his conjured image.

"Anything?" Oriana asks.

Jermaine shake his head, but keeps his eyes closed. Continues to concentrate, hoping, wishing even. But still nothing.

"Can you give me an explanation now?" Dr. Woodall asks.

"We're trying to tap into the collective unconscious." I inform him totally mystified as to why it hasn't worked.

CASH

I'm walking back to AppleCore with Jackson, who is going on to his office at the City, but offered to accompany me. One way to have some alone time.

"I'm still not sure I understand what I just witnessed," he confides.

"I'm not either, so that makes two of us," I respond knowing he wants to talk about other things but is curious about what he's getting into with A'zam and now this demonstration that makes no sense to him.

"You have to have more insight than I do." Jackson protests. He's not about to let me off the hook that easily.

"Some people think we have deeply embedded experiences that guide our behavior unconsciously. Experiences that we had thousands of years ago as a species that helped us survive the perils of that time."

"I'm a machine shop kind of guy. Hand me a block of metal and a specification and I'll cut you a figure of angels dancing on the head of a pin. Unconscious stuff? That's a bit beyond my normal everyday conversations. But you're an engineer. So why are you so knowledgeable about the unconscious? I thought that was for psychiatrists or the clergy guys."

I smile as Jackson's description of himself. He is definitely not a machine shop kind of guy. If he were he'd not be mayor and running a very successful business from all appearances. The fact that AppleCore is using him, A'zam is using him for a key part and I am using him indicates he's able to inspire confidence. From all appearances his shop does excellent work. In fact I'm now carrying around a part he made just for me. "You're a public official," I decide to try a different way of helping him understand what I'm up to. "You ask the people every few years to select representatives to decide on matters of collective concern."

"Every four years for Mayor."

"So, for four years the people delegate their authority to make decisions on their behalf to you."

"They do."

"But during the colonial times we had town meetings where everyone came out to discuss and make decisions on those things that were of collective concern."

"I remember it like it was yesterday," Jackson laughs.

"What if…" and I hesitate to set this up. "What if we went back to the style of governance where everyone has a say on every issue of collective concern?"

"Only a few would show up. Most people just don't have the time or the interest."

"But what if…they didn't have to participate consciously?"

"You mean your unconscious self would go to the meetings and you'd just be there on your cell phone texting your stockbroker or boyfriend or class mate?"

"No, but you're not far off." I try to help him understand. "Think of it this way. You decide you're going to rob a liquor store."

"Not like me, but whatever."

"And everyone else who lives in Cupertino is suddenly pulsed with your intention. They're not aware of it, but their unconscious is." I'm trying to keep this close to home and simple. "The unconscious then pulses you back saying 'Don't.' And we're not talking just one person in Cupertino, but everyone who lives here. They aren't aware of who you are or what your intention is. They're not even aware they are reacting to your intention. But all at once you get this pulse from thousands of people saying 'Don't.' What do you do?"

"I think about it long and hard. If everyone is telling me don't. That's a pretty strong indicator I shouldn't do it."

"But what if you don't know who is reacting to you?" He's getting the concept, but not entirely. "It's just an impulse you get? But it's a strong impulse. Does that tell you what you should or shouldn't do? Does that give you permission to do something someone else may have told you not to?"

"Like my father or mother?"

"Something like that," I judge is close enough.

"Priest, maybe?"

"Something like that."

"If the person who told me to do something was someone that is important to me, like my father, then I'd probably have to listen to him regardless of this impulse." Jackson responds. "That is unless I know the impulse is from everyone else who lives here. That may make me think about it differently. Make me question why my father wanted me to do something everyone else here is against."

"In a nutshell, that's what I was hoping you would say. Apparently, I'm not as close to a working solution as I hoped. Not sure I'm even going in the right direction." I try to finish the explanation.

"You don't know?"

I shake my head. "I was hoping for an indication. An impulse. From two people. I didn't know if it would be one impulse or more than one. And if more than one I was going to have to figure out if maybe it was just an echo of the first impulse. I still have a lot of work ahead of me to prove the concept works. At the moment it doesn't appear to."

Jackson stops me. "You're on the right track."

"You're an optimist." I suddenly realize.

"Have to be to either own a machine shop or be a politician these days. If I were a realist I probably wouldn't be either." He leans forward and kisses me. A long and languorous kiss. He's telling me he is an optimist. I eventually end the kiss realizing there may be media types around and that would be a wonderful image any one of them would love to put out for the consumption of all who pay them for the inside story.

And then I get a ring on my phone. My personal cell. I pull it out to find it's Dietrich. "Excuse me. A work call."

Jackson frowns, but steps away to give me space, if not privacy.

"Yes?"

Dietrich sounds weary. "You know that little investigation you wanted me to conduct?"

"Yes."

"Well, I'm sitting in Petra's office. She's been doing a little investigation of her own at my request."

"And?"

"Smoking gun."

"I'm ten minutes away. Wait there." I disconnect and put the phone away.

"Why do you still use one of those? Haven't you figured out how to build one in?"

I have but don't tell him that. "I have to go."

"I know." Jackson sounds disappointed. Apparently was hoping to get me to detour. No such luck. "All your conversations so detailed and descriptive?"

"What?"

"'Yes, yes, and?' Not exactly the kind of discussions I usually have with my teams, at the company or the city."

"I'm sorry." I hesitate, wondering how to explain this one. "That wasn't deliberate to exclude you. It was just the most appropriate response to the news I got."

"Not good?"

"Just one more thing to deal with. AppleCore business. I already know what I have to do, but I need to get the details before I do anything."

"So, I need one detail. An evening alone with you where AppleCore business doesn't interrupt us as it has every time I've had even a moment with you."

This time I kiss him, a hurried kiss, but hopefully he understands. And I'm walking fast towards AppleCore. The guard sees me coming, opens the door and herds me in, following behind. I touch his arm to thank him and he smiles at me. I'm glad Mrs. Walker reminded me that people like to be touched.

Up the stairs, down the hall and I'm standing in Petra's office door. Dietrich and Petra are looking at a monitor in deep conversation. They look up when they hear me arrive. "That was quick." Petra remarks.

"I was just up the street, on my way back here, in fact."

"There's a problem," Petra begins. If you remember I told you I thought A'zam may have been doing something... not necessarily illegal, but at least outside the corporate charter."

"I remember."

"Well, I was right, but I wasn't completely right." Petra shakes her head and changes the image for me to see. "A'zam set up a dummy corporation, entered them into the vendor system and wrote purchase orders for them from our systems. He then sent invoices to fund his dummy corporation."

"How did you figure this out?"

Dietrich responds, "I checked his name against corporate filings. The curious thing is there are none. But I found a tax ID for a company in his name and traced it down from there."

"So, you gave that name to Petra who checked in our systems and there it is," I suggest to show I'm listening.

"New Vision. That's the name of the company," Petra answers.

Bingo. Same name as the one Jackson gave me for A'zam's company. "How much has he laundered through this company?" I ask.

"A lot. And I'm sure I haven't found them all just yet," Petra is clearly unhappy.

"Can't you just do a search under that name?" I'm confused as to why she doesn't think she's found all the money.

"I did, got that number. But if he set up one dummy corporation, there could easily be more," Petra confirms.

"Wouldn't Dietrich's search have brought up those names as well?" I'm still lost.

"Not necessarily." Dietrich responds. "They could have been set up under someone else's name. If the company isn't registered, he could have used any name."

"Is he trying to go into competition with us?" Petra asks me.

"I don't know." I answer thinking about her question. "It doesn't make sense to me. He can buy anything he wants through AppleCore. Why set up a dummy corporation that isn't even registered to do it?"

"Could it be he wants to capture all the profits for himself? Lots of CEOs have done similar things. Set up companies to own the real estate the company leases from him. He gets the equity growth in the building but doesn't have to pay taxes on it until he sells it, usually to the corporation."

"If this were just another version of the same thing, why should we be concerned?" I have to ask.

"Because we are a major public corporation and subject to Securities and Exchange Commission regulations. He's violated a bunch of them from what I can see," Petra answers my question.

"Do we have any idea what he's using the money for?" I doubt it, but maybe Petra has some means of finding that out.

"Entering into contracts of some sort." She suggests apparently not having anything firm. "Probably buying components to build something, or hiring people to do so, or deliver some kind of services. Maybe even marketing, although I've not seen anything where New Vision has been marketing a product. Could be they're doing the marketing research or something preliminary that just hasn't hit the street as yet."

I nod in understanding. "Smoking gun that he's misappropriated corporate assets. Diverted them through a dummy corporation. Doing something that is off the corporate books and records. And we're talking big dollars."

Dietrich grimaces an agreement. "We have verified that much. I fear there is more we haven't seen as yet. If A'zam was willing to go to all this trouble and not bring any of us into it, whatever we haven't seen can't be any better."

"What kind of action are we subject to from SEC and whoever else?" I ask Dietrich.

"Minimum, if we have a good explanation, heavy fine. Possible removal of A'zam from office and maybe the three of us."

"Even though we are the ones who discovered it?" I wonder aloud.

"SEC would say we have inadequate controls and would hit us under Sarbanes-Oxley as not ensuring the accuracy of the books and records of the corporation such that investors could put reliance in them." Petra recites as if she'd memorized it.

"Remember that certification you sign once a year? It makes you personally responsible." Dietrich points out.

"You're saying we can't simply blow the whistle and have their auditors do the dirty work." I realize one option is off the table.

"We have to address this. Take the actions we would expect them to if they had discovered it. And we have to do it quickly." Dietrich informs both of us.

"I understand." This is not going to be pretty and A'zam is going to skewer me no matter how I handle it. "How much more investigation do you need to do before we take action?"

"The first thing you need to do is inform the Chairman of the governance committee of the board. She will have to keep it to herself until we present the full report. But you have to do that today. We have enough evidence to warrant a full investigation and you also need to put that in writing today."

"What good news do you have for me?" I ask hoping to at least walk out of here with something positive to think about.

"Our cash position is the best it's ever been." Petra informs us.

"White Rabbit?" I assume since it set first day sales records.

"Don't you check sales figures?" Dietrich asks. "Mad Hatter broke the first day sales of White Rabbit. Back to back record setting sales of industry leading products. Not a bad few weeks."

AN INTERESTING WEEK

The Night Club has our regular table waiting as we arrive. Reese is at the bar already. Must have been a bad week. Delilah is talking with someone she knows that I don't. But that's not unusual since we generally don't travel in the same circles for work. MC is in the lobby on her phone talking one of her patients down from something. Windy is walking towards the table from the ladies room. Apparently, she got here early enough that she wanted to powder her nose first. I walk up to her and exchange our usual hug before taking our usual seats.

"Let's screw with them," I suggest. "You sit in MC's seat and…" I glance at Reese at the bar. "I'll sit in Reese's."

Windy's eyes get big as she breaks into a broad smile, slides into MC's usual seat. Reese looks over and I give a big wave, so she sees we're here. She finishes her drink, which appears to be hard liquor, something I don't think I've ever seen her consume. She's a dyed in the wool red wine drinker. The redder the wine the better. Must be her West Texas upbringing or something.

The waiter brings our usual opening round, but looks at us, confused as to where she should put the drinks down, apparently not knowing where anyone is going to sit tonight. I help her out, "Red wine there, white there and the scotch and water there." She knows what Windy and I drink so she put them down first.

Reese is the first to arrive, looks confused but finally identifies her wine, comes for hugs from both of us and sits herself down behind her wine. She takes a sip first thing. Must have been a hell of a week. "What's going on? We letting work get in the way of gossip?" Reese wants to know.

"I think MC is talking her dog down off a window ledge," I begin. "And Delilah is apparently making plans for later after we're done skewering friends and family."

"I understand A'zam called her up." Reese looks around to see who Delilah is talking with. "Told him she was busy with a sensitive type who has a bigger dick."

"Did she really?" Windy can't believe it, probably because A'zam must have a bigger dick than her husband Tom. What was it she said, 'Filled me up and carried me over?' And that was before he got his inflatable play toy that automatically inflates to fill the welcoming cavity.

MC is walking about two hundred miles an hour, comes around for perfunctory hugs, probably only because it's the tradition, and goes right for her scotch and water. Why is it psychologists always seem to be the ones who can consume just ungodly amounts of alcohol and never show any signs? MC looks at Windy in her seat, shrugs and sits down. "You all having a wonderful day too?"

"Hell of a day." Reese responds but doesn't give any details.

"I'm having my period, so yes, it's a good day," Windy offers.

"I got another glimpse into the soul of the one man we all love, literally, with the exception of Reese." I respond eager to hear about Delilah's conversation with the man.

"Are you going to share?" MC asks before taking another sip.

"Only if you share what's going on with you." I toss back.

"We going to wait for Delilah?" MC asks. "That's the tradition. We can't say anything bad about anyone unless we're all here."

The guy Delilah has been talking with rises... to his full height of six foot something north of eight inches, leans over and gives her a hug and then a departing kiss, which shows he's not her cousin. She has a big smile on all the way over to the table. Apparently still enjoying that hug, or maybe it was the kiss, I don't really know, she exchanges hugs with each of us before realizing MC is in her seat and everyone else is out of place. She sees her white wine at the open seat and frowns before settling in behind her glass. Contrary to the established pattern of the evening, she doesn't drain half of it before asking her first question. "I got something to look forward to tonight. How about the rest of you?"

Windy asks, "Who's leaving here for A'zam's place?"

No one answers, which tells me it must be Petra's night, but of course they don't know about her.

"Does that mean he's dumped all of us already?" Windy follows up her question.

Reese doesn't let that one go by, "I understand Delilah dumped him."

"Who told you that?" Delilah wants to know. "I didn't. In fact, I didn't tell anyone."

Reese doesn't answer the question which makes me wonder where did she hear that little tidbit since Delilah isn't denying it. "Well? Did you?"

"Nothing to dump." Delilah responds as if it were no big deal. "He called, but I didn't go, if that's what you mean."

"Heard it was a little more… direct?" Reese continues.

"Well… you know. I wasn't up for another night of him fulfilling his dreams while I'm kind of left hanging out there. No big attraction. I certainly wasn't going to change my plans for the evening just for him."

"What were your plans?" MC is glancing back at the guy she'd been talking with.

"Not him." Delilah picks up on the glances. "He's dessert tonight."

"So, he's bigger than A'zam?" Windy asks, probably unable to contain her curiosity.

"Hell yes," Delilah smiles broadly. "I'm not lowering my standards just because the guy's rich and all that."

"What are your standards?" MC is curious. I'm actually surprised we haven't had this conversation before.

"Size matters," Delilah begins. "But he better be into me and not himself. Happy to have him enjoy me, but it's got to be a slow and patient mutual affair. You know? He's got to satisfy me or there's no reason to try it again. That's kind of where I am with A'zam. It wasn't mutual, he wasn't patient, and I wasn't a satisfied customer, no offense Sage. I know you wrote his software, but frankly it sucks."

"Only because you didn't, probably," Reese teases her.

"No, I didn't." Delilah responds with an emphasis on didn't.

"I would have," Windy volunteers. "But then I don't have dessert coming."

"Be my guest," Delilah nods towards Mr. Tall. "See if you can get him to change his plans."

Windy picks up her white wine and inhales the bouquet before answering. "I've never been into competition for a guy. If he can't see what I have to offer, I don't want to chase after him to try to convince him of what he's missing."

"Glad to see you've learned from your investment in Tom." MC responds as she lifts her scotch and water to polish it off.

"Touché," Windy raises her wine to MC.

"So, what are you going to do? Chase after A'zam?" MC

continues. Glad to see her in her therapeutic frame of mind tonight. That always makes the evening interesting.

"I figure since I was the first, he'll come back when he's tired of all of you because he'll want something that lasts."

"He's going to live a million years." I point out. "How you going to keep up?" I'm giving her an opportunity to tell the others of her request.

She looks at me sternly, as if she wished I'd not brought it up, but we don't keep secrets in this group and the others have a right to know about that and MC's request.

"I have a plan. But it's up to Sage whether it happens."

MC sits up, "You want to transition too?"

"And my kids. That's part of the deal. I want them to be with me."

"Do they have any idea what that means?" Reese, the earth mother asks immediately. "I don't want to rush my kids through their childhoods."

"What I want isn't what you all want." Windy observes. "I want, no I need to be successful in something in my life. I screwed up out of the gate. Transitioning gives me a leg up on all those who will after me. I'll be able to get entrenched somewhere. Be important. Responsible. You know? It will be harder for those who come after me. Fewer opportunities. Harder to establish themselves. And that's why I want my kids coming over now. Get in ahead of everyone else."

"You make it sound like all those people who were hovering over their devices to order the Mad Hatter when it went on sale." Reese notes. "People aren't appliances, or platforms or whatever it is you're calling your latest product Sage."

"No, we aren't." Windy concedes. "But we are looking at the most fundamental transformation of our society probably since Homo sapiens displaced the Neanderthals."

"You don't really believe that?" Delilah chimes in. "Sage, I love you honey, but you're not transforming anything. And neither is that boss of yours. He's not as good as he thinks he is. I know. And I'm the only one here with enough experience in that department to be an expert."

"Are you suggesting you don't think Windy and her kids should transition?" MC asks, saving me the need to do so.

"That's exactly what I'm suggesting." Delilah looks directly at Windy. "The worst thing you could do is change your kids into something they never wanted to be. You and they will regret it for the rest of your lives. And if you really are immortals, well, that could be a while."

"What about me?" MC asks Delilah. "Should I transition? I don't have a husband or kids. It's just me. If I wanted to transition because I think I can help all those who do, isn't that a good enough reason?"

Delilah frowns. "You too? What the hell is this? Has everyone suddenly got a God complex or something?" She nods to me. "Sage I can kind of understand. Not completely. But she never wanted anything but to not die. And she got all this other baggage that came with that. Not to say it's not all been bad, but she's stuck with A'zam now. Probably for a million years or something. I wouldn't want to be in her position for all the gold in the universe. But you? I hear what you're saying about being able to help those who transition. But why would you have to in order to help them? There's got to be another reason."

"So, if that was my only reason you wouldn't do it." MC confirms.

"I wouldn't but I'm not the one selling out to the man." Delilah responds and looks to me.

"I'm not selling out." MC responds sharply.

"Sage was the first of us to sell out. It's taking the rest of us a little longer." Delilah looks directly at me not angry, not with a superior attitude or anything. Almost like she feels sorry for me.

"Why you saying I sold out?" I respond, not sure I'm following her analysis.

"You went to work for a corporation right out of college. I remember all those parties when we were undergrads where you'd get drunk and rail on and on about how you were never going to let yourself spend your whole life putting your genius into what someone else sold and made a mint off of. You'd always say AppleCore was using Rocky up and someday they were going to throw him away without so much as a thank you."

"There's making a living and there's selling out." I respond.

"You sold out." Delilah responds. "You were a janitor just selling hours to make a living that's one thing. But you were giving them your creativity. You helped change our world. How we communicate, what we talk about, set an expectation that the future is right around the corner if we are just patient. That was you, but you didn't do it for you. You did it for the man. The corporation. AppleCore. The very same company that was using Rocky."

"But look where I am? I can do so much for so many where I am. My impact would have been near zero if I'd been a clerk at Wal-Mart or Costco. Or a teacher even. Sure, I could have inspired kids to be more, but I inspire people with the products I'm able to provide to change their lives, do more than they ever could have foreseen. And not just a few thousand over my lifetime, but billions around the world. How is that selling out?"

"My, aren't you full of yourself tonight." Delilah shoots back, and she's right. I drop my head realizing I'm congratulating myself for achieving things that were important to me and extrapolating that the rest of the world appreciates it.

"I'm sorry." I admit. "I've been having a hell of a week. I can't talk about what's going on, but it will be consequential for all of us and people we don't even know."

"C'mon Sage." Reese chimes in. "We've had some interesting weeks too. So, don't think we give a shit about what you're doing for the rest of the world."

"Other than Delilah, who's going out for dessert later, Windy who's hoping I can help her and her kids transition, and MC who is hoping the same, what's going on?"

"I have a patient who's out on a ledge as we speak." MC offers. "But it's no big deal. He's out there every Thursday night about this time. He's supposed to call me when he decides to go back inside. That's our deal. If he decides he's really going to jump, then he's supposed to call the fire department because they will have to scrape up his remains."

"Is this gallows humor or something?" Windy asks.

"No. He decided hanging would take too long. And besides he's on the window ledge of his bedroom and he owns a one-story house. So, I'm not too worried."

"You want to give up patients like that for patients like Sage?" Delilah asks almost seriously.

"I know. But I need to stretch myself. I've been cruising for a while now and really need a challenge to grow again." MC winks at me with a smile. She never winks at me, but I let it go.

"Well I've had an interesting week." Windy offers to contribute to the conversation. "Nothing as consequential as Sage's week, but important just the same. "My divorce is final today, so I'm a free woman in Paris and it only cost me half of everything I owned. Tom kept everything he had, which was essentially the clothes on his back and his car. But I have full custody of the kids which was all I really wanted anyway."

"So why aren't you the one working on your third drink of the night?" I ask.

"It's a matter of putting it all into perspective. If the kids and I live forever and he dies in the next fifty years, let's be generous, who's going to have the last laugh?"

"Just so long as you don't think A'zam is going to live with you forever?" Delilah reminds her. "That's probably the worst bet in the universe right now."

"I still don't see why you think I have no chance with him." Windy scowls.

"He's had all of us except Reese, and he was putting the full court press on her the last time we got together." Delilah explains. "So how could you expect him to suddenly want to be monogamous? That's something a woman with kids wants, not one of the richest men in the world who can have anything and practically anyone he wants. Present company excluded, Reese."

Delilah looks at me, then offers. "Yeah, I've had a pretty shitty week too. Mr. Dessert? Well, he's getting married and not to me. So, tonight's that last tumble. Last time I'm going to enjoy him. I tried to convince him I was a better choice, but he's made up his mind he wants a fashion model and not experience. I keep saying she may be good to look at but she's never going to bring a lifetime of experiences to make it interesting. You know how men are. She gets him hard if he just looks at her. I get him harder, but I have to work at it longer. Some things just aren't fair."

"There's always A'zam," Reese suggests.

"Don't think so." Delilah is quick to respond. "But what about you Reese. You've been pounding down the alcohol tonight."

"It's been an interesting week."

"Really?" I ask. "That mean you finally slept with A'zam?"

THOUGHT

Maybe it was Delilah talking about Rocky being used up and thrown away by AppleCore that spooked me and made me decide I need to see him. So here I am in a Googlecar on the way to his house while Delilah is on her way to a fulfilling evening with Mr. Tall, even though it's their last night together. Maybe that thought of a last night together made me want to see Rocky tonight. I don't know.

The car comes to a stop at the usual point in front of his house. He doesn't know I'm coming so I have to go to the door and wait for him to override the biometric screen and let me in. "Rocky. It's me. Can I come in?"

I wait a long moment and the door unlatches. I open it and wonder if he's still in the kitchen teaching Anna Laura how to cook a hamburger with fries or in his lab working on his secret project for A'zam. Clearly, I hope he's taking his time on the latter. I go to the lab first because that's where I've found him ninety-nine of a hundred times. And of course, tonight is one of those one in a hundred nights. No Rocky. In fact, I'm pleasantly surprised that it doesn't look like Rocky has been working in here for a few days. So, I follow my nose to the kitchen. Only I'm sure this is spaghetti sauce and not a hamburger. That makes sense since Rocky used to buy a bottled sauce and cook up a pot of pasta which he would keep in a pot in the refrigerator for up to a week while he ate a little out of the pot each day. He used to say that was a highly efficient use of his time. He really didn't get anything done when he was eating other than ensure he had the strength to get through another day.

"Hey, Rocky." I call before I can see who is in the kitchen. I'm surprised there is another woman with him besides Anna Laura. The other woman's back is to me, so I only see her shape. She is looking at Anna Laura. Like they had been having a discussion. I wonder, is this the mystery woman Rocky intends to marry? Rocky motions me to come over next to him. I hesitate, not sure I really want to meet this woman who as I get closer doesn't seem to be much older than I am.

Rocky looks at me, but doesn't say anything as I come and stand next to him. I see the woman's face for the first time. There is something familiar here, but I can't place it. "Sage," I offer my hand. "Rocky's daughter."

She returns the gesture but is a bit slow in responding, "Tabitha."

It all comes back now. I ordered a Tabitha android at Rocky's request and simply lost track of when it was going to be ready. Here she is. My sister grown to be the age she would have been.

"I've down loaded my remembrances." Rocky informs me. "Now it's your turn."

I sit down in the chair Rocky had been sitting in. I see the neural lace hat that will capture my memories if I put it on, but the cable I used with Anna Laura is still on the table. I pick it up and plug it into Tabitha, behind her left ear and under her long dark hair. Then I plug the other end in my port. I think about the memories of Tabitha and send them to her. Tabitha looks at me as I see her react to the memories flashing past her. The Anna Laura android comes over and puts her hand on my shoulder just the way the real Anna Laura used to.

Rocky settles himself into another breakfast table chair and glances down at a tablet, scrolling through something that seems to completely occupy him. I'm glad it's Tabitha and not the mystery woman. That means my experiment is still keeping him engaged. I don't know if it's because he needed to build and install another master controller or he's really wanting to understand what he's missed for the last two decades. I hope it's the latter.

"What do you think about having women in the house again?" I ask Rocky.

"They're more bother than they're worth." Rocky shoots back. Of course, Anna Laura isn't about to accept this kind of behavior. She gives him the evil eye and picks up his cup of half consumed coffee. "Hey. I'm not finished with that."

"Maybe I'm finished with you, if that's your attitude about me." Anna Laura responds. I'm surprised. She's closer to the real thing than I feared she would be.

"Think you need to apologize." I tell him.

"If I apologize will you bring my coffee back?" Rocky asks Anna Laura.

"I'll think about it."

Wow! She's got that part down. "Well, Rock. What's your plan now?"

Rocky rolls his eyes. "I'm sorry, you're not more bother than you're worth."

Anna Laura brings the coffee cup back and sets it down in front of Rocky with a thud. "You need to appreciate what I'm doing for you." She then walks back to the other side of the kitchen and stands there looking at him the way she always did. Half looking like she's wondering why she ever gave up her former life for this bozo and half like she wouldn't want any other man in the world.

"Now that you two got that settled, what's the plan for Tabitha?" I ask.

"She's going to live with you." Rocky states simply as if a foregone conclusion.

"This is her home," Anna Laura offers.

"I'm good either way," I begin. "But someone has to bring her up to speed. You know. Help her fill in the blanks like you have been doing for Anna Laura. Do you remember what she talked about wanting to be when she grew up?" I ask Rocky.

"Which day of the week." Rocky responds immediately, but then adds, "Which year?"

"Wasn't there something she was more interested in than others?" I pursue.

"Teacher." Anna Laura offers unexpectedly. "She wanted to be a teacher. Work with little kids like herself."

"That was probably a result of being so young that it was her only point of reference." Rocky reasons.

"So, we have a problem." I begin. "She doesn't have a high school diploma, she doesn't have a college degree, and she doesn't have a teaching certificate. So, a teacher is probably not possible without her going back to school to get all three. We need to find something she can be that doesn't require the formal education."

"That eliminates nearly everything." Rocky points out.

"Except a software coder. Most of our best coders don't have college degrees since they really don't teach the creative part of coding the best of them understand. We can provide the knowledge she will need though a simple download. And she can learn what she needs on the job to increase her skills and ability."

"You're thinking AppleCore." Anna Laura is the first to clarify.

Rocky nods in understanding. "If anyone can get her in now, it's got to be you or A'zam. But I doubt he would even listen to a request to bring her in. He's got his own approach to solving the world's problems. At least the problems he has deemed important to solve."

Rocky seems to be telling me something about A'zam without telling me. I need to keep him talking so I understand what he's referring to, but knowing Rocky if I ask him directly he'll never answer. If I circle back around I may have a chance.

"So, Tabitha lives here initially. When you've been able to bring her up to speed then I'll have someone at AppleCore transfer the coding skills memory and we'll put her on some entry level tasks until she can demonstrate proficiency."

"What then?" Rocky pursues a clear plan which I'm trying to avoid for the moment.

"Hopefully she gets a full-time job at AppleCore. And we'll see what makes the most sense for her and all of us."

"I knew it." Rocky jumps on me. "You're already backing away from your earlier suggestions. You think I'll want her to stay after I get used to her. Just like you're still expecting I'm going to want to keep her here." Rocky nods towards Anna Laura.

"Give it time Rocky." I push back. "When we have Tabitha employed and secure, then we'll talk again about logistics."

"Logistics being code for her living with you along with her mother." Rocky is giving it to me even though I hear some doubt in his voice. "I got a woman who wants to marry me. I'm not going to give up a real live woman for…" Apparently Rocky remembers Anna Laura not being happy with his earlier characterization of her.

"Not a problem," I decide to be agreeable and see how he really behaves when the time comes. Don't want to over-react. "I've got room and you can just put them in a Googlecar when the time comes."

Rocky seems to have run out of objections and the memory transfer completes. I remove the cable from Tabitha first and then from my own neck. I decide to talk to Tabitha, which I haven't yet because I wanted to give her my memories to work with. "I'm so happy you're here. It's been a long time since we had a chance to talk and gossip like we used to."

"We used to gossip?" Tabitha responds, tentatively as if she's searching for that memory. I wonder if there's an integration problem.

"Would you mind if I do a diagnostic?" I ask her.

"That would be all right." Tabitha responds slowly. Something isn't right.

I pick up the tablet and pull up her profile. I run a diagnostic on her and wait for it to process. "This will only take a minute. Hopefully if something isn't set right I can take care of it from here." I show her the tablet.

"What is that?"

"A tool that lets me see if everything is set up right or if I need to make an adjustment."

"Are you a doctor?" Tabitha asks.

"Yes," I answer even though I know she's thinking of the medical doctors we used to see once a year or so when we were kids.

"Then I will be all right soon?"

I reach out and touch Tabitha to reassure her. I think she has memories of reassurance. "Yes."

The diagnostic completes and it shows a number of settings that are incorrect. I don't know if she came this way or Rocky reset a few things hoping to make the master controller work better. I don't want to embarrass him, so I have the diagnostic reset to defaults and wait to see what happens.

"That's better." Tabitha starts looking around. "I recognize this place. This is home. I recognize mom and Rocky, but who are you?"

"I'm Sage, your sister."

"You look so old." Tabitha seems confused. "Why do you look so old?"

"Maybe because it's been twenty years since your last memory. We're both older now. But we're still very much sisters."

Tabitha reaches to squeeze my hand. "I'm glad we're together again, Sage. It seems like a long time since we were."

"It has been." I squeeze back, but then let go. "I need to talk with Rocky for a minute. We'll have a lot of time to talk and catch up." I nod to Tabitha and she smiles as if she's happy. That's exactly what Tabitha used to do. I turn to Rocky, "Delilah reminded me tonight that I was a bit of a rebel when we were undergraduates. Was I?"

"How the hell would I know?" Rocky shakes like he's remembering being angry with me, but I know he's not. It's just a memory of how he felt then. "You never talked to me after you went off to school. I have no idea what you did, or thought or what philosophy you espoused to your girlfriends."

"Did I ever talk about how I'd never sell out to the whole corporate way of life?"

Rocky looks at me with a hard gaze as he tries to remember something, "You used to say I'd sold out. Is that what you're talking about?"

"Did you?" I have to ask.

"Every day of my life." Rocky is most definite. "Every day of my life. The only thing I had to sell was my mind. Look at me. I'm not good for farming, or raising chickens or flipping hamburgers. In fact, I really can't even cook them today. That's why I need her." Rocky nods towards Anna Laura. "So, what have I got to sell? Nothing anyone wants to pay me for. So of course, I sold out. I had to pay for this house, to keep you all fed and buy you school clothes and supplies and toys and all that. Anyone who tells you they didn't sell out is blowing smoke. We all sell out. We have to in order to survive."

I note Rocky admitted he needs Anna Laura, smile slightly. "If I'd come to the conclusion that I'd never sell out it was because I didn't understand the world. Is that what you're saying?"

"We never understand the world. It keeps changing on us every day. Just look around. Last week it was just you and me and my lady. Then all of a sudden you complicate matters for me by delivering Anna Laura. I've got to go invent something that didn't exist, so she could fulfill her promise. I just started getting used to her and the new world order and then Tabitha arrives. Now I got to build another master controller and start the process of bringing her up to speed all over again. Different world today than yesterday. Different yesterday than the day before. So don't even try to understand the world. You and I occupy such a small segment of it that we have no chance of even seeing what's over the horizon or what's coming tomorrow, let alone understand what happened to that world we had been occupying until last week."

"Do you understand your lady friend?" I ask trying to understand how he really feels about my grand strategy and how that changes his life.

"I understand her better than I do you." Rocky responds, not bitterly, but almost with an air of resignation. "She's kind, gentle and caring. She's not hung up on herself. Doesn't feel she'd be lowering herself to my level. Not at all. She would actually welcome having someone who cares about her as much as she cares about me."

"Are those her words, or your interpretation of the situation?"

"A little of both." Rocky admits. "There may be some wishful thinking on my part. I can't deny that. But I think I know enough about her I can count on her when I won't be able to take care of myself anymore. She'll love me for what I am, regardless of what that is at the time."

"And if she has breast cancer and a year to live, with radiation and chemotherapy, you're ready to take care of her? Clean up the mess, wait on her hand and foot because she can't do anything for herself?"

Rocky looks at me as if this thought had never occurred to him.

DIGNITY

I wait in the lobby at Symbol Ventures. It seems like months ago that I came here for a brief discussion with Howard Fisher, the Chairman and CEO about AppleCore's interest in merging our companies. Howard was reluctant to discuss it that day, but said if the offer was a fair one he was obligated to take it to his board. I doubt the offer we sent over would be deemed 'fair' by someone who had made the creation and growth of this firm his life's work. But he would have to listen to his bankers because if he did not act on their advice he would have to be ready to explain it to the board and his shareholders.

He keeps me waiting for a long time, in my view of things, but as an immortal whose brain is working at increasing multiples of a mortal's clock speed, however long it's been has seemed a lot longer to me. Howard's assistant comes through the doors and stops there. "Good morning, Miss Washington. Howard will be through with his meeting shortly. He asked me to take you to the conference room."

I follow her since the conference room indicates a polite meeting, not an intimate conversation. I remember this room. I was here once for a meeting with Simpson, their SVP of software when we were working together on a legislative priority for our trade association. About the only time such a meeting would have been possible, and even then, we had to sign off on documentation indicating that nothing of an anticompetitive nature would be discussed. It wasn't. Symbol Ventures at that time was much closer to us and a fierce rival. Simpson thought he had us on the ropes, but I came up with a novel solution to an annoying problem most users were experiencing, and it pulled sales our way. We've not looked back since.

Good to her word, Howard keeps me waiting longer than is polite for a CEO, but I'm not about ego and only consider it as a passing thought about how he is handling this opportunity to make a good impression. Evidently, he doesn't give a shit about a good impression.

I hear someone talking in the hallway. The voice sounds like Howard and it is getting louder. He's apparently on his way to meet with me, finally. The door bursts open and there he is in full stride, pushing the world ahead of him to make way for him. No smile of recognition. No indication he is happy to see me. Just the same determined to right all wrongs scowl I've come to recognize in our few meetings.

"Dr. Washington." At least he got the title right.

"Good morning Howard." I deliberately use the familiar even though he did not. Want to let him know I'm trying to make a deal that would make us partners.

"No coffee? Oh, that's right you don't drink it. I was about to have a conversation about being rude to our guests."

"No need, she remembered from last time. I assume you received our offer to purchase all of the assets and liabilities of Symbol Ventures."

"I did. I was pleased to see you used all the right words, throughout. But I was disappointed. For some reason you didn't use the right numbers anywhere I could find them. Would you take a moment to point me to them if in fact I overlooked them somehow?"

"Since it is a rather brief document I'm sure you haven't overlooked them." I can play this game too, although I'd rather not. But then I'd rather not be here at all, but that's another matter.

"If those numbers truly are your offer to acquire my company, could you tell me if they are A'zam's numbers? If they are then I understand them. But if they are A'zam's numbers then he should be the one here negotiating on behalf of AppleCore. If they are your numbers, then I simply have to say that on balance you have displayed a wholly inadequate understanding of the value of this enterprise."

I lean forward, "Howard," I make sure my voice is rock solid. "You will run out of cash in five weeks if you stretch all of your suppliers to 120 days rather than the customary thirty. Your sales have tanked to the tune of only forty percent of your year ago sales this month, you launched the lifeboats and sent anyone who you could get off the payroll to the nearest shore, your retailers are sitting on double the inventory they had just two months ago and you're on the hook to buy all of that back in sixty days if they can't move it. The market has frozen for you because of White Rabbit and Mad Hatter. Nobody is buying what you're selling until they know if this change is the way of the future or another great concept that doesn't deliver sales with legs." I wait just a moment for Howard to fix his face. It appears he dropped his jaw and isn't sure where to find it. "Now the rumor on the street is that you have a major new contract in the wings. The problem is no one knows anything about your customer, whether the company is for real, whether the product is or whether it will have long legs. It is said to be a retirement contract in that once you build the product you will have the operations and maintenance for life. From what little information is available, this contract may enable you to shrink your way to survival, but you will be a much smaller entity than today. Either way, the offer we have provided to you is fair and reasonable as validated against all market comparables by our independent bankers."

"I understand why A'zam sent you over. He could never have delivered that analysis and I've known him nearly thirty years. I'm pleased to see you have done your homework. I would have expected nothing less from AppleCore and from all that I've learned recently, from you as well. But as I indicated, your offer fails to recognize the value intrinsic in this enterprise. You allude to it in your mention of the mystery contract. You actually know much more about it than you are indicating, and that would mean either you are trying to down play it to get the price you want, or you don't recognize the real value yourself."

"We have attempted to assign a generous value to that purported contract, but would be happy to consider a purchase price adjustment if one is merited during due diligence."

Howard smiles a rueful smile. "You would have to double the value you have proposed for me to be comfortable taking it to my board in the first place. And then a purchase price adjustment may still be necessary."

Suddenly I think I may know what the contract is. I can think of only one new market out there that could have that kind of impact on a company the size of Symbol Ventures. And I know the person who would have brought the opportunity to them. Damn.

"In that case I should expect you to be sitting on this side of the table in about a year, with your offer for AppleCore between us." I'm testing the theory since I know he will never tell me anything about the contract.

"I would love to be in that position, but with the way you whipsawed us in the last few weeks I doubt anything could slow your march to immortality."

Bad choice of words, Howard since you've just confirmed A'zam has given you a contract to build all of the immortal bodies and evidently something more. But what? And if that's the case, what's the game he's playing by having me nearly put them out of business, so he can swoop in to be the white knight in response to an offer from his company. Except his company can't execute a contract of this size without an AppleCore guarantee, which I know we haven't given because the board would have to approve it, requiring me to take it to them. I can't believe how screwed up this whole thing is getting. "Of course, you're referring to AppleCore."

"Of course," the disdain is heavy in the room. Howard must think I'm really enjoying whipsawing him as he put it and he's enjoying trying to put me in my place by making me look foolish and powerless to bring him to the table.

"What do you know of White Rabbit?" I ask in such a way that I know he will understand there is more there than he appreciates, which I know to be the case.

"That you've solved some very difficult technical issues to create an internal platform which essentially obsoletes all of the external platforms we have been building forever."

"Essentially we have created a mechanism whereby you and Beth and your janitor can have the same ability to process internet enabled information and data, almost the same way as I do."

Howard blinks rapidly. I've seen him do this when he realizes something for the first time. He refocuses on me and the rapid blinking stops. It's as if he is seeing something clearly, he had not before.

"Now do you want to rethink our offer? I think you must realize now that the market for the contract you are hoping to sign, I would know if you had, isn't as big as you expect. You will have to invest massive cash you don't have to gear up for a contract that won't deliver the volumes, cash or margins you have been led to believe they will. You see, we both know the same master salesman who has been known to do anything to win. And driving your value even lower after you've spurned my offer is not beneath him. We both know that."

Howard begins blinking again. That goes on for a long few seconds then Howard refocuses on me. "Would you excuse me for a moment? I need to have a conversation."

I rise, "Certainly. I'll wait in the lobby."

As I reach the sliding doors to the lobby I catch a glimpse of Beth walking quickly in the direction of Fisher's office. When I reach the lobby, I walk straight to the window to look out to the circle in front. AppleCore has just such a circle where dignitaries can be delivered by a limousine. The building is here to house the employees who create the value of the firm. But the architecture is for a visitor who has come to sign a contract to buy product or sell parts. The intent is to impress them that this is a substantial company. You should be glad it is willing to do business with you. It is well run and will be here long after you have passed on to your next state of being. But again, I have changed all the expectations Fisher and A'zam's predecessors had for their businesses. They grew them from concepts to reality to market leading forces for innovation and change in our very social structure. Now, because I was going to die at a very young age, a lifetime of problem solving in an industry I wasn't following and knew practically nothing about, has changed nearly everything for both Symbol Ventures and AppleCore.

Howard comes out to the lobby himself with Beth hanging back near the entrance to his office. He approaches me looking much less confident and disdainful. "I don't know if the two of you rehearsed this or what."

"We didn't. My offer was developed independently of A'zam although he was aware of it and reviewed it at the board meeting where it was approved. As Chairman he did not vote and it received a majority vote of the independent board members."

Howard nods, understanding that we followed protocol in how the bid was developed, approved and presented to him. "But you're aware of New Vision."

"I am," is all I will say.

"I thought A'zam was my friend," Howard sounds disoriented. Clearly A'zam sold him a bill of goods and now he has come to realize the contract he expected to save him will destroy him surely.

"What do you know of immortals?" I ask to help him understand.

"That you have infinite capacity for growth and will live forever. That means in time you will make mortals obsolete. Enough of you will be able to replace all labor and reshape the economy of nations. And the world. It's inevitable. A new world order driven by the innovation of AppleCore and its partners."

"What part of that is not an exact quote from A'zam?"

"None of it. I think I captured it almost word for word." Howard is proud of his memory.

"But the problem is it is A'zam's picture of the world that could be. But if you've been following the ACLU proceeding you see there are the stirrings of a resistance to that world view. And as far as the public is concerned there is only one immortal in the world at this time, although Dr. Woodall has left some room for interpretation there."

Howard looks upset, "What are you saying? A'zam has given me assurances…"

"A'zam can give you all the assurances you want. He's not talking with our attorneys. I am. Has he ever explained our reorganization to you?"

Howard looks totally lost. "I am CEO of the products company. Essentially the AppleCore you know. I design, build and sell all of our products and provide after sales support. A'zam is responsible for non-core development. That includes the work of New Vision, which by the way hasn't even been incorporated yet, has not been given any backstop guarantees, and is basically A'zam working on his own to build something from nothing all based on an emerging market, maybe, that he personally intends to dominate."

"No guarantees?" Howard gets pale.

"So A'zam can just let it collapse and it goes away. You and every other party to a New Vision contract will have no recourse to any assets whatsoever."

"This is worse than I thought." Howard turns to look at Beth. He shakes his head. I see her drop hers as she slowly walks towards us.

But then Howard suddenly gets a new thought, "Are you playing good cop/bad cop with me?"

"No Howard. You don't know me at all, but Beth does. Ask her if I would be a party to something like that. I don't operate that way. I don't operate the way A'zam apparently is. If New Vision doesn't deliver value, he simply lets it go and comes back to AppleCore where I've doubled the value of the company in my short tenure. He can't lose, but he intends that you will lose everything. And that's the opportunity you have at the moment. If you accept the offer I made, you get that much. For where you are at the moment it's a fair offer. If you wait, you will probably get nothing for your life's work. That's why it's structured as an asset purchase rather than a stock deal."

Beth joins us. I shake her hand, "Beth."

"Sage."

"Howard has a question. Would I deliberately lie or mislead you in any way to get a better deal for AppleCore?"

Beth hesitates probably only having a sketchy understanding of the conversation Howard and I'd just had. "I've known Sage since high school. I have never known her to lie to me or misrepresent something. Now that she's a CEO would she do the kinds of things you've been known to do Howard? I honestly don't think she would. Even if ordered to do it by A'zam. She has too much integrity."

Howard shakes his head in realization he has been set up to lose whichever way he goes. "I need some time to think this through, talk with my advisors. I never thought A'zam would do such a thing."

"We never know who we are dealing with until they and we are put under pressure. Then the measure of a man becomes clear. I'm sorry we didn't have more time to get to know each other. I think you and I see the world in much the same way. It would have been a pleasure to work with you to see what we could have built together."

"You talk as if there's no way I can recover, Symbol Ventures can recover."

"My pipeline of products is full and growing around the new architecture. How long will it take you to even get into the market?"

Howard Fisher doesn't answer my question. He knows he has run out of time. I don't know if he is aware of the number of immortals we have working at AppleCore or the number that will be joining our ranks in the coming months. If he did he wouldn't need to talk to his advisors. I'm not even sure if he knows A'zam has transitioned. I have been a party to killing an institution. But if I can convince Howard to sell to me under my terms and conditions, I may be able to salvage jobs for his team, dignity for them in the emerging economy and society and an opportunity to help build the new community I envision, hopefully not the one A'zam has in mind.

RESPECT AND LOYALTY

A'zam greets me at the door to his apartment with surprise. Although I see him wondering if I've come for another Kama Sutra marathon. He's still dressed for work, which is a relief. I really didn't want to catch him in a towel having just come out of the shower. That would have been awkward as he would have expected at least a half dozen positions if not all one-hundred. "To what do I owe this pleasure?"

"We need to talk about New Vision," I respond and push past him into his living room.

"Please sit down," he offers after I already have.

"New Vision," I repeat. "It's time you fill me in. I've had to open an investigation into your activities since more and more violations of policy and now law are coming to light."

A'zam listens to me without commenting. He is apparently reviewing something in his head and when he finishes finally looks at me again. "Not so bad."

"You think the investigation won't lead to your resignation?" I push.

A'zam shakes his head. "I hand-picked the board. I did that for a reason. I have nothing to fear from the board or the law for that matter. So what else do you want to know?"

"What New Vision is doing and why you're having to operate a rogue operation when you have all the staff in the world you might want at AppleCore who can do it all within policy and within the law."

"That's the problem. If I did it within AppleCore it would fall under your supervision. You'd question what I'm doing, why am I doing things this way rather than that way. Why don't you try a different approach altogether? That's not what I want. I'm used to making the decisions and in setting up this new venture I didn't want anyone else's eyes on how, what or why I'm doing what I'm doing."

"What are you afraid of?" I instantly react to what he's saying.

"I'm not afraid of anything."

"Listen to yourself. You're afraid of me. Afraid I'll question you, just like I'm doing right now."

A'zam looks at me curiously. "You work for me, so why should I be afraid of you?"

"Only you can answer that." I push back. "But you are."

A'zam looks away, apparently thinking about something he's not willing to share.

"If you're not afraid, then prove it. Tell me what you're doing, what New Vision is doing and why."

A'zam finally sits down across from me. Looks at me, apparently trying to decide what, if anything, he might want to share with me. I give him time to think it through and he finally decides. "You're absolutely the last person I should discuss New Vision with. You have been trying to undermine everything it stands for. If not overtly, covertly. You've been making it hard for me to reach full capability, but now that's changing. The pieces are coming together. I now have enough that no matter what you do, I'll still achieve my objective."

"Which is?"

"To be the richest person, with the most influence and power of any being on this planet."

"Not God?" I cut to the chase since his response seems to skirt what I've interpreted his actions leading to.

A'zam smiles. "That would require too much work on my part. To be responsible for twelve billion people? I couldn't possibly do it justice."

"Tell me more about how you're going to become the person you hope to be without being God."

"You're thinking about how rich the Catholic Church has become and that it is only able to gain those riches by controlling the lives of the members of the church." A'zam assumes.

"I'm just looking at your behavior." I disagree. "We've been making the technology that intermediates human relationships. Pushes people apart while enabling them to communicate almost constantly. White Rabbit and Mad Hatter are the first products we've put out that actually are intended to bring people closer together by internalizing the communications. Now you're building capabilities outside our formal structures that limit the freedoms of immortals like us. And yet you exempt yourself from the limits you intend to impose on every immortal. Why would you do that unless you were intending on being 'God' and deciding what they can and should do?"

"I like to think of it as more like being Santa Claus. Determining who's been naughty and who's been nice. The fact that those who have been naughty must be punished and those who've been nice should be rewarded, well, doesn't that sound more like Santa Claus?"

"What's your point?"

"My point is you're interpreting without facts. You assume I'm trying to become God, when that's really not my intent at all."

"What is your intent then?"

"To create a different world, most assuredly." A'zam visualizes something. "A world that precludes the self-destructive impulses of mankind. Precludes want and starvation. Enables peace and tranquility. A world that may be boring because of the sameness across all men and women, but is infinitely more predictable and equitable."

"How do you get there? By making immortals the enforcers of your will?"

A'zam shakes his head. "Better living through chemistry."

"What does chemistry have to do with immortals?" He has completely lost me now.

"Have you heard of gene editing and gene splicing?" A'zam starts to zero in on an answer.

"CRISPR-cas9?"

"That's the original technique." A'zam acknowledges. "But it's evolved a lot since then. I was actually working in this area before you transitioned. I thought it was going to be the next big thing for AppleCore. But then you showed me another path to immortality. While it has slowed me down a bit and caused me to spread resources much differently than I intended, I have actually made progress on both simultaneously. I've delegated the immortals work to you..."

"Not all of it." I remind him.

"You're right. Not all of it. But you have the most important part which is getting people through the transition and working on making AppleCore the one indispensable company in the world."

"And you've been acquiring the rights to all the technology that makes immortals possible."

"I have done that, yes."

"You've also made promises to companies you can't fulfill." I seek to confirm what I suspect, "Signed contracts that you will walk away from at some point and put them out of business."

"They won't go out of business, but their assets will be available on much better terms."

"Fisher doesn't want you to think he's a fool."

"What did you just say?" A'zam wants to clarify what he thinks he heard.

"Fisher took our offer. He knew you were playing him for a fool, but he also knew you don't trust anyone, so he was just waiting for our offer." Not the way it happened but the result is the same.

A'zam stops to think for a moment, but then shakes it off and continues. "May have to have the board reject the final deal. We can get them for less."

"The board already approved the deal. There is no going back now." I inform him.

A'zam considers my data point but isn't about to let it go.

"So, what exactly are you doing with Gene editing?" I bring him back to my conversation.

A'zam holds up what looks like a White Rabbit pill. "New Vision is producing these. A pill that edits genes. I can custom make any biologic entity either in vitro or even after they are fully grown. This pill would make any one of your posse members forget how to love. Adjust their metabolism rate to melt away that unwanted celluloid. Improve their hearing. Improve their memories. I can even adjust their DNA, so they will follow whatever suggestions I make."

"Which makes you God."

"You keep coming back to that. You really need to move on. Get with the program. You can only seem to focus on the power I will have and not the good I will do."

"Three hundred years ago, no one would have even noticed." I point out. "But today everyone wants to self-actualize. To be in control of themselves and the world in which they live. You are trying to take everyone in exactly the opposite direction. Make the world they will inhabit. Set the boundaries of their choices. Ensure the world is just as you want it, regardless of the opinions of the other twelve billion residents of planet Earth."

"Why are you hung up on free will? It doesn't really exist. Never has. You aren't free to do as you please because we have set all these rules you must comply with every day. You can't kill your neighbor or at least I can't rape his wife. I can't take someone else's house to live in without paying him or her. I can't even visit certain countries without getting permission in advance in the form of a visa. So, you see, neither of us have free will. We only have freedom within limits. And that's what kind of world I'm proposing. An extension of what is, only with adjustments to make it a more harmonious place for all of us to live."

"I agree we all live within limits. What I'm suggesting isn't appropriate is that you become the sole arbiter of those limits. What we have now has evolved from man over thousands of years. Everyone had a set of shared experiences that led us to a set of shared expectations, norms and behaviors that transcend rules and laws and human decency."

"You obviously don't get out much." A'zam responds ruefully. "I could take you to places where the term human decency never existed. Where shared expectations and behaviors are all those things you abhor. Killing someone just because they worship a different god or gods. Raping your neighbor's wife because he is too weak to protest. Keeping children on the brink of starvation, while living in disease riddled villages and tenements. Segregating boys from girls such that girls never have the chance to even learn how to read or do math. Human decency may be the product of the places where you live and work. But it is not a universal right, behavior or even expectation."

"And your pill will solve all that?"

"Just as your pills will speed up life for all who dare to ingest them." A'zam pushes back on me. "You may think your cause is nobler than mine. But you would leave the chaos that is mankind to rule itself. Isn't it evident to you that approach doesn't work? Mankind isn't capable of ending conflict without some external force that makes it impossible. The fact I have chosen to be that force should be a relief to you. If for no reason other than I'm someone who you have known for a long time. You know I won't be arbitrary or capricious. I won't set limits or enable groups such that they would destroy each other. If there is a God, she must be enjoying the show mankind is putting on. The only thing that is predictable is mankind will continue on its march towards self-destruction."

"My posse, as you referred to them…"

"Only because that's what you refer to them as." A'zam corrects me.

"Pointed out to me recently that we grow, we change, our beliefs change, our values adjust with the times and the changing societal norms." I begin to try to understand the depth of his considerations. "How does your gene edited individual continue to grow, change, adjust values and norms?"

"The same as they do now." A'zam is trying to sound like he has his plan all thought out, but I'm getting the impression there are holes. "All I'm doing is setting boundaries, just as your parents set boundaries for you and you would set for any children you might have had."

"Even though they are no longer free to decide for themselves anything you have elected to determine for them."

"We're back to the same argument about limited free will."

"You said you don't want to be God because you don't have time to worry about twelve billion people. So how do you decide who gets what pill?"

A'zam grins, "Took you long enough. I thought that was the question you came to ask." He rises and takes me over to his desk where a monitor shows a dashboard. "Every known person is loaded in here."

"Known meaning?"

"Have a platform, whether an AppleCore platform or someone else's. A means of communicating with every known person."

"Why would you want to communicate with them?"

"To monitor their behavior. You see I can set a profile for each person and bulk load it with the base profile of permitted and prohibited behaviors. Then I can add new restrictions or relax existing restrictions on what that person can do."

"A universal control platform." I pronounce.

"If you will."

"But you don't have time to monitor twelve billion people, you said so yourself."

"No, but Santa here monitors who's been naughty and who's been nice. You see, it's driven by artificial intelligence. I give it parameters and it takes care of the rest, including punishing and rewarding all my children."

"Who you define as everyone in the world." I clarify.

"Including all the immortals. I limit them in much the same way, but it's actually easier because it's just an over-the-air software update."

"If you've automated the management of everyone in the world, who maintains your systems? Who updates the software to ensure it's what you want? Who's reviewing the data logs of behavioral exceptions that require you to change a profile or everyone's profile?"

"I have a helper. Someone you know well."

I can't imagine who would have come to work directly for A'zam without me knowing about it. At least Desiree, our HR person would have informed me. She didn't. "You mean you actually trust someone to enforce the norms you want? To limit everyone in the same way. Not play God and set people or groups against each other for the fun of it?"

"Trust. Now there is a word I didn't expect to hear from you because I've never been able to trust you. You know why? Because you never trusted me."

"You trusted me to deliver results, which I did for ten years. At the same time I watched you operate." I point out. "How could I trust someone who has never lived up to a commitment he ever made, who changes his mind capriciously, who punishes people, in some cases for no good reason?"

"Because I chose you and you work for me. I deserve respect and loyalty.

SANTA CLAUS

Dietrich stops by my office. He often does this just to see what frame of mind I'm in. If I didn't know better I'd think he was sleeping with MC. But she only has eyes for A'zam along with the rest of my posse.

"You been following the proceedings?" He asks, knowing I would know instantly he was talking about the hearings on immortals. Those are the only proceedings of interest to us at the moment, but that changes from time to time. There are countries that want to ban the use of our technology. Can you imagine that? Whole counties that don't want their citizens to have the same access to communications with each other and the world. I've been amazed at the picture of the world I've developed since I've been in this role. When I was Software SVP everything was a focus on what the competition was doing. What were people buying from them and why? Was it better than what we offered or only different? Some functionality that we didn't offer they wanted.

"Time, Dietrich. I just don't have enough time in a day, even though it's now 24 hours versus the old eight to ten."

"That's why I'm here. To bring you up to date."

I look past Dietrich and notice Petra sneaking in behind him.

"Come on in. The water's fine." I inform Petra. Dietrich looks around and he is smiling as he turns back to look at me.

"Heard Dietrich was giving you a brief, so thought I should come down and save him the trouble of repeating himself. Besides, I was hoping you might update us on your conversation with A'zam since he doesn't come in anymore."

"You're not seeing him outside work?" I ask, knowing Dietrich is aware of their relationship.

"Ever since he got that friend of yours into the sack. What's her name?"

"Reese?" I suggest.

"That's the one. He's just not been as interested in me."

"Don't feel bad." I try to put it all into context for Petra. "I was the one before you and he seemed to have lost interest for the longest time. But eventually he seems to come back. There was this song I remember from when I was a kid. Was an oldie goldy back then. Can't remember the name of the band, but I remember the song. Something about 'Did you ever have to make up your mind?' That's A'zam."

"Loving Spoonful." Dietrich rattles off."1965. Album was Do You Believe in Magic."

"What?" I have to ask. "You're a rock and roll historian?"

"I know my music history. Who wrote what. Who performed what. Can I sing? Please don't ask. It wouldn't be a pleasant experience for any of us."

"But you know the words?" Petra asks.

"Every one." Dietrich admits.

"Nice detour into who we all are, but what about the proceeding?" I have to change the direction of this conversation or we will be here revisiting lyrics all day.

Dietrich seems as if he'd rather talk music, but pulls himself back into reality. "Right. The proceeding. Jane Williams has been earning her money."

"That doesn't sound good," Petra ventures.

"It isn't." Dietrich admits. "She's scored points in cross examination of each witness."

"So how do we recover?" I have to ask knowing this isn't going to be a short conversation.

"We don't have to." Dietrich checks my reaction then checks Petra.

"And why is that?" I have to ask.

"Because she's walked right into the trap I set for her."

Trap? I wasn't aware of a trap in our strategy briefings. "Tell me more."

"Yes. I'm all ears." Petra confirms.

Dietrich is smiles from ear-to-ear. I've never seen him this happy with himself. As a good German he is usually restrained in his responses. Not today. Must be a real triumph for him. "Miss Williams has established that society has winners and losers. Government policy can either enhance those divisions or seek to address them by taking from the winners to give to the losers."

"Robin Hood." I respond without thinking.

"And there are equivalent characters in nearly every societal subgroup at one time in their history or another." Dietrich clarifies.

"Sounds ominous for us." I point out. "So how is this a good thing?"

"Jane has walked into a trap." Dietrich smiles broadly. "The natural order of things is that there are winners and losers in every transaction. Big fish eat little fish. Faster animals hunt down slower animals. Charles Darwin established the order of species survival two centuries ago. This is nothing new."

"I don't understand your point." I respond. "Our opponents have known this. It doesn't make any difference to them."

"But we aren't arguing the case in front of them. They aren't the judge in this case. The judge is constrained to uphold the law. And we can go back to natural law, which predates man-made laws as the governing doctrine. We can show that if we try to change the priorities of nature we are trying to change the natural order. And judges hate to be evaluated as making a ruling that can be shown to be contra to the natural order."

I shake my head. "Are you saying we have nature on our side?"

"We do." Dietrich responds. "And a lot more. I've not been this confident of a verdict in all my years practicing law. The judge may want to find in favor of the plaintiff, but if she does she will be severely criticized by her colleagues, the judicial review boards and the legal establishment. Sure, judges want to make landmark decisions. But they have to find a place in the law that supports them. In this case, Jane Williams is out at sea without a paddle or even a friendly breeze."

Petra shakes her head. "You may be brilliant in a court of law, but you have no clue when it comes to politics."

I remember that Petra grew up on the streets of St. Petersburg, Russia and lived to tell about it. I would trust her instincts above anyone else on my team having only survived because she developed them to a high degree.

"Really?" Dietrich isn't happy at her response.

"Think about it." She begins. "This judge is only in this position because she's rendered controversial decisions that have favored the plaintiff, which in every case, until this one, has been one or another environmental group. Never an individual. Always a group, or organization, or voluntary group that is advocating for a position they know she will support because she gets all her campaign contributions from them and the various unions. She has no sense of her peers. She could care less about the people. She is only interested in being re-elected to the bench where she has a ten-year guaranteed salary. The problem is that while she became more accessible to reason in her fifth and sixth years, she is now concentrating on re-election. So for the next four years her decisions will be made by her major donors and not the legal mind sitting on the bench."

"Are you just trying to balance Dietrich's enthusiasm?" I ask.

"Someone has to. Listening to him I'd believe there was no way the ACLU could win this case. As a realist, I don't think there's any way we can win it. All the social causes are lined up against us. And they've become the dominant voice in California politics. They make the decisions not with the facts, but in spite of the facts that are brought before them."

"What happened to truth and politicians who did their homework?" I have to ask.

"No one knows what to believe." Petra responds. "The Russian government perfected this approach to preservation of power. Unfortunately, the political parties around the world noticed and adopted the Russian model rather than rising above the petty disinformation campaigns that make people unable to determine truth from alternative truths."

"What's your recommendation?" I ask Petra.

"Proceed as if you expect to lose. Take whatever actions you would take if you do. Get out in front of it so you have established your position and can drive public opinion because it's not just a reaction. It's what you've been saying right along."

"And your message would be?"

"White Rabbit and Mad Hatter get you as close to immortality as possible without transitioning."

"Think you have a future in marketing." I point out.

Dietrich removes his glasses and rubs his face with his left hand. "Wrong." He puts his glasses back on and takes a long look at Petra. "Wrong. You don't want to seem commercial in this proceeding. The judge thinks you're using it to promote your products and you might as well report to the minimum-security prison closest to you."

"You're exaggerating." Petra responds, dismissing the picture Dietrich is painting. "It's all about spin. How can you spin the situation, so you look like a saint on earth? I know it can be done because we see it all the time. Besides I think you look good in white," she says to me.

"Thank you," I respond imagining myself in a flowing white gown. Blowing in the wind. Revealing only what I want, but enough to keep the attention and interest of all the men in the room. "But if in fact I lose, and they decide there should be no immortals. That we have to transition back with no bodies to go to? What then?"

"Do you think there is any possibility of that Dietrich?" Petra asks.

Dietrich shakes his head. "That would be arbitrary, capricious and unsustainable by any law I am aware of. They couldn't make anyone transition back who transitioned before a law prohibiting it. There's just no precedent for it."

Petra seems satisfied, asks me, "You talked with A'zam. What happened?"

This is the question I've been expecting. But I'm not ready to address it just yet. I need to change the vector. "Did you find any other accounts where he was transferring money out of AppleCore into his side ventures?"

Petra looks at me as if she were now the one who wished she didn't have to answer the question I'd just asked. "I have. Not in his name, but they are clearly linked to him."

"How do you know?" I pursue the line of reasoning.

"The name on the accounts is one of his people."

"Who is that?" I have to ask since I don't know him to have any 'people.'

"You know him. In fact, he was one of your team leads once upon a time."

"I instantly go way back, but she stops me. "In fact, I'm sure he picked him up because you were going to transition him back to being a mortal."

"Moshe?" almost leaps from my lips.

Petra nods, "A dozen companies. None of them registered. He's the applicant on each of them. Each one has done billions of business with AppleCore. And I can't find any records that show they have delivered anything."

"Services?" I ask. Knowing services often don't have a recorded deliverable.

"Some of the contracts are service oriented, but not all." Petra clarifies.

"Moshe." I repeat to myself aloud. I know that means A'zam is deliberately seeking out people to join his team that will be antagonistic to me because of past decisions I've made.

"You aggregate everything and he has enough to fund a start-up. No problem." Petra assesses. "So, what's going to change as a result of your discussion with him yesterday?"

"I still don't have an effective response to his strategy." I admit.

"So, he wins?" Dietrich summarizes.

"Unless my failed approach suddenly works." I respond unhappily. "I thought I had it all figured out, but it didn't work."

"And you're the only one between A'zam and his grand vision?" Petra asks, apparently having heard all about it during their many sexual liaisons.

"No one else has taken it seriously." I confirm.

Dietrich tries to change the direction of the conversation. "You have enough."

"For what?"

"To ask the board to remove him as CEO of AppleCore, Corp."

"They're his friends." I respond. "He hand-picked them. Do you really think they would vote to oust him?" I ask.

"Board has fiduciary responsibilities." Dietrich tries to frame the situation. "If they believe they might be held personally responsible in any suits filed as a result of his violation of federal laws, they would cave in a New York minute."

Petra grimaces, "Not going to happen. A'zam has them in his pocket. He's convinced them that if there are any lawsuits the corporation will defend them and indemnify them even if the law says they are personally responsible."

"How do you know that?" I have to understand her perspective as this is crucial.

"A'zam. He was bragging about it."

"When you were…" I lead her to confirm without having to say where she was.

Petra notices and nods. "So, Dietrich. What do you think?" she finally asks.

"I'm of the opinion that we're fucked on more than one plane. A'zam is going to keep on transitioning people regardless of the trial's outcome. He's going to build an army of product development immortals that will change the very nature of what it means to be human. And anyone who doesn't transition? Well, as far as A'zam is concerned, it's all just too bad. He doesn't give a shit about any of them. He's all in for A'zam."

"Yes and no." I respond.

"C'mon Sage. Don't give me this equivocation bullshit. What's going on?" Petra responds.

"You ever hear of Santa Claus?" I respond.

HUMANITY

Landon sits across from me in my office. Mindi is at her desk, listening to every word I'm sure. Landon has a date to transition. Mindi is pregnant. She also has a date about three months after she delivers the child. I did that deliberately, so she can bond with her one and only child.

"You have not been looking at the numbers." Landon sounds exasperated with me. "How can a CEO not know what her company is doing? That is your primary function. To look at the numbers and order your staff to make the necessary adjustments."

"If you were on this side of the desk, Landon, what adjustments would you make?" I ask hoping to get insight into his decision-making process.

"The data shows me that India is not accepting Mad Hatter at the same rate as the Chinese. This is all relative in that their adoption rates are well below western nations, meaning both the Western hemisphere and Europe. All I can attribute to the data is a mistrust that the Chinese will come out with a comparable capability."

"That they will reverse engineer it." I clarify.

"Yes. But what is interesting is that India is expecting a Chinese alternative to a US product that is setting a new world standard. Even more so than the Chinese population itself."

"What would you suggest I need to do?" I ask, not sure where he is going.

"You need to change your advertising in India. You need to show more Indian specific applications. Why is this such a good product for the way they have used AppleCore and competitor tools in the past? They need to understand this is an extension of all they know, but a revolution in how information is presented to them. And if they wait for a different platform, they will be left behind."

"Being left behind." I muse. "Is that what our Indian customers are afraid of?"

"They are very competitive when it comes to China. They think of the Chinese as a wave of cheap labor. They think of themselves as the civilization that should rightfully be the leaders of the world. They have one of the oldest civilizations, comparable to the Chinese. But they believe they add more brain power. Whereas the Chinese have been focused on Artificial Intelligence because they don't think they alone can compete on an even playing field with India or the western nations."

"Still doesn't tell me how to sell one more unit of Mad Hatter in India." I point out.

Landon thinks for a long moment. "Did you ever get that capability you asked me to help you with working? You've never asked me to do anything since."

I shake my head. "The lab is working on it, but no."

"Then Mad Hatter is not the revolution you were expecting." Landon surmises.

"Doesn't appear to be." I confirm glumly.

"That would have been a differentiator it would have taken our competitors a long time to catch up to." Landon observes.

I consider the information Landon has given me. The fastest adoption for a new product ever. Uneven adoption rates with western nations insatiable and eastern nations skeptical still. I need to do something that captures the world's attention if I want this to truly be a global product. Move past the skepticism. It's also time to confront A'zam. I can't put it off any longer.

"Time to go." I rise and shoo Landon from my office. As I come out after him Mindi looks up at me expectantly.

"You're going out?" She inquires looking at my schedule and knowing I have meetings stacked up for the rest of the day and night.

"I need to visit with A'zam. Is he in his office?"

Mindi checks his schedule. "Yes, but his day is even worse than yours. He's down to ten-minute appointments.

I nod and wander down the hallway. I'm not sure what kind of reception I'm likely to get given our last discussion. As I turn into his reception area, Brit, his gorgeous admin looks up. I wonder where she fits into the pecking order of women for him. Clearly the most stunning in terms of her appearance, but for some reason that has not been the driver I've noticed for A'zam. "Sage." She seems disoriented, as if she'd memorized his schedule for the day and can't understand why I'm here but not on it.

"Need five minutes with him now." I respond so she knows she won't find me on his schedule but that shouldn't matter.

"He's almost finished, but he's running behind and there are several others stacked up and waiting."

I look into the conference room where she has parked those waiting. Of course, Moshe is sitting in there, but is unwilling to look at me. Probably hoping I don't notice him. I wonder if Moshe is afraid I'll tell A'zam why I transitioned Moshe back. Apparently, he doesn't know A'zam doesn't give a shit about my opinion. Moshe wouldn't be sitting in that room if he did.

"I need to see him now." I reaffirm.

Brit holds up her finger for me, buzzes A'zam. I listen and in a moment A'zam responds with an acknowledgement that doesn't include him saying anything. Just a tone so Brit knows he's listening.

"Sage." Is all Brit says.

I hear a click. I'm not sure what that means. Is he acknowledging I'm here, or did he simply hang up on Brit?

In a moment Jackson comes out of A'zam's office, followed by the man himself. Jackson looks embarrassed, nods to me and keeps on going. A'zam comes out right behind him. "This has to be in person? You can't send me a text or visual message?"

I walk up to him, push him back into his office and close the door behind us. "It's over."

"What? I've hardly begun." He assures me.

"Santa Claus won't work."

A'zam gets a cynical look. "You may be right. You know I'm glad your friend is so much better in bed than you are. Since I'm going to have to destroy you I won't be missing out on anything."

"Is that all I am to you?" I challenge him hoping he will see all I've delivered to the company.

"You can't imagine the difference." A'zam responds, clearly trying to belittle me.

"Actually, I can." I push back. "Delilah has given me perspective about your inadequacies in that regard, and Jackson has shown me the inadequacies of your design discipline."

That stops A'zam in his tracks. "Bullshit."

"Thank you for verifying. Anytime you have no facts or alternative facts to draw on your default is to go to profanity."

A'zam shakes his head as if he's not sure how to proceed. "What is it you want? You're wasting my time and putting me behind."

"I want you to resign." I say as simply as I can, as if it were a foregone conclusion, at least for me if not for him.

"Really? Maybe I want the same thing." He continues his stare, although I ignore it.

"You've created the situation." I continue. "The board no longer trusts you. I am obligated to present the findings of the internal investigation and have done so. I'm sure you know it's not pretty."

"The board isn't going to do anything. Every one of them owes me big time. So you can just park that threat."

"Not a threat. Stephenson already has the file. She is obligated to call the committee together to review it."

"So what? She's also obligated to call me in to explain my behavior. When I tell them what I've been up to they'll be wanting to increase my compensation package."

"You do realize they're personally liable for incomplete and misleading financial filings."

"What I've been doing isn't material." A'zam dismisses my clarification.

"Under Sarbanes Oxley it is and that's the governing law in this instance."

A'zam is agitated, crosses to me and grabs me, pressing his mouth against mine in what he hopes is going to be a kiss that causes me to stop, relent my pursuit of him.

But it doesn't. I push him away "You can't insult me, saying my friend is better in bed, and think I'll believe you care about me one bit."

"I haven't done the Kama Sutra with her."

"Twice." I remind him. "But that was all mechanical. I never thought you were doing anything other than trying to establish your dominance over me. Not exactly what someone does who's trying to establish a trusting relationship."

The door opens. Moshe comes in. I take a quick look and realize he's still an immortal. Somehow A'zam was able to save him from transitioning back, over riding my instructions. What I'm wondering is how I was never informed of this change of plans.

"Moshe," I acknowledge him but then turn back to A'zam.

A'zam nods to Moshe who I hear going to A'zam's desk. He sits down in A'zam's chair and brings up a screen that only he can see. He looks up at A'zam and waits.

"Sure you won't join the march to world domination? You've already moved most people in that direction. My team is working on how to exploit Mad Hatter. You've accelerated my plans and you didn't even know what they were. I find that delightful. But also ironic. Since we started down this whole path you've led the way. But you never understood the opportunity. Never understood how we change the world one person at a time. You've thought you were working to limit me, but all the time you've been working against yourself. Ensuring you won't be part of the leadership. The global leadership that will transition the world to peaceful co-existence. To unparalleled economic prosperity. To harmony amongst all peoples. That's achievable. But instead you were on a quest to preserve what is human as you define it. That's the problem. You're trying to define humanity and there is no definition. When you define it, all you've done is impose your world view on everyone. I've not tried to do that. I don't want to impose anything. I want everyone to be what they can and want to be. All I want to do is limit their ability to self-destruct. Limit their worst tendencies so they will be supportive of each other. Create harmony world-wide."

"With you as the supreme leader." I point out. "With you determining what freedoms they have to give up."

"In my world no one will care. Everyone will be the same. Everyone will see things the same. What's wrong with a world of unity of principle?"

"Your principle." I point out, "Not theirs. Why should you be exempt from the restrictions you want to impose on them?"

"You read too much philosophy." A'zam dismisses me still one more time, but with each dismissal I realize I'm gaining power. He can't dismiss me in reality because if he could he would have the first time. And here he is doing it one more time.

"And you think you're the philosopher," I respond. "Only you're not. You're no different than me or Moshe or anyone else who has transitioned. The only difference is you've convinced the board to support your strategic plan to make them individually richer than they would be otherwise. Only now that they've seen how you've run fast and loose with their fortunes, they may not be as sanguine about letting you just continue to reshape the world they've known and understand how to make money in. Don't underestimate where you get your power from."

A'zam looks at Moshe, as if to say to him it's time to do something. Moshe responds, entering something into the monitor he alone sees. He looks up and A'zam grins at me. I wait. Nothing happens. A'zam looks at Moshe, who concentrates on the monitor, apparently trying to up whatever it is he is attempting to change. He looks up at me, glances at A'zam and looks confused, but his look is no more confused than A'zam who studies me.

"I take it Santa Claus is trying to punish me?" I show as much disdain as I can, surprised nothing is happening, but not wanting them to see my surprise.

"Moshe," A'zam sounds desperate.

"She should have shut down with this much force concentrated on her."

"Obviously I haven't. There are over a billion mortals who are counteracting Santa's wishes." I inform them. "Your great plan has been defeated by those you dismissed as unimportant."

A'zam rushes over to the monitor to see what its showing. "How do we fix this?" he asks Moshe.

"You wanted me to understand that I can't judge people who are different than me in their approach. That's why you salvaged Moshe from his return transition. But what you didn't stop to consider is that there may be a reason why Moshe didn't conform to the expectations of an emerging society. You only wanted me to think I was wrong. And you overlooked the fact that Moshe doesn't have the technical skills or experience to understand the complexity of the system you wanted to deploy. You always relied on me to provide that for you. I did. And in the process, I developed the expertise you need but now don't have. So, this conversation is done and so are you."

A'zam looks up over the dash board, "What are you saying?"

A knock on A'zam's door and it opens. Stephenson, the governance committee chairman of the board enters with Randall, our security chief.

"What's the meaning of this?" A'zam greets them.

"The board has voted to remove you from office, for ten counts of Sarbanes Oxley violations, deliberate defrauding of company records and misappropriation of company funds. Your actions have jeopardized the funding of approved company initiatives at the expense of pet projects you've never had the courtesy to brief the board on. We've known each other a long time. Been good friends most of that time. You were excellent in painting a vision I and the other board members embraced. But since you transitioned you seem to have lost the humility a CEO needs in relation to his or her board. We can't give you carte blanche to spend funds without proper accounting, without proper approvals, without periodic evaluations. Your time is up."

"Since you're Vice Chairman this would be considered a coup." A'zam shouts at Stephenson.

"I'm not acting as Vice Chairman, I'm acting in my capacity as Chairman of the Governance Committee to ensure we have appropriate checks and balances to meet our fiduciary responsibility to the Security and Exchange Commission and our shareholders. You'll be lucky not to spend time in prison for your dereliction of duty and criminal behavior."

Randall crosses the room and takes A'zam's arm. A'zam pulls away from him, glares at me, glares at Stephenson and then a final disgusted look at Moshe. Reluctantly he walks out of the office with Randall just behind him.

Stephenson approaches me, "Did the collective unconscious really work?"

I nod. "We have what we need to create a more just society. AppleCore will lead the way."

Stephenson nods and leaves me to decide what to do with Moshe and humanity.

BRAND NEW DAY

A year later.

I am shuffling from the bedroom to my kitchen. It seems I don't spend much time here anymore. Haven't since I transitioned. But that seems to be changing now that Jackson has moved in. "Morning." I greet Tabitha.

She sits at the kitchen table in her bathrobe, which means she has nothing on beneath. Anna Laura has tried to get her to just wear regular clothes, but she's taken with the idea of bathrobes. She's reviewing the newsfeeds. I never do that, but like so many she is obsessed with knowing what is going on in the world. I don't care. "I see your judge has finally ruled." She remarks matter-of-factly. Your attorney will probably contact you shortly if he hasn't already."

"What did she decide? "I ask, not sure I want to know. The testimony had gotten so strident I'd given up trying to follow it.

"That you're a menace to society and should be walked back to be like everyone else." Tabitha's voice betrays her attempt at pulling my chain.

"What did she rule?" I correct my question.

"As much as she wanted to find a sinister plot to rob all citizens of their god given rights as well as those given everyone who lives in the glorious state of California, she was unable to find that the preponderance of the evidence supports such a position. That through much testimony, there was a paucity of facts, as facts can be defined as no contested or contravening theories of what the state of the world actually may be for the next twenty-seven seconds."

She's been listening to talk radio again.

"Can I take it the court chose to rule against the ACLU complaint?" I clarify.

"That is correct." Tabitha concedes, although I know she would have preferred not to, just to see how far she could have taken this discussion before I discovered the truth.

"How's work?" I change the subject. Tabitha is working for the City of Cupertino as the Director of Public Information. She's responsible for communicating with the citizens who pay their taxes for the services the city provides. It's sort of a marketing job, sort of communications and sort of public affairs. She needed a job where her lack of formal degrees would not prevent her from meeting certification requirements to do the job. Jackson helped her get the position.

"We're trying to mandate that everyone must have a Mad Hatter or equivalent ability to receive communications from the city."

"Is there an equivalent?" I ask, not being aware of one. But I set my mind to researching that question and the answer comes back almost immediately that a Chinese equivalent at fifty percent of the cost has been introduced in Shanghai, but the availability is limited at the moment.

"There will be," Tabitha confirms.

"You seek Rocky and Anna Laura last night?" I change the subject not wanting to talk business with my younger sister's android.

"Rocky is finally getting used to the fact he's got his family back." Tabitha seems curious about this situation. "Never thought it would take him this long. Even though I know how stubborn he is."

"What about Anna Laura? She still threatening to come live with us if he doesn't get his act together?"

"Rocky sees right through that." Tabitha responds. "She's not going anywhere. He could murder someone on the front lawn, drag the body through the house and bury it in the back yard, never having wiped up the blood stains and she still would deny he was responsible to the police when they came to investigate."

I instantly have a flashback to a man with a knife and my spinning around to hit him in the head. But I put that aside. That was a different life, a different me and the police closed that case a long time ago. "You're suggesting Rocky has settled in, that Anna Laura is content and dinner once a week with them isn't the end of the world for you."

"It would be nice if you came to join us once in a while. Have the whole family there. I'd like it and I know Rocky will never admit it, but it would mean a lot to him as well."

"I'll think about it," I respond, knowing it's not high on my priority list, but is something I should do more often because I never know how much longer I have Rocky there, acting as a catalyst of ideas and approaches I need to be successful.

"What about you?" Tabitha asks. "Another application for White Rabbit? Another wonder drug from New Vision? It seems the solutions are coming so fast from both companies that you're solving societal issues society hasn't figured out it has. How long can you continue to do that?"

"You want a job at one of my companies, just say the word. You'd get along famously with Landon and Suwanee."

"Who's Suwanee?"

"Head of marketing at New Vision," I respond.

"You going to put the two companies together so you can better articulate the product lines?"

Tabitha's vocabulary is growing exponentially. "I established a team to do that, for the purpose of avoiding having to put two very diverse companies together." I respond.

"Your world is so much more interesting than mine." Tabitha observes.

"Patience." I respond. "A year from now you still want to make a move, you know where I live."

Tabitha smiles in recognition that is where she also lives.

Jackson comes out of the bedroom, all showered, shaved and smelling nice for the many babies he will have to kiss along with the asses of the corporate big shots like me. Those are the same corporate big shots who have come to expect that behavior from the mayor of their favorite city in order not to threaten to move work elsewhere. Jackson explained to me once that is the least desirable part of his job. He wanted only to provide better service to the people who live here. But so many corporate big shots want to leverage him into doing something for their company that he has lost sight, in all too many instances, of the common person. He would love to get back to pure democracy where no one person has a greater voice than another. But he knows that won't happen in his lifetime. At least within his lifetime if he doesn't transition. He hasn't raised the question and neither have I.

Jackson kisses me on the cheek as he retrieves a cup of black coffee from the coffee machine. "Tabitha." He greets her. "Anything I need to know before I appear at City Hall?"

"Last reading of the charter amendment tonight."

"That the one to eliminate term limits?" I ask, knowing Jackson hopes to run again, but is currently limited.

"I can expect a big crowd tonight. Folks don't like change especially since you feed us all a steady diet of it with all your miracles." Jackson comes up to me and gives me a hug. "When are you coming home again?"

"With the new battery upgrade I only need to charge once a week now." I point out.

"So, Friday night is now our date night?" Jackson asks.

"It's in my calendar." I confirm. But then I stop. "Oops. I have the posse for drinks next Friday. Can we do Saturday instead?"

"Windy gotten over A'zam yet?" Jackson asks since he's met them all.

"Windy's good. No man in her life, but she's coming up to speed real quickly since her transition. She's been keeping real close to her kids. Making sure they can navigate their new world."

"And the others?" Tabitha asks. I'm surprised she didn't wait for Jackson.

"They're all good."

"Even MC, who chose not to transition, but is working with those who are?" Jackson inquires.

"MC is seeing Dr. Woodall." I admit. "Amazing what they have in common."

Jackson kisses me, I rub Tabitha's back and we all go off to our brand-new day.

TRANSITION

Ten years pass quickly. I didn't know Rocky had cancer. He never told anyone, never sought treatment, never complained. I saw him getting weaker, but I took his explanations at face value. I did not push to know more, wanting to give him the privacy he always sought when it came to his health.

I tried everything I could think of to convince him to transition so the whole family could stay together, forever. But Rocky would always invoke that life wasn't always as grand as it was now, and he just couldn't conceive of being a circuit designer forever.

As the casket is lowered into the ground, Anna Laura is next to me on my left and Tabitha is on her left, all three of us dressed in black. I feel a tear form and run down my right cheek. And then I notice first Anna Laura wipes away a tear followed almost instantly by Tabitha.

In ten years, we've made progress. We have a semblance of feelings. Memories are no longer the only source we have of reacting to others. But still, we are becoming a different humanity. Less emotional, but more balanced than when I transitioned so long ago. White Rabbit and the Mad Hatter have enabled all men, women and children to understand what is right, what is wrong and how each of us should behave. That has made the world a more predictable place. Less conflict. More harmony. A world similar to what A'zam described to me was his plan. But the major difference is we all have a vote in what is right and wrong. We all have the opportunity to ignore it and do as we please, rather than being limited by one immortal's view of the world. The question is whether it will be enough to keep those who would subjugate us from finding a way to defeat the collective unconscious. A'zam is out there, attempting to rewrite the immortals software to re-enable his trap door that I closed when he went to jail. So far, we have been able to prevent that. But one never knows how long it will be before someone discovers a way. And then all bets are off.

THE END

ABOUT THE AUTHOR

dhtreichler toured the global garden spots as a defense contractor executive for fifteen years. His assignments covered intelligence, training and battlefield systems integrating state of the art technology to keep Americans safe. During this time he authored seven novels exploring the role of increasingly sophisticated technology in transforming our lives and how men and women establish relationships in a mediated world.

Keep up with all of dhtreichler's latest work and essays at

www.dhtreichler.com.

Also by dhtreichler

Barely Human

The Ghost in the Machine: a novel

World Without Work

The Great American Cat Novel

My Life as a Frog

Succession

Life After

The Tragic Flaw

Lucifer

The End Game

I Believe in You

Rik's

The Illustrated Bearmas Reader – Ralph's Ordeals

The First Bearmas

16883323R00243

Made in the USA
Middletown, DE
02 December 2018